UNSEEN PRESENCE

He came to the forest and found his cottage and knew something had changed. He could sense it, even before he entered the small building.

Some two-legged creature had been there.

He felt suddenly afraid, and drew his knife, inspecting the cottage.

Nothing was missing, so he sheathed his blade and went outside. He sniffed the air and found it normal—all forest smells, and that of the chickens and pigs that came rushing to him in search of food. He stared around and felt as if he were watched, but he could see no one. He paced the margins of his holding, staring at the encircling trees, but saw nothing untoward. Save he felt that odd sensation that eyes studied him, invisible behind the woodland canopy.

"Who's there?" he called. "Shall you come out?"

There was no answer, but still he felt he was watched. The short hairs of his neck tingled and he felt suddenly wary. He had not felt afraid before—not in the friendly forest—but now. He wondered who watched him.

Or what.

YESTERDAY'S KINGS

ANGUS WELLS

BANTAM BOOKS
New York   Toronto   London
Sydney   Auckland

YESTERDAY'S KINGS

A Bantam Spectra Book / April 2001

SPECTRA and the portrayal of a boxed "s" are trademarks of
Bantam Books, a division of Random House, Inc.

ISBN 0-553-57796-4

Published simultaneously in the United States and Canada

Bantam Books are published by Bantam Books, a division of
Random House, Inc. Its trademark, consisting of the words "Bantam
Books" and the portrayal of a rooster, is Registered in U.S. Patent
and Trademark Office and in other countries. Marca Registrada.
Bantam Books, 1540 Broadway, New York, New York 10036.

PRINTED IN THE UNITED STATES OF AMERICA

OPM   10 9 8 7 6 5 4 3 2 1

In memory of Laurence James, my best friend

ONE

❧❧❧

HE RESTED AGAINST the bole of a massive oak until the squirrel chattering a warning above lost interest and went away. Then he waited some more, listening to the birds that moved amongst the branches and the ferns, before he moved—cautiously—from the oak's shelter. His bow was half drawn, an arrow set firm on the string, and he knew that the deer he hunted was not far ahead. He crouched, a motley figure, dressed in a homespun shirt and old leather breeches, all melding with the natural shades of the forest, as if he were part of the great woodland that stretched from the Alagordar to the farmlands beyond, where men had taken command and shaped the land to their desires. There were fields there now, tilled and hedged and marked off in orders of possession; cottages that connected with one another along roads of hard-packed dirt, some packed at the sides with dry stone walls. Some even had walls about them in memory of the Durrym raids, before order was imposed on Kandar and the firstcome folk driven out.

The nearest village was Lyth, and that was walled round, as if ancient memories could not be forgotten. There was a wide road leading there, and then on to the keep that dominated the hill above, with stone at its base and great wooden ramparts above, patrolled by Lord Bartram's soldiery, who wore mail and even plate armor, and looked down on the few who chose to continue their lives in the forest as if they were traitors, allied to the Durrym.

Cullyn could not understand that. He had encountered Lord Bartram's folk from time to time, and knew that most of the soldiers were from other provinces, or recruited from the fishing villages along the coast; few—if any—had ever seen one of the fey folk. He was not certain he had himself, although there were times he wondered, as he wandered the forest, if he were not watched. It was a curious feeling, a prickling down the nape of his neck, the sensation that *something* was watching him. Not an animal—that he'd have recognized, for he had lived in the forest all his life—but something else, that he could never quite spot or find. He'd turn around, bow drawn or knife ready, only to find himself staring at shadows, listening to the rustle of leaves and the birdsong, wondering what was there when there was nothing.

He was forest-birthed, and knew the place as few other men did. His father, Mattias, had carved out a clearing and built the cabin where Cullyn now lived. Because, he had told his son when Cullyn grew old enough to understand, he was sick of deceptions. He had fought in the Great War, when men came together and resolved their differences so as to drive the Durrym out of the land. And he had taken up shield and spear to fight the fey folk and claim the country for men. But had grown weary of the slaughter and chosen to have no more part of it. Not least because he had met Cullyn's mother, who came from Tyris, the fishing village on the coast, and wanted to take her away from the threat of Durrym raids. So they had gone into the forest and cleared enough land to build a cabin and grow vegetables, and raise such pigs and chickens and cows as could keep them alive. It was enough for them, and they lived happy.

Cullyn remembered it. There were eggs for breakfast, and rich pork; milk to drink. At times an exciting journey to Lyth. The cabin was well built, warm against the winter winds and cool in the summer's heat. There was an order to the seasons: the planting of seeds, and later their harvesting; the raising of animals that were later slaughtered, that his family might eat bacon and beef through the hard time of winter. The chickens tasted good, even when they were familiar friends that had pecked him as a child.

He had no problem with that: it was part of the cycle. But he never could understand why men warred against the Durrym, and when he was old enough to question his father, he had asked why.

"Because they are different," Mattias had said. "I can give you no better answer, save that perhaps men are foolish and listen to those who'd be kings and lords and look to vaunt themselves over all others. We came to this land from the west, and found the Durrym here. And our forefathers wanted the land, so they drove the Durrym out."

"But you fought in that war," Cullyn said.

"I did," his father answered, "and now I regret it. The Durrym have as much right to this country as do we, but they've gone away across the Alagordar now and they've magic to deny us entry. But remember, they are not evil, only different, and they've as much right to these lands as we."

His parents died as he came into his manhood. He and his father had taken several deer, and two boars, that they intended to trade in Lyth. His mother came with them, intent on purchasing new cloth and threads in the village. It was early spring, and the melt water from the hills set the rivers swirling, running with ice pack and torrents.

It was over in moments: the horse started as a dredge of ice struck. It plunged and fell. Mattias was dragged from his seat by the reins, and carried into the water. Cullyn sprung after him as his mother screamed, but he could not catch his father, who was borne away by the river, tumbling over and over as he shouted and thrust up helpless arms, then drowned. Cullyn struggled back and did his best to comfort his mother. He found the horse, near drowned itself, and they went on to Lyth, drenched and wretched, and traded their forest meat for what the village had to offer. Then he took his mother home, and not long after she died of a fever. Since then, Cullyn had lived alone in the cabin, taking what he needed from the forest, where—perhaps—the Durrym still lived, venturing into Lyth only to procure such things as he could not manufacture himself, like milled flour and salt, well-baked bread; even though he preferred his life in the forest to that of the village.

He had lived alone in the cabin since his mother's demise, rejecting all offers of hospitality, for he could not imagine living anywhere else. Surely not in a place where buildings faced one another, with streets between and constant voices. He loved the sounds of the forest: the rustling of the leaves as the wind blew through, and the cries of its creatures, birds and deer and boar, fox song and the grunting of badgers, the messages of owls and the hymning of doves. He could not imagine another life, and when the priest had come, intent on persuading the young man to find a home in Lyth, Cullyn had driven him off with harsh words that he later regretted, for he recognized the priest to be a decent man who sought only to do good. But he did not understand the appeal of the forest. None could, Cullyn thought, who did not live there; and those who did not perceived the forest as magical, the domain of the Durrym, and therefore dangerous. To them it was an enchanted place, where men became lost and were taken by the fey folk into the unknown country across the Alagordar where the gods alone knew what happened to them.

Cullyn believed some of this might be true. Certainly, he had never attempted to cross the river— why should he? He found all he needed on the Kandar side, and the Durrym had not, in all his eighteen years, offered him any threat. Did they sometimes watch him, as he suspected, he did not consider them dangerous. Curious, perhaps, but no more than that, and so he ran the forest freely, and enjoyed its bounty and his life within its confines. He had no real idea of its size. He knew that it stretched to the high cliffs that loomed above the Southern Sea, and for long miles eastward, and for at least a week's march north—the farthest he'd ever ventured—but how much farther north, or how far east, he had no conception. He was content with his own small piece, and wanted no more. So far as he was concerned, the Durrym were welcome to the farther side of the river.

He shook himself from his musings as he heard the deer stir. It was within bowshot, and comforted by his silence. There was a clearing ahead where he'd guessed it would stop to browse, and he was right. He went soft-footed and crouched through the bracken until he saw the animal—a fine, high-antlered stag—that raised its head at his approach, so that he crouched anew and held his breath until the lofting antlers dropped and the beast set to cropping the clearing's rich grass again. Cullyn took a soft breath as he drew his bow string and sighted down the shaft. He wet his lips, testing the breeze, and adjusted his aim. He drew the string back to his cheek and rose, loosing the arrow. It flew straight, taking the stag behind the left shoulder, so that the great beast snorted and staggered and went down on its forelegs. Cullyn dropped his bow and charged forward as he drew his knife. Before the stag could rise, even before it had time to wonder, he was on it. He drove his blade deep into its throat, severing the great arteries, so that the stag snorted blood from its nostrils and mouth even as a great gout spurted from its neck. It was slain in moments, falling as Cullyn clutched it and begged its forgiveness.

"I must eat," he murmured, "just like you. And I could die here like you."

He was aware of that. For all he loved the forest, he knew its dangers. There were savage boars in the woodlands, and bears, and forest cats—all of which would slay a man for presuming to enter their domain. It was no easy life, but it was what Cullyn loved, and it was all he knew.

He cleaned his knife and worked his arrow loose and then took up the deer and began the trek back to his cabin. The corpse was heavy, but he was strong, broader of shoulder than most men of his age, and taller, worked hard by all his years in the forest. His arms were muscled from hewing wood, and his legs from chasing down prey. His hair was brown as oakwood, and long, drawn back in a tail for want of trimming, and a thick beard grew around his mouth and cheeks. There had been young women in Lyth who'd called him handsome, but he was too shy to heed their calling, and was not at all sure what he looked like, save himself. He knew only that he enjoyed his life, and were he sometimes lonely, there was always the forest, with all its wondrous sights and sounds.

And the mystery of the Durrym.

He carried the deer back and hung the carcass in the butchering shed, where he bled it and carved it, taking enough for himself to cure and keep, the rest to trade. He hacked off the head and set the skull to boiling. Someone in Lyth would likely buy it. Cullyn had no time for trophies: they seemed pointless to him, like keeping one's own stool preserved for memory.

He thought that when the skull was bleached he'd go into the village. The meat would surely be ready by then, and he could trade sufficient to afford a jug of ale, which he enjoyed no less than the attentions of Andrias's serving wench, who seemed particularly fond of him. Surely she served him sooner than others, and bent lower over his table, and smiled at him so fondly that he felt himself stir. Perhaps this time, he thought, he'd not collapse into embarrassment and turn his face away. Perhaps this time he'd accept her offer and follow her to her room. Perhaps.

He set a small portion of the venison on the fire and began to cut vegetables, and when they were done he ate, and settled to sleep, listening to the sounds of the forest. As ever, they lulled him into slumber, even though he felt both apprehensive and excited by the prospect of visiting Lyth again. It was like another country, mysterious and enticing, albeit frightening. He was not much used to people.

❧❀❧

WHEN THE VENISON was properly cured and the stag's skull bleached dry, he packed his gear and set out

for Lyth. The horse that had carried his parents into the
river was long dead, and he had never been able to afford
another, so he loaded a cart he had built himself and set
the traces about his chest and shoulders and began to
trudge the forest paths until he came to the road leading
to the village. It was a journey of some two days by foot,
but he had no qualms about sleeping on the roadside,
and he had sufficient to eat, and water to drink from the
freshets that fed the Alagordar. He wore his finest
clothes: a linen shirt woven by his mother and breeches
that were not entirely stained with animal blood and leaf
mold. He had also combed his long hair and tied it with a
strap of leather; even trimmed his burgeoning beard as
best he could with a hunting knife. He felt ready to face
civilization.

The road stretched across rolling farmland after the
forest ended, where dales and vales ran toward the
plateau that held Lyth and the great keep. Cullyn felt
somewhat uncomfortable there, for he was more accustomed to enclosing timber than this open landscape, but
he pressed on, contemplating the reward for his burden,
and when farmers offered him shelter, he thanked them
and continued, preferring to sleep in the open. At least,
until he came on the village.

He found that on the fourth day, by which time even
his strength was waning. He halted at the open gate and
shouted his name, but no one answered and so he went
through, wondering why the villagers maintained their
wall if no one guarded it.

Past the empty gate the road narrowed, running
through the center of the village. It was flanked by
houses, most plain cottages, but some larger, offering hospitality or stabling. Alleyways ran between, out to the
walls, like the spokes of a wheel, and at its center was the
village square. There was a pond there, on which sat fat

ducks and two graceful swans; a weeping willow draped its branches over the water, and grass surrounded it. All around were the finest houses. None stood higher than a single story, but their windows were glassed and their doors set with metal, their porches intricately carved and painted in bright colors. They spoke to Cullyn of wealth, and he halted, his wonder at such extravagance reawakened.

And then, as ever, his eyes were drawn to the keep. That stood atop a knoll that overlooked the village like some immemorial guardian. It seemed to brood over Lyth, like a mother over a vulnerable child, stern and demanding, but ever watchful and protective. Cullyn wondered what it might be like to live there, behind walls. He could not imagine it.

He gathered up his strength and hauled his cart to the hostelry named the Golden Goat, dragging his burden to the rearward yard, where a gate gave access to a paved area that contained a well and the odors of cooking emanating from the kitchens. He felt his mouth water and his belly rumble as he ducked clear of the cart's straps and went to the back door. He knocked and waited.

After a while a buxom woman of indeterminate age appeared. Her face was round as a cherry, and near as red, girded with a circle of graying auburn hair that was gathered into a bun surmounted by a white cap. She was brushing flour off her hands as she came through the door, wiping them on the voluminous apron that she wore over a long blue dress. The latter matched the color of her angry eyes.

"What, another tramp?" Then she started as she saw Cullyn, and her expression shifted to a warm smile. "Cullyn, by all the gods! How are you, lad? Come in. What have you brought us?" She stepped somewhat ponderously off the porch and flung her hefty arms around him. "Are you well? Gods, but you've grown!"

Cullyn felt himself engulfed in her weight and warmth, and for a moment enjoyed it; then he stepped free and gestured at his cart.

"The better part of a good deer, Martia; and the skull for selling. It's a twelve-point spread."

"Well, that shall fetch a handsome price." She surveyed the antlered skull with professional expertise, then hefted the weight of meat in the cart. "And this, too. Come inside and take a cup."

Cullyn followed her through the kitchen, listening to her shouting orders that the meat be taken from his cart and stored, and the skull set aside. Her helpers ran to her commands as Cullyn went with her into the main room.

"Hey, Andrias, see who's here?" Her shout cut through all conversation, and her husband turned from scrubbing glasses. He smiled and came out from behind the bar.

"Cullyn, lad, it's good to see you. How are you? What shall it be—ale or wine? Brandy?"

Cullyn felt embarrassed as the occupants of the hostelry turned their eyes his way. He shrugged and said, "Ale, if you will."

"I shall," Andrias said with great enthusiasm, "and welcome a friend. Here." He drew a full measure into a pewter mug and passed it to Cullyn. "Drink deep on the house."

Cullyn said, "My thanks," and swallowed.

The ale tasted good. It was dark and clean, bitter on his tongue, then warmer in his belly. It had been a long time since he'd tasted ale, and Martia's arm was around his shoulders as he remembered his mother's, and Andrias was beaming at him and already pouring another measure as he asked, "You'll be staying, no? We've rooms enough."

Cullyn nodded, more than a little embarrassed. "If I can . . ."

"Silly boy." Martia hugged him closer, deepening his embarrassment for all the pleasure he felt. "Of course you can. You know you've always a place with us. Did we not know your parents before—"

"They died," Cullyn supplied pragmatically.

"They were our friends," Andrias said, "as are you."

"And I worry about you," Martia added, "living all alone in the forest. What life is that for a young man?"

"I survive well enough." He'd have shrugged had the weight of her hefty arm not rested across his shoulders. "I've brought you meat, no?"

"Surely," Martia said. "I've no doubt at all that you're a great hunter. But what of friends? What of . . . women?" She loosed him long enough to cast an eye over the room. "See Elvira there? She fancies you, and always has. You could do far worse than bed with her."

Cullyn blushed and said, "I know. But—"

"Ask her," Martia said. "Take her upstairs, eh?"

"And then?" Cullyn asked. "Would she come live with me in the forest?"

Andrias snorted laughter. "I doubt that. Elvira's a taste for tavern life."

"So there's no point to it," Cullyn said.

Andrias laughed again, joined by his wife. "There's always a *point* to it. It depends what you do with it."

"I think," Cullyn said nervously, "that I must think about it."

"So be it, but don't strain your bow hand." Andrias laughed, joined by Martia. "Now, are you hungry?"

Cullyn nodded.

"Then find a seat and we'll bring you food."

He found a table and sat, feeling awkward. He thought that all the folk in the place stared at him, and talked about him: the forest strangeling, his parents dead and he a hunter along the edge of the fey folk's barrier. Not one of them.

He was grateful when Elvira brought him a bowl of soup, and bent low across the table so that her flounced blouse exposed her cleavage, and smiled at him, as if she knew some secret they shared. Save he was not sure what secret that might be.

He sat, drinking another mug of ale as she delivered a platter of roasted pork, with bread and vegetables, and all the while wondering what her smiles meant. Promise or only enticement? He could not be sure; neither of her intentions nor what he wanted. He felt curiously afraid.

The hostelry closed. Folk quit the place, leaving Cullyn alone with his wonderings. Andrias and Martia came to him, suggesting he find his bed, for he was more than a little drunk now. Then Elvira suggested that she take him to his room, which he thought a fine idea. He rose from his seat to fall into her strong arms as the hall spun around his eyes and he felt his legs weaken.

He was vaguely aware of standing up; of throwing his arm about her shoulders as she held him upright. He could smell the sweet scent of her, perfume and kitchen smells mingled, and knew that she was strong. He kissed her ear and said, "I love you." She tossed blond hair against his face and said, "You don't; you're only drunk."

He said, "I do. I swear it."

She said, "You'll think different come the morning. They all do."

"No!" He shook his head as solemnly as he could. "I shall feel the same."

"We'll see," she said.

❧❦❧

HE WOKE THICK-HEADED and alone.

She was gone, and he lay stranded on an isolated bed that stank of sweat and booze and sex. He could smell what they had done together and regretted his drinking, which had made it less than his expectations, and lay a while wondering why they had come together, save they had both wanted it. But then they found it did not fulfill their expectations, and so she had left him.

He rose and bathed his face. He felt somehow sad, and not at all eager to meet her again, for he was no longer sure of his feelings. He had wanted her, but now he was no longer certain, as if the accomplishment of the promised act had taken away the pleasure of anticipation. But still he went down to the hall, because he was hungry. He wondered how he should greet her—as a lover or a serving wench?

She made it easy for him. She was clearing tables and met him with a cheerful smile and a hearty "Good morning." He wondered if he should kiss her, but she seemed too busy, so he only gave her back the same greeting and found a cleared table to which she came when she'd cleared the last of the others.

"Breakfast?" Her smile was wide and cheerful—as it always was—and he wondered if the last night had meant anything to her other than the satisfaction of a purely carnal appetite. "Are you hungry?"

He nodded and she bustled off to return with a platter of bread and a mug of steaming tea that she set down before him with the same encompassing smile. He sipped the tea and nibbled at the bread, and then a platter of eggs and ham and sausage was set before him, and he realized how hungry he was. He set to eating even as she bent toward him and whispered, "I enjoyed last night. Shall you stay?"

He felt his cheeks grow red and heard her laugh, and said, "I don't know. Andrias is to sell my stuff, and I don't know how long that will take."

She shrugged as if it mattered not at all, but her smile stiffened a little and she turned away, busying herself, and he dug into his breakfast as he wondered if he wanted to remain or return to his familiar surroundings. He found it difficult to understand these transactions of men and women.

Andrias emerged from the kitchen to rescue him. The landlord was wiping his hands on a greasy apron. "Leave the tables for now, Elvira. Go help Martia in the kitchen, eh?"

She shrugged again—or was it a flounce?—and disappeared through the rearward door. Andrias grinned at Cullyn. "How was it, then?"

Cullyn blushed anew. "It was . . . Well . . ."

"Your first time?" Andrias supplied.

Cullyn nodded.

"It's not always the best," Andrias said. "You need to practice. It gets better."

Cullyn hid his fresh embarrassment behind a mouthful of food. "What about the stuff I brought?" he asked. "Can you sell it?"

"Easily." Andrias waved an expansive hand. "I'll take most of it, and sell the rest. That skull alone should fetch a good price."

Cullyn asked, "How long?"

And his friend laughed and said, "You'll need to stay a while yet, and decide about Elvira. But . . . a day? Perhaps two?"

Cullyn smiled and asked, "What shall that cost me?"

"Little," Andrias said. "I'll take the cost out of the meat, and charge you the least I can."

Cullyn nodded. "I need salt," he said, "and flour. I made a list."

He drew the scrap of paper from his tunic and passed it to Andrias, who studied it a moment, his lips moving as he read the words. Then: "Once the meat and the skull are sold, I can get you all of this, and coin left over."

"How much?" Cullyn was abruptly eager. "Enough to buy the horse?"

It was his ambition to purchase such a mount as Lord Bartram's cavalry rode. A horse that he could ride swift through the forest, yet with muscle enough to haul a cart. He had saved toward this end for years, hoarding what coin was left from purchasing supplies against the time he might afford the beast. Horses were in short supply in the Borderlands, mostly the property of the Border Lords and their men. The farmers used mules, or the great plough-dragging shires, but Cullyn was intent on owning a hunter, and had stored his coin with Andrias to that end.

"Perhaps this time you've enough for a mule or a plough horse."

"I want a hunter," Cullyn said.

"Then likely you'll need to wait," Andrias replied, "until the Summer Horse Fair."

Cullyn sighed. That was three months off.

"You'll get the best bargains then," Andrias said.

Cullyn nodded and drank the last of his tea. "Get me a good price, eh?"

"My word on it," Andrias promised. "Do you want to come with me, when I sell your meat?"

Cullyn shook his head. He hated bargaining and would sooner wander the small confines of Lyth, or take the road out to stare at the keep. He wondered, briefly, if he should invite Elvira to accompany him, but then de cided against it. He felt a need to be alone, so h scrubbed up the last of his breakfast and went out int the streets of the village.

He wandered a while, wondering at the houses and how folk could live so close-packed, then found the roac that led to the keep. It went into the open country where the slope rose toward the fortress. Up toward th great stone walls and wooden buttresses of the castle which stood on sparse moorland that had been stricker of trees and undergrowth so that the keep might not b approached unseen, but sit alone and defensive behinc its great walls.

He could not understand how anyone would choose to live so confined. But still it was fascinating. As is a spi der to one who finds arachnids frightening.

He halted not far from Lyth's walls and stared at th mighty structure. And then he saw the gates open anc the drawbridge fall down across the moat, and a troop o riders come out.

Their horses made a great clattering on the draw bridge, and then a steady thunder on the roadway be yond, so that Cullyn was standing beside the track a they passed by, darting aside so that he not be run down.

The column was led by a handsome man whose long blond hair streamed from under his half-helm. He wore a mail shirt and carried a cross-picked boar lance, and the horse he rode was such as Cullyn wished to find. Beside him was a fair-haired woman, pale-featured and lovely, dressed in hunting clothes. And then . . . Cullyn's heart beat faster . . . a younger woman whose hair was red as an autumn sunset, her face an oval of desire even though her lips were pursed in an expression of disapproval as she glared at the two riders ahead.

He stared at her, and for a moment their eyes met.

He smiled and ducked his head. She stared at him, irritably, and then was gone, followed by a small squadron of horsemen. Cullyn was not sure how many because his attention was occupied by her face, and he could see little else.

He watched them go down the road into Lyth and he followed after, even though—as he descended the slope—he saw them emerge from the farther gate and ride toward the forest.

❧❦❧

"WHO WERE THEY?" he asked Andrias. "I've never seen a woman so lovely."

"Do you mean Vanysse, or her daughter?" Andrias asked.

"One was fair and older," Cullyn said. "The other was . . . beautiful."

From across the room, Elvira scowled at him.

"Vanysse is the elder," Andrias told him, "married to Lord Bartram, but . . ." He tapped his nose. "Word has it that she favors her husband's captain. Likely you saw her riding out with Amadis. He's captain of the guard."

"And the other?"

"That would be Abra," Andrias said. "Lord Bartram's daughter by his first marriage. Don't you know?"

Cullyn shook his head.

"Bartram was made a Border Lord by Kristoferos," Andrias explained. "Then Kristoferos died and Khoros came to power. Didn't your father teach you any history?"

Cullyn shook his head again.

Andrias sighed. "Well, anyway, we're now ruled by Khoros, who mistrusts anyone appointed by Kristoferos. But . . . to avoid civil war, he could not risk offending the Border Lords appointed by his brother. So he left them in place and sent them captains of his own persausion who'd watch and report back to him. Amadis is one such. The king's man. And—is rumor true, the lady Vanysse's lover."

"Why," Cullyn asked, in his innocence, "does Lord Bartram allow that?"

"Politics," Andrias said bluntly. "As I understand it, the lady Vanysse was chosen for Lord Bartram by Khoros himself, as a marriage of convenience. Her dowry was substantial and she is, undoubtedly, beautiful—and half Bartram's age." He grinned cynically. "I imagine she favors Bartram once in a while, so he accepts her favors and turns a blind eye. And should he argue, he'll find the king's troops knocking on his door. He'd not want that any more than Khoros—it'd occupy too many men, to no one's good, and leave the way open for the fey folk to come back."

"Do you believe they would?" Cullyn asked.

Andrias shrugged. "Perhaps."

"They've not," Cullyn said. "Surely not since my father fought the Great War."

"As did I," Andrias told him. "But I'd not see them back."

"Why not?"

Andrias shrugged again. "They're *different*. They're not like us. The gods know, they set up the Barrier across the Alagordar."

That barrier no man could cross, or return from. There was no understanding of it, save that it confused mens' minds and turned them around. The great river ran through the heart of the forest, from the Kandarian side to the other, which men named Duran. Cullyn had been there often enough, watching the farther bank, where willows drooped as naturally, and waterbirds—coots and moorhens, ducks and stately swans—went about their business as if all were normal. Otters swam there, hunting the fish that he sometimes caught. Neither was the river very deep: a horseman might ford it easily . . . but if he tried, either he disappeared forever, or found himself fording back to the Kandarian side. It was Durrym magic—what the fey folk had established to protect themselves after the Great War—and no man understood quite how they had gained that magic.

"Perhaps," Cullyn said, "because we drove them out and they wanted their own land, without us."

Andrias laughed and shook his head. "You've lived alone too long in that forest, lad. You should listen more to what the Church says."

Cullyn shrugged in turn.

"Anyway," Andrias said, "I shall get the best prices I can. Give me a day, eh?"

Cullyn ducked his head in agreement, and then wondered what to do with the remainder of the day. Elvira was gone and he could hardly hope to see Lord Bartram's daughter again, for all her beauty occupied his mind. There had been something there in that flash of contact and irritation that . . . he was not sure; only that it was hopeless.

He went out from the inn to wander the small streets again, studying such things as he could not afford. Swords, and handsomely tooled scabbards; saddles accoutred with gold and silver chasings; bright brass stirrups and cooking pots beyond his means. He grew miserable and returned to the inn, where he knew friends and would not feel so alone and poor.

The common room was empty of guests at this hour. Martia stood behind the long serving table, polishing mugs and glasses, beaming at him as he came in.

"Andrias is off selling your bounty," she told him. "A mug of ale?"

He nodded and she drew him a tankard of the dark
bitter beer.

"You seem"—she hesitated—"unhappy."

He took a mouthful of the ale before he replied. "
saw someone today. I . . ."

"Abra," Martia nodded. "Andrias told me. An odd
lass, that one—and far beyond *your* reach. She resent
her stepmother, and has little time for anyone save he
father." She shrugged her plump shoulders. "Forget such
dreams, lad. Abra's prideful, and besides, she's betrothed
to Wyllym of Danzigan Keep."

Cullyn grinned and took another sup of ale. "I'd no
think to bed a lord's daughter."

Martia chuckled, reaching across to pat his cheek
"And before last night, you'd not thought to bed any
one, eh?"

He felt his cheeks grow warm and hid his face in his
mug. Martia laughed aloud. "Elvira's a fine girl," she said
"You could do worse. Listen." Her laughter faded as her
tone grew earnest. "Why don't you give up forest life and
live here? With us? We could use a strong young man like
you. You'd be useful here, and you'd find a decent enough
living. And Elvira to warm your bed."

Cullyn set down his mug. "My thanks," he said,
"but no."

"Is living alone in the forest so wonderful, then?"
Martia fixed him with accusing eyes. "Do you enjoy it so
much?"

He thought a moment and then nodded. "Yes.
It's . . ." He shrugged. "I enjoy it."

"Wondering if you'll have enough to eat? Snowed in
come winter? Dragging that cart here to trade what
you've hunted down?"

"Yes," he said. "But I'll have a horse soon, and be
able to ride."

"Obstinate boy." Martia shook her head in maternal irritation. "You'd be better off here. You could have a warm room, good food. And Elvira."

Cullyn emptied his tankard and smiled at her. "I have a warm room," he said, "and the snow's not so bad. And I doubt I *could* live here. I think I'm too used to the forest."

"I give up! The gods know, but perhaps you're fey yourself."

"Perhaps," Cullyn agreed as she drew him another tankard.

"But don't say that to anyone else," she advised. "Folk here think you're strange enough already. Don't give them further cause to doubt you."

"Why should they?" he asked.

"Because you live solitary, in the forest, where the fey folk set up their Barrier. Some wonder why you stayed, after your parents died. They wonder if you're not in league with the Durrym."

Cullyn laughed. "I've never seen a Durrym. I've heard my father's stories about the Great War, but he said they looked much like us. And he thought they were only fighting us to protect the land that was once theirs."

"Likely so," Martia allowed. "But Lord Bartram's got a new churchman, who preaches that the Durrym are an abomination, as are all who mingle with them. Which might be you, simply because you live so close to the Alagordar. So be careful, eh?"

Cullyn nodded, wondering why the Church must make such a fuss of nonevents. The Kandarians had driven the Durrym eastward across the river, and since the Great War there had been little enough fighting. There *had* been raids in the early years, but nothing since he had grown to what he supposed was his manhood. It seemed to him that the fey folk had gone away, that the

Alagordar was marked as division between Kandar and
the Durrym. So why condemn anyone for living within
the forest?

"I'll be careful," he said. "Indeed, does Andrias find
me good prices, I'll be gone tomorrow."

Martia sighed and he drained his mug, announcing
his intention of finding his room. He had again drunk
more than he was accustomed to, so he found his chamber and stretched on the bed, closing his eyes on hopeless
memories of red hair and angry eyes.

It was twilight before he woke, and his belly rum-
bled, so he went down to the common room and waited
to be served.

Elvira came to him with a mug of ale and asked what
he'd like. He looked at her and thought of Abra, and
asked that she bring him whatever was available. He
dined on roasted beef and dumplings in thick gravy, and
a bowl of vegetables, and then cheese and bread, and still
more tankards of ale.

After, he slept for a while, until Elvira came to him,
stripping off her gown as he lay, more than a little drunk
on the bed. He watched her, thinking that she was beautiful . . . but not like the girl—or was she a woman?—
he'd seen that day. But Abra was beyond his grasp and
Elivira was present: he smiled and welcomed her.

But all the time he was with her, he thought of Abra.

TWO

ABRA SAT SULLENLY beside her father in the Great Hall. She was to his left, her stepmother to his right, and Amadis beyond her, whispering in Vanysse's ear even as Bartram cut into his meat, all smiles and good humor. He seemed unaware of what transpired between his wife and his captain, innocent of their flirtation. Indeed, he raised his goblet to toast the captain.

"So it was a good hunt, eh? My congratulations, Amadis. And to you, my love." He ducked his head toward his wife, then turned to Abra. "And did you enjoy it, sweetling?"

Abra forced a smile and nodded. What could she tell him? What *should* she tell him? That Amadis was likely Vanysse's lover? Most folk believed that, and the pair gave every impression that it was so, but her father seemed to accept it. He seemed so besotted with his new

bride, and—she was sure—would dismiss her suspicions
So she said, "It was a most interesting hunt, Father." And
smiled piercingly at Amadis. "And our captain was most
brave."

Bartram nodded solemnly. "I hear that you faced the
boar alone, Amadis." He stroked his graying beard, ab-
sentmindedly wiping meat juices from fingers that he
then stroked against his shirt. Abra saw Amadis smile, as
if her father amused him with his uncouth habits.

The fair-haired man shrugged negligently. "There
were none others present, my lord, and it was not so large
a boar."

"It was *huge*," Vanysse declared. "A veritable monster. Amadis was a hero to slay it alone."

Abra winced. Her stepmother gazed adoringly at
Amadis; less tolerantly at her older husband. Why, Abra
wondered, had her father taken up with this trollop who
flaunted her infatuation before him? Were his eyes
blinded, could he not see what went on?

Presumably not, save that he was besotted, or accepted the arrangement. It was, after all, a marriage of
convenience: it linked holds, and Vanysse's dowry had
strengthened Lyth's fortunes. Perhaps that was why he allowed it. Perhaps it was only convenience, and her father
the wiser man. Accepting what he gained and willing to
share it—her!—with another. Save she remembered, dis-
tantly, her mother and father's devotion, and could not
accept Vanysse.

Lord Bartram beamed approval and raised his goblet.
"To my captain," he announced. "A toast to his courage."

Below the high table the soldiery of the keep dutifully raised their mugs. Abra saw Laurens, the master-at-
arms, frown as he joined the accolade. "Amadis," they
shouted, but she thought that Laurens's lips shaped different words.

She studied his grizzled face, wondering if he shared her dislike of Amadis. He had served her father for as long as she could remember. Indeed, it had been Laurens who first set her on a pony, when her mother was still alive, and taught her to ride. It had been Laurens who first taught her to use a bow, and a boar spear. She was no longer sure how old he was, for he seemed ageless. His hair was as gray as her father's, but he could still master the younger men in the practice yard, and ride with the best of them. He lacked Amadis's fine-featured looks—his face was lined and his nose broken askew—but to Abra he was solid as the northern mountains. Trustworthy and loyal. She wondered if she should speak with him of Amadis and her stepmother.

But then the priest spoke to her, and she was forced to answer him politely, as he asked: "You seem unhappy, demizzel."

She smiled courteously. "Why do you say that, Per Fendur?"

She liked this priest no better than Amadis. He seemed an oily fellow, for all he was as handsome as the captain. And—like Amadis—there was something about him she could not take to. He was young, and the silver fillet that marked him as a churchman held back thick, black hair and accentuated his aquiline features. His dark robe flattered his slender body, and in other circumstances, she might have found his attentions welcome.

But there was still something about him that she could not trust. It was not simply that Khoros had sent him here, although she was sure he was the king's spy—or the Church's. There was something else about him that made her think of lies and betrayals. But she held on to her smile: no point to offending the chosen of the gods.

"I see your expression," he murmured. "And wonder
why you seem so"—he shrugged eloquently—"*disturbed?*"

Abra felt suddenly cold. Per Fendur was not at all to
her liking, but he was perceptive. Indeed, she wondered
if he saw past her courtesy to what lay beneath. She took
a sip of wine that she might find the time to compose a
diplomatic reply, and said: "It was a *small* boar. I find my
father vaunts Amadis overmuch."

"Such is the way," Fendur replied, leaning toward her
as if they spoke in confidence. "But still he slew the
beast."

"And much impressed my stepmother," Abra said.

"Ah!" Fendur smiled at her. "But even so, is he not
brave? Does he not make a fine captain?"

"I suppose he does," Abra allowed. "Surely he drills
the men enough."

"Which is as well," Fendur said, "should the Durrym
come against us again."

"Think you they shall?" Abra was thankful that the
conversation moved away from Amadis and Vanysse.
"Surely they're gone away behind the Barrier."

"Perhaps." Fendur shrugged. "But who's to say they'll
not come back? Or we seek to cross the Alagordar?"

"Why?" she asked.

"To own new lands," the priest answered. "Kandar
fills up with folk now. The Vakyr intrude eastward, and
there are the Almyrian barbarians to the north, and perhaps someday we shall need more space. Where can we
go, save across that river?"

"But none can cross," she said, intrigued despite her
antipathy. "Any that have attempted the crossing have
been tricked back by Durrym magic, or disappeared forever."

"So far," Fendur said, "but now . . . the Church finds
new powers. Perhaps before long . . ." He stroked his

hands, eyes hooding. "I must not say more. Save that our domain might well extend."

"Kandar," she asked. "Or that of the Church?"

"Is there any difference?" Per Fendur returned.

❦❧

CULLYN WOKE EARLY, with an aching head and churning belly. Birds sang outside his window, and he heard dogs barking as the sky brightened into day. For a moment he thought he was home, back in the forest, but then reality impinged and he looked at the shape still sleeping beside him. For one insane moment, as he shifted from sleep to wakefulness, he imagined that it was the woman he had seen. Abra. But then Elvira's blond curls tossed on the pillow as she turned to smile at him.

"Come here," she said, opening her arms.

He did, and it was good. But still he imposed Abra's face on hers.

The dawn grew brighter still and she rose, businesslike, washing swiftly and gathering up her discarded clothing. Cullyn lay in bed, exhausted and confused.

"I must go make breakfast," she told him. "What shall you want?"

"You," he said, not meaning it; or did he? He was no longer sure. "Eggs and ham. Bread. And plenty of tea." He rubbed his eyes and his swirling skull. "I drank too much last night."

"Even so," she said as she fastened her skirt, "you were . . ."

She blushed, which surprised Cullyn. "What?" he asked.

"Why do you live alone in the forest?" She laced her skirt in place and found her shoes. Pulled them on. "Why not here?"

"Here, in Lyth?" He shook his head. "I can't."

"You'd have me," she said. "Alone."

He watched her button her bodice. The corset settled over her breasts, and he remembered the taste of her nipples in his mouth. And all else.

"I don't know," he said. "I . . ."

She pulled her blouse into place, and rose.

"I couldn't live here," he said.

She said, "It's not so bad."

"Could you live in the forest?" he asked.

She shook her head.

"Then . . ."

She shrugged and kissed him. "I'll see to your breakfast."

❧❧❧

HE LAY A WHILE, confused. Then he rose and washed and went down to the common room. He had achieved a goal—he had lost his virginity and found a woman who wanted to be with him—but that seemed only to render his life complicated. It seemed simpler—and far easier—to live alone. Save for the sensual pleasures of being with someone.

He smiled at Elvira as he found a table, but she only set his food before him and said, "Decide. I wait for no man!"

He nodded and set to his breakfast. He knew he'd not stay in Lyth, for all Elvira's charms, and so he'd sooner depart as early as he might. He thought that another night here could confuse him beyond sorting, and he missed the forest. He pondered as he ate.

Elvira's charms were enticing, and he thought that were she willing to come live with him it could be pleasant. But she was not, and he was not willing to live in the

illage, so there was no hope. He felt sad and at the same
me excited to be going home again . . . once Andrias
paid him.

Martia came to his table, scrubbing flour from her
ample arms, and set a dusty, maternal hand on his head.

"Have you chosen?"

He nodded. "I'm going home."

"I'm sorry," she said. "I worry about you, living all
alone But if you've decided . . ."

"I have," he said.

"So be it, then. When shall you leave?"

"After I've spoken with Andrias," he replied. "All
well, today."

"I doubt he'll be long." She stroked his head a while,
embarrassing him, then bussed his cheek and went back
to her kitchen.

Andrias appeared, his face stretched in a smile, and
took a seat across from Cullyn.

"Good news," he said. "Indeed, most excellent
news."

Cullyn waited, but Andrias chose to draw it out. He
turned and called for Elvira to bring him tea. She served
him a mug, not looking much at Cullyn, who watched
her walk away, wondering as he observed the sway of her
hips if he had made the right decision.

"I got you good prices," Andrias said. "Two more deer
and I think that come the Horse Fair you'll be able to afford the animal you want."

"You're sure?" Cullyn asked. "A good horse, mind.
Not some hack!"

"A charger such as Lord Bartram's men ride,"
Andrias declared firmly. "My word on it."

Cullyn said, "Thank you."

"Thank me? The gods know but you've worked hard
enough toward that aim. Why thank me?"

"For all you've done," Cullyn answered.

Andrias laughed. "Just keep me supplied with venison, eh? That's thanks enough. Anyway, here are you takings." He tossed a small bag of coin onto the table.

Cullyn scooped it up, marveling at the weight: he could now purchase all the supplies he needed.

Andrias said, "I got you what you wanted—the flour and salt, and the rest. You need only collect them." Cullyn smiled his thanks. The bag sat heavy in his hand. Indeed, he thought there must be four or five coins inside, and he needed no more than Andrias had bought him. He pushed the bag across the table.

"Hold it for me, eh? Set it toward the horse."

"You're sure?"

Cullyn nodded. "What shall I do with it, in the forest? Save it for me, please."

"As you will." Andrias shrugged, scooping up the sack.

"Thank you." Cullyn wiped up the last remnants of his breakfast and emptied his mug. "I think I shall go now."

"You could stay a while," Andrias suggested. "Are you in such a hurry?"

Cullyn looked to where Elvira scrubbed the tables and nodded. "I think it best I be gone," he said. "I'll see you again when next I take a deer."

"You know that you're always welcome," Andrias said.

"Yes, and I thank you for that." They shook hands and Cullyn rose and went out, suddenly anxious to be gone.

He wondered if Elvira watched him leave, but he did not look back. He could seldom stay away from the forest long, as if the woodlands called him home. So he found his cart, already loaded with those provisions he had asked Andrias to purchase, and took up the straps and set out.

He was halted at the gate by Martia, who tossed a cloth-wrapped bundle onto the cart.

"Some sustenance for the road," she said. "Must you go?"

"I must. But thank you."

She hugged him a moment, and then watched him go out through the gate and down the street to the village wall.

It was a fine, bright day and he felt invigorated by the prospect of returning home. It was as if his feet bounced on the hard-packed dirt of the road, the earth itself propelling him onward. The sky was a hard blue, decked with drifting billows of white cloud like great ships sailing on some ethereal ocean. Birds darted there—swifts and swallows and skylarks—and the air was fresh and clean after the odors of the village. He thought a while of Elvira and her charms, and wondered if he regretted leaving them, but then decided not. The woods called him, and he knew he could never live the way she'd like, or she his way, so it was better that they part. He saw a hawk circling overhead, then hanging on steady wings as it studied the ground below. He watched it stoop and rise again, clutching some tiny animal in its talons before it dropped behind a hedge to eat its prey.

He halted around noon, shrugging off the cart's straps from his sweating shoulders, and opened the package Martia had gifted him. It held sufficient food for two days: roast beef and sweating cheese, hard bread, several apples. He ate enough to satisfy his hunger then marched on. He could see the forest's margin ahead, hazy in the distance, and it called to him.

That night he slept in a stand of birches that

surrounded a freshet where he caught a trout that he charred over his fire, and settled happily to sleep under a sky all filled with stars and the pale light of a half-grown moon. The grass smelled sweet, and night birds sang, and he slept until dawn, when he rose and ate the last of Martia's bounty before setting off.

The next day he came to the forest and found his cottage and knew something had changed. He could sense it, even before he entered the small building.

Inside, there was a difference: a pot misplaced, a book left out of place, a cup not where he'd left it. He saw that his bedding was disturbed, and as he examined the cottage he smelled a musty, leafy odor. For a while he wondered if the pigs had got inside; but they could not have closed the door behind them, nor reached up to the shelf on which he kept his few books.

No—some two-legged creature had been here.

He felt suddenly afraid, and drew his knife, inspecting the cottage.

Nothing was missing—only the disarrangement of inspection—so he sheathed his blade and went outside. He sniffed the air and found it normal—all forest smells, and that of the chickens and pigs that came rushing to him in search of food. He stared around and felt as if he were watched, but he could see no one. He paced the margins of his holding, staring at the encircling trees, but saw nothing untoward. Save he felt that odd sensation that eyes studied him, invisible behind the woodland canopy.

"Who's there?" he called. "Shall you come out?"

There was no answer, but still he felt he was watched. The short hairs of his neck tingled and he felt suddenly wary. He had not felt afraid before—not in the friendly forest—but now . . . He wondered who watched him. Or what.

"Shall you meet me?" he called, thinking the while that perhaps he should purchase a dog. "Are you afraid of me?"

No answer: only the rustling of leaves and birdsong.

He shrugged and shouted, "So be it, then," and set to unloading his cart.

He stored his supplies and fed the animals, then fed himself and settled to sleep. But for the first time, he bolted the door.

❧❧❧

HE WOKE WITH THE DAWN light and the birds' song and felt afraid. He rose and went outside—as much to prove to himself that he was not afraid as for any other reason.

Sunlight wafted brilliant through the trees' canopy, patterning the grass in dappled shades of green. The chickens clucked about their business and the pigs—those not already gone into the forest—snuffled at the ground around the cottage. All was normal.

Cullyn gathered eggs and went back inside. He made his breakfast, thinking of Elvira and Abra, and then took up his bow. Andrias had said that two more deer would buy him a horse, and the sooner he took them down, the sooner he'd be able to ride.

It was easy for him to find the deer trails. They cut through the bracken to the waterholes and grazing places, where he could follow them and wait and take what he needed, and today he decided that—no matter who or what watched him—he'd take at least one deer to buy his desired horse. So he checked his bow and oiled the string, then checked all his arrows and their fletchings, and went out into the woodland.

He felt curiously uneasy, thinking of his unknown visitor.

It was another sunny day, light drifting down through the canopy of overhanging branches to dapple the grass below with harlequin patterns of sun and shadow. A gentle breeze stirred the leaves and the ferns, so that their soft rustling was a whispered counterharmony to the trilling of the birds that filled the trees. It was a day that in other circumstances he'd have enjoyed for its beauty, but now felt somehow menacing.

He had felt watched before, but had never known the watchers to intrude on his home. That made a difference.

He shook off the feeling, intent on taking his first deer, telling himself there was nothing he could do. If the Durrym watched him, then they watched him. If they chose to show themselves, he'd face them. He had no argument with them, nor wanted any. But still, as he found fresh tracks and crouched to examine a pile of dung, he felt uneasy. It was as if the forest had changed.

He followed the trail, knowing it led to a spring, and circled around so that he approached the water with the breeze on his face.

The spring was set between outcrops of stone that thrust up from the grassy sward, birches growing silvery from between the rocks, and all the circle surrounded by stately oaks. Three deer drank there: a young stag and two hinds. Cullyn nocked an arrow and sighted down the shaft at the older hind. The stag looked up, antlers tossing as he scented the wind. He raised his head, mouth opening to bell a warning. Cullyn drew back and loosed his shaft.

The arrow flew true, taking the hind behind the left shoulder as she rose from the water. She coughed and stumbled a few faltering steps back. The stag and the other hind turned and ran even as Cullyn charged out, bow dropped and knife in hand to plunge the blade into her throat. He slew her swiftly, as she deserved, standing back as she fell, blood coming from her throat as her gentle eyes dulled. He waited until her last kicking was done and then lifted her across his shoulders and started back to his cottage.

It was mid-afternoon before he reached home and halted in amazement as he saw the horses there.

He'd seen them before: the dozen or so he'd watched riding out from the keep. Big hunters, handsomely accoutred, the riders making use of his well, and staring at him as if he had no right to approach his own home. They were, he realized, Lord Bartram's men, for they wore such gear as only keep folk owned—metal-plated leather and mail, half-helms atop their heads, swords in scabbards, even some shields slung on the saddles. He felt affronted by their imperious gaze.

He dropped the deer as a tall man, old enough to be his father, came toward him. He was grizzled gray, with lines on his face, and a long scar that ran from hairline to chin, but he was smiling, and as he reached Cullyn he ducked his head and said, "I apologize for this intrusion. I am Laurens, master-at-arms to Lord Bartram."

Cullyn nodded, confused. "What do you want?"

"We were hunting," the old man said, "and we came upon your cottage. The lady Vanysse and her daughter, the demizzel Abra, wished to rest, so . . ." He shrugged. "They chose to rest here. I trust . . ."

What else he might have said was cut off by the man who emerged from the cottage. Cullyn recognized him as Amadis. He was dressed in hunting gear, and carried his helm so that his long, blond hair waved free, his handsome face set in a casual smile.

"So who's this, Laurens?" He glanced enquiringly at Cullyn, as if he inspected some prospective target.

Laurens said, "The cottage's owner, captain. I don't know his name."

Amadis nodded and went on smiling. "Which is?"

"Cullyn," Cullyn said. "And this is my home."

Amadis shaped a mocking bow. "And I trust you'll forgive us for making use of your humble abode, but my lady and the demizzel were in need of rest and shelter. And . . ." He gestured at the cottage, the waving of his hand making it seem somehow smaller and poorer than it was. "We found this. So . . ."

"Be welcome," Cullyn said. "The ladies are inside?"

"Taking their rest." Amadis nodded.

Cullyn stepped toward his door and Amadis moved to block him.

"They'd have their privacy."

"This is my home," Cullyn said.

"Even so." Amadis shrugged, a negligent hand touching his sword's hilt.

His intention was obvious and Cullyn felt anger swelling. He realized that his own hand was on the hilt of his hunting knife, and Amadis was smiling at him as if in challenge.

Then Laurens stepped between them. "Shall I call to the ladies, Captain? They'd likely enjoy meeting their host."

He turned before Amadis could reply and bellowed at the house.

"Mesdames, the owner is come and bids you welcome. Shall you greet him?"

Cullyn saw Amadis scowl, but the two women emerged from the cottage and he recognized them both. One was Vanysse, Lord Bartram's wife, dressed in hunting green, her long blond hair tousled, her face flushed.

She was, Cullyn thought, beautiful, but not so lovely as her red-haired stepdaughter.

Abra wore the same tunic and divided skirt, which flattered her slender body and set off the color of her hair in different hues, like oak trunks to autumnal leaves. Her eyes were large and very blue above a tip-tilted nose and full, naturally red lips. Cullyn felt his breath catch in his throat; almost, he bent a knee.

But then she smiled and said, "Please forgive us, but we were tired," and it was as if the sun emerged from behind gray clouds and bathed him in its radiance.

All he could do was nod and mumble, and say, "Welcome. My home is yours."

Her stepmother laughed and said, "How charming." And glanced at Amadis before she added, "And you are?"

"Cullyn," he said. "Cullyn ap Myrr."

"And you live here?" Vanysse waved a casual hand toward his cottage. "Alone in the forest?"

He looked at Abra as he said, "It suits me, lady. My father built this house after the Great War. He brought my mother here, and I was born here. I have lived here since."

"What of your parents?" Abra asked.

"They died," Cullyn answered.

"And now you live here alone?"

He nodded, and she asked, "Is it not lonely?"

He shrugged and shook his head. "Sometimes, perhaps, but not much."

"I doubt I could survive it," she said, smiling at him so that his heart warmed to her as it had not to Elvira. "I think I must be too content with life in the castle. Is it not uncomfortable in winter?"

"It's cold," he said, "but I can build a fire." He laughed, charmed by her easy manner and her beauty, and gestured at the trees. "I've enough wood."

She smiled and he was entranced.

He asked, "And what is life in the castle like?"

But before she could answer, her stepmother interrupted.

"Enough, eh?" Vanysse glowered at her stepdaughter. "We've taken sufficient of his time."

"And hospitality," Amadis added. "So let's be on our way."

He reached into his sabretache and tossed two coins to Cullyn.

Cullyn watched them fall, insulted. A pig came to investigate the downfall. He kicked it away as Abra blushed. Her stepmother smiled as Amadis helped her astride her horse. He watched Abra mount, and then felt a heavy hand on his shoulder.

"He knows no better," Laurens said. "Take the coin and no insult, eh?"

"He's . . ." Cullyn struggled to find the right word.

Laurens swung astride his horse. "Arrogant? Rude? Presumptious? Name it, lad—I know it. But take the coin—the gods know, he has enough to spend. Use it, eh? And if you ever think of being a soldier, come see me in the keep."

"I don't think," Cullyn said, "that I'd like soldiering."

"There are worse lives," Laurens answered. "The gods know, but I've been at the trade for forty years and more. Think about it, eh?"

Cullyn nodded and watched them ride away, all set up on great, grand horses, bound for the keep where servants would prepare them baths and set their food before them, cooked and ready to eat, and after take the plates away and clear the tables, while he must butcher the deer he'd taken and trudge afoot into Lyth if ever he hoped to own a horse.

He sighed, and carried the deer to the outhouse; it

was dark before the butchering was done and he washed and settled to sleep.

Which was disturbed by the insensate notion that he was still being watched.

❧❧❧❧

HE WOKE UNEASY, the smell of strangers in his nostrils and the memory of odd dreams in his head.

It was as if Abra had imprinted her scent on the cottage. Then he recalled the coins the captain had so casually tossed him and found them in the pig-grubbed dirt outside as he went to the well. He grinned wryly as he scooped up the silver discs—they'd go some good way to buying his horse—before he drew a bucket from the well and bathed. Then he fed the animals and watered his small vegetable garden before making himself a simple breakfast; and all the while he thought of Abra and Elvira, and weighed the proven charms of the one against the untasted charms of the other, and thought that both were unobtainable.

He checked the butchered carcass of the deer and found it sound, so he took up his bow again and went out to hunt another.

He realized that he wanted to wait no longer to purchase his horse. It was as if his unwelcome visitors had started up some desire he had not previously known, so that he was now consumed with impatience. He would, he decided, take a second deer and go straight back to Lyth, not wait for the Summer Horse Fair, but buy an animal as soon as possible.

He was firm in his purpose as he stalked the deer trails through the forest, and equally uneasy, for he felt he was still watched. It was as if some shadow trailed him, unseen amidst the bracken, and although he would halt and glance around and sniff the breeze, he could not see his follower.

It was like chasing a dream: a thing perceived on the edge of vision, shapeless and unfocused. Sometimes he thought he caught a glimpse of some shifting shape that crouched inside the tall ferns or darted behind the bole of an oak, but there was never any firm sighting. Only the sensation of eyes upon his back, as if he were the hunted.

He took a deer with a single clean shot, and as he cut the throat a figure emerged from behind a lowering oak.

Cullyn stared, grasping his bloody knife, ready to defend himself. Save the man—a Durrym, he supposed—raised opened hands in gesture of amity. He was as tall as Cullyn himself, and dressed in similar garb, save his blended better with the woodland, all motley patternings that melded with the trees and bracken and seemed, even, to ape the shadings of the sunlight. He was slender for all his broad shoulders, and long, leaf-brown hair was drawn back in a tail from a narrow face that was simultaneously alien and handsome. He carried a bow strung across his back, and a long knife was sheathed on his hip, but he smiled in a friendly way, so that Cullyn felt a little more at ease.

"Who are you?" he asked.

"I am named Lofantyl," the Durrym said. "Who are you?"

"Cullyn."

The Durrym nodded. "I have watched you a while now. You love this forest, no?"

Cullyn nodded. "It's my home."

"I love it, too. Almost as much as Coim'na Drhu."

Cullyn frowned, and Lofantyl added: "Our new homeland. Since you drove us out of Coim'na Hass." He shrugged. "I don't know what you call it."

"Kandar," Cullyn supplied.

"An ugly name, but no matter." Lofantyl gestured at Cullyn's still-ready knife. "Shall you put that blade away and we talk?"

Utterly confused, Cullyn nodded.

THREE

❧❦❧❦

CULLYN STARED in amazement at the Durrym, but Lofantyl smiled at him, as if this strange meeting were normal.

"I've watched you a while," he said, "and I think you know it."

Cullyn nodded, and mumbled, "I sensed you there. Was it you who went into my cottage?" He wondered if he should draw his knife and attempt to kill this stranger, considered a mortal enemy by Church and State. But the Durrym seemed friendly, as if they were two chance acquaintances met by accident or, perhaps, design, and he felt no wish to fight.

Lofantyl ducked his head, shrugging a gesture of apology. "I was curious. Your ways are different, and I wondered how you lived. I had never seen the inside of a Garm's home before."

"Is that what you call us?" Cullyn asked.

"Garm'kes Lyn. In our language it means 'taker,' " Lofantyl said. "Because you took our land. What do you call us?"

"Durrym. That means 'exile.' "

"We obviously have our own names for one another," Lofantyl said, smiling, "but I wonder if you and I could not be friends."

It occurred to Cullyn that this was a most odd conversation. The Durrym were the creatures of nightmare, proscribed by the Church as godless outcasts; they were the reason the great border forts had been built after the war. And they, in turn, had created the Barrier to hold men from the land Lofantyl named as Coim'na Drhu. They were the ogres mothers warned their children of. Cullyn could remember his own mother telling him that a Durrym might come in the night and take him away, if he was naughty. Yet now he sat speaking with one such monster—who seemed not at all menacing.

"Perhaps," he allowed.

"Save?" Lofantyl asked, hearing the hesitation in Cullyn's voice.

"I . . ." Cullyn shrugged, his voice faltering.

"Don't trust me?" Lofantyl chuckled, a musical sound. "Because I'm . . . What is that name you have—*Durrym*?"

"No; yes," Cullyn spluttered. "But mostly because you spied on me."

"I wanted to know you," Lofantyl said calmly, "before I spoke with you."

"Do you often speak with us Garm . . . whatever?"

"Garm'kes Lyn," the Durrym supplied. "No. Sometimes we come across the river to watch you, but not often. I am considered . . . odd, for my interest in you. But . . ."

He paused, and Cullyn sensed something behind his calm expression that was not at all calm. "What?" he asked.

"The woman," Lofantyl said. "I've seen her before, and . . ." Cullyn wondered if the Durrym blushed, for surely Lofantyl's face grew red as he added, "I believe myself in love."

"What woman?" Cullyn asked.

"The young one," the Durrym returned. "The one with the red hair, like oak leaves in the autumn. The one with the face that—"

"Abra," Cullyn interrupted. "Lord Bartram's daughter."

"She's noble born?" Lofantyl asked.

"Her father's a Border Lord," Cullyn said. "Sworn to defend our land against the likes of you."

"The likes of me?" Lofantyl chuckled. "My own father would defend *our* land against the likes of *you.*"

Cullyn shrugged his incomprehension, and wondered if he were not dreaming. He sat in conversation with one of his people's enemies, who seemed entirely friendly. Indeed, love struck; yet he found the *man*—he could somehow not conceive Lofantyl as enemy—most likable.

"My father is *Vashinu* of the *Kash'ma Hall.* He commands the south of Coim'na Drhu." Lofantyl chuckled again. "Forgive me—that means that my father is what you would call a Border Lord. His fortress is Kash'ma Hall, and his duty is to hold the south of Coim'na Drhu safe against you . . . What are you called?"

"Kandarians," Cullyn said, feeling his confusion grow by the moment. "I don't understand this."

"It's really quite simple," Lofantyl said. "You drove us out, so we retreated across the river—"

"The Alagordar."

"Which we call the Mys'enh, and set up the Barrier, yes. I suppose it was better than fighting you. But I always wondered what our old land was like, so I came across the river to find out." He shrugged, chuckling. "My father considers my interest strange. I think he indulges my fancy only because he has my brother, Afranydyr, to name as heir. But, anyway"—he beamed amiably at Cullyn—"I came and watched you, and saw *her*. Abra, you said was her name?"

Cullyn nodded. He felt confusion drape him like a cloak, like some wild dream that wrapped him up and carried him off into such realms of fantasy as he could not imagine. He thought that likely he blasphemed the Church's doctrines by speaking with Durrym; that he betrayed King Khoros and Lord Bartram, both. And yet he could not help liking this man.

"And fell in love with her," the Durrym added.

"You, too?" Cullyn asked.

"Are we rivals, then?"

"I've hardly seen her," Cullyn mumbled. "Twice, perhaps."

"When she came to your cottage?"

"You saw that?"

"I was watching. Her guards are not very observant."

"They're not so used to the forest," Cullyn said. "Save for hunting, they tend to avoid the woods. When they come here, they come in numbers."

"How strange." Lofantyl shook his head thoughtfully. "The forest is *our* friend."

He said it in such a way as to imply that he spoke not only of the Durrym, but also of Cullyn himself, as if they were somehow bonded by their love of the woodlands. Cullyn could only nod his agreement. And then ask the inevitable question: "How can you cross the Alagordar? How can you cross the Barrier, when we cannot?"

"I've the key," Lofantyl answered, as if that were all that needed saying. At least, until he saw Cullyn's incomprehension. Then: "We always lived *with* the land—we came to know it, and understand it, and thus made it work for us."

"Like farming," Cullyn interjected.

"No!" Lofantyl shook his head emphatically. "We do not parcel up the land in little bits and pieces as you do. We live *with* it, and take what bounty it offers—which it does in abundance." He frowned, his tanned face wrinkling like a nut. "I've ventured farther than I should from the forest margins, and seen what you do. All those *walls* of stone; everything fenced off. How can you live like that?"

"I don't," Cullyn said, feeling a degree of sympathy.

"Not you, perhaps." Lofantyl smiled an apology. "But your people . . ."

"It's how they . . ."—Cullyn corrected himself—"*we* live. Each family has its own piece of land. They own it and tend it. It belongs to them."

"How can the land belong to anyone?" Lofantyl asked. "The land is itself, not yours or mine. We only share it, live *with* it."

"I suppose," Cullyn said, struggling with concepts alien to Kandarians, "that we have a different way of thinking." He shrugged, seeking an explanation he was not at all sure he understood himself. "What if I could cross the Alagordar and find Kash'ma Hall? Could I walk in as you did to my home? Wander round and inspect the place?"

Lofantyl nodded. "Of course, and you'd be welcome."

"And you'd let me go, after?"

"*I* would. But"—he smiled—"I doubt my father or Afranydyr would. They trust you Garm no better than you trust us."

"So I'd be trapped?" Cullyn wondered.

"Not by me," Lofantyl answered. "But I was too young to fight in the *A'sh im'whey*." Cullyn guessed that meant the Great War. "My father did, and Afranydyr is old enough to remember some of it. They'd not let you go."

"What would they do with me?"

"Kill you," Lofantyl replied. "Or set you to work."

"Is that why no one has ever come back?"

The Durrym nodded his agreement. "Very few can find their way past the Barrier. Those who have . . ." He shrugged again. "Either they're slain or become our servants." He chuckled at Cullyn's expression. "What do you do to us?"

"Those captured," Cullyn acknowledged, "are executed."

"We're not so different then."

Cullyn shook his head.

"I think," Lofantyl said, "that I'd like to show you Coim'na Drhu. After all, I've seen your home."

"And could I come back?" Cullyn asked.

"Aye, there's the rub." Lofantyl laughed. "Perhaps one day, eh?"

"Perhaps." For all the Durrym's easygoing manner, Cullyn could not help a degree of suspicion. The fey folk were, after all, known for their seductions, and perhaps this was somewhat of the same.

"But to other matters," Lofantyl declared. "You say the woman is named Abra, and she's this lord's daughter?"

"Aye, Lord Bartram's," Cullyn replied, wondering which direction their conversation now took.

"And she lives in that great stone place on the hill?"

Cullyn nodded. "How else do you build a castle?"

"With trees," Lofantyl answered, as if that were only normal. Then, "And she hunts these woods?"

"You know that."

Lofantyl smiled and ducked his head. "Yes, I do." He pondered a moment, then rose in a single swift movement. "I shall see you again, my friend. I trust we *are* friends?"

Before Cullyn had a chance to answer, the Durrym was gone, fleeting as a shadow into the forest. He made little sound and seemed to leave no tracks—it was, Cullyn thought, as if the woodland itself gave him shelter: hid him so that no human might see him come and go.

Cullyn picked up his deer and carried it back to his cottage, which no longer felt the same. It had always been a haven to him, and it now felt violated—by both Lofantyl and the hunters from the keep. It was as if his privacy were stolen, and he became privy to unexpected visitors, who came and went at will. Even did he feel an instinctive liking for the Durrym, still Lofantyl had entered his home uninvited.

He hung the deer beside the other and set the carcass to bleeding. Then, shutting the outhouse door on the eagerly squealing pigs, he went into the cottage.

Bright sunlight set motes of dust to dancing in the shafts that fell across the interior, and where one landed on the plain oak table, something glittered. Cullyn gasped as he picked it up: a dagger such as he'd never seen before. The hilt was some hardwood, a deep brown carved with intricate patterns that were both beautiful and securing, so that as he held it, it seemed to meld with his palm. The quillon was a span of similar wood that seemed less set into the jointure of hilt and blade than grown there. And from it extended a wide, double-edged blade that was manufactured of no material he could define. Certainly it was not metal, but when he touched it to a finger it cut him clean as any razor, and it shone bright as he raised it to the light. He wondered if it was a gift from Lofantyl, an apology for intrusion, and thought that if that were so, he'd received far less from the keep folk.

He took the knife and set to butchering the deer.

❧❀❧

ABRA SAT FLANKED by Per Fendur and Amadis in her parents' private chambers. It was a circular table, so that she faced her father and Vanysse, with Amadis to her right and Per Fendur to her left. No servants were present, having delivered the food and wine and departed. This was a discreet meeting. Indeed, so discreet that Per Fendur had suggested she leave. To which her father had voiced opposition, explaining that he had no secrets from his daughter, who would, after all, inherit the keep on his death.

"Save she's trothed to Wyllym of Danzigan," Fendur murmured. "So on your death—which I pray the gods delay for many years—this keep shall come under his command."

And he, like his father, Abra thought, is Khoros's man, and a weakling. She wished she might speak aloud, but that would only endanger her father's position. Bartram had fought for Kristoferos in the war between the brothers—the War of Succession—and he held this castle only because he commanded the loyalty of the Border folk, and should Khoros look to replace him, the king would likely find himself embroiled in rebellion. So Bartram remained keep lord, but—Abra knew—Amadis was Khoros's man, and so was Fendur; save the Church looked to its own ends.

She smiled politely back at Fendur, and then smiled brighter as her father said, "She's trothed, aye. But when it comes to it, she'll decide for herself." He stroked his thick beard, winking at her. "The gods know, but Wyllym's an ugly fellow."

"Even so," Fendur said, "it was agreed."

"By Khoros, when they were both still children," Bartram returned bluntly. "Never by Abra. Now she's near grown, and can make up her own mind."

"You'd go against the king's wishes?" Fendur asked.

"No," Bartram answered, "I'd do the king's duty. But I'll not go against my daughter's wishes."

Abra saw Vanysse scowl at that, touching her husband's hand as if in warning. Amadis sat stroking his clean-shaven chin with one hand, the other hidden. Abra wondered if it touched her stepmother's thigh. Fendur nodded, looking from one to the other.

"The marriage would please both our king and our Church," he said.

"No doubt." Lord Bartram smiled, teeth showing from under his moustache. He looked, Abra thought fondly, like some great bear, perhaps past its prime, but still powerful—muscle hidden under a weight of comfortable living, but nonetheless dangerous—and smiled at his answer. Vanysse favored her with an angry glance that she ignored.

"I serve our king and the Church, but my daughter comes first."

"Of course. But . . . A promise is surely a promise, and your lovely daughter was promised to Wyllym. *Trothed* to Wyllym. Does that not bind both her and you?"

"Trothed on the king's command," Bartram said. "Not hers or mine. Nor her mother's."

"Her mother is dead," Fendur said.

As Bartram nodded solemnly, Vanysse said, "I am her mother now, and I approve this betrothal."

Amadis voiced his support, and Per Fendur beamed. But then Bartram said, "It's for Abra to decide," and looked at her.

She thought of her father's future. Did he offend Khoros, who knew what might happen? But he had spoken out for her and left her to decide, so she said, "Does Wyllym wish to court me, I'll consider his proposal. But I'll not marry to order. I shall make up my own mind." She looked toward her father, avoiding her stepmother's angry stare. "With my father's permission."

Lord Bartram nodded.

Vanysse glowered, and Amadis held his expression in check—ever the diplomat. Fendur smiled his oily smile and said, "Then of course it must be so."

Bartram laughed and said, "My daughter, eh? She's a mind of her own."

"And it would take me away." Abra rose. "Do you forgive me, but I'd find my bed and think on all you've said." She kissed her father on the cheek and bowed to the others. "Good night."

Per Fendur rose from his chair to make the godly sign; Abra quit the room thinking that she was well done with such prevarications and politics. Did her father wish to marry some western whore, that was his affair. It had, after all, been a marriage of politics—to unite the eastern borders with the west—but perhaps her father loved the woman, for all Abra could not see how. But . . . She climbed the stairs from the chamber to her bedroom, thinking.

There were two images dancing in her mind like remembered dreams.

One was of a tall young man with long brown hair caught up in a tail . . . a beard . . . broad shoulders, and eyes that stared at her as if she were a jewel he could not properly comprehend. Cullyn, he'd said his name was.

And he lived in that sorry little shack in the forest
where she had rested and wondered how anyone coul
live so poorly.

The second was less distinct because it was far mor
akin to a dream: a matter of eyes on her as she rode th
woodlands, aware of some watcher who seemed obser
vant and benign, as if she were protected under the gaz
she could not see, but still felt safe, as if nothing unto
ward could happen to her while she was watched. It wa
a feeling of utter safety, and at the same time a feeling o
simplicity, as if the politics of Kandar meant nothing t
the forest, and that she might enter it and find peace—a
she thought Cullyn had—and forget Kandar's problems
and hers.

She thought that would be a fine thing as she
climbed to her chamber and prepared for sleep.

Save she could not: she felt too exasperated, think
ing of how Khoros and the Church would decide her life
for her, as if she were nothing more than some mino
piece in a Game of Stones. Amadis would agree with
them, as would Vanysse—if for no other reason than t
rid herself of a troublesome stepdaughter. Only her father
took her side, and no doubt even now Per Fendur and
Vanysse were bent on persuading him to their wishes—
and the gods knew, that woman could bend Bartram to
her desires. Abra ground her teeth in frustration, and
found herself not at all composed for sleep. She rose and
poured a glass of wine, pacing her bedroom as she wondered if it would have been better to remain in the dining chamber.

Only that would have curtailed whatever significant
conversation it was that Fendur sought with her father.
Per had made it clear his words were not for her ears—as
if she were some silly slip of a girl who would not understand.

But there were ways to circumvent the oily priest's secrecy: the keep was well built, with fireplaces and chimneys that heated all the rooms, and ventilation shafts built into the stone, rising from the ground floor to the upper reaches. Sometimes, from her bedroom, she could hear conversation from below—if it was summer and the hearths not lit, so that she could kneel and set her head inside the fireplace.

Which she did now.

". . . madness," she heard her father say, his voice a whispery echo in the chimney shaft. "They offer us no threat."

"They are always a threat," came back Per Fendur's solemn answer, incanted as if he spoke a catechism. "They are godless savages who'd steal our land."

Abra heard her father splutter. Then: "Steal *our* land? It seems more like that you'd steal theirs."

"They've no right to it," Fendur said.

"As much as we've right to Kandar," Bartram answered. "Remember, this was their land first. We drove them out."

"That," Fendur intoned, "was the gods' will. Else they'd have won, and we would have been expelled."

Bartram's snorting was contemptuous, even muffled by the chimney. "I'd thought," he said, "that it was more a matter of expediency and arms—we needed the land, so we went to war and drove off the original inhabitants. I fought in that war, and I can tell you that it was bloody. Far worse than the War of Succession."

"My lord Bartram, you border close on heresy."

"Do you threaten me?"

"Only point out fact. Your bravery is proven, but your loyalty—"

"Is to Kandar."

"Which means to King Khoros and the Church."

"And to the people, perhaps?"

"The people are guided and guarded by Church and king, who have only their best interests at heart."

Abra heard a gust of humorless laughter as her father said, "And you think the people shall welcome another war?"

"They may not have any choice," she heard Fendur say. "We need more land. Since we expelled the Durrym, Kandar has grown. There are more children born, more fields tilled; folk live longer. Kandar is greater than it has ever been, and we need more space. We *need* that land across the river."

"You've seen incomers," Amadis said in support. "Folk come from north and west, looking for land to settle."

Abra heard Vanysse agree.

Bartram thought a while. Then: "We took this land from the Durrym. Shall we now seek what they found after we drove them out?"

"Neither the king nor the Church sees any other choice."

Abra heard her father sigh gustily. "Another war?"

"Another chance," Fendur said. "More land for Kandarians."

"I see one problem here," Bartram returned. "How do we cross the Barrier? How do we find a way past the Alagordar?"

"The Church works on that even now," Fendur replied. "We believe we can overcome the savages' magic and find a way into the eastern lands. We believe the land itself owns magical power that the Durrym have learned to use. We believe the river is a crossing point between two worlds."

"That do not accept one another."

"Save we find a way." Abra heard Fendur snort triumphant laughter. "Which I believe we have."

"And if you can? What, then?"

"We shall have all the land we need. We believe the eastern forest stretches across the world—we can hew it down and build farms and villages, keeps and castles. We can make the Durrym land our own."

"And they'll not fight?"

"Of course," Fendur agreed. "But we defeated them before, and what are they, after all? Only savages."

"I think your . . ."—Abra heard her father hesitate—"optimism is misplaced. I think you make a grave mistake."

"It is written," Fendur said. "Decided by the gods and our king."

Abra lost the voices for a while then, but could hear the faint shuffling of feet, and guessed that her father paced the room, as was his wont when he pondered weighty matters.

Then: "Is this why you'd see my daughter wed to Wyllym?"

"It should be better," Fendur answered, "that all the Border keeps are bound together. Indeed, Wyllym's brother is trothed to Saryn of Andar Keep."

Abra heard laughter gust up the chimney as her father said, "She'll eat that little squit alive. The gods know, but she'll make him dance, and throw him out."

"Perhaps, but the keeps will be bound by marriage and loyalty. As would you be if—"

"I told you!" Abra heard her father's voice ring loud and angry. "That shall be her decision. Not mine or yours; neither the king's nor the Church's—only hers!"

There was a long silence then, before Fendur said, "So where shall you stand when the blades are drawn?"

"On Kandar's side," her father answered. "And now this discussion is ended. I shall find my bed and think on what you've said."

"I trust," Abra heard the priest say, "that you shall make the right decision."

There was shuffling then, and a loud slamming of doors. Abra withdrew from the fireplace to brush soot from her hair and pour another glass of wine as she considered all she'd heard.

There was much to ponder, and outside her windows the night was very black. She emptied the glass and climbed into bed, wondering about her future. Wondering about Kandar's future.

❧❧❧

CULLYN SET THE TWO BUTCHERED DEER on his cart and started off for Lyth. He was determined that this time he would come back with a horse. He'd not wait for the Summer Horse Fair, but buy one now—even did it cost him more.

He reached the village and dragged his cart into the yard of the Golden Goat, where both Martia and Andrias met him with surprise.

"Two, you said, eh? And here they are!" He dropped the straps as they stared at him. "Now find me a horse."

"Now?" Andrias asked.

Cullyn nodded.

"Eat first," Martia suggested.

"And let's talk," said Andrias.

He went inside the hostelry to encounter Elvira's . . . he was not sure whether it was smile or scowl. But he grinned at her and took the mug Andrias offered, and felt pleased with himself. After all, he had brought in the two deer Andrias had said would purchase him the horse. And he might see Abra again.

He drank the ale thirstily, then settled at a table to which Martia brought a venison pie.

"Yours," she said, "cooked of what you brought us be-fore."

He smiled and waited for Elvira to bring another mug.

When she did she was not so friendly. She set the cup before him and stood waiting until he asked, "Shall I . . . see you tonight?"

"I don't know." She set hands on hips and tossed back her blond curls. "I've other friends."

"I thought . . ." he said, and shook his head. "I don't understand this."

She said, "No, you don't," and walked away.

He called after her, remembering the pleasure they'd found, but she ignored him, so he ate his meal and drank his ale, thinking that he did not understand women. And when he was done, he found Andrias to ask about the horse.

"It'll take all you've saved with me," Andrias said, "but it's a fine mount. And Jordia will throw in all the trappings, but you'd still be better off to wait for the Horse Fair. It's not the friendliest of animals. Indeed—"

"Just show me," Cullyn grunted. He felt excited at the prospect of buying a horse, but also disappointed by Elvira's rejection. He wanted to get out of Lyth as quickly as possible. Save that staying might catch him another sight of Abra—for whatever that was worth.

Andrias shrugged. "Come look at it, then. I'll let Jordia tell you about it."

They went down through the narrow streets of Lyth to the stable, where a gray-haired woman greeted them and looked Cullyn up and down before she looked at Andrias and said, "He might be able to handle the bas-tard."

Andrias said, "If anyone can. He'd not listen to me."

Cullyn wondered what was wrong with the horse.

"Well, let's see." Jordia grinned at him. "Perhaps he *can* manage the beast. And at least it's cheap."

Her face was as nut-brown as Lofantyl's, and massively lined, but she walked with a fine stride, skirts swinging over wide hips with a vigor that belied her obvious age. Her arms were muscled from handling the horses.

She took them to a stall at the end of the stable, where a tall, black horse stood, stamping its feet. It rolled its eyes when it saw them, and bared its teeth.

"Why should he be cheap?" Cullyn asked. "He's superb."

"He killed his last owner," Jordia said. "Stamped him to death. I was going to sell him for meat until Andrias spoke to me."

Cullyn stared at the horse. It was big as any hunter out of the keep, and sleekly black as midnight. It flashed its teeth as he watched, and rose up to paw its fore hooves at the watchers.

Andrias said, "You'd be better to wait for the Horse Fair."

And Jordia added, "He's a killer."

Cullyn stared at the splendid beast and said, "How much?"

Jordia quoted a price and Cullyn shook her hand.

"That," Andrias said, "includes the tack, no?"

"And well rid of it," said Jordia. "It's bloodstained from the last owner."

Without further ado, Cullyn swung up onto the stable's gate and dropped into the stall. He ducked as the stallion snapped its teeth, avoiding the vicious bite, and then again as hooves swung toward his skull. He turned aside as the hind legs kicked at him, and jumped to grab an ear, and bit it and hung on as the horse struggled. He held his teeth firm in the ear as he settled one hand under the snapping jaw and the other in the mane and struggled to force the beast down. It snorted and bucked, but then fell over so that he could hold it, lying across its neck as he whispered to it.

"I'm your friend," he murmured. "I'll take you out of here to places you can run free. Believe me, eh?"

After a while the horse calmed, and Cullyn let it loose to rise, and when it did, it looked at him and ducked its head, and let him stroke its neck.

"I never thought to see that," Jordia said, amazement in her voice. "Has he fey blood?"

"He's an odd fellow," Andrias replied, grinning. "But he's got a way with him."

"For sure." Jordia brought a saddle and bridle from her tack room. "You know how to ride?"

Cullyn said, "I'll learn."

❧❧❦❧❧

THEY LED THE BIG BLACK STALLION back to the stables of the Golden Goat, where Cullyn fed him oats and saw him watered and settled. Andrias watched in amazement as the horse ate from Cullyn's hand.

"He killed his last owner," the landlord said. "Aren't you afraid of him?"

"No." Cullyn shook his head. "I think his last owner didn't understand him."

"Even so."

"You brought me to him."

"You were anxious for a horse."

Cullyn said, "Aye, and now I've got one. Even better than the keep's."

"If he doesn't kill you."

Cullyn laughed, rubbing the horse's nose. "He'll not—trust me."

"What shall you call him?"

Cullyn thought a moment, then said, "Fey."

"*Fey?*" Andrias stared at him. "What kind of name is that?"

"The one I want to give him," Cullyn said.

"Perhaps it is like they say." Andrias shook his head. "You are crazy."

"Perhaps." Cullyn stroked the sleek neck and Fey nuzzled his face. "Who cares?"

"Folk in Lyth," Andrias said. "They wonder about you."

"Let them wonder." Cullyn was altogether too happy with his horse to worry about mankind's concerns. "Do they not like it, let them come tell me."

"Someday," Andrias warned, "they might."

Cullyn shrugged. "So be it, and do they find me, I'll answer them. But now . . ." He stroked his magnificent new horse again. "Let's celebrate."

"Celebrate?" Andrias frowned. "Have you so much coin left?"

Cullyn shook his head. "No, but I thought you might . . ."

"Another deer," Andrias said.

And Cullyn said, "A deal."

They went back into the tavern, where Martia met them with a worried expression. "You didn't . . . He didn't . . ."

Andrias shrugged. "He did—he liked the beast."

Martia frowned, angry with her husband, and turned to Cullyn. "He's a killer. Why don't you wait for the Horse Fair?"

"I like him," Cullyn said. "And I think he likes me. Anyway, he's mine now."

Martia sighed, clutching a moment at his shoulder. "I

just pray he doesn't kill you." Then an ominous glance at her husband. "And if he does, someone else shall suffer."

"So be it," Andrias declared. "But I'll tell you that if anyone can handle that beast, it's our Cullyn. Now, let's celebrate his purchase."

They drank well, and ate better, and as the inn closed Cullyn felt wrapped in the comfort of good friends, and—as before—more than a little merry. Indeed, when he rose, he watched the room revolve slowly around him, and had to clutch at a chair to stay on his feet. He looked for Elvira, anticipating, but she was nowhere in sight. And when he asked, Martia said, "She's gone with a friend," and Andrias clapped him on the shoulder and said, "I doubt you'd be up to her this night. Best find your bed and sleep, eh?"

Cullyn felt disappointed and relieved at the same time. He swayed a while until Andrias set a hand on his shoulder and helped him to his chamber, where he collapsed onto the bed and fell instantly into troubled sleep.

He dreamed of Elvira, and of Fey, and Lofantyl, and Abra, and they were all mixed up together in confusions that had him tossing and turning, so that he wrapped the sheets around himself and thought he was entrapped. And at some point in the long night he vomited into the chamber pot, and then slept more peacefully until dawn and the stirring of the inn woke him.

His head ached then, and the sun coming in through the windows hurt his eyes; his mouth was parched, but he'd drunk all the water in the room, which now stank of his vomit. So he struggled into his clothes and went, embarrassed, to the yard, where he ducked his head under the well pump and swallowed copious mouthfuls of fresh water.

The sun was not long up, but at this time of year it

already filled the sky with light, and birds chorused a welcome that sent splintery shards of sound through Cullyn's
head. The clanging of the kitchen pots did him no good,
and it was worse when he saw Elvira emerge from the
kitchen.

Her hair was tousled, and she smiled when she
saw him.

"You slept well?"

He shook his head—and wished he'd not. "I'm
sorry," he said. "I wish . . ."

"You lost your chance," she told him.

"But . . . perhaps . . . I hoped . . ."

She looked him in the eyes. "I'd have been with you,
had you not been more interested in that horse."

"I *need* a horse," he said.

"And I need a husband, or someone to protect me.
Do you think I want to live here all my life? Serving tables, and . . . well, the rest?"

Cullyn shook his head. "You could live with me."

"In the forest?" She shook her head in turn. "No."

It was what Martia and Andrias had told him, so he
looked at her and gave up all his wonderings, and said,
"Goodbye."

Elvira nodded and bussed his cheek. "Goodbye," she
answered, and went back inside the tavern.

Cullyn went to the stables, where Fey met him with
an anxious stare. The horse rolled its eyes as he
approached its stall. The stallion's ears flattened and
its lips came back off big teeth. Cullyn leaned against
the bars, murmuring softly, and after a while the
horse calmed and stretched out its head so that he might
stroke it. He breathed into the velvet nostrils, and
rubbed at the muscled neck. He felt a kinship with this
wild horse.

He saw the grain basket filled and went into the inn, where Martia served him breakfast, and Andrias asked when he might deliver the promised deer.

"I don't know," he said. "Another month? Perhaps sooner."

He could see Elvira serving a merchant, who smiled at her and touched her in a familiar way, and wondered if he felt jealous.

"When you can," Andrias said.

"The sooner the better." He did not like the way Elvira served the merchant. He knew he had no right to resent it, but even so, he could not help it. So he finished his breakfast quickly and said, "I'll be gone now. And bring you back that deer."

He went out to the stables and found his cart. He loaded the tack he'd bought and brought his new horse out of the stall. Fey came willingly enough until Cullyn set the saddle on his back and hiked up the traps of the cart.

Then Fey began to buck, and in moments the cart was reduced to splinters.

Andrias emerged from the inn. "I doubt he's a carthorse."

Cullyn eased his hold on the lunging horse's reins and shrugged. "No," he allowed, facing the inevitable.

"More a rider's horse," Andrias suggested.

Cullyn extricated the cart's traps from the saddle and calmed the big, black horse. "One deer?"

"And do you need a healer, I'll pay."

"Thank you, but I'll not." Cullyn set a foot in the stirrup and swung astride the stallion.

Then he had no time to answer whatever it was Andrias shouted, because he was sitting astride a bucking monster that was intent on throwing him from the saddle and likely—he now remembered the warnings—stamping him dead.

He felt the world spin around—it was as bad as his hangover—saw the courtyard revolve, and felt the saddle smash against his buttocks, sending pain up through his spine into his still-aching head. He clung to the reins and wrapped his legs about the horse's ribs firmly as he'd swung them around Elvira's.

Then Fey calmed. He was unsure whether it was because he had beaten the horse, or because Fey accepted him. He only knew that the big stallion settled as Andrias opened the gate, and charged out.

The cart was left splintered and forgotten as Cullyn thundered down the road, heady with the excitement of this wild ride. He felt the big black horse pounding toward the forest and savored the whistle of the wind in his hair. He charged through the village, and onto the fields beyond. He had a horse—and such a horse as could *run*, and he exulted in the sensation.

Then, after he'd reached the forest's edge, he was spilled from the saddle.

He was unsure why—perhaps a low branch, or only his ineptitude—but Fey came back to nuzzle his face, as if in apology, and he climbed to his feet and mounted the horse again, and knew that he loved the animal.

He rode home and put Fey into the fenced area behind his cottage. He set out water and grain, and watched the pigs squeal around this newcomer.

And then he prepared a meal as the sun went down, and thought of Elvira and Abra and Lofantyl.

The one was lost to him, and he felt no great regret for that; the other was beyond his reach—a keep lord's daughter with an orphaned forester? But Lofantyl intrigued him. He picked up the knife the Durrym had gifted him and turned it about in the light of the setting sun. It glistened as no metal did; it was more like wood or stone, picking up the dying rays as if it embraced them and took them into itself. He thought on what Lofantyl had said about living with the forest, and how Kash'ma Hall was built of wood. He thought that he'd like to see that place.

FOUR

ABRA WOKE to the sound of birdsong, and sunlight on her face. Dawn's brightness came in through her bedroom windows and the chorus of the avians seemed to accompany her troubled thoughts as she lay contemplating what she'd heard the night before. For a while she rested, then determination overcame her and she arose, washing quickly and dressing faster. It was her father's habit to rise early—far sooner than his wife—and take his breakfast with his men.

Abra went to join him.

She found him in the dining hall, a plate piled with bacon and eggs before him, a loaf of fresh-baked bread at one elbow, and a mug of mulled ale at the other. He smiled as he saw her, and drew a hand through his beard, scraping off crumbs that fell onto the table.

"You're up early, child."

"I was thinking," she said.

"About Wyllym? Don't worry—you'll wed by your choice. Say nay and I'll support you."

"It wasn't that." Abra took the mug of tea a servant offered, and helped herself to a measure of eggs. "I heard what you said after . . ."

She wondered if Bartram might be angry, but he only chuckled and said, "I wondered. The chimneys, eh?"

She nodded, and he laughed aloud. "When I was a child," he said, "and my father was lord of this keep, I used to listen all the time to the chimneys and the vents. There's much information you can learn from holes in the stone."

"And not all welcome," Abra said.

"No." Her father shook his head, and his expression become solemn.

"Invasion of the fey lands?" Abra asked

"I think," her father replied, "that that's a dream concocted by Khoros and the Church. As I told Fendur—and you doubtless heard—I don't think we can cross the Alagordar; and I see no reason why we should. Leave the fey folk to their country and we to ours is my belief. Why fight another war?"

"So what *shall* happen?"

Bartram shrugged and shoveled a fresh mouthful of eggs into his mouth. "I don't know for sure. Were it my decision, I'd find land in Kandar for our burgeoning population. But it seems that Khoros is intent on crossing the Alagordar and taking over the fey folk's land."

"Is that possible?" Abra asked.

"I don't think so," her father answered. "I think they command some greater magic than the Church can raise, or blades defeat. But Per Fendur says the Church has new magic. He says they've ways to circumvent the Barrier. Did you not hear as you spied on us?"

He smiled benignly and Abra giggled as she shook her head. "Not that part. The wind was too strong."

Bartram lifted bacon to his mouth and chewed a while before he spoke again. "Per claims that the Church has learned somewhat of the Durrym magic. It comes from the land, he claims, and is far stronger across the river—but still works here. He says that the Church *absorbs* it and has learned how to use it against the Durrym to cross the Barrier. That's why he was sent here: to investigate that power."

"Do you believe him?"

Her father shrugged again. "Perhaps; but if he does, I've not yet seen it. I wonder if it's not just wild hope." He chuckled, spilling breadcrumbs and fragments of bacon over the table, brushing more from his ample stomach. "I'd as soon leave things as they are. Better than another war, eh?"

"But if he can?" Abra asked. "If the Church *can* defeat the Barrier—shall you go with them?"

"I'm sworn to defend Kandar," Bartram answered. "Does Khoros ask it, I must obey."

"Even though . . ." Abra left the question hanging in the air between them.

"Even though," her father replied.

Just then Vanysse entered the hall. She looked sleepy, but her hair was dressed and her gown fresh-pressed, and she smelled of perfume. She bussed her husband on the cheek and took the chair beside him, favoring Abra with a casual smile.

"Look at you." She drew long-nailed fingers through Bartram's beard. "What have you been eating?"

"My breakfast, darling."

Abra winced as Vanysse simpered and said, "You eat too much."

"I was hungry." He scooped up the last of his breakfast, and beamed at her. Abra felt forgotten. "Shall we hunt today?"

Vanysse shook her head. "I'd sooner rest."

"As you wish," Abra heard her father agree, and saw Amadis enter the hall; Vanysse smiled at his entry.

Abra felt a moment's anger—with her father and Vanysse and Amadis, as much as with herself. And decided that she wanted to go somewhere clean and honest. At least, somewhere away from her stepmother.

So she excused herself and went out to the stables, and found her horse, and ordered the stable boy to saddle the gelding.

And was halted by Laurens, who asked: "Where are you going?"

She stared at him, angered by his blunt inquisition. "I'd take a ride."

"Not alone."

"By whose order?"

"The keep's," he said. "Your father's." And grinned, "I suspect you've heard what's afoot."

Abra nodded.

"So you understand?"

She nodded again.

"Then I'll come with you. I could use a ride."

"If you can keep up." Abra swung astride the gray gelding, and stared irritably at Laurens as he mounted a bay mare.

He shouted at the stable hands that he'd accompany the lord's daughter on a morning ride, and smiled at her.

"I think I can match your pace," he said. Then, over his shoulder as they rode out, "Tell Amadis where I go."

The gods knew that he was old and grizzled, but he still matched her pace as they went out through the gates and cantered through the village to the fields beyond.

Swallows darted above them and the sun shone

bright. It lit the stone walls with golden radiance, and set the fields to glistening with multiple shades of green. The air was warm and heady against her face as she urged the gelding to a faster pace that Laurens matched. He only followed, though, so that she took them down through the fields and farmlands toward the forest that somehow seemed to call to her.

He came alongside then and said, "Is it wise to go in there?"

She shrugged off his warning hand and galloped to the edge of the woods.

They stood decked in sunlight, leafy and enticing, and she rode toward them as Laurens followed after.

She crossed the bracken and brambles that edged the main timber and rode through the skirting of lesser trees into the forest proper. Saplings gave way to older timber, ancient oaks spreading massive limbs over the trail she followed, which she supposed was some hunter's path such as Cullyn might use, or a deer trail. But it was spaced with ash and beech, so that all the time the colors changed and shifted, and the ferns that grew tall whispered, and she could imagine how the Durrym turned her own folk around. She felt suddenly afraid.

She halted her horse and looked about, and was grateful to hear the pounding of hooves behind her. Laurens came ducking under a low-hung branch to join her.

"It's a strange place, no?"

She nodded.

"A fey place," he said.

"But folk live here."

"Not many."

"There's that one we met—Cullyn."

"The forester." Laurens ducked his head in agreement. "There's folk say he's fey."

"He seemed friendly enough to me."

"He was. But even so . . ." Laurens shrugged. "It's said the fey folk are often friendly—so as to deceive."

"How many do you know?"

Laurens shrugged again. "Two, perhaps. There's Eben . . ."

"Who is?" Abra demanded as the husky voice fell silent.

"A man who lives alone," Laurens answered. "Has your father not told you?"

Abra shook her head.

"Then perhaps I should not. It's not much spoken of."

"Why not?"

Laurens grinned. "He's an odd fellow. I've met him a time or two. He lives with animals—foxes and dogs and cats, owls and badgers. Folk say he was birthed by the Durrym. Conceived in a raid, when some fey warrior had his mother. And she a widow then, so Eben was both Kandarian and Durrym. I think the Church took him for a while, but then he . . . *escaped*? And came to live alone in the forest." Laurens shrugged. "I've only met him a time or two, but he's likable. Who knows, perhaps you'll meet him. These are, after all, strange lands."

Abra shook her head and urged her horse deeper into the woods. Laurens followed after.

They came to a clearing where a spring bubbled up from between rocks and roots, and drizzled away down a narrow freshet that disappeared under folds of bracken and overhanging ferns. Abra had not realized how long they'd ridden until she dismounted and looked up to find the sun directly above her head. She let her horse drink and then herself, and looked at Laurens and said, "I'm hungry."

"As well I thought before, then." Grinning, he

reached into his saddlebags to bring out bread and cheese, a few apples. "Soldier's habit, eh?"

Abra laughed, nodding, and took what he offered. She began to eat, thinking that for all his bluff and grizzled appearance, Laurens was a considerate man.

It was pleasant here, and it seemed to her that if the seduction of the woodland was Durrym magic, then that magic was benign. Light filtered down through the branches above and sparkled on the spring, which gurgled merrily, as if in accord with the gentle swaying of the ferns. Birds sang overhead, and insects buzzed through the lazy air, which was warm and soft, and rendered her sleepy.

"I think," she declared, "that I shall nap a while." She felt tired after her restless night, and the warm air and the buzzing of the insects urged her to sleep. Indeed, the forest felt somnolent, as if all its sounds and patterns urged her to stretch out and close her eyes.

Laurens nodded and settled against the bole of a massive oak. "I'll keep watch," he said.

Abra stretched out on the springy grass and soon fell asleep.

She wondered if she dreamed then, for it seemed that a soft voice whispered in her ear. It was not so different from the rustling of the leaves, or the lazy chatter of the insects, or the chuckling of the spring as it gurgled over the rocks. It was a comforting voice, and it called to her, urging that she rise and meet the speaker.

It was so insistent that she rose—not sure if that were reality or dream—and walked toward the beckoning voice. She thought that she looked back and saw Laurens snoring against the oak. He held his sheathed sword in his arms, like a mother held her child, but he did not stir, and her feet seemed to make no sound on the forest sward as she followed the call.

I must be dreaming, she thought.

And then an entirely realistic voice, which at the same time was no more than the rustling of leaves, said, "No. I called you."

Abra started, knowing that she was now awake, and some distance from Laurens. She set a hand on the hilt of her belt knife and stared around.

"Are you afraid of me? You shouldn't be."

A face appeared, upside down, hanging from the branches of an oak. It was a handsome face, tanned brown as an autumn nut, surrounded by long brown hair, with startling eyes that glistened amusement to match the smile on the wide mouth. She drew her knife and opened her lips to shout for Laurens's help.

And bit off her cry as the face reversed itself, the owner swinging down from the confines of the tree to land lithely before her. He was still smiling as he bowed elegantly and said, "Welcome to the forest, my lady Abra."

"You know my name?" She held the dagger extended.

He smiled—the gods knew, but his teeth were white—and said, "Cullyn told me. You are Abra, daughter of Bartram, who commands the stone place."

"Cullyn?" She remembered the young forester. "What does he know of me? And who are you?"

"My name is Lofantyl." This was accompanied by another extravagant bow. "I am the younger son of Isydrian, who is Vashinu of Kash'ma Hall, the southernmost of all Coim'na Drhu's holdings."

"You're a Durrym!" Abra held her knife firmer.

"Indeed, I am," Lofantyl agreed. "But I offer you no harm. In fact—"

"Then why did you lure me away?" Abra gestured at the path she'd tracked through the bracken, and raised her blade.

Lofantyl smiled. "Because I wished to talk with you."

His smile could dazzle. It was seductive, so Abra held her blade as she'd been taught, thumb to quillon so that the cut would go deep into the belly.

"You should not fear me," Lofantyl said. "I mean you no harm. I've seen you out riding, and . . ." He paused, his smile faltering for a moment. "I fell in love with you."

"What?" Abra stared at him, surprise overcoming fear. "You're mad."

"With love. I've watched you, and . . ." An eloquent shrug.

"But you don't know me." She shook her head, baffled and flattered and somewhat frightened. She wondered if he were mad, or played some game with her. Surely he'd used magic to speak into her dreams and bring her here, with Laurens sound asleep behind. So what might he plan? To carry her off, perhaps? Away into the fey lands, a captive? She held her blade ready.

"I've seen you," he said, "and I know."

She was barely aware that she lowered the knife; only of those deep brown eyes staring into hers.

"I *know*," he repeated. "I love you."

This was, Abra thought, insane. She stood in a forest glade speaking with a Durrym who declared his love for her. Worse, she listened to him and—the thought amazed her—believed him. There was an intensity in his gaze that convinced her; such sincerity in his voice that she could not deny it. Save all Kandarian lore spoke of the Durrym's seductions—how they'd lure human folk across the Alagordar to the fey lands beyond. She wondered if this handsome fellow intended to carry her off.

"How do you know Cullyn?" she asked, thinking to buy herself time.

"I've watched him, too," Lofantyl replied. "He's near as close to the land as Eben."

"Eben?" Abra was utterly confused.

"I've met him a few times," Lofantyl returned. "He lives even lonelier than Cullyn." He gestured vaguely to the north. "I know little about him, save my father says he was birthed of Durrym stock and yours."

"And you are only fey?"

Lofantyl laughed aloud at that. "Does it worry you so much? Is it not more important that I love you?"

"You don't even know me," Abra repeated.

"I know I love you. Come with me to my father's hall."

She shook her head. "No."

"You break my heart," he returned gallantly. "But I shall win yours."

"How?" she asked. "Shall you court me? Shall you present yourself in my father's hall and ask for my hand?"

"Cullyn said you'd likely execute me," he answered. "So, no, not a formal courtship. But perhaps I'll come to you in secret. Would you like that?"

Abra thought of Wyllym and their arranged betrothal, and the fascination of a clandestine affair intrigued her. Was this madman truly prepared to risk his life for his declared love?

"My father or any of his men would slay you on sight."

"They'd not see me," Lofantyl returned confidently. "We could meet here, or I could come to your chambers."

"In the keep?" She stared at him, wondering if he boasted.

"I'd attempt it," he said. "For you."

"And how should you know which are my chambers?"

"Leave out a sign—a ribbon, or some such—and if I see it, I'll come to you." He bowed again. "With your permission, of course."

Intrigued and flattered, Abra nodded.

"Then I shall," Lofantyl promised.

"How?" she asked.

He chuckled and said, "I shall find the ways, now you've agreed."

He stepped closer and set his hands on her shoulders, and she smelled leaf mold and earth, and the sap of growing leaves and buds. She allowed him to kiss her, and felt her head spin. She clutched him and felt alive and frightened, all at the same time.

And then it was over, and he stepped back and said, "I shall come for you."

And he was gone, like a shadow disappearing into the forest, and she was left confused, the taste of nutmeg and cloves in her mouth.

She stood a while, tasting him on her lips. She was aware of her heart pounding quickly, unsure of whether she felt flattered or frightened, and then went back to where Laurens still slumbered against the oak. She wondered if this was some manifestation of Durrym magic. Had Lofantyl entrapped her; cast some spell over Laurens? She was not sure. She only knew that she had met a Durrym who declared his love and promised to come to her—although she could not envisage how that might be, or how he could survive the attempt. But it was as fascinating as a fairy tale, and every bit as unlikely. And he was surely far more exciting than Wyllym. She stared at the slumbering master-at-arms and thought that she should wake him—warn him of the Durrym and flee the forest. But . . . she could not forget that kiss, or his face, or the honesty she sensed in him.

Or was that only Durrym magic? Did he look to seduce her to some secret end? To find a way into her father's castle, perhaps, so that he could bring others and they take the keep? Yet he had seemed entirely honest.

There was about him some sense of integrity she'd known only in her father, or perhaps in the forester, Cullyn. It was not a thing she could properly define, only sense.

So she decided to say nothing, and await the outcome.

She shook Laurens awake, and sprang back as he came to his feet with his sword in hand.

She was startled by his energy. He was on his feet with the blade up in defense, sunlight sparkling off the steel, the point angling at her belly, so swift she'd barely time to avoid the stroke.

"Laurens!" she shouted.

He lowered the blade, his face reddening as he recognized her.

"Forgive me." He sheathed the sword and ducked his head. "I must have fallen asleep."

"You did." Abra waved a hand at the surrounding forest. "Who'd not, here?"

"And you?" Laurens asked.

"I slept, too," she said. And lied, "I only just awoke."

"We'd best return," he said, yawning.

"Yes, I suppose we should." Abra could still taste Lofantyl's kiss. "I expect they'll be wondering where we've been."

She waited as Laurens brought up their horses, and let him help her mount, then rode back to the keep, where she said nothing at all about her strange meeting.

❧❧❧

CULLYN WAS PREPARING his supper when he heard Fey snort and the grubbing pigs squeal a warning. He left the stew to simmer and picked up the Durrym knife as he went to the door and flung it open. The sun was setting behind the forest and the eastern sky was already dark, albeit pocked with stars and the bright shape of the risen moon, so that all his little yard was dappled with light and dancing shadows.

From across the clearing before the cottage he heard a voice.

"You took my gift, then?"

"Lofantyl?"

"Who else?"

The Durrym came out of the shadows and Cullyn wished he might blend so well with the woodland. He watched as Lofantyl walked through the pigs—which no longer squealed—and went to where Fey stood watching. The Durrym stroked the stallion's glossy nose and Fey ducked his head, as if in obeisance.

"You've a fine horse." Lofantyl came to the door. "Where did you find him?"

"I bought him," Cullyn said. "Not long ago."

"*Bought?*" asked Lofantyl.

"Yes. I take deer from the forest and trade them—I earned some money, and—"

"*Money?*"

"Traded it for the horse. You don't have money in Coim'na Drhu?"

"No." Lofantyl shook his head. "Are you going to invite me into your home?"

Cullyn hesitated. This Durrym had already entered uninvited. But then again, he had left the gift of the knife; and Cullyn could not help liking him.

He stepped aside, gesturing that Lofantyl enter. "Have you eaten?"

Lofantyl shook his head.

"Then eat with me."

"Thank you." The Durrym stepped inside the cottage, staring around as if it were all new and marvelous to him. "That smells good."

Cullyn went to the stewpot. Lofantyl settled on a chair. "So tell me, what is *money?*"

"Coin," Cullyn said, thinking hard. "We decide that a deer is worth so much; a parcel of salt, so much; a loaf of bread, so much. We then decide that each thing is worth a certain amount of money, and trade in coin."

"Why not just trade?" Lofantyl asked. "A deer for so much salt and bread, and so on?"

"Is that how you live?" Cullyn returned.

"Don't you?" Lofantyl replied.

And Cullyn shrugged. "I suppose so; but I'm—"

"Different?" Lofantyl grinned. "Like me, eh? Have you anything to drink?"

"Yes," Cullyn said, answering the first question. "It seems that folk believe I talk too much with fey folk."

"As my people believe of me. Now answer my other question."

"What question?" Cullyn stared at the Durrym, wondering if Lofantyl joked with him or tormented him.

"Do you have anything to drink?"

"I've water." Cullyn remembered his hangover. "Or tea."

"Nothing stronger?"

"A jar or two of honey wine."

"We make that," Lofantyl said. "Where is it?"

Cullyn pointed at his shelves and the Durrym fetched a jar. Filled two cups and settled in as if with an old friend.

"I . . . encountered Abra today," he said. "I pledged my troth. I trust that shall not make us enemies."

"Why should it?" For a moment Cullyn's mind returned memories of Elvira and the smug merchant, and glimpses of Abra. "But how shall you pursue that affair?" He set plates on the table and spooned stew into them.

"With great difficulty," Lofantyl said. And then, "This is very good."

"Thank you. But why are you telling me this?"

"Because I'd not have enemies here, and I think of you as a friend. Like Eben: a Garm who has some sympathy for we Durrym."

"Eben?" Cullyn said. "I thought he was only a legend."

"No." Lofantyl shook his head. "He's alive. I've no idea how old he is, but he lives. I was telling Abra about him—he dwells north of here. Alone even more than you."

Cullyn wondered for a moment how anyone could live more alone than he. Elvira had rejected him, and Abra was beyond his grasp—and, if Lofantyl spoke true, thinking of a Durrym lover.

"It would be interesting to speak with him," he said.

"Eben doesn't speak with many folk," Lofantyl answered. "Neither your kind nor mine. But that's beside the point."

"So what *is* the point?" Cullyn asked.

"That you help me see Abra," the Durrym said. "That we not become enemies because of this. Shall you agree?"

Cullyn thought a while. There seemed no point to pursuing Abra. She was, after all, daughter of the keep. Whatever he felt for her, likely her father would reject him. Just as Elvira had rejected him. She'd found a better lover, with more to give her than a penniless forester could hope to muster, and wouldn't Abra do the same? He spooned up stew and wondered why he discussed this with Lofantyl. The Durrym was, after all, a traditional enemy; save he could not think of the fellow sitting across his table as an *enemy*.

"I don't know," he said cautiously.

"But I *love* her," Lofantyl declared. "You must help me."

"But . . ." Cullyn sought the words "You're Durrym. You're our enemy."

"*I'm* not," came the answer. "I'd see peace between us. Do you think me your enemy?"

Cullyn shook his head.

"So do you trust me?"

Cullyn hid his face in his cup. Then, "I don't know."

"I left you that blade," Lofantyl said. "Do you understand what that means?"

"No, save it was a splendid gift."

"It was a . . . we name it *lyn'nha'thall*—a gift between brothers. It means 'a bonding . . . trust.' We give such a knife only to those we believe we can trust."

Cullyn studied the knife, and Lofantyl. "So you trust me so much?"

Lofantyl nodded.

"Why?"

"Because," the Durrym said, "I feel that you are a brother. You've the forest in your blood, as it's in mine. I feel a kinship." He grinned from across his bowl. "You could almost be Durrym. I feel that I know you, and I trust you."

"We've met, what? Twice? And now you ask me to aid you in the seduction of Lord Bartram's daughter?"

"Not the seduction," Lofantyl said. "Only the pursuit of the woman I love."

"And what would you have me do?"

"Allow us refuge," Lofantyl said. "Let us use your cottage."

"So I become a pander?" Cullyn shook his head. "No!"

"I'll only bring her here," Lofantyl returned, "if she's willing. And first, I intend to visit her in the stone place—that she agreed to."

"You're mad," Cullyn said. "They'll slay you."

"She's worth it." Lofantyl emptied his bowl. "I'd die for her."

"And likely shall," Cullyn said as the Durrym—his friend?—went to the door.

"But shall you aid me?"

Cullyn said, reluctantly, "Yes."

"Then you've my thanks."

And Lofantyl was gone into the night, leaving Cullyn to wonder.

❧❧❧

As was Abra.

She could not forget that nut-brown face that had smiled at her from the tree. She could not believe he'd risk her father's keep to find her, but that night she hung a ribbon from her window and wondered.

❧❧❧

Lofantyl came up through the village at midnight. Dogs came out to challenge him, but he spoke to them and they did not bark, and so he reached the edge wall of the keep and climbed the wall without the guards seeing him. He crossed the ground between and saw the ribboned window of the castle. It was a high climb, and difficult even for him, but he set his hands and his feet against the stone and commenced the ascent. He did not like the feeling of this textured, man-made stone, all carved and cut, but he endured it for the prize above. And like some clinging spider, he reached Abra's window—and, because he could not open the shutter, tapped.

Abra appeared.

She opened her mouth to scream as she saw him there, and then, as she recognized him, opened the window and said, "I didn't believe you'd come."

"I promised," he said.

He dropped into the room and she stared at the window, obviously thinking of the wall and the guards and all he must have overcome to be here, with her.

"How could you do that?" she asked.

"For love," he said. "I told you, no?"

"Are you found you'll be slain."

"You're worth it."

"You're mad."

"For you, yes."

She stared at him, clearly wondering if he were insane, and then seemed suddenly aware that she wore only a nightgown. She blushed, and hurried to find her robe.

Lofantyl remained by the window, but when she turned back toward him, he reached inside his tunic to extract a somewhat crushed and wilted bunch of flowers.

"I chose these for you, in the forest." He proffered the bouquet, and as she took it, their hands touched and he felt a thrill run through him.

"Thank you."

He bowed, all courtly, and smiled at her. "It is my pleasure to bring you what small gifts I can offer."

"Even at risk of your life?"

"So small a price to pay for your smile." He came farther into the room. "May I sit down? That was a hard climb—even for a Durrym."

❧⊱⊰❧

ABRA GESTURED at the chairs, still clutching the
bouquet of wildflowers, utterly confused. She was flattered that he'd risk his life to see her, and not yet quite
sure of his intentions. The teachings of the Church
warned her of Durrym seductions, but when she looked
into his eyes and saw his smile, she could not believe him
other than honest.

Lofantyl took a chair and glanced around. "A drink,"
he said, "would not go amiss.

"I've water and wine."

"Water, please."

She filled him a glass that he drank with obvious
pleasure, then settled in a facing chair, wondering
at what she did. Duty ordered that she call out for the
guards and have this Durrym taken; but she could not
do that, for it would surely mean his death. So she remained silent, and waited for him to speak. She had
never before entertained a man in her private chambers.
She felt her face grow warm and knew she blushed; but
she was unsure whether that was embarrassment or excitement.

"I'd see you again," he said. "With your permission."

It was madness, but before she knew what she said,
she heard herself saying: "You have it."

"It will not be easy."

"No."

"But if you are willing . . ."

"I am."

What did she say? Lofantyl was fey, a Durrym—enemy of Kandar—save when she looked into his eyes she
forgot the realm.

"I spoke with Cullyn," she heard him say, as if in a
dream.

"The forester?"

A memory then of another handsome man, but un-couth—not like Lofantyl.

"A friend. He's agreed that we might meet in his cot-tage."

"That would be difficult."

"Truly?"

"Certainly."

"But shall you?"

She looked at him and ducked her head as she said, almost against her will: "Yes; when I can." His eyes and his smile persuaded her.

"Tomorrow?"

"Perhaps. It shall not be easy." She was not at all sure she *could* meet Lofantyl again—although the gods knew she wanted to—and so she chose to hold her own coun-sel and see what transpired.

"Promise me," he asked.

"I cannot say. It might not be possible."

He took her hand and said, "I'll wait for you in the forest. Save you invite me to stay the night."

A question hung in his brown eyes. To which Abra answered: "Not yet; it's too soon. I must think."

"What's to think about?" he asked. "I love you. Don't you—"

She raised her free hand. "I don't know—not yet. I must think."

And so they sat through most of the night, and Lofantyl was most gentlemanly. And Abra wondered if the Durrym fell in love so easily. Certainly he declared his devotion but, for all his handsome face and earnest eyes urged her to agree, she hesitated. They were, after all, old enemies, and Per Fendur had spoken of the Church's newfound magic that could find a way through the Barrier so that Kandar could invade the fey lands.

And she was Lord Bartram's daughter, and her father sworn to defend Kandar against the Durrym.

Her head spun as the night grew older, and she wondered if it would not be easier to marry Wyllym, rather than entertain the notions that wound through her head as she looked at Lofantyl's earnest face.

Only those notions brought a flush to her cheeks, and she could not take her eyes from his face as he told her of Coim'na Drhu and Kash'ma Hall, and she found herself intrigued, and wondered what that unknown land might be like. And the sun edged a way into the sky and birds began to chorus.

"You'd best go now," she warned.

Outside the windows a pale sun was rising to wake the birds. He nodded, and kissed her hands, and she felt her skin thrill and her heart beat faster. And then he rose and said, "As you say, I'd best be gone."

Abra looked at the window and realized that they'd talked the night away. The sky was shifting into dawn's pearly gray, and birds began to sing, chorusing the advent of morning. She felt fear then, that Lofantyl be found and slain.

"But I'll see you soon, eh?"

She ducked her head in agreement, unable to do else, nor wanting to.

And watched him slither out of the window and clamber down the wall and run through the early morning shadows to disappear over the outer wall and . . . become no longer visible, as if the dawn swallowed him up and he became a part of the land.

She sighed and went back to her bed, and thought of their next meeting—which, she was decided, should be as soon as possible.

FIVE

I SYDRIAN BECKONED the raven in from the window ledge with a summons and a bowl of nuts.

He sat quietly as the avian hopped from ledge to desk and eyed him with a beady yellow curiosity. They were poor enough messengers, but the best Coim'na Drhu had—save Lofantyl return—so he waited until the bird finished its inspection and dipped its beak into the bowl. Then he grabbed it, ignoring its squalling as he took the tiny cylinder from its leg and broke the seals. The raven eyed him angrily, ruffled its feathers, and then went back to pecking up nuts.

The lord of Kash'ma Hall read the message. It was encrypted, but he knew the codes well enough that he needed no help to decipher the symbols. And it was a plain enough message: Lofantyl had encountered the keep lord's daughter and won her affection; the Garm'kes

Lyn planned a war. Their *church*—Isydrian wondered what exactly that word meant—believed its officers had found such power as could gain them entry to Coim'na Drhu. He doubted that—the Durrym magicks set on the forest and the river were strong, and turned invaders away. He doubted that any Garm could find a way past the river that divided the two lands and held the Durrym safe from the depredations of the barbaric Garm.

But it was interesting information, and he silently praised his younger son for his acuity. Lofantyl was wayward, and far too interested in the Garm, but he had the sense to keep his ear to the ground. Or to windows and locked doors; and that was all that mattered. Afranydyr could never have managed such a task: he was too blunt, perhaps too honest to ever be a spy. But Lofantyl . . . Isydrian chuckled, and reached out to stroke the raven, which squawked and pecked at his hand.

He stared at the bird even as he sucked at his bloodied finger, concentrating his will so that the bird turned away and returned to its feast. His younger son, he thought, had little idea what potentially valuable information he sent back from his travels. Indeed, he was not so dissimilar to the raven: a messenger.

Isydrian took up a quill fashioned from a black swan's feather and set the pen in the inkpot. From a drawer in his desk he extracted a scrap of parchment no larger than Lofantyl has used, and in a minuscule hand composed his reply. Then he dusted the scrap with fine sand and carefully rolled it into the message cylinder.

The raven squawked a protest as he lifted it from the bowl and fixed the cylinder to its left leg. He allowed the bird to peck up a few more nuts before he grabbed it and carried it, protesting, to the window. He stared into the avian's eyes and fixed its objective in the tiny brain.

Then he flung it away, watching as it swooped, and then lofted over the walls to wing westward.

All went well so far, and was Lofantyl's information correct, he could likely drive the Garm against Ky'atha Hall, and let Pyris fight them—if they *could* find a way past the Barrier.

It hardly mattered: there was a war coming, and he would benefit from it. He might emerge a heroic defender, or a savior—if he warned Santylla of the Garms' plans. But would he advise Dobre Henes, or hold it to himself? He was not yet sure—he thought he'd wait for further news.

❧❧❧

"I CAN FIND A WAY," Per Fendur said. Then corrected himself, "The Church can find a way. We work on it even now."

"No one has ever crossed the Alagordar." Amadis sipped his wine. "Or if they have, they've not come back."

"We've new magicks." The priest stared at the soldier. "We've studied the matter, and decided it's something to do with the land. Do you believe me?"

"I'd like to," Amadis said. "But . . ."

"The Durrym are not like us. They are the creations of nature, not God. They live with the land and its animals, and shape those things to their own designs. We control it; we own it; we make the land and all that inhabits it subservient to us. That is what God intended for us when we came to Kandar. How else could we conquer the savages and drive them out?"

Amadis shrugged. "Lord Bartram says because we owned the greater numbers, and steel."

"Lord Bartram"—Fendur filled the title with

contempt—"is an old man, with old ways. Would you not enjoy this keep?" The priest waved an expansive hand. "You could be lord here."

"What of Bartram?"

Fendur poured the captain a fresh glass of wine. "Men die in battle, no? And their wives grieve, and seek others."

"But I am sworn to defend Bartram's hold."

"But if he were to die in battle—a hero—what then?"

Amadis drained his glass; Fendur poured him another.

"You've . . . *feelings* . . . for his wife?"

Amadis ducked his head in acknowledgment.

"Would she marry you? Were Lord Bartram to die?"

"I believe so."

"Then you'd become lord of this keep, my word on it. Does that not interest you?"

Amadis nodded.

"So persuade him. Lend your arguments to mine and we'll go to war with the fey folk. You'll emerge a hero and become a keep lord."

Amadis thought a while—not long—and nodded. "I've your word on that?"

Per Fendur smiled and said, "My word and bond, both."

"Then," Amadis said, "we go to war." And raised his glass in agreement before he added, "Save do you betray me, I shall slay you—priest or no."

"Why should I betray you?" Fendur asked innocently. "Are we not allies in this venture, bonded by our common purpose?"

"Save you've the Church at your back," Amadis said, "and I've only your word."

"Which you can trust," the priest assured him.

"And you'll make me keep lord? And I'll have Vanysse?"

"My word on both."

Dreams spun through Amadis's mind. Lord of the keep; Vanysse in his bed, his wife; the hero who led Kandar into the Durrym lands; the approval of the Church.

He smiled and raised his glass.

❧❧❧

ABRA DREAMED OF LOFANTYL, and rode into the forest whenever she could. It was not so easy to meet him, but when her stepmother went out—inevitably with Amadis—Abra would accompany them. And then it was not so difficult, because Vanysse would find reasons to ride off alone with the captain, and then Abra was able to drift away and find her fey courtier in some glade, or Cullyn's hut, and lose her escorts for a while. Long enough, at least, that they could spend time together.

She wondered, sometimes, if she were no better than Vanysse—for surely she betrayed her father's sworn duty when she took Lofantyl's hands and allowed him to kiss her. He was, after all, Durrym.

But he was unlike any man she had known.

Not that she had known many.

Indeed, were she honest, none. She was virgin and pledged by the king's word to Wyllym. She considered Wyllym, after their few meetings, ugly and uncouth. And she was afraid that whatever her father said, King Khoros might impose the marriage. She had seen the forester, Cullyn, and felt a . . . stirring. But it was an impossible notion. A keep lord's daughter and a forester?

Lofantyl was different, even be it no less likely.

A Durrym and a Border Lord's daughter? What
would the Church, the king, have to say about that?

But he was surely a lord in his own right: a younger
son of some great Durrym fortress. And gentle in his attentions; courteous and subtle. He showed her the forest
in all its sylvan glory, but made no attempt to bed her;
only took her by the hand and showed her the nests of
mated birds, or badger setts, or forest springs she'd not
known existed. Pointed out high squirrels' dreys. Took
her to glades where deer grazed, the stag calming his
harem when Lofantyl murmured—as if all the forest and
its denizens obeyed him. And then he'd find her flowers
and present the bouquet with a courtly bow, and bring
her back before her escort wondered where she might be.

He was gentility personified, and through the summer's courtship she came to love him—and to trust him.
So she told him all she knew of the Church's plans, and
her father's attitude, thinking to deliver peace, and
Lofantyl listened and kissed her cheek, and held her
hands, and was a perfect gentleman.

❦❧❦

THEY TRYSTED OFTEN as not in Cullyn's cottage,
and Cullyn wondered at his feelings. Abra was beautiful,
and he could not deny his desire for her. But he regarded
Lofantyl as a friend, and so wished them well, and pondered what he did. If not the gods, then surely the
Church and Lord Bartram would find him guilty—of
heresy and betrayal, both.

It was a difficult time for him, torn between desire
and friendship, wondering at his own motives. And all
the while thinking that were they discovered, he would
be branded a traitor and executed. But Abra was obvi-

ously in love with the Durrym, and Lofantyl was charm
personified—cheerful and friendly, such as few Cullyn
had known—that he felt incapable of doing other than
aid them in their trysts.

Which was not always so easy, for the master-at-
arms, Laurens, appeared to have taken a liking to him,
and would visit him as Vanysse and Amadis slipped away
into the forest, and Abra found excuses to seek Lofantyl.
Then, Laurens would come to Cullyn's cottage and idly
wonder where Abra might have disappeared to.

"And her stepmother?" Cullyn asked on one occasion. "Don't you wonder about her?"

"I know where she's gone." Laurens chuckled, tap-
ping a callused finger against his broken nose. Cullyn
raised questioning brows, pretending innocence, and
Laurens said: "Off to some glade with Amadis. But say
nothing of that!"

Cullyn shook his head in confirmation. "But does
not Lord Bartram suspect?"

"He knows." Laurens shrugged. "Knows and closes
his eyes. He's twice her age, and . . ." He shrugged again,
expansively. "Does she take our vaunted captain for her
lover, still Bartram shares her bed, and likely makes do
with that."

"How could he?" Cullyn asked, horrified. "If I had a
wife, I'd not share her."

Laurens laughed and glanced around the cottage,
much as Lofantyl had once done, then asked if Cullyn
had aught to drink.

Cullyn brought out the flask of honey wine, from
which Laurens quaffed deep, declaring the brew excellent, and said: "It's politics, lad. I've little time for such
niceties, myself, but . . . The Lady Vanysse is western
born—out of Yrin hold, daughter of Lord Mykael, who

commands at least half of the western coast. Bartram married Vanysse on order of our king—who looked to bind east and west together. Bartram agreed and fell in love." He laughed again, reaching for the flask. "Wouldn't you? Or at least want her in your bed? She's lovely, no?"

"She's pretty enough," Cullyn agreed, thinking of Abra.

"But not so desirable as Bartram's daughter?"

Cullyn blushed.

"Who said she was coming here," Laurens declared, his voice mild. "So where is she?"

Cullyn hoped that the heat he felt on his cheeks did not show. "She stopped to take a drink of water," he mumbled, "and then went on."

"Truly?" Laurens drank more honey wine.

"Truly," Cullyn answered, hoping the master-at-arms would take it as a question.

"And you've no idea where she's gone?"

Cullyn shook his head.

"I'd wondered," Laurens said easily, "if she'd taken you for her lover. The gods know, but you'd be better than that sorry Wyllym."

"I wish it were so," Cullyn said without thinking. Then bit his tongue and added, "But it's not."

"So where has she gone?" Laurens leaned back, sipping his honey wine.

"I don't know," Cullyn answered honestly.

Laurens emptied his cup and studied Cullyn from hooded eyes. "I think you know more than you admit."

"She came and went." Cullyn shrugged. "And who am I to question her?"

"No one," Laurens returned cheerfully. "You're an orphaned forester, with no right to question Lord Bartram's daughter. No more right than I have to question the Lady Vanysse or Amadis. But . . ."

"What?" Cullyn asked nervously.

Laurens guffawed. "I think I know what Vanysse and Amadis do."

"So?"

"And I think you know what our fair Abra does. And if not with you, then with whom?"

Cullyn shrugged again.

"I should arrest you," Laurens said. "I should do my duty and take you back to the keep—where you'd be put to question. Our new priest would get answers."

"Shall you?" Cullyn asked, suddenly chilled.

Laurens shook his head. "No. I like you too much. The gods know why, but you've something about you. But I still think you admit less than you know."

Abra appeared. Her hair was disheveled, and leaves clung to her gown. She was obviously startled to find Laurens in the cottage, but she composed herself and asked, "What do you do here?"

"Wait for you," Laurens said equably.

"I . . . wanted to be on my own."

"Of course." Laurens set down his cup, his grizzled face blank. "And so I waited for you. Cullyn explained."

Abra's cheeks reddened. Cullyn busied himself with cups, trying not to look at either of them. "I told Laurens that you went riding alone," he said.

"Which is not wise in these woods," Laurens said. "Fey woods, these. Who knows whom you might meet?"

Abra blushed afresh.

And Laurens chuckled and rose, then suggested that they find their horses and return to the keep. As he quit the cottage he favored Cullyn with a wink, and left Cullyn wondering if he were condemned a traitor or had found a friend.

❦❦

"THIS IS EXTREMELY DIFFICULT," Lofantyl said. "I love her, but what shall I do? What *can* I do? Should I take her back to Coim'na Drhu? Would she come with me? I cannot see you Garm accepting me as her husband." He sighed, dipping his face into his cup. "What shall I do, Cullyn?"

"I don't know." Cullyn wondered how long his honey wine would last between Lofantyl and Laurens. "What does she say?"

"I haven't asked her," the Durrym returned.

"Perhaps you should. Let her decide."

"But if she says nay?" Lofantyl shook his head. "I doubt I could bear that."

"Sometimes," Cullyn said, with a degree of bitterness in his voice, "we must accept disappointment."

"I cannot lose her!" Lofantyl declared. "I *cannot*!"

Cullyn felt sympathy: it seemed he could accept loss better than his Durrym friend. He thought of his own desire for Abra, and what he'd felt for Elvira, and said, "We do not always get what we want. Sometimes, I think, we must accept that."

"I *cannot*," Lofantyl moaned. "I *need* her."

Cullyn did not know what else to say, so he poured out more honey wine and set venison steaks to cooking as Lofantyl bemoaned his fate.

❦❦

IT WAS A MOST CURIOUS TIME for Cullyn, a summer of uncertainty. He saw Abra come and go, on her trysts with Lofantyl; heard them both tell him of the problems they faced. And then he'd sit with Laurens, and listen to the master-at-arms discourse on warfare and politics. And between, he must hunt and feed himself and earn what he might from Lyth.

He never could train Fey to drag a cart, but the stallion would carry a carcass over the saddle, and he did well that summer. He wondered if it were Lofantyl's forest magic that brought the deer to his bow; indeed, there were times the Durrym went out with him, and summoned the animals that he might bring them down. And must he ride into Lyth all bloody from the deer he carried, still he rode, and his conquest of Fey was considered a marvel. He earned enough that he became well equipped, and laid in sufficient supplies to last him through the winter, which Lofantyl warned him would be harsh.

He became as friendly with Laurens as he was with Lofantyl, and wondered at that dichotomy, but liked them both, and wondered if he was a traitor.

※❦❧※

SUMMER TURNED TO AUTUMN.

The forest faded, green leaves becoming red and gold and brown, and falling from the trees to layer the ground with crispness that became moist as the rains came. The squirrels busied themselves with the storing of nuts, and migratory birds passed noisily overhead. It was a time Cullyn enjoyed, in a melancholy way, for it presaged the cessation of summer's heat and the coming of winter's quiet time. Some days were pure blue, with a high, fine wind; others were dismal, all gray skies and scudding rain that left the trails muddy so that Cullyn had sooner stayed inside his cottage, by the fire.

Only Lofantyl would come to him then, and talk, and ask when Abra might next visit, which Cullyn could not tell him. And when she did come it was with

Laurens, who'd settle himself in the cottage and sup on Cullyn's depleting store of honey wine—even did he sometimes deliver a flask from the keep, or a small keg of ale—and wonder where Abra had gone in such dismal weather, so that Cullyn could only answer that he did not know, and see the older man's face wrinkle in disbelief, although Laurens never questioned him too deep.

And then the winter snows came.

They were hard that year, and deceptive.

They came gentle at first, then falling wind-driven and sharp from the east to strip the trees of their last autumn leaves. Then easing so that the forest filled with soft drifts that blocked the trails and the road to Lyth with impassable snow. And after that came howling winds that made his cottage shudder and stripped away the topmost level of snow so that when next the heavy falls came they draped the woods with such white as blocked all the trails and froze the pools like cold emeralds. Frost hung icicles from the branches and turned the ferns to wondrous spectacles of glittering jewels. Spiderwebs hung crystal, and trees stood rimed, leafless black limbs draped with trailers of winter, and the ground was all white and hard beneath, as if all the world were filled with ice, and metal stuck burning to careless hands.

Cullyn hunted little then: he had sufficient meat laid in store that he could last out the cold weather, and vegetables in his root cellar, and enough wood to keep the cottage warm, despite the ice-breathed winds that blew outside to deliver great banks of snow that piled in the yard so that he must go out with a shovel to clear the ground for his animals. The pigs fared well enough, for they were sufficiently hardy that they'd grub down through the frozen earth, but the chickens and the cow needed tending, and Fey grew restless.

The stallion's coat grew thick with winter hair, and

he protested the confinement the snows imposed. He grew irritable again, and when Cullyn came to him, he'd snap his teeth and sometimes rear. So Cullyn took to riding through the snow, which was hard going but worked off Fey's energy, leaving the stallion sweating and wearied so that Cullyn must wipe him down and drape him with a blanket before returning him to the stall.

It was a strange winter—harsher than any he'd known, and lonely. He saw nothing of Abra or Laurens, for the roads and trails were all sealed deep and impassable, and the keep folk held tight to home. Neither did he see Lofantyl, for the Durrym told him that he'd winter at home, in Kash'ma Hall. So Cullyn was left alone—which was not unusual, save lately he had grown accustomed to company, and consequently found its absence disturbing. He had not been aware of loneliness before, but now he felt the emptiness of the long winter and wished for company. He read what few books he owned—none for the first time—and grew bored, and prayed for spring's advent.

❧❧❧

IN WHICH ABRA JOINED HIM.

The keep was winter-locked. Frost rimed the bastions and icicles hung sparkling from the balconies and ramparts. The world was all gray—save when it grew white with snow—and fires blazed constantly in the hearths, filling the keep with an indolent warmth that seemed to suck out her breath and leave her sweating when she was not shivering. Neither could she—with the hearth ablaze—listen to those conversations that went on below. But worst of all was Lofantyl's absence.

He'd told her he must go away for a while, but she had not understood how long that while might be. It seemed an age, and she wondered when he might return. Nightly, she hung the ribbon from her window; and daily, she drew it in, crusted hard with frost, as she watched the guards patrol the ramparts from brazier to brazier, warming their hands before the guttering fires.

❧❧❧

"YOU'VE DONE WELL." Isydrian slapped his younger son's shoulder. "The information you've delivered is most useful."

"Thank you, Father."

Isydrian poured wine, watching his two sons eye one another like fighting cocks. They each had their own virtues, he thought, their own strengths. Afranydyr was hard as a blade, with no more love for the Garm than Isydrian himself. Lofantyl was softer, but also more subtle. He had too much time for the Garm—too much interest in their ways; and this talk of the Garm woman troubled him. But even so, it *was* useful information.

Afranydyr interrupted his father's contemplation in typically blunt fashion. "Is this information truly of such worth?"

"That the Garm find ways to cross the Barrier?" Isydrian returned. "Yes! I'd know if they come against us."

"Save it's only hearsay," Afranydyr objected.

Isydrian glanced at his younger son, who shrugged and said, "It's what Abra told me."

Afranydyr snorted. "The tales of a woman besotted. And likely only pillow talk."

"I've not bedded her," Lofantyl objected. "I . . . respect her too much. I think I love her."

"A Garm?" Afranydyr's lips pursed in disapproval. "How can you love a Garm?"

"They're not so different," Lofantyl answered. "And she *is* beautiful."

Afranydyr glowered at his brother.

"It matters not," Isydrian interjected. He looked at Lofantyl and said, "You can have her, if you want. Persuade her to come here, or take her as a captive . . . either way, you can have her. What's important is that we know what the Garm plan."

He pondered a moment. "This war can do us good— if they *do* find a way past the Mys'enh, then we can direct them against Pyris, and let the walls of Ky'atha Hall take the brunt. You, my son, might suggest that. Tell your Garm that, eh? Tell her how her folk can find Ky'atha Hall, and let her pass it on." He chuckled, pleased with his plan, and rubbed his hands in happy anticipation. "You might even show them the way through the Mys'enh—to Ky'atha Hall. Let the Garm take that, and then we come to the rescue. That, or leave Pyris to his fate."

He smiled, contemplating the future. Let the Garm come across the Barrier against Ky'atha Hall, and Pyris might fail and die. It was his ambition to see both his sons enthroned in their own halls. Afranydyr would inherit Kash'ma. And if Pyris should fail, then Lofantyl could be established as lord of Ky'atha. It was, he decided, up to the gods and his own cunning.

"This is devoid of honor," Lofantyl protested.

"This is politics," his father said. "We could own the whole of the border. Let Pyris face the Garm and we reap the rewards."

"My little brother objects," Afranydyr chuckled scornfully.

"I'd behave with honor," Lofantyl said, glowering at his brother as fiercely as Afranydyr glared at him.

Isydrian shook his head and folded his hands inside the deep sleeves of his bearskin robe. As a Durrym, he felt little cold, but he grew old now—both his sons were late-born, and Lofantyl the last, for Aederia had died in that birthing. But he'd leave them a great heritage—if all his plans worked out. He studied them, wondering that they could not see his intent. Perhaps Afranydyr sensed it; but surely not Lofantyl. One day, he'd explain it in detail—that if the Garm came against Coim'na Drhu, and only he knew of their plans, then he had the opportunity to realize that dream and leave both his sons a heritage worthy of his own father. Worthy of himself and them.

And perhaps, with his sons lifted up so high, even come to challenge the Dur'em Jahnt, so that one or the other, or their children, might take the throne of the Floating City.

But that was the future—if all went well—and the moment demanded decision. So Isydrian chuckled and said, "I think you should go back and talk more with this Garm lord's daughter."

"I'll not betray her," Lofantyl protested.

"I don't ask you to," his father said. "Only let me know what plans the Garm have. For the sake of Coim'na Drhu."

"And his love for the Garm?" Afranydyr grunted.

"I doubt it shall cloud his judgment." Isydrian smiled benignly at Lofantyl. "Shall it?"

Lofantyl looked at his father and shook his head. "No, my lord."

"Then go back, eh? Learn all you can and send a raven as soon you know."

Lofantyl nodded. "As you order, my father."

THE SNOW WAS CRISP under his feet, crunching despite his light tread, but no dogs barked at him as he made his way through the village, for he was fey and communed with the animals in ways the Garm'kes Lyn could not, so they let him pass without interruption. He stared at the little buildings and wondered how they could live there, all winter-hidden behind their walls, with shutters closed against the honesty of the snowy night, lit only by the fires inside and what few braziers burned in the streets. His own people would be outside in such weather, glorying in the sky, which was hung thick with stars and a great, dim moon. In Coim'na Drhu they'd be celebrating the festival of Lyris now, but here all the Garm did was huddle. He felt sorry for them as thick flakes fell down to mask him and he made his way through the empty streets of Lyth to the walls of the keep.

Those he climbed easily, and dropped to the yard beyond.

That was swept clear of snow, but the cold wind held the guards inside their revetments, or concentrated on warming themselves at the braziers that burned along the walls. And he was fey, and quick, so he was across the yard and clambering up the stone wall before any saw him.

He felt the stone slippery under his fingers. And they numbed as he climbed, all time waiting for a shaft to pierce his back and drop him from the wall. His hands and feet grew cold as his body, and he gritted his teeth that they not chatter.

And climbed, and came to her window.

And found it shuttered against the cold.

He perched himself precariously on the ledge and

tapped, wondering how long he could hold on before his
frozen hands gave up all their feeling and he fell away.

❧❦❧

ABRA HEARD THE KNOCKING and dismissed her
servants. One woman giggled, wondering aloud who—or
what—might come visiting her lady on so bleak a night.

"Likely it's some luckless bird," Abra extemporized,
"seeking shelter." And shooed her attendants away with
the excuse that they'd frighten off the bird.

She wondered if they'd accept her excuses—which
seemed, even to her, lame—but she had no doubt at all
who knocked on her window.

She opened the portal and he clambered in, all wet
and icy. He put his arms around her and said, "I missed
you. I could no longer bear to be apart."

"Nor I."

They embraced, and she felt the cold in his body and
clung to him.

And then the door burst open and Amadis came in
with a drawn sword, Per Fendur and six guardsmen at his
back. Abra screamed; Lofantyl pushed her away and drew
his dagger, which was the only weapon he carried.

Amadis laughed. "Not enough, boy. Lay it down else
I slay you here and now."

Per Fendur smiled his oily smile and said, "Did you
truly believe you could enter this keep unnoticed? Are
you Durrym so stupid as to forget *my* powers?"

Lofantyl glanced like some cornered animal at the
blade and the soldiers.

Abra saw him look toward the window and weigh his
chances as Amadis raised his blade. She screamed and
threw herself at the captain.

"Thank the gods you came! He burst in on me!"

Her slight weight took Amadis by such surprise that he was flung back. Lofantyl gaped.

"I thought it was a bird." She clung to Amadis. "You saved me! The gods alone know what might have happened, else."

The captain lowered his blade for fear of damaging Abra, and barked that his men take the Durrym.

Lofantyl stared at Abra as he was dragged away, confusion and resentment in his gaze.

SIX

ABRA KNEW BETTER than to scream as they carried Lofantyl away, though it was hard to bite off her horror and her grief. She saw him struggle, and a thick-knuckled hand slammed against his jaw, so that his handsome head was snapped back even as another fist landed in his belly and doubled him over. Then Amadis stepped forward and drove the heavy pommel of his sword into Lofantyl's face. Lofantyl gasped, blood running from his nose, and slumped unconscious against his captors.

Amadis raised his blade and looked to Per Fendur for instruction. "I could slay him now."

"No." Fendur raised a hand, and set the other on Abra. "Best we hold him alive and question him."

"He's Durrym," Amadis spat. "Let's be done with him now, the bastard!"

"Hold him," Fendur insisted. "Take him to the dungeons—and keep him alive, eh? I will question him, so I need him sensible."

Amadis scowled, but lowered his blade.

"He can tell us much," Fendur said. He smiled horribly at Abra. "And you, also, my lady."

Abra struggled in the priest's grasp. It was surprisingly strong, his fingers biting like claws into her arm so that she felt it go numb. Pain shafted up into her shoulder and neck so that even her jaw ached and she found it hard to cry out as Lofantyl was dragged away. Fendur thrust her back into her chamber.

"So you entertain the Durrym?" he murmured when Lofantyl was gone.

"I thought it was a lost bird," she reiterated. "I had no idea it was a man. Ask my attendants."

"I shall," the priest promised, his dark eyes glinting with a wicked light. "I shall question them and the Durrym. And you."

"Me?" Abra broke from his grasp and faced him with all the courage she could muster. "You'd question *me*?"

"A Durrym was found in your chamber," the priest said, and shrugged eloquently. "That renders you suspect."

"I explained that." Abra heard the terrible threat in his voice, saw it in his eyes, and struggled to maintain her composure. Was she found guilty of consorting with Lofantyl she'd be executed beside him. "Do you suggest that I consort with the enemy?"

"I know what I know," Per Fendur said ominously. "And I know what I suspect."

"I think," Abra said, with all the dignity she could find in the midst of her terror, "that you should speak with my father."

"I am the Church incarnate," he returned with a

smug confidence. "I speak for the prelate and the king, and do I find you guilty, you'll decorate the gibbet beside the Durrym."

Abra felt a terrible cold then, as if the ice she'd felt on Lofantyl filled her veins and set her skin to prickling. She was tempted to fall on her knees and beg Per Fendur's forgiveness but she could not. She loved Lofantyl and despised this oily priest, so she steeled herself and fought the trembling that threatened to wrack her body.

"Shall we speak with my father? I believe he might have a view on this. And does he not agree, I wonder if *you* might not find yourself on the gibbet."

Fendur started back at that. "Treason!" he gasped. "Is all this keep given over to treason?"

"My father is a just man," Abra said, sensing an advantage. "So shall we go speak with him?"

❧❀❧

LORD BARTRAM WAS NOT HAPPY to be roused from his bed, though his wife seemed not to mind: they consented to an audience in their private chambers, where anxious servants stoked the hearth and lit candles, and brought wine.

Amadis was there, and Per Fendur and Abra, and a sleepy-eyed Laurens.

The hearth was built high against the cold and filled the room with somnolent heat. Abra's father wore a bearskin that covered his belly and muffled him as if he were the animal. His wife wore a thick silken gown and fluttered her eyes at Amadis. Laurens stood stolid, dressed in his usual leather and metal. He kept, as ever, a hand on the hilt of his sword.

Amadis pranced in fancy armor as he described his

capture of the Durrym, and Per Fendur folded his hands into the wide sleeves of his black robe and agreed with the captain.

According to them, they had taken a Durrym captive—a foul fey who'd seduced Lord Bartram's daughter and suborned her to his wicked purpose.

"And where is he now?" Bartram asked.

"Locked safe inside the dungeons," Amadis replied.

"To be questioned later," Fendur added.

"And what's my daughter to do with this?"

"Seduced!" Fendur declared, his dark eyes flickering hostilely at Abra. "She welcomed the Durrym to the keep—and that's treason!"

Vanysse nodded eagerly.

Bartram looked at his daughter. "Is this so?"

"Seduced?" she returned. "No. I've not slept with him."

"But you've . . . *consorted* with him?"

"I've known him as a friend, an admirer."

"A *Durrym?*" her father asked. He was torn between disbelief and horror. "How could you?"

"I knew him only as a handsome man," Abra lied. "He complimented me. How should I know he was Durrym?"

"But even so," Fendur declared, "she admits that she consorts with the Durrym, and that's treason."

"*That,*" Lord Bartram said, "I shall decide. Did she not, originally, know he was Durrym, then there's no sin or treason."

Fendur spluttered. "And meanwhile?"

"We hold him in the dungeons. Until *I* decide what's to be done with him." Bartram looked at his daughter. "You speak the truth?"

Abra nodded, forcing herself to meet her father's eyes as she said, "Yes."

"Then go back to your room."

"*No!*" Per Fendur cried. "She's guilty, and must be punished."

Abra saw her stepmother nod agreement. But her father shook his head and stared angrily at the priest. "She's my daughter," he said, "and I trust her before you, so still your accusations and be gone. I shall consider this matter in the morning."

Abra saw the priest study her father, and wondered what trouble she had initiated. But then he waved a hand and said, "Go back to your chambers, daughter, and we'll speak of this tomorrow."

Abra curtsied and quit the room, grateful to be gone. She hurried to her chambers and flung herself on the bed, weeping as she thought of Lofantyl.

❧❧❧

LOFANTYL REGAINED HIS SENSES in a pool of ordure that seeped from a crack that he supposed must bleed from some midden above. He heard the door slam shut and picked himself up, groaning as his ribs ached, wiping at the blood that still ran from his nostrils. He stared at the horrid, blank stone walls. He could climb them, for Abra's sake, but that was outside—where wind and weather shaped the stone and gave it some semblance of nature. Here—in this dungeon—it was all confined and unnatural. Here there were only cold, man-made blocks of granite that were designed to hold prisoners. There were bars of thick metal on the solitary window, and more spread down across the door. The floor was all stone—cold—and spread with so little straw that he could not find any warmth. Moss grew down the walls, and rats scuttled over what little straw covered the floor.

His body hurt and he wondered what his fate might

be. He went to the window and saw a sky that faded from night to dawn, and thought of the forest and Coim'na Drhu, and wondered if he had made a terrible mistake. He had not thought to fall in love with Abra, and that emotion confused everything. And now he was captured, and consigned to this horrid dungeon. He sighed, turning from the window, and curled on the floor. He summoned the rats, which curled around him and over him, and kept him warm with their bodies until the sun rose and the door opened. Then they fled, as if terrified.

Per Fendur stood there, smiling. Amadis stood behind the priest, and four soldiers behind him.

"I'd talk with you," Fendur said mildly. But his face was stretched in a gloating smile. And to the soldiers: "Pick him up."

Lofantyl rose of his own accord, but still they grabbed him and carried him out of the cell and down a long corridor of dank stone to a room where strange machines waited. He had never seen such machines, but he felt them malign, and wondered why so many irons sat in glowing braziers.

"Put him there!" Per Fendur indicated a contraption that seemed to be a wide table equipped with straps at either end, and a wheel between.

Lofantyl was picked up and deposited on the table. He fought his captors as best he could, but they beat him down and fastened the leathers around his wrists and ankles.

Per Fendur smiled at him. "We'll stretch you now," he said, and turned the wheel. Lofantyl felt his body drawn taut. "And stretch . . . and stretch . . . until you admit your guilt and tell me what I want to know."

"I've nothing to tell you," Lofantyl returned. "Save that I fell in love with Abra."

"Who consorts with Durrym." Fendur turned the

wheel a notch tighter; Lofantyl felt his limbs stretch.
"Such as you."

"She did not know!"

"Are you sure?" The wheel turned another notch.

Lofantyl felt his body drawn out, as if all his bones
and muscles threatened to tear apart.

"*Yes!*"

"So what did you do here? Why did you consort
with her?"

The wheel turned again, and Lofantyl thought his
shoulders must tear loose from his arms, his legs and
knees and ankles from his body.

"I disagreed with my father," he screamed. "I came
across the Mys'enh—the Alagordar—and I met . . ."

He hesitated, and the wheel turned, dragging his
body tighter against its own limbs.

Then: "*Abra!*"

"Who aids you?" Per Fendur asked.

"*No!*" Lofantyl groaned. "No help at all. I met her in
the forest and fell in love with her. She did not know
what I am."

"No?" Per Fendur turned the wheel another notch
tighter. "Then why come to her chamber?"

"Because I love her," Lofantyl screamed as he felt his
limbs stretched out again. "Because I love her!"

Fendur eased the wheel. "Enough for now," he said,
turning to the guards. "Take him back to his cell." And
to Lofantyl: "We'll speak again—soon."

❧❧❧

HE HURT as he was flung into the cell. His limbs ached
as if all his joints had been prised apart. He wondered if
his feet were still connected to his ankles, his knees to
the bones above. His arms ached and he was unsure he

could move his hands, for they felt dismembered from his wrists, and those from his elbows, and he could not, in the magnitude of his pain, feel his shoulders at all.

He tasted the filthy straw in his mouth and lay there as the rats—his only friends, it seemed—gathered around him. They were nervous, but they once again warmed him, so that after a while he felt his body reconnect to its strained limbs and was able to crawl to the bucket some guard more caring than his torturer had left. He dunked his face and sucked up water, and then forced himself upright that he might stare from the barred window at the sun, and wonder on his fate.

It seemed that the Garm'kes Lyn had the better of him, and he doubted Abra's intent. She had protected him against the Garm priest—who stank of evil—but . . . Could he trust her? She was Garm, after all, and clearly her father's daughter. Faced with the choice of execution at his side, would she still support him, or deny him? He felt his wrists ache as he clutched the bars and stared at the sun; and wondered if he was to die here, in this stone prison.

❦❦❦

"NOW TELL ME THE TRUTH," Lord Bartram said. "We are alone, and you can be honest."

Abra smiled wanly and said, "I love him."

"A Durrym?"

She shrugged. "He seems not so different."

"He's *Durrym*." her father said.

"And the priest would have you go to war against them. Lofantyl would make peace." She rose from her chair to pace the room, summoning arguments for Lofantyl's survival. "He'd see this enmity finished! He'd see men and Durrym live together."

"He told you that?" her father asked.

Abra nodded.

"Then why not approach me? Do the Durrym truly seek peace, why did he not come to me?"

"How could he trust you?" she asked. "A Border Lord, sworn to defend the frontier against such as he?" She shook her head. "And Per Fendur speaks of war— he'd invade the fey lands, and drive Lofantyl's people off again. How could Lofantyl come to you?"

Bartram sighed. "There's more to it than that, my daughter. Do you not understand? We grow too strong, too fast. We took this land from the Durrym, and now we increase in numbers, so that Kandar becomes too small for all its folk."

"So we must invade the fey lands?" she asked. "Because we are threatened, we must threaten others?"

"I'd sooner it were not so," her father replied. "But our king sees it differently. He'd prefer to place his trust in the Church, and hope the priests find a way east— across the Alagordar. Into new lands."

"That's madness," Abra said. "To fight the Durrym to gain what's theirs?"

Bartram shrugged. "Khoros commands me. He's my king—and yours."

"And listens to the whisperings of such as Fendur," Abra snapped.

"And rules this land," her father reminded her. "And I am pledged to him."

"So you heed Fendur?"

Bartram's ruddy face flushed at the accusation in her voice. "No more than I must," he said. "But he represents the Church, and Khoros trusts the priests. Do I argue, he'll replace me, and then what might happen to you?"

Abra frowned, confused. Her father laughed cynically and said, "You'd be given to Wyllym like some prize. You'd be wed and I'd be . . . executed? Or . . ."

"*No!*" Abra cried. "Not even the king would dare that."

"Perhaps not," Bartram allowed. "For that might well foment civil war, but even so . . . I might be ordered to some lesser hold, stripped of my position."

"And who'd hold this keep?" Abra gestured at the walls of the chamber.

They were composed of hard gray blocks, albeit decorated with tapestries and paintings, and the hearth blazed bright in rejection of the cold. Rugs covered the stones of the floor and there were trophies set about the walls: old swords and boar tusks, ancient banners. The memorabilia of several lives. The windows were thickly glassed, and set in polished wood—her father's work—and she thought that all this keep was his, and could not imagine him losing it. And certainly not because of her.

"I think," her father said, "that Khoros might give it to Amadis. Or hand it all to the Church—to Fendur."

Abra felt her eyes fill with tears. "And this is my fault?"

"It's not come to that yet." He leaned forward to take her hands. "I'd not see you unhappy; nor Kandar delivered to unreasonable war. I'd sooner see us make peace with the Durrym."

"Then free Lofantyl," she asked. "Let him go."

"I cannot," he said. "He's Durrym—the enemy. But I shall do what I can. Believe me, eh?"

Abra had no choice save to agree.

❧☙❧

LOFANTYL LAY IN HIS CELL, hurting, and waited for Per Fendur to return.

He knew the priest would, for that had shone like evil lamplight from his black eyes: a dismal promise of pain to come. And the next morning he did return, smiling.

"Shall we speak again?"

"I've not been fed," Lofantyl replied. "And I'm mightily hungry."

"No doubt." Per Fendur aped apology. "You must forgive me my faulty memory—I thought only of getting answers from you." He bowed, elaborate and mocking. Then, to the hulking soldiers who accompanied him, "Bring him!"

Lofantyl was once again dragged from the cell and flung onto the rack. Per Fendur smiled at him as the straps were buckled about the wrists and ankles.

"A little tighter, today," he said. "Perhaps enough to break your joints. Are Durrym limbs stronger than ours? We'll see, eh?"

"I cannot tell you anything more," Lofantyl declared. "No more than what I've said."

"We shall see." Per Fendur smiled equably and turned the wheel.

Lofantyl screamed, for all he'd vowed he'd not. He could not help the shriek that burst out as his hurting body was stretched farther.

"That hurts, no?" Per Fendur leaned close, smiling. "I cannot imagine how much it must hurt. And so much more to come. Until I'm satisfied."

"With the truth or the pain?" Lofantyl moaned.

"Are they not the same?" The priest swung the wheel a notch tighter. "Truth is often painful—and the sooner you give me yours, the sooner this can end."

He turned the wheel again; Lofantyl howled.

Per Fendur laughed.

And then the dungeon door slammed open and Lord

Bartram entered. Laurens stood behind him, and six solid men.

"What is this?" Bartram's voice echoed the expression of disgust on his face.

"I question the prisoner," Fendur said.

"You torture him." Bartram stared at the rack. "I'd forgotten this existed."

"It's a useful tool," the priest returned.

"Let him up!" Bartram gestured and Laurens stepped toward the horrid table.

Fendur darted in front of the master-at-arms. "Leave him be! He's mine to question."

Laurens hesitated, looking back at Lord Bartram, who smiled sardonically and repeated, "Let him up. Get him off that thing!" And then: "Put your sword into any who oppose you."

"Treason!" Fendur howled. "You defy the Church and your king! Disobey me and you shall be excommunicated!"

Laurens glanced at Bartram, and saw his lord nod. So he cut the straps and lifted Lofantyl from the rack.

"I'll see no man tortured in my keep," Bartram said.

"He's not a man," Fendur snarled. "He's a Durrym!"

"Even so," Bartram replied, "he deserves respect." He looked to Laurens, who held Lofantyl upright. "Take him back to his cell. And see it's decent, eh? Fresh straw and clean water; and see him fed properly."

Laurens ducked his head and hauled the stumbling Durrym away.

Bartram and Fendur glowered at one another, mutual dislike in their eyes.

"The Church shall hear of this," Fendur threatened, "and not like what it hears."

"Likely so," Lord Bartram agreed. "But for now get out of my sight, lest I lose my temper."

He watched as the priest quit the torture chamber. It was an afterthought to command the guards who'd aided Fendur to stand the midnight watch until he changed his mind. And then he ordered the men with him to destroy the apparatus of torture that filled the room. He saw the horrid instruments torn down and hammered; the tables set ablaze, until the dungeon was filled with smoke and fire. And then he wondered what he'd done, and if Per Fendur might not still bring him down in disgrace.

Save, he thought, it would not be disgrace, but only whatever honesty he could find.

SEVEN

Abra wondered how Lofantyl fared. She was terribly afraid for him, and for herself. She sensed that if Per Fendur had his way, they'd both be executed—save her father intervened, which might well lose him his holding, or worse. She thought, as she lay restless on her bed, that the worst had arrived and all her roads were come together in a ghastly tangle that could leave only sorrow in its path. Had she refused Lofantyl's advances none of this would have happened. He'd not have risked the keep's walls to visit her, nor been captured, and then her father would have not have been in opposition to the Church.

She poured a glass of wine and stared from her window at the bleak walls of her home.

The snows had ceased now, and froze under a cold east wind. The keep's walls were glassy with ice, and the land beyond lay frozen and white, as empty as her hopes. A new moon rose, a yellow sickle that mocked her, looking as lonely as she felt, but more regal. She made a decision.

She tugged on a robe and found her way to the dungeons.

There were no guards—the night was icy, and who'd free a Durrym? The key to the outer gate was hung in a box by the wall, the turnkey gone to his dinner. She took it and opened the gate. There was a flight of stairs, descending into darkness and the stench of ordure and ancient straw, so that she coughed and muffled her sleeve about her nostrils as she found a lantern and carried it lit before her, calling Lofantyl's name.

He answered and she brought the lamp to the front of his cell. Then dropped it as he took her hands and drew her against the bars.

"I love you," he said.

"And I you," she answered. "But what can we do?"

"Are you safe here?"

She nodded. "The dungeons aren't guarded."

"Then—if you can, safely—bring me paper and pen."

"To what end?" she asked, clutching his hands.

"I can send a message to my father. Does he hear of my plight, he might well sue for peace—agree to some treaty between us."

"I'll do it," she promised.

❧❦☙

LOFANTYL RETURNED to his straw-laden bed. His cell was cleaner now that Lord Bartram had ordered he be tended well. He had fresh water and decent food, but even so he was held prisoner by the Garm'kes Lyn. And even did he trust Bartram, he could not trust the priest, or the one called Amadis. He thought that in time they'd put him back on the rack, or send him to the Church or the capital, where he'd be hung or burned. Unless he could escape, which would be difficult without help.

Without Abra.

He waited for the sky to brighten and then summoned the raven.

The bird settled noisily on the ledge of his cell, where he spoke to it and told it to return at sunset.

Which it did. But before then Abra had brought him a scroll and a nib and an inkpot, so he was able to compose a message that he fixed to the raven's leg before he bade it fly.

❧❦❧

THE BIRD LOFTED over Lyth, black wings beating. It crossed the forest and the Alagordar, and came to a gentler land, leaving winter behind. It rested a while in the sun and then, compelled by Lofantyl's command, flew onward, over such country as the Kandarians had never seen. Ahead lay Kash'ma Hall, all glossy and wooden in the late afternoon light, set in a great clearing, yet still part of the expansive woodland.

The bird landed on a tree that had no right to grow so green in winter—save it was not winter here—and waited until a caller, whose name was Arym, came and brought it down. It sat atop his wrist as he took off Lofantyl's message, then hopped onto his shoulder as he brought it to the aviary and fed it nuts and grain.

Arym took the message to Isydrian.

The High Lord of Kash'ma Hall was settled by a hearth that burned so bright it should, in Kandar, have devoured all the keep, did they not live inside stone places. In Coim'na Drhu, however, the flames only caressed the wood, decorating the hearth with reflections of fire, giving back only warmth.

Isydrian felt the cold now: he was growing old, and he felt a terrible presentiment as Arym delivered the message, bowed and departed. He doubted it was any good news.

His courtiers rose as he opened the scroll; he waved them back. This was something he'd read alone.

He held his aquiline features steady as he read of Lofantyl's plight. Then beckoned Afranydyr to his side.

"I've a task for you."

Afranydyr bowed his head. "As you command, Father."

Isydrian said, "Your brother is held captive by the Garm. In Lyth Keep. The barbarians have tortured him, but the Garm woman aids him. She'll help him escape, all well. I want to rescue him."

"How?" Afranydyr demanded. "Kandar's snow-bound—how shall we make the way?"

"I don't care—make it!" Isydrian glowered at his older son. "Your brother is held prisoner by the Garm. Shall you see him executed?"

Afranydyr shook his head.

"Then go!"

"How many warriors shall I take?" Afranydyr asked.

"Ten should be enough," Isydrian replied. "You face, after all, only Garm'kes Lyn."

"Yes, my father." Afranydyr ducked obeisance. "As you command, my father."

❦❧❦

COIM'NA DRHU RESTED AUTUMNAL. The grass grew green and the trees were still leafed, so from Kash'ma Hall to the Mys'enh they made good time.

Beyond the river, however, winter locked the land. The west bank of the Alagordar was all snowy, and the big Durrym chargers protested the cold with snorts of disapproval. They were larger and fleeter than any Garm horse, but accustomed to the benign climate of Coim'na Drhu, so their riders must urge them on, themselves shivering as the cold gripped, watching their mounts blow great steamy breaths into the chill air.

"It's my brother we come to rescue," Afranydyr declared dutifully. "Shall we let a little inclement weather halt us?"

Gofylans, who was his second, blew on his hands and said, "No. But I cannot like this miserable country. I wonder if the Garm didn't do us a favor when they drove us out."

Afranydyr chuckled. "Coim'na Drhu is surely more pleasant. I think the Garm don't understand the country. I think they only seek to own it, and make it theirs."

Gofylans stared at him. "How so? How can anyone own the land?"

"They're Garm," Afranydyr said. "They don't understand."

Gofylans shook his head in disbelief.

❧❧❧

THEY REACHED THE EDGE OF THE WOODS, with Kandar stretching out before them. They halted inside the forest and built a fire, spreading their bedrolls on the snow. Afranydyr and Gofylans sat together, discussing their strategy.

"The keep is there." Afranydyr tapped the parchment his father had given him, drawn from Lofantyl's raven-delivered instructions. "There are farms between here and there, and a village below the keep."

"So we've little chance of approaching unobserved."

Gofylans snorted laughter. "What do we do? Ride through the village and storm the walls? And then die?"

"No." Afranydyr shook his head. "The girl aids us. Lofantyl promises that she'll let us in when the moon is full."

"And you trust a Garm?"

"What other choice?" Afranydyr sighed. "He's my brother, no?"

"And I'm your friend," said Gofylans, "but I doubt the wisdom of the venture."

"It's my father's command," Afranydyr replied. "And my brother in the prison. Honor demands I rescue him."

❧❧❧

"REMEMBER, THEY'LL COME for me when the moon grows full." Lofantyl clutched Abra's hands through the bars. "You must open a gate for them."

She shook her head. "How can I? You ask me to betray my father."

"Then Per Fendur shall have me. He'll rack me and then send me off to die. Do you want that?"

"*No!*"

"Then you *must* help me. Else I'm dead."

"I must think on it," she said, and left him before any guards came.

She returned to her chambers and thought on all he asked—on what it must mean for her and her father. And wondered, torn between love and loyalty, what she should do.

❧❧❧

"IT SHALL SERVE YOU WELL, that we've a Durrym to question." Per Fendur raised his glass in toast. "He might well give us information of their land, and make our conquest easier."

"Under torture?" Lord Bartram shook his head. "A man racked will tell you anything."

"Even so," the priest returned, "we can learn. The rack gives answers."

"But not necessarily the truth."

"You dispute my methods?" The priest fixed the keep lord with an accusing stare.

Bartram nodded. "I do. I've no taste for torture."

Fendur smiled, directing his gaze to Vanysse and Amadis. "A squeamish Border Lord?" He chuckled, taking the sting from his taunt. "I'd thought you hardier."

"I'll face any man in battle," Bartram replied indignantly. "Or any Durrym. But I'll not condone torture."

Fendur's smile evaporated, his eyes growing cold as frozen stones. "You'd defy the Church?"

Vanysse said, "Heed him, husband." And Amadis nodded his approval.

But Lord Bartram shook his head and said, "I'll not agree to torture."

Fendur exaggerated a sigh. "Then I must send a message to my prelate, who will doubtless speak with Khoros, and . . ."—he let a breath go by—"you shall receive *orders*."

"Perhaps," Bartram said. "And does my king command, I must obey. But that shall take a while, no?" He gestured at the misted windows. "Traveling is hard out there, Per Fendur, and I wonder how long your message shall take. And until you've sent it, and I've a response, you'll not touch the prisoner."

Fendur glanced at Amadis, who shrugged and said, "Weeks, in such weather as this."

"So be it." Fendur nodded. "I shall compose a letter." He looked to Amadis rather than Bartram. "You'll see it sent?"

Amadis ducked his head.

"And meanwhile," Fendur said with oily mildness, "I see fit to question your daughter, my lord."

"*No!*" Bartram shouted.

"Why not?" Fendur asked. "If she is innocent, she's nothing to fear."

He fixed Abra with a smile, and she made her decision.

❧❧❧

AFRANYDYR HALTED HIS MOUNT with Lyth in sight. The moon stood full above, painting the snow with silvery light, so that he could see the sleeping village clear as day. It was shuttered against the chill, and he grinned as he gave his instructions. Unlike his brother, he savored the prospect of combat.

"We'll skirt around," he told Gofylans, "and approach from the north. There should be a lantern to mark the gate."

"And if there's not?"

"Then we'll do what we can, no?"

"Which is what?" Gofylans asked.

"Fight our way in and rescue my brother," Afranydyr said.

❧❧❧

THEY REACHED THE WALLS and waited.

"They're sleepy folk," Afranydyr remarked, studying the ramparts. "We could easily take this place."

Stretched flat against the frozen snow, Gofylans was in worse humor than his commander. "Until they wake up," he said. "Then it might be different."

Afranydyr chuckled. And then a light showed as a sallyport opened.

"*Now!*"

❧❧❧

THEY RAN TOWARD the lantern Abra held and swept her up in their charge. She opened her mouth to scream, startled by their onslaught, but a hand clamped firm over her mouth and she heard her captor whisper, "One sound and I slay you."

His tone left her in no doubt, and she nodded as best she could against his hard, musky hand.

It went away and she looked up at a Durrym who seemed a larger, sterner version of Lofantyl.

"I am Afranydyr," he whispered. "Lofantyl's brother. Where is he?"

She saw that he held a sword made of no metal she had ever seen, perhaps no metal at all. It was against her neck, and his eyes told her he'd not hesitate to use it. She felt very afraid. "There." She pointed toward the dungeon's entrance, and Afranydyr took hold of her arm and urged her in that direction. His cohorts followed, moving silent as shadows across the frosted courtyard.

❧❧❧

THE WIND BLEW cold as Abra made her way to the dungeons. She wore a cloak, but even so the chill gripped her like panic, and she could hardly stop her teeth from rattling as she heard her feet crunch—loud—on the ice. Sentries manned the walls, but they were cold as she, and held mostly to their posts and, anyway, looked for assault from outside rather than within.

She found the entrance to the dungeons and took the great key from its hook. It chilled her fingers and she could not insert it in the lock for the trembling of her hands. Afranydyr took it from her, wincing as he touched the metal. Then he inserted key to lock and, with a grunt, turned it.

He shouldered the door open and Abra stared around, terrified that the grating sound it made should alert the guards. She stared at the walls, where the sentries were, and saw the night all still and cold, and heaved a sigh of relief when no alarum sounded.

"Show me where he is."

Afranydyr's blade rested on her shoulder and she led him down the damp steps to Lofantyl's cell.

The turnkey was long gone to his bed, the dungeons lightless save for a single torch that spread long shadows over the miserable confines, rats and cockroaches scattering at their entrance. Afranydyr snorted his disgust.

"This is no way to imprison a son of Kash'ma Hall."

"Nor my way," Abra returned. She found Lofantyl's older brother uncouth, not at all like her Durrym lover. But she set that thought aside as she took him and his men to Lofantyl's cell.

"We honor our prisoners," Afranydyr muttered. "We treat them well."

Abra had no answer for that, so all she said was, "He's here," as she pointed at the barred gate.

Lofantyl rose, scattering his blanket of rats, and stared at the gate.

"Abra? I'd scarce dared hope . . ." He reached through the bars that he might touch her fingers. Then, "Afranydyr?"

"Our father ordered me." Afranydyr studied the bars and the lock, and looked to Abra. "How do I open this thing?"

Abra shook her head helplessly. "I've only the outside key. Not those to the cell."

"Garm," Afranydyr muttered. Then: "Gofylans, bring up that axe."

Gofylans stepped forward, hefting a sickle-bladed axe. Afranydyr pointed at the cell's lock, and Gofylans swung his blade.

There was a clatter that Abra feared must alert the sentries, but the lock parted and the door swung free.

Lofantyl stepped out of the cell and kissed Abra. She kissed him back.

"Thank you. You saved my life."

"And I?" Afranydyr demanded.

"You've my thanks as well, brother," Lofantyl returned. "You also, no less."

"So now we're done with thanks," Afranydyr said, "let's be gone. The sooner we're quit of this Garm place, the better."

He turned to leave, his men lining the stairway, alert against attack.

Lofantyl said, "Wait," and looked to Abra. "You'll come with me?"

"To your land?"

He nodded. "To Coim'na Drhu. To Kash'ma Hall. I'll wed you there."

"And what of my father?" she asked. "What shall happen to him?"

"I don't know," he said.

"Per Fendur would pronounce him guilty—and me! Likely he'd be imprisoned, and I'd be executed."

"Then come with me!"

"And leave my father?"

They stared at one another and found no secure answers until Abra said, "Do you not go now, you'll not be safe."

And Lofantyl said, "*Shall* you come with me?"

She shook her head and said, "I cannot desert my fa
ther."

"I'd find it hard to live without you," he declared.

"And I without you."

Afranydyr said, "Enough of this nonsense," and
slammed his sword's hilt against Abra's neck, so that she
gasped and fell down unconscious.

❧❦❧

LOFANTYL CAUGHT HER as she fell and held her in
his arms, staring aghast at his brother.

"We've not so much time," Afranydyr snarled, "so
bring her with us. You want her, no?"

Lofantyl nodded.

"So we'll take her with us. Come!"

Not waiting on a reply he headed back up the dungeon's steps. Lofantyl followed, cradling Abra in his arms

The Durrym spread shadowlike into the courtyard
Afranydyr in the lead, Lofantyl and the unconscious
Abra hustled on by the others. They came unnoticed to
the open sallyport and found their horses.

"So, little brother," Afranydyr chuckled as the
Durrym chargers stamped their eagerness to be gone
"all's well, no? You're rescued and you've the woman you
want. Now let's go home."

"Before the Garm wake up, eh?" This from Gofylans
"We've a ride ahead."

"I know," Afranydyr retorted, and stared at Lofantyl
"Well, brother? Shall you bring the Garm along, or leave
her in the snow?"

Lofantyl studied Abra's face and knew he could not
bear to leave her.

"You've a horse for me?"

"Of course. But not for her."

"She'll ride with me."

"So be it." Afranydyr beckoned a man toward him, bringing up a big bay charger. "Now shall we depart?"

Lofantyl nodded; he could not bear to leave Abra behind. Gofylans helped him throw Abra across the saddle. He mounted and they set off across the snow-scaped land, toward the Alagordar. Toward Coim'na Drhu.

EIGHT

ABRA LAY CONFUSED and frightened across the saddlebow of the Durrym charger. Lofantyl kept a hand pressed against her back as he steered the big horse with the other, and all she knew was speed and the sweetly musty odor of the animal as they thundered northward. They rode like the wind, and even as the saddle ground into her ribs and drove the breath from her aching body, she realized that they put the bulk of the keep between them and Lyth before turning eastward, toward the forest and the Alagordar.

She was not sure how long they rode, for the journey became agonizing, her legs kicking and her head bumping, and all she could see was the moonlit snow glinting under the pounding hoofs. She wailed in protest, but Lofantyl gave no sign of hearing until they halted before a stream that fed across snow-covered grazing land into the Alagordar. Then he sprang from the saddle and eased her down, all solicitous.

"Forgive me, please." He touched her face. "I had no other choice."

"No?" Abra rubbed her aching ribs and waited for the world to steady itself as she composed her response. She wiped horse sweat from her face and studied his. The others dismounted around them, tall men dressed in leather and homespun, and armed with swords and bows. One, she recognized—Afranydyr—who spoke with a hawk-faced Durrym whose eyes surveyed her coldly.

"You've kidnapped me," she said, indignant. "I told you that I'd remain with my father, but you took me anyway."

"Afranydyr left me no choice." Lofantyl gestured at the larger man, who now came toward them.

"Brother! It's good to have you back." He clasped Lofantyl's shoulder before turning to Abra. He bowed with cold courtesy. "I apologize, my lady. The manner of your taking was not what I'd have wished, but . . ." He shrugged. "There was little other choice."

"Save to leave me!"

"To give the alarm?"

"I set Lofantyl free," she returned, torn now between anger and confusion. "Was it likely I'd give the alarm?"

Afranydyr opened his mouth to respond, but Lofantyl spoke faster. "No! I owe you my life—but think on the circumstances, eh? Had you remained would the priest not have questioned you? Perhaps set you on the rack?"

"What's that?" Afranydyr asked.

"An instrument of torture that stretches you until your limbs come apart," Lofantyl replied.

"Obscenity!" Afranydyr frowned. "The Garm truly use such things?"

"I'm proof," Lofantyl said. "The priest would have stretched me to breaking had Lord Bartram not intervened." He looked to Abra. "He's a decent man, your father. But that priest . . ." He shook his head. "There's evil incarnate in him."

Abra could only agree, and wonder what was to become of her. Lofantyl and Anfranydyr watched her as the others opened saddlebags and ate. The moon was close on its zenith, and the keep lay farther behind than she could believe—testament to the speed of the Durrym horses. The land was quiet, save for the snuffling of the chargers and the soft conversation of the Durrym. The snow glittered all silvery under the moon's light, and choices stood before and behind her.

At her back was the keep, where—she supposed—her father slept unaware of her deeds. To go back was to face Per Fendur's questions, which she doubted she could answer. Might he not use his magic on her to learn the truth? And what then should be the outcome—the rack, or execution? Ahead was Coim'na Drhu, the unknown land: a strange country filled with her traditional enemies. She looked at Lofantyl and knew she loved him, and then at his brother, who studied her with cold, unwinking eyes.

"You could leave me here," she said. "Before long, they'll know you're gone and send men out, who'd find me."

"And you might freeze before they did," Lofantyl said. "I cannot allow that."

"Build me a fire, then."

"No!" Afranydyr spoke harshly. "A fire would be a marker. They'd find us."

"So soon?" Abra asked defiantly, not liking this Durrym at all. "Shall you not be gone into your secret lands before any pursuit can catch you?"

Afranydyr chuckled sourly, and gestured to the south. "They've already noticed, my lady. Likely they're abroad now, in search of you. You Garm are hard hunters."

Abra turned. Far off in the distance, light blazed about the keep. Fluttering torches moved back and forth, and bonfires were lit along the castle's walls. In the still, cold night she wondered if she could hear her father calling.

"And our horses are weary," Afranydyr continued. "I'd not see them put to the chase until they're rested."

"She'll freeze without a fire," Lofantyl said.

"Then we've no choice. She comes with us."

Afranydyr turned as if all discussion were concluded.

"It's hard," Lofantyl said, "to argue with my brother. He cares so much for Coim'na Drhu, for our hall. We disagree on most things, but in this . . ."

"So I must come with you?"

He smiled at her. "Shall that be so awful?"

She shook her head, still frightened by the unknown, but comforted by him.

"Ride with me?" he asked, and helped her onto the saddle.

She sat behind him, her arms about his waist, and Afranydyr shouted for his men to mount and they set out across the snowy fields toward the Alagordar.

❧❧❧❧

'WHAT IN THE NAMES of all the gods is this?" Lord Bartram demanded when the officer of the watch woke him. "How could he have escaped?"

None could say for sure, only that the dungeons had been opened and a discarded lantern found by the northern sallyport.

Bartram checked for himself and found the cell empty, the lock smashed off and the prisoner gone. The sallyport stood open, deep hoofprints in the snow beyond. He was not in his best humor as he summoned his officers.

Amadis came tousle haired and smelling of Vanysse's perfume; Per Fendur hollow eyed and irritable; Laurens calm as ever.

"We should have chained him," Fendur said. "Had you agreed with me, then—"

"I did not, and he's gone!" Bartram hammered a fist against the table, ending the priest's argument. "Where?"

"The tracks go north," Laurens said, "but they'll turn east before long—to the Alagordar."

"Then send riders!" Fendur barked. "Capture him again!"

"They've a decent start on us," Laurens said. "It could be difficult to catch up with them."

Before Bartram could respond, Fendur spoke. *"Do it! In the name of the Church, I command you!"* His voice was harsh, his eyes bleak. "I want him back! I want—"

Amadis said quickly, "Your wish is our command." And to Laurens: "See two squadrons mounted. Now!"

Laurens looked to Bartram, and only when the keep lord had nodded his agreement said, "Then I shall, as you order." He rose with deliberate ponderousness, and looked to Amadis. "Shall you go forth, Captain? And if so, to which point?"

"I'll take a squadron east," he said. "You go north."

"Before you leave," Per Fendur said, looking hard at Lord Bartram, "shall we discover the lady Abra's whereabouts?"

"Why?" Bartram glowered at the priest. "What's she to do with this?"

"Who knows?" Fendur replied. "Save she's consorted ith the Durrym—which makes her suspect."

Bartram scowled, but consented that Abra's chamers be searched. And when they were and she found one, he sent all his horsemen to find her.

❦❧❦

'HE TRACKS WENT NORTH, and Laurens chuck-d, turning his men eastward.

"They're Durrym," he shouted, "they'll be making for heir own land. So we ride the bank of the Alagordar and ut them off. Come on!"

He turned his troop eastward, riding hard through he cold night until he came through the edge of the oods and into the true forest, the river before him, wide nd mystical. Ancient oaks grew there, and old birch, azel and walnut, great drooping willows, and the sky ung brightly dark above, and all the world was filled ith frozen snow. His men's breath blew pale mist before heir faces, and the horses gave off the sweat of their ex-rtions.

Then night gave way to pale dawn. What few birds emained in snow-rimed Kandar set to singing as the sky eluctantly brightened. Laurens had halted his troop for a hile, lest horses and men come upon the enemy weary; hey had settled in a stand of frost-hung willows that sur-ounded a frozen pool. Now light filtered through the ici-led branches and spread the surface of the pool with an yellow, sick as a leper's features.

Laurens checked the watchmen and kicked the rest wake.

"Up, eh! We've a treasure to recover."

If we can, he thought to himself, as they rose. If the Durrym aren't already gone across the river. He helped himself to tea and ate a piece of cold meat, and wondered what might become of Abra, and what of his men if they encountered the Durrym.

He took his troop north along a trail crusted with ice and overhung with frozen branches. The Alagordar—too fast to freeze, or perhaps draped with Durrym magic—ran loud to their right. To the left, the forest spread rimed and silvery.

And where the frozen trees opened on a ford they saw the Durrym.

❧❦❧

LAURENS DREW HIS SWORD and shouted for his troop to follow him as he charged at Abra's captors.

They were ten against ten, he estimated; but the Durrym were mounted on higher horses, and they had bows. He ducked as an arrow whistled past his head and wished he'd thought to armor up and carry a shield, but he'd had no time.

He felt a shaft pierce his left side. It hurt, but he did not let it slow him as he plucked it out and cast the bloodied stump aside. And saw Abra carried off across the river even as he raced forward to drive his blade against the hawk-faced archer's neck.

He saw the Durrym tumble from his charger, his body cloven from windpipe to waist. And for all it was larger and more muscular than Laurens's horse, the Durrym animal was smashed aside by Laurens's charge, and fell down shrilling.

Laurens turned back, sword raised, and charged again into the melee. He cut at a Durrym and saw the fey topple bloody from his mount. And then all was confusion and sword work save that he was aware of Abra clutching a Durrym's waist as he drove his mount across the river.

And then a horn sounded, silvery as bells in the cold air. The Durrym turned away and crossed the ford in a single charge, and were gone.

Laurens bellowed at his men and swung his horse in pursuit.

They followed the same ford as the Durrym had taken. It was easy, until they reached the farther bank, where ice and snow gave way to warmth, and the ground grew sticky with the aftermath of sunlight. Willows overhung the path, trailing great branches in their way, so that they must duck under the massive limbs as birds and squirrels chattered at them angrily. Then enormous ferns concealed the trail, as if there had never been any way through here at all. There were clear hoofprints coming up from the river, where the ground was still soft, but then it grew hard and there were no more, and all Laurens could do was follow the trail as best he could through a great swath of forest that seemed to have nothing to do with Kandar's winter. It was another country here, one that had little to do with men.

But he knew where the Durrym had gone. Save as he followed them he found himself turned around so that even as he followed where he *knew* the Durrym must have gone, he found himself facing the Alagordar again. He cursed and returned back along the path, and was again faced with the river. His side hurt where the arrow had gone in, but he ignored the pain and brought his troop around to retrace their path, back through the willows and alders, where deep hoofprints showed in the muddy ground; back to where the soil became hard under an impossible sun, and autumnal trees spread low branches in defiance of their passing. He took his men on, following the trail, and was every time brought back to the river. And all the time with his wounded side hurting worse.

Three more times he tried to follow, until the sun was setting. It was as if the trees and shrubs, the very foliage itself, conspired to defeat him. And he'd not spend a night in this weird country for fear of his soul.

"Durrym magic," he declared. "She's lost now, and we must return to the keep." He looked back at the impossible landscape and waved his sword in frustration and fury.

The land darkened. Birds he thought were swallows hunted the overhanging sky. He heard their calling and watched them in wonderment until his head began to spin and a warrior called Drak came up beside him.

"Best we cross now, before the night comes on."

Laurens nodded, suddenly aware of the pain in his side.

"You need tending," Drak said. "That shaft pricked you somewhat."

Laurens looked down and saw dark stains spreading over his shirt and breeches. Abruptly, he felt a rush of nausea, and wondered how much damage the Durrym arrow had done. He hoped it had not been venomed. "There's a place we can rest," he said. "A forester's hut. I know him. Now, lead on."

Drak nodded and waved the troop forward, riding alongside Laurens. He held his mount tight against the master-at-arms's as they forded back into winter.

It was as if some invisible curtain hung across the Alagordar from north to south. On one side the climate was mild, on the other wintry. Laurens wondered at the Durrym's magic that could turn aside the seasons, and what a boon that could be for Kandar.

They splashed across the ford with dying sunlight warm on their backs and cold against their faces as they climbed the farther bank into frozen snow. Here, all the timber was frosted and hung with icicles, the trail frozen hard, and all the undergrowth caught down beneath the weight of snow. Laurens looked back and saw the river running free and clear, and wondered if its gurgling was Durrym laughter. He ducked beneath an ice-hung branch and cursed volubly as the hole in his side protested the movement. He glanced down and saw the stain on his breeches descending farther. His boots darkened, and his mount's side was tainted. He gritted his teeth and pushed through the winter-hung woods as pain filled him. He watched frosted oaks spin above, and all the stars he could see combined to turn his world into a whirligig of pain and frustration and disappointment. He spat, wondering if he spat out blood, and urged his troop onward.

Worse, it was night here: the early darkness of Kandar's winter. Moonlight dappled the frozen ground in harlequin patterns of light and shade that tricked his eyes and started up an even greater turning in his head that he struggled to ignore as he forced himself upright in his saddle.

He was embarrassed to find himself leaning against Drak, but the soldier's arm was the only thing—were he honest—that held him astride his mount.

"You'll not make the keep like this," Drak said bluntly.

Laurens sighed, acknowledging the inevitable. "So we must do as I said and find Cullyn. Hold me up, eh? And I'll show you where."

If I can, he thought, as he watched the forest whirl about his head.

❀❁❀

CULLYN WAS GROOMING Fey as the troop rode in. He'd taken the big stallion for a gallop now that the forest trails were frozen hard enough to make for safe running, and the horse was lathered from the exercise. It raised its head and whickered as it sensed the approaching riders, and Cullyn turned from his grooming to gasp as he saw Laurens drooping in his saddle, held upright by a younger man whose face was lined with concern.

"What's amiss?" He left Fey to fret as he vaulted the fence and ran toward them. "Laurens?"

"I got pricked." The master-at-arms grinned at Cullyn, who thought his face was very pale. "I need a place to rest a while."

"I'm Drak," the young soldier said, and ducked his head at Laurens. "He took a Durrym arrow in his side, and brought us here. He said you'd succor him. He'll not make the keep so wounded."

"My apologies," Laurens grunted, "but I could think of nowhere else."

"You're welcome," Cullyn returned, and held out his arms as Laurens slumped, taking the weight Drak let down until Laurens was on the ground and leaning against him. Drak sprang clear of his saddle and swung an arm around Laurens.

"I can walk," the master-at-arms protested, and promptly fell between them. "Dammit, I've had worse hits than this."

They carried him into the cottage and set him on Cullyn's bed.

Laurens protested as they stripped off his shirt to examine the wound, which was bloody, gouged through by a warhead arrow, and worse for his tearing it out. Cullyn fetched what was almost the last of his honey wine and fed Laurens a big cupful. The older man drank it gratefully.

"Can you help him?" Drak asked.

"Perhaps." Cullyn studied the wound. "I'm no healer, and he'd be better off in the keep."

"He'll not make that distance," Drak said, "else I'd have taken him there."

"I've herbs and poultices." Cullyn stared at the bloody hole. "And I'll do my best."

"Thank you." Drak set Laurens's stained breeches aside. "What can I do?"

"Stoke that fire." Cullyn indicated the hearth. "Set water to boiling, then leave the rest to me."

"And the men?" Drak spoke over his shoulder as he drove an iron into the fire. "They're hungry and cold."

Cullyn sighed as he envisioned his winter's supplies eaten. "There's not enough room in here for all of you—and they'd best stay clear of Fey—so let them bed where they can. I'll bring them food later."

Drak nodded and went out to the waiting soldiers, and Cullyn looked to Laurens.

The man's face was gray with pain, which was not surprising—Cullyn had seldom seen a worse wound. It was as if a boar had tusked him, thrusting through his side to open holes in front and back. Blood decorated his ribs and sweat beaded his forehead, running down the channels of his face to gather in the grizzle of his beard. He held his teeth clenched as Cullyn fed him more honey wine and lifted the pot from the fire, then fetched herbs that he set to boiling, and when they were ready set them on the wounds.

Laurens grunted and his body lurched as the steaming poultice settled on his flesh.

Cullyn wrapped the holes in moss and spiderwebs and tore up a sheet for the bandage that he wound about Laurens, who sighed gustily and settled back with a mumbled, "Thank you." And closed his eyes.

Cullyn left him, going out to find the troop settled in the yard. He went to his smokehouse and fetched a side of cured pork that he gave them, along with sufficient wood from his stack that they might build a decent fire.

"Shall he live?" Drak asked.

Cullyn shrugged. "Likely, but he'll not be fit to ride for a while."

"We need to get back to Lyth," Drak said. "How long before he *can* ride?"

"Days," Cullyn answered. "That wound needs to heal. Put him on a horse and he'll bleed to death."

"We've not that much time." Drak wiped an anxious hand across his face. "You know what's happened?"

Cullyn shook his head, and Drak explained. Cullyn gasped: "*Abra?*"

"Taken by the Durrym," Drak expanded. "Or seduced by them. By Lofantyl, at least." He slapped his sword's hilt angrily. "And to think we had the Durrym bastard in our dungeons! Per Fendur was right: we should have kept him chained. Or slain him straightaway."

Cullyn offered no answer, thinking of the friend he'd known, and of Abra; and decided that he would speak of all this with Laurens, whom he trusted. So he bade Drak good-night and returned to the cottage where Laurens slept feverishly, and waited for a clearer morning, when Drak left with the troop.

"We'll leave him here," he said, "until he's fit enough to ride. But I must go tell Lord Bartram that his daughter's lost to the fey folk. Doubtless Lord Bartram will reward you for your aid."

"I need no reward for helping a friend," Cullyn said, and watched them gallop off through the snow before he returned inside to check on Laurens.

Who stared at him with glazed eyes and asked, "Where am I?"

Cullyn explained, and Laurens struggled to sit up. Cullyn pushed him back.

"Drak's gone to the keep," he said, "to take word to Lord Bartram."

"I need to report." Laurens struggled against Cullyn's restraining hands. "I was in charge. I must report to Lord Bartram."

It was an unequal dispute. Laurens was weak and feverish, and Cullyn could shove him easily back against the pillows. "Listen," he said, "you've a hole in your side that will kill you if you get on a horse. You'll bleed to death if you do."

"But Abra's taken by the fey folk, and I could not get her back. I *must* tell her father."

"Drak will do that," Cullyn said—even as he wondered if Abra had not gone of her own accord. "And you'd best wait here—until you heal."

"I've a duty to Lord Bartram," Laurens mumbled.

And then he closed his eyes and drifted into healing sleep.

Cullyn wiped his sweaty brow and saw him comfortable, then went out to check his animals even as he wondered at these strange events.

So Lofantyl had been captured and rescued—with Abra's aid, it seemed—and then Abra had been taken across the Barrier into the fey country. He threw feed down for the pigs and forked out Fey's stall—set fresh hay in the manager—and gathered eggs that he took into the cottage and set to scrambling, with bacon and what little bread he had left.

He fed Laurens as if the soldier were a pigling in his care, a deserted shoat that must be mothered and tended. Yet even as he watched over Laurens he had decided what he must do.

🐛🐝🐛

"Tʜᴇʏ ᴡᴇʀᴇ ɴᴏᴛ ᴛʜᴇʀᴇ. We could not find them," Amadis said. "We sought them long enough, but . . ." He shrugged and ducked his head. "Forgive me, my lord, but I believe your daughter is seduced and taken into the Durrym country. She's gone away with the fey folk."

"And perhaps," Per Fendur said, "of her own choosing. After all—"

He closed his mouth as Lord Bartram glowered at him. "And the other patrols?"

"No word as yet."

Then Drak came into the hall. He was hollow eyed and weary from his ride, and he swayed on his feet as he gave his report.

"So my daughter is taken away by the Durrym," Lord Bartram said when Drak finished. "And Laurens lies wounded in this forester's hut. What shall we do?"

He stared at Per Fendur, who said: "Does this not prove all I've told you? Do you want your daughter back, we must go to war."

"How?" Bartram demanded. "The gods know, Drak has just told us there's no way across the Alagordar. We are defeated by Durrym magic."

"Save the Church finds a way," Fendur said. "Trust me, my lord. And should we not speak with your master-at-arms, and also this forester? I wonder if they might not tell us the truth—surely more than they admit."

"Laurens is honest," Bartram said. "I cannot doubt him."

"But the forester?" Fendur asked. "This . . . *Cullyn*. Is he trustworthy?"

"I don't know him," Bartram said.

"I've encountered him," Amadis declared.

"And?" Fendur asked.

"A surly fellow, who dwells alone in the forest. Close on the margins of the river."

"He seems friendly," Drak ventured. "And surely served Laurens well." He fell silent as Amadis glowered at him.

"Then perhaps we should question them both—in the name of the Church." Fendur smiled, turning back to Lord Bartram as if Drak had not spoken. "After all, your beloved daughter is gone into the fey folks' land—likely seduced by one of them—and should we not seek to get her back?"

"For that," Bartram declared, "I'd sell my soul."

"No need for such expedition," Fendur said. "Only let us go talk with this forester, and with your master-at-arms—who seem to be in concert—and we shall have answers."

NINE

I APOLOGIZE," Lofantyl said as he helped Abra dismount. "This was not of my choosing."

"No, but even so . . ." She looked around at a landscape that had nothing to do with Kandar. Here the woodland grew green, barely faded into autumn's colors, let alone the snows that gripped her homeland. The sun was setting—she supposed the Durrym could not control *that*, but it seemed they commanded all else, as if they governed the seasons. For here they stood on bright green grass, with birds singing and the sun lowering slowly in the west so that long, hot shadows stretched leisurely across the glade. A brook babbled there, and the big Durrym horses drank thirstily.

"This is my land." Lofantyl took her hand and led her to the stream. "I hope you like it."

"Have I any choice?" she asked.

"I'd have courted you otherwise," he said, "had that been possible."

"Save it was not, and so you're here." Afranydyr came to them. Lofantyl favored his brother with a sour glance that Afranydyr ignored as he spoke to Abra. "You are taken, my lady. My hapless brother declares himself in love with you, and perhaps he is, but even so—you are come into Coim'na Drhu now, and shall not go back to your Garm land."

"So I am kidnapped?" Abra touched the hilt of her belt knife and contemplated stabbing him. But Lofantyl set an arm around her.

"Afranydyr speaks bluntly," he said, "for he's a blunt fellow. But I *do* love you, and I think you shall enjoy your life here."

"And do I not?" she asked. "Can I return?"

Afranydyr barked short laughter; Lofantyl smiled easily, drawing her closer. "Come see Kash'ma Hall," he said. "And then decide."

And without choice, she could only agree.

❧❦❧

"I MUST BE GETTING OLD. Wounds never hurt like this before."

Laurens eased upright, leaning on Cullyn's shoulder.

"You were stuck through," Cullyn said, "and bled like a butchered pig. It's a wonder you're alive at all."

Laurens grunted what might be laughter and hobbled to the table, where Cullyn set him down. "I've suffered worse."

"When you were younger?" Cullyn stirred the venison broth he'd set to simmering.

"Aye, perhaps that," Laurens allowed. Then, "Have you any of that honey wine left?"

Cullyn laughed. "You've drunk most of it already."

"Even so." Laurens rubbed his bandaged side. "It does me good, no?"

Cullyn brought the flask and poured his friend a measure. Laurens raised the cup in toast and said, "Your health, my friend. I'd likely be dead were it not for you."

"I'd do as much for anyone," Cullyn said, embarrassed.

"But you did it for *me*," Laurens replied. "And so I owe you."

"You owe me nothing," Cullyn returned.

"Save my life."

❧❧❧

THE NEXT DAY, when the first thawing set in and the hard snow began to melt, Amadis and Per Fendur arrived with a squadron of twenty men.

They trampled Cullyn's yard, setting his pigs to squealing and Fey to snorting anger. The chickens fluttered their wings and squawked alarm.

Cullyn went out to meet them, with Laurens limping at his back.

"I'd speak with you," Amadis said to Laurens.

"And I with you," Fendur said to Cullyn.

The thaw had set the trees to dripping and the squadron sat disconsolate and damp. Drak sat his horse with his head down and an embarrassed expression on his face. Amadis shook out his cloak and shoved past Cullyn. Per Fendur entered the cottage with an oily smile and shook the moisture from his black cloak when he stood before the hearth.

"You might have sent a healer," Laurens said. "Were it not for Cullyn, I'd likely have died."

"You lost Abra," Amadis returned.

"I lost her?" Laurens gaped at his captain. "She was taken by the Durrym, and I did my best to find her. What did you do?"

"This matters not at all," Per Fendur said, staring at Cullyn. "What do *you* know?"

"That Abra's been taken," Cullyn said as the priest's black eyes bored into him. "No more than that."

"But you consort with the Durrym."

"No."

"You deny that Lofantyl was your friend?"

"No!"

"A Durrym?"

"I knew him first for a friend," Cullyn gasped, "and only after for a Durrym."

"Our enemy," Fendur declared. "Our traditional enemy!"

"He was my friend," Cullyn said. "He offered me no harm, nor could I believe he threatened Kandar."

"*Heresy!*" Fendur shouted, and turned to Amadis. "They must be questioned."

"It's a good day's ride to the keep," Amadis said.

"Then we'll spend the night here," Fendur decided, "and take them back tomorrow."

Laurens looked at Amadis and asked, "Do you truly doubt me so much?"

Amadis blushed and turned his eyes away.

Per Fendur shouted: "Take them both away! Secure them."

So they were dragged out of the cottage and thrown into the stable, condemned.

❧❦❧

"THIS IS NOT RIGHT," Cullyn said.

"*Right?*" Laurens eased himself to a sitting position,

taking care to avoid Fey's stamping. "What's *right* got to do with it?"

Cullyn stroked Fey's neck as he answered, calming the stallion for fear he'd trample Laurens. "You did your duty," he said, "and what offense have I given?"

"None," Laurens replied, "save to tend me."

"And for that we're to be taken for questioning?"

"It's the way of the world, lad," Laurens said. "Amadis needs an excuse and Per Fendur a victim. Neither can admit they failed, so they need scapegoats— which are you and I."

"So what shall become of us?"

Laurens chuckled cynically. "You've admitted the Durrym's friendship—so most likely the Per will torture you until you give him whatever answers he seeks. I've acknowledged our friendship, so I imagine my fate shall not be so different." He clutched his side as he spat into the straw. "And then . . . we die."

"And Lord Bartram has no say?"

"Lord Bartram's a just and decent man," Laurens returned. "But his beloved daughter is taken by this Lofantyl, and he's crazed with grief. I think he'll give Fendur his way." He rubbed his side again. "And Vanysse will support Amadis, who'll coddle her and sympathize as we are turned on the wheel."

"So we shall be tortured?" Cullyn stroked Fey's steaming nostrils. "Even though we are innocent?"

"Are we taken back," Laurens said. "And then likely executed."

"How can we avoid that?" Cullyn asked. He stared around the stable as Fey fretted beside him. Laurens's bay stood nervous in the adjoining stall. There was a single window that let in pale light, and the one narrow door, outside of which stood guards. He could not imagine escape. "What can we do?"

Laurens groaned as he hauled himself upright. "Drak might aid us, for he's a good lad. Otherwise . . ." He steadied himself, leaning on the rails. "You keep the tack in here?"

Cullyn nodded, gesturing at the saddles hung along the wall.

"Well, that's a start." Laurens went to the door and set an eye to the crack. "I suppose my blade's in the cottage?"

Cullyn nodded.

"And you've no weapons here?"

"Only this." Cullyn drew the knife Lofantyl had given him.

"A Durrym blade?" Laurens chuckled. "That alone would condemn you. Your bow?"

"In the cottage."

"Then we must make do as best we can. Shall you saddle those horses?"

"What do you intend?" Cullyn asked.

"To avoid the rack. In my condition I'd not last a day under Per Fendur's attention, and I'm too old to suffer torture."

"So?"

"Saddle the horses and get ready to depart."

"But where shall we go?" Cullyn asked.

"Away from here," Laurens replied. "Or would you give yourself up to Per Fendur's attentions?"

Cullyn saddled the horses.

"Excellent," Laurens declared when they were accoutred. "Now wait on my word—but when I give it, mount and ride! No hesitation, eh? Just ride as if all the hounds of hell were barking at your heels."

Cullyn held the two horses steady as Laurens went to the door and shouted for Drak.

Outside, the day was fading, afternoon giving way to

dusk. There was a steady dripping as the snow melted, and the light that entered the stable was mellow. Winter birds sang their chorus and Cullyn's pigs shuffled through the snow, their hunting echoed by the clucking of the chickens.

"What?" Drak asked.

"I'd speak with you," Laurens answered.

"I'm forbidden to speak with you." Drak sounded embarrassed.

"Then the gods damn you!" Laurens hammered a fist against the door. "Shall you not exchange a word with an old friend?"

"What word?" Drak asked.

"Face to face," Laurens demanded, and gestured that Cullyn bring the horses up.

The door opened and Laurens snatched Drak inside.

"My word," he said as he swung the younger soldier against a stall, "forgive me." He slammed a fist into Drak's face. And then, as Drak slumped against broken fencing, he cried to Cullyn, "Mount up and ride!"

Cullyn swung astride Fey. Laurens climbed slower onto the bay's saddle. And then he shouted and charged out of the stable, and they hurtled across the yard into the forest beyond.

It was all confusion then, and Cullyn wondered at what he'd done, for men came running to block them and Laurens rode them down and sent them spinning, and Fey snorted and bucked and snapped his teeth. Cullyn thought—in the brief moments of clarity as he fought free of clutching hands and ducked away from swords—that this must be what combat was like.

He glanced back to see Amadis and Per Fendur emerge from his cottage and then he was off, following Laurens.

They rode hard, putting in miles as the sun settled.

Horses came behind them, the tramp of hooves and the shouting of the riders warning of determined pursuit. The ground was thick with the snow's melting, slowing them as much as their pursuers, and melting icicles dripped from the overhanging branches, so that they were soaked and chilled before they halted.

"A while farther," Laurens said, "and they'll give up. I hope."

"And then?" Cullyn asked, thinking that he'd lost his home now, and all he had was Fey and what little he'd stowed in the saddlebags.

"We're alive, no?" Laurens said.

"And outlawed."

"But not racked."

Cullyn looked at the soldier. Laurens was likely old enough to be his father, and his face was still gray with pain—their reckless ride had done little for his wound. Cullyn could see the blood that oozed afresh from his side, and the way he clenched his teeth.

"You'll not last long," he said bluntly.

"Drak said the same," Laurens replied, "but he was also wrong. So trust me, eh? You know this wood. Find us trails that bring us northward."

Cullyn nodded, and rode ahead of Laurens as the day dimmed and a pale moon rose to illuminate the forest. He took them north along deer trails that began to freeze again, even as melting ice dripped over them and the horses' hooves came sludgy from the ground. Every so often he looked back to find Laurens clutching at the saddle horn as if that were all that held him upright. Behind, he heard shouts, and as the night settled in saw torches burning, coming after them through the trees. He reined in where a glade gave them space to talk.

"We must find somewhere to rest."

"Do you know anywhere?" Laurens swayed in the

saddle, and under the moon's wan light his face was hollowed. Cullyn saw that his eyes were dulled with pain, and that blood still oozed from the wound in his side.

"Not readily. I'd thought we'd have lost them by now."

Laurens spat and smiled at the same time. "We've a priest on our heels, lad, and he's got Church magic at his command. Like a hunting dog that's got its nose. Don't you understand?"

Cullyn shook his head. "I've had little to do with priests until now. There was one came when my parents died . . . a kindly man."

"That would have been Fra Robyrt." Laurens smiled grayly. "He *was* a kindly man, but not . . ." He paused, sucking in breath as he rubbed at his side. "Not *gifted* with the talent that raises the priesthood up. He cared for people, not power."

Cullyn frowned his incomprehension. Laurens pressed his side, husking out cynical laughter. "There are two kinds of Churchmen, lad. One cares for his flock, the other for his ambition. The ambitious ones own the magic—which Per Fendur says is to find a way into the fey lands, to defeat the Barrier. Priests like Fra Robyrt seek to serve their gods and tend their flock. Priests like that bastard Fendur seek only to advance themselves. And as they find more magic with which they might overcome the Durrym's, so they find ways to cross the Alagordar and take war to the fey folk."

"Why?" Cullyn asked innocently.

"Because they can." Laurens spat noisily. "Because they wish to extend their power. Because they'd bring all the world under the control of the Church, and they'd sit happy and fat atop it all. They'd command kings and dominate the world."

"I'd thought," Cullyn said, confused, "that priests were supposed to help us."

"Some do," Laurens replied. "Fra Robyrt was one. But Per Fendur . . ." He shook his head. "He's of the other persuasion. He seeks only command and conquest. He'd invade the fey lands for want of power. And hunt us down like dogs."

"So what do we do?" Cullyn asked. Laurens could never last out a gallop, and he felt no wish to be set on Per Fendur's rack.

"So we go where they'll not find us."

"Where?" Cullyn asked.

And Laurens said, "Across the Alagordar."

"You're crazed! How shall we find our way back?"

"It turns you," Laurens said, "and the Durrym magic shall likely confuse Fendur's."

"Save we become trapped there."

"We're trapped here," Laurens grunted. "Can you not find us some hiding place, they'll take us—and Fendur shall bring us back to the keep and *question* us. So—have you a better suggestion?"

Cullyn shook his head.

"Then let us find the river and cross it."

Cullyn nodded and heeled Fey across the glade, down between looming oaks to the willows that flanked the river.

Moonlight shone in silver filigree over the water, its ripples glistening. The tumbling of the Alagordar was a subtle, sensate temptation that frightened him. But behind came the torches, and the threat of the rack and execution, and Laurens shouted for him to continue. So he heeled Fey into the water and heard Laurens splash down behind him, and went into Coim'na Drhu.

On the farther bank there was a subtler night: no snow, but the same moon, the ground firmer, the air warmer, so that they might come swiftly into the trees beyond.

Where Laurens fell from his saddle.

Cullyn swung down from Fey and ran to his wounded companion.

Laurens clutched his side, watching blood spurt over his fingers.

"I used," he said slowly, "to take worse wounds than this. But . . ."

Across the river torches gathered and Cullyn heard shouting.

Laurens groaned. "Leave me and go on."

"*No!* Besides, where should I go?"

"Home."

"To Per Fendur's attentions?"

"Not those. But . . ."

"Get up! Damn you—get up."

"You're friends with the Durrym—go there."

"I'll not leave you!"

The torches that blazed across the river came closer. Cullyn hauled Laurens upright and set him astride the bay. "I'll not leave you," he said, as he heard the splashing of hoofs, saw the torchlight come closer.

"But you might kill me," Laurens said.

"This was your idea."

Laurens sighed out a rueful chuckle. "Perhaps not my best, but all we had, eh? So let's head north and see if we can lose them."

Cullyn was not sure Coim'na Drhu had a *north*. He wondered if all the compass points were not confused here, and whichever direction they took should lead them back to Kandar, with Per Fendur and Amadis hot on their heels. But with little other choice, he obeyed Laurens and rode what he supposed was northward. Surely the moon sat in the right quarter and the river ran to his left, but this was all fey land now and so he wondered where they might end up.

He followed some sort of trail, unsure what had made it, and found himself in a grove of dense birches that shone silver under the moon's light. Great stones protruded from the grass that filled the space between the trees, like batholith monuments. The trail ended there, at a stone circle, and there was a sense of power, as if trees and stones and moonlight combined to imbue the circle with magic. He felt the hair on his neck stand up, and was abruptly cold and hot at the same time. He wondered if the combinations of light and shadow he saw amongst the stones were the products of moon and rocks, or capering spirits. Fey snorted, stamping restless hoofs, and Cullyn looked to Laurens.

The older man slumped in his saddle, one leg stained with the opening of his wound. The bay horse fretted, smelling the blood, and Cullyn walked Fey to stand beside.

"*Can* you go on?" he asked.

Laurens groaned and looked back to where the torches moved bright through the trees. "I'd best. They'll be on us soon."

"Where do we go? This trail ends here."

"Hold northward. Keep the river on our left until we find another ford."

"Which they'll find."

"Perhaps, perhaps not; this is a tricksy land. Who knows where we'll come out?"

"All well," Cullyn said, "back into Kandar."

"But ahead of our hunters," Laurens returned. "Now go!"

He pointed to where two vast stones stood upright and apart, allowing sufficient gap that the horses might pass between them. Moonlit grass and shining trees stood

beyond, but when Cullyn trotted Fey through the opening he found himself riding a gentle sward that was
flanked leftward with alders and willows, and the ground
was moist, almost swampy. Laurens followed, still swaying in his saddle, but with a grin on his grizzled face as he
looked back.

Cullyn followed his eyes and saw small, ancient
stones looming amongst marshy trees, but somehow
overlaid with monoliths that shimmered as the torches
approached. He watched them slow and skirt around,
and wondered at the marvels of Coim'na Drhu.

Then Laurens said, "The priest will likely find a way
ere long, so shall we go?"

And they set off again.

They halted as the sky woke up. Birds began to sing,
and dawn's pallid entrance gave way to sunlight. They
stood in a grove of wide-branched alders whose branches
split and curled like broken limbs across the ground. The
Alagordar mouthed its passage to their left, and to
the right—eastward into the heart of Coim'na Drhu—
the forest deepened into oaks and birch and hazel.

"We need to keep going," Laurens said. "Fendur will
find a way around the stones . . . Likely already has."

"And you'll bleed to death if we go on." Cullyn took
the older man's weight as he pitched from the saddle.
"And then I'd be lost in this fey land."

Laurens chuckled as he closed his eyes. "You think *I*
know where we are?"

Cullyn dragged him to a stand of clean grass and left
him there as he tended the two horses. Both were
sweated by the long run, so he rubbed them down and
walked them a while before he let them drink. Then he
hobbled them and left them to crop the grass and marsh
plants as he tended Laurens.

Without his herbs and poultices there was little he

could do other than staunch the bleeding wound, and wonder how Laurens had stayed astride his horse. The man grew feverish: sweat beaded him, and even when Cullyn cut strips from his shirt to bandage him afresh, blood oozed through the cloth.

He built a fire, deciding that neither the glow nor the smoke would be seen as the day brightened. And Laurens needed warmth. They had no food; nor had Cullyn any idea of how long they might run—how long the pursuit would continue. But he'd not quit Laurens.

❦❧❦

"WHERE AM I?" Laurens woke. "What are you doing?"

"Warming you."

"A fire?" Laurens struggled upright. "Per Fendur will sense that. Do you want to light a beacon?"

"You fell off your horse."

Laurens shrugged. "I'm not so fit as I used to be—so, thank you—but now shall we go? Else . . ."

"I think we've lost them," Cullyn said.

"Let's hope so." Laurens coughed dubious laughter. "But with Per Fendur's magical nose . . ."

"So what do we do?"

"Run and hide. Kick out that fire, and let's ride."

Cullyn stamped the fire to embers and helped Laurens astride the bay, and they went north again until Laurens pointed them westward.

"How can you know?"

Cullyn halted Fey at the fording Laurens indicated.

"Trust me, eh?" Laurens drooped over his saddle horn, his face pale. "I've been here before, in pursuit of the Durrym."

The day had once more lengthened into evening. In Coim'na Drhu it was mellow autumn. Across the

Alagordar it was winter's ending, the commencement of
spring. On one side of the river the trees blushed and
faded into autumn's mildness; on the other, they were
stripped and bare and bled moisture onto muddy paths.

"They'll find us there," Cullyn protested. "If Per
Fendur can find us, he'll follow us."

"Trust me," Laurens said. "It's likely our only
chance."

Cullyn shrugged. It seemed he had little other
choice, so he walked Fey down the bank and into the
river.

Laurens came behind on the bay horse, leaning low
over his saddle, leaving droplets of blood in the stream
behind.

They crossed into winter's aftermath, where snow
gave way to mud, and Cullyn halted again and turned to
Laurens. "Where now?"

"North."

Cullyn stared at the trees, dripping, the evening dark
and cold. And he trapped in a forest he did not know.

"Where are we?"

"Hopefully safe from Per Fendur and Amadis,"
Laurens muttered. "Go on, eh?"

Cullyn went on, and after a while of riding through
winter-hung trees came to a clearing where a cottage not
unlike his own stood. It was wood-built, with a stone
chimney that bled smoke into the winter sky, and a
thatched roof. And there was a stall beside, and pigs
grubbing in the wet earth.

An old man came out. His hair was white as the winter and his face lined with wrinkles like some piece of ancient leather. He wore a long robe that was very dirty,
drifting shapelessly from neck to feet. It might once have
been decorated with sigils, but they were now either covered with dirt or so faded they had become unrecogniz-

able. He seemed ancient, save for his eyes, which were a piercing blue, bright as a summer morning.

Cullyn stared at him, and Laurens said: "Eben, we meet again."

"I'd not thought that should happen," came the answer. "Save you came to take me captive for your Church. Have you a squad of soldiers with you?"

"Hardly." Laurens coughed out bitter laughter. "But a squad behind, and we in need of refuge."

"And wounded, no? What happened?"

"I took a Durrym shaft," Laurens said. "Were it not for him"—he gestured at Cullyn—"I'd be dead."

"Through your thick hide as best I judge." Eben stared at the bloody wound in Laurens's side. "Best come in and let me tend you."

"There's more," Laurens said. "We're pursued. Outlawed, I suppose."

"How so?"

"We fell afoul of the Church, and perhaps Lord Bartram."

"Like me?" Eben smiled. "Come down off that horse before you fall off, eh? Come inside and explain."

He turned to Cullyn. "Shall you help me?"

Cullyn nodded, not quite sure of what went on. He helped Laurens down from the bay horse and carried him into the hut, then saw Fey and the bay stabled, and went to find Laurens.

To be sure his friend—and savior?—was well.

TEN

THE COTTAGE WAS much like Cullyn's—a single room with a hearth that served also as a stove, a table set close to the fire, four rough chairs about it, and a narrow bed overlooked by one of the three windows. What made it different was the proliferation of books and animals that seemed to merge into one great mass. Shelves filled with tomes and dusty parchments hid one wall, and on them lay squirrels and rats, while bats hung from the edges and sleepy birds rested above them. More books lay scattered across the floor, dogs and cats spread over and amongst them. Cullyn gaped in amazement as a fox rose from a bed of ancient tomes, yawned, stared at him, and sauntered past. A dog eyed him, barked indolently, and then wagged its tail before settling back on its book-bed. A massive cat, all ginger, stretched and came to rub itself against his legs.

"Dammit!" Eben gestured at the multiplicity of animals lying on the bed. "Get off, eh? We've a hurt man here. And you!" He turned to Cullyn. "Stop gaping and help me. I'm not so young as I was, and Laurens is damnably heavy."

Cullyn obeyed as cats and dogs and badgers and rats clambered from the pallet. He set an arm around Laurens and helped Eben settle the soldier on the bed.

"He took a Durrym arrow in his side," Cullyn said.

"I'm old, not blind." Eben shoved him aside with more strength than his narrow frame suggested. "And he's been bleeding since, no?"

"I did my best to tend him, but I'm no healer. And—"

"Explain later." Eben pointed toward the shelves around the hearth. "For now, fetch me that blue bottle."

Cullyn obeyed as Eben stripped Laurens naked and studied the ugly holes.

"A typical Durrym wound. Only the gods—if they exist—know how he survived it. A lesser man would have died." He took the bottle from Cullyn and bled a few drips of some dark liquid into Laurens's mouth. "Fine archers, the Durrym." He patted Laurens's shoulder. "You should have taken more care extracting the shaft: you'd have done yourself less harm."

"I had no time," Laurens mumbled. "I was in a fight."

"Blood and blood and blood, eh?" Eben watched as Laurens's eyes closed and his breathing grew deep and steady. "Is it not always the way?"

"Can you save him?" Cullyn asked.

"Perhaps; I shall do my best. And I need your help."

"Tell me what to do," Cullyn asked.

"Fill that pot with fresh well water and set it to boiling."

Cullyn took the indicated pot out to the well,

escorted by a coterie of animals. Bats fluttered by him as
he went out, and rats and badgers scurried past his feet.
He began to wonder if he were still in Coim'na Drhu, for
surely there was magic at work here.

When he returned inside, Eben had numerous pots
set on the table, and was busily grinding a pestle into a
mortar, crushing ingredients. "When the water boils," he
said, "bring it to me. Until then, keep silent."

Cullyn stood watching as the silver-haired man bent
over Laurens. Eben raised his hands and shaped signs in
the air; then he took the blue bottle and splashed some
of its content over Laurens's side, then drew his forefinger
through the liquid, marking out sigils.

"Does it boil yet?"

Cullyn started and looked to the pot: "Yes."

"Then set it on the table, damn you."

Cullyn found a cloth and brought the pot to the table.
Eben rose from beside the bed and kicked a sleepy cat aside
before he set to spooning the hot water into a bowl, into
which he tipped his medicaments. He mixed them and
then went to Laurens, who now lay sound asleep, and set
to pasting the mixture over the wounds. Then he produced swathes of linen that Cullyn thought—consider-
ing the circumstances of the cottage—were remarkably
clean, and wrapped the bandages around Laurens.

"That's as much as I can do." He settled a blanket
over the supine form. "I'll pray for him, but that's a bad
wound."

"I know," Cullyn said. "I doubted he'd survive our
ride."

"Which you must tell me about." Eben gestured at
the table. "I suppose you're hungry, so you can tell me as
we eat."

"I need to see the horses bedded first," Cullyn said.
"They've run hard of late."

"Admirable." Eben chuckled. "I could like a young man who cares for his animals. But don't worry." He raised a hand as Cullyn began to rise. "They're tended. Stripped and rubbed down and stabled safe."

"How?" Cullyn stared at the silver-haired man.

Eben smiled enigmatically and said, "Magic, my boy. Trust me, eh? Why else would Laurens have brought you here?"

"I don't know," Cullyn said nervously. "We were running from Per Fendur, and Laurens found a way. He said it should be safe."

"And so it shall be," Eben promised. "Few people can find this cottage—Laurens is one of the few."

"I don't understand," Cullyn said. "Are you a wizard? I thought only the Church commanded magic."

"And the Durrym," Eben said. "They command—what should I call it? Land magic, I suppose. They *live* with the land, and consequently have learned to use it. To bend its power to theirs. You folk look to own it. No more than that."

"So how is Laurens your friend?"

Eben sighed and rose to bring a flask from his shelves. Filled two mugs with tea and honey wine.

"He's a good man." He gestured at the sleeping soldier. "He found me once, when I was sore hurt, and succored me."

"Why?" Cullyn asked. "What happened?"

"I was a runaway, like you, and Laurens saved me." Eben grinned. "My father was Durrym, my mother Kandarian. The Church looked to take me, to . . . study me, I suppose. Which it did for a while. But then I escaped and ran to the forest. Like you?"

Cullyn shrugged.

"I was pursued," Eben said, "and took an arrow in my back. It would have slain me had Laurens not found me.

He took it out and tended the wound—then left me to heal. He saved my life. So when I came into my power I thanked him, and that's how he knows where I live. So now tell me your story."

Cullyn told him, their conversation interrupted by trips to the hearth, from which Eben produced a stew, the taste of which Cullyn could not define, save that it was good.

"So you're likely proscribed," Eben said when Cullyn was done.

"Likely to be racked and executed," Cullyn agreed.

"Because Lofantyl stole Abra."

Cullyn nodded.

"I must think about this," Eben said.

The stew was finished and Cullyn took the plates and pots outside to wash them as Eben returned his attentions to Laurens. Animals trailed around him, dogs snapping for his attention, cats cradling his ankles, three foxes grinning at him, four badgers and a hedgehog studying him solemnly.

When Cullyn returned inside, Eben said, "So you're pursued?"

"By Per Fendur and Amadis."

"The soldier's of no account. But the priest . . ." Eben sighed. "He might find you. And me."

"I thought you said this place was warded against discovery." Cullyn felt mightily tired—would sooner have found a bed and slept than have this discussion. Save a troop led by Per Fendur came after him as Laurens lay hurt.

"Against most intrusions," Eben replied, "but is all you've told me true, then the Church *has* found more magic—and this Per Fendur might well find you here."

There was an echo in his voice: of fear or regret, Cullyn could not be sure. So he asked.

Eben said, "Do I guess aright, then the Church has found ways to circumvent the Durrym's magic. Is all you tell me true, then this priest can find a way across the Alagordar and not be turned back. Which means he can follow you here—is his magic stronger than mine."

"Think you it is?" Cullyn was suddenly no longer tired; fear woke him.

Eben shrugged. "Who knows? I suppose we'll find out in time."

"And your magic? Where does that come from?"

"I am a half-breed," Eben answered. "My father was Durrym, my mother Kandarian. I own somewhat of the Durrym magic, somewhat of the Church's. They'd have taken me for a priest, save I could not like what Kandar and its Church did to the Durrym, so I chose to live here—alone, and separate from both. Until now." He sighed, studying Cullyn with his clear blue eyes.

"I'd only see Laurens able again," Cullyn said. "And both of us safe."

"And then?"

Cullyn shrugged.

"What do you think shall happen then?" Eben poured them both more honey wine. "Shall you go back to your hut and Laurens to the keep, and you both live happily ever after?"

"I don't know." Cullyn longed for sleep, and a return to normality: to collect his morning eggs and feed his pigs, milk the cow—how did she fare with him gone? It seemed that all his world was turned upside down and shaken, and nothing was *normal* anymore.

"Not likely," Eben said. "Not with this priest on your heels, and Laurens hurt."

"Then what?" Cullyn asked.

"Rest," Eben said, "and we shall talk again in the morning."

He stoppered the flask and spread two great bearskins on the floor. "Laurens needs the bed," he said, "so we sleep here."

Cullyn stretched out, and Eben's pets came to surround him. He fell asleep encompassed by dogs and cats and rats and badgers, whose bodies warmed him and filled his nostrils with sleepy scents, so that he felt safe and for a while forgot his troubles.

❧❧❧

THE DAWN SUN SHONE harsh on his eyes, waking him afraid and mistrusting. He spilled complaining animals from his makeshift bed and rose.

Eben slept on, snoring loudly. Laurens lay silent, breathing shallowly but easily. Cullyn looked at his wounds and saw no fresh blood. His face was pale, but somehow seemed healthier than before.

"Leave him be." Eben rose through an explosion of animals, scratching vigorously at a scrawny chest that seemed more bone than muscle. "He needs to rest—if we've the time."

He flung the bearskin aside, standing naked as he ran fingers through his long hair and set to scratching again. Cullyn turned his eyes away: it was like watching a skeleton fidget.

"Boil us up some water, eh?"

Cullyn took the pot to the well and washed hurriedly before carrying the bucket back to the cottage.

"What took you so long?"

"I washed."

"Ha! An overrated habit. Dirt can protect you, boy. Excessive cleanliness can damage your skin and leave you vulnerable to diseases."

"The Church says it's next to godliness," Cullyn ventured.

"And the Church knows best, eh? Do you always do what the Church tells you? No! Else you'd not be here. You'd have given this priest—what's his name? Fendur?—what he wanted. You'd not have named a Durrym your friend, or helped him meet this young woman."

"Abra," Cullyn said.

"Whatever." Eben struggled into his robe. "A foolish girl by my guess. But even so . . ." He gestured at the pot. "Are you going to set that on the fire, or stand gaping me?"

Cullyn set the kettle to boiling. Eben went to Laurens and, with a gentleness that belied his irascible manner, removed the bandages and set fresh ointments over the wounds. Laurens stirred in his sleep, and Eben dripped more of the liquid in the blue flask between his lips. Then turned to Cullyn again.

"Boil us up some tea," he ordered. "There's fresh bread, and plenty of bacon. Eggs in the coop, most like—can you find them."

Cullyn poured boiling water into a kettle and went outside, wondering where his life had gone. He seemed to have stepped into a strange world of magic and wonder that he did not understand.

The day was bright—brighter, it seemed, around the perimeter of Eben's cottage than beyond. There it was still early spring, with melting snow dripping from the trees and the woodland yet decked with icicles. But for an area around the cottage it was pleasant as Coim'na Drhu's autumn. Birds sang, louder within the confines, and overhead the sky shone blue, decked with white, billowing clouds that ran before a brisk, warm wind. Cullyn stared a while, wondering, then fetched the eggs from the coop.

"At last," Eben snapped. He was at the table, a mug of tea in his hand, a cat settled on his knees, a squirrel on his left shoulder and a rat on the right, two dogs and three more cats by his feet. "What took you so long?"

Cullyn shrugged. Eben pointed at the pans hanging around the hearth. "Make yourself useful, eh? Cut us some bacon and get our breakfast ready."

Cullyn took down the pans and drew his knife, ready to cut the slab of bacon that hung by the hearth.

"A lyn'nha'thall?" Eben asked. "Lofantyl gave you a friendship knife?"

Cullyn nodded, torn between gratitude and resentment.

"That means a lot." Eben sipped his tea. "Not least that if the Church had found it, you'd be outright deemed a traitor. No question of it!"

"I already am." Cullyn set the bacon to grilling.

"And all because you made a friend." Eben lifted a fox cub from the floor and tickled its stomach, then replaced it with a cat that curled against him and purred. "Life is hard, no?"

"Sometimes." Cullyn turned the bacon, splashed fat over the eggs.

"And there's little justice."

"I only wanted to be left alone." He set bread to frying. "I sought no trouble."

Eben laughed noisily. "Trouble finds you, boy. Look at Laurens—a good soldier, but now an outlaw. Do you think he wanted to give up his keep? A sound bed and ready meals . . . a warm place, with duty easily understood. And where is he now? Renegade, like you and me. Why do you think he gave all that up?"

"Because . . ." Cullyn shrugged and brought their

breakfast to the table. "I don't know. I understand little of this."

"Because he has *honor*," Eben said. "He has a code that has nothing to do with Per Fendur or Amadis, but only himself. Do you understand that?"

"I'm not sure," Cullyn said.

"You'll learn," Eben returned cheerfully, and set to eating his breakfast.

He spoke no more until the plate was wiped clean and all the tea drunk. Cullyn ate in equal silence, utterly confused by the turn of events. He had run with Laurens because he had no other choice. He was still not entirely sure who or what Eben was, so he waited for instructions.

Eben swept animals from his lap and stood abruptly upright. "Come, we've business to attend."

Cullyn wiped crumbs of fried bread from his mouth and stared at the wizard. "What shall I do?"

"You've delivered me a problem," Eben said, his mood switching abruptly from good humor to irritation. "Do you not understand how long I've lived in peace here? No, of course not; how could you?" He sighed gustily. "You only did what Laurens asked. And I suppose I shouldn't blame you for that. Or Laurens. But even so . . ."

He moved around the cottage as he spoke, collecting bits and pieces of equipment: sprigs of herbs and small vials of indefinable liquids, a sharp-looking knife such as the chirurgeons used.

"Laurens took you across the Mys'enh, and I suppose I cannot blame him for that. But . . ." He shook his head, speaking mostly to himself. "With a priest on your heels? Even so . . . I suppose he had no choice. . . ."

"They'd have taken us else," Cullyn protested.

"Yes, yes; most likely they would." Eben set his gatherings on the table. "But now?"

"I'd thought," Cullyn said, "that we'd be safe here."

Eben frowned. "From all you've told me, this priest can find the way. He followed you across the Mys'enh, no?"

"Yes," Cullyn agreed. "Across the river, and then through the stones."

"Not many can do that." Eben studied the materials set on the table. "Boil another kettle, eh?"

Cullyn complied, thinking that lately all he did was obey.

"Then fetch that bowl." Eben indicated a pot that was somehow neither metal nor wood nor clay, but hard as the one and smooth as the other, all carved with intricate designs.

Cullyn fetched the pot down, disturbing a sleeping bat in the process. "So we're in danger?" he asked. "Have you a bow? I'm a good archer."

Eben snorted. "You'd face a Churchman and twenty riders with a bow? Are you a fool, boy?"

Cullyn blushed. "I'll not leave Laurens," he said.

Eben worked busily. "Neither would I, for our fates are all entwined, I think. So . . . Is that pot ready?"

The water was seething. Cullyn took a cloth and brought it to the table, where Eben dumped in a selection of herbs and weeds. Then took up the knife and slashed his wrist so that blood dripped, bright, into the stew.

"Now give me yours," he commanded.

Cullyn gasped and shook his head.

"Dammit, give me your arm! I need your blood."

"What for?"

"To make fends," Eben snapped. "Else likely we all die."

"I don't understand," Cullyn said, reluctant to lend his blood to the pot.

"You wouldn't." Eben flourished the blade. "But I'll have it anyway. I'm not ready to die yet. I've lived too long to give it up for such stupidity. Now do as I say!"

Cullyn backed away, shaking his head vigorously as Eben came around the table with the knife upraised. He was prepared to fight the strange old man, but suddenly he found his path blocked by animals: dogs barked at him and cats mewed, exposing their claws; badgers and foxes nipped his heels; rats clambered up his breeches, and birds came fluttering around his head until he tripped and fell down and Eben was on him, brandishing the shining blade.

He shouted, more in surprise than pain, as Eben slashed his wrist and he saw hot, red blood spurt.

Then he was yanked upright, his shirtfront grasped by the silver-haired man, who was far stronger than he'd guessed, and his arm extended over the pot so that his blood dripped in to join the wizard's.

"Excellent." Eben let him go and he collapsed onto the floor. The wizard gestured at the animals clustering around Cullyn. "Stay there."

He had little choice: there was a weight of beasts holding him to the floor, and many wore sharp teeth that snapped and flashed when he tried to rise. Dogs barked in his face and badgers opened wicked jaws; cats set claws on him as rats gnawed on his hair and foxes set fangs about his wrists. He could not move: only watch as Eben carried the pot to the bed and cut Laurens's wrist, dripping more blood into the kettle.

"What are you doing?" Cullyn wailed past the weight on his body.

"Protecting us all," Eben snapped. "Now be quiet! You begin to annoy me." He flung a dirty sleeve loose from his wrist and cut his own flesh again.

Cullyn lay still as the wizard studied his own thick

droplets of blood dripping into the pot, then stirred the potion and called the animals to him.

Cullyn rose slowly, wary of attack, but none came and Eben only smiled as he dipped his fingers into the horrid brew and began to decorate the animals. He painted five badgers and six foxes; nine birds; seven dogs; eleven cats; and as many bats as he could catch before they fluttered away. Then he opened the door and ushered them all out into the burgeoning morning.

"That should do it. For a while, at least."

"What?" Cullyn clutched at his bleeding arm.

"Confuse the priest with fends," Eben said, "Give me your arm, eh?"

Cullyn extended his arm and watched Eben set salves on the wound and bandage it, then tend to Laurens before he wrapped himself.

"Fends?"

Eben chuckled. "You've little knowledge of magic, boy."

"None."

"And yet you wear a lyn'nha'thall. The gods know but Lofantyl must have seen *something* in you. Though I cannot imagine what." He sat down at the table, gesturing that Cullyn join him.

"A fend is a trickster: it deceives pursuit because it's disguised. Do you understand?"

Cullyn shook his head, and Eben said wearily, "Dear gods, protect me from such innocence. This priest seeks you, no? He'd have you for his own purposes—and he's found a way to follow you across the Mys'enh and likely even here. So I must confuse him, else we shall all be taken. I needed blood to make fends, which shall carry our magical scents and—all well—find groves and burrows and dens and confuse the pursuit. Does this priest follow the blood-trails my pets take, he'll be utterly confused, and have no idea where *we* are. For a while, at least."

"And if not?" Cullyn asked.

"Then he'll find us," Eben said. "And you and Laurens shall die—after the torture, of course."

"And you?"

Eben shrugged. "I'd likely escape. I've succeeded thus far, no? But . . . now you come to disturb my solitude."

"So why bring us in?" Cullyn asked.

"I don't know," Eben said, "and I don't care to explain. Ask Laurens when he wakes."

"*If,*" Cullyn said.

"I think he shall," Eben returned. "I gave him my best tending. Because . . . I care about him. But I need time. *He* needs time."

Cullyn stared at the wizard, and Eben shrugged and said, "Ask him."

᙭᙭᙭

AMADIS HALTED THE TROOP on Per Fendur's order. The sun fell away to the west and a swelling moon rose into the blue velvet sky. It was poor tracking weather—the melting snow produced slush and mud that left the ground roiled with the tracks of animals, and all the surrounding trees dripped meltwater, so that the trails were indistinguishable. Amadis felt as miserable as his men. He longed to return to the keep, but he was under Fendur's command, and the priest would have his prey. So the captain of Lord Bartram's guard sat his horse and thought of his lord's wife, and how soft was her bed and how firm her body, and of Fendur's implied promises. He watched as the priest cast about, turning his mount slowly from one branching track to another, and for want of anything better to do called, "Steady, men! We wait on Per Fendur."

The soldiers gave back no answer. Like Amadis, they were troubled by their journey into the Fey lands. And to make matters worse, they pursued a man they liked and respected. Indeed, Amadis wondered if they did not respect Laurens more than him, and could not understand why Laurens had done what he had. But . . . and it was a very large *but* . . . Laurens *had* chosen to side with the forester, Cullyn—who was of no account, save he consorted with the Durrym and consequently found disfavor in Per Fendur's eyes.

Therefore, Amadis thought as he watched the priest study the ground and sniff the air, Laurens and the forester were proscribed, and *he* would side with Per Fendur and hope to become master of the keep, and somehow find himself in Lord Bartam's place—lord of Border Castle and bed, both. He contemplated the prospect until a voice interrupted his musings.

"What?"

"Do we make camp?"

He glowered at Drak and rose taller in his saddle. "No. We've quarry to pursue, so we wait on—"

"This way." Per Fendur swung astride his horse. "Come!"

Amadis waved for the disgruntled troop to follow.

❧❧❧

EBEN BENT OVER LAURENS, examining the wounds and easing more of the blue liquid into the man's mouth.

"At least three days," he muttered, more to himself than Cullyn. "Then, perhaps . . ."

"Perhaps what?" Cullyn was confused and frightened and irritated. He understood that he and Laurens were pursued, but little of what Eben did, and he had sooner quit the cottage to find refuge in the forest. Nor did he enjoy the wizard's shifting humors.

"Before he's well enough to travel," Eben grunted. "Put him on a horse now and he'll be dead, despite all my care."

Cullyn felt fear overcome his other emotions; he did not want Laurens to die. "And so?"

"We wait and hope," Eben said. "Hope that my fends distract the priest; hope that he and his soldiers do not somehow stumble on my home; hope that Laurens does not die."

"And if not?"

"Then we *might* be safe. You and Laurens *might* not be put to the question. I *might* not be hung and burned for a Durrym wizard." He settled wearily at the table. "The gods know, boy, but you delivered me trouble. I wonder if you're not a *syn'qui.*"

"What's that?" Cullyn asked.

"A Durrym word," Eben replied. "It means a . . ." He shook his head angrily, as if he could not quite grasp the point, or understand it. "A *confluence.* It means . . . a person who gathers events to themselves, so that the world revolves around them, and others are swept along in the train of events."

"*Me?*" Cullyn stared at the wizard.

Eben shrugged and said, "Perhaps. I wish you'd not come here. I was happy before you came."

"And I was happy in my cottage," Cullyn returned.

Eben laughed and rubbed his hands over his eyes. "The way of the world, no? We're all happy until something happens to disturb it. Then . . . Oh, gods, boy, fetch me that flask and let's have a drink while we decide what to do."

Cullyn fetched down the flask and filled their cups.

❦❧

"THIS WAY!" Per Fendur beckoned the troop. "They went this way—I can *smell* them."

Amadis urged his tired horse forward. His men came behind, weary and cold and thoroughly disgruntled. The sun was down now and the night chilly. The moon illuminated their way, casting long shadows over the mud and the glistening snow. They were all hungry and tired, and wanted nothing more than to halt, make a fire, and sleep. But Per Fendur took them onward until the moon was overhead, shining its cold silvery light over the grove where they finally made camp.

"We need to rest the horses and the men," Amadis insisted. "Neither can go on much longer."

"But we ride on come dawn," Fendur decided. "The heretics are in sight now."

They rose to a wet morning. A wind blew from the south, and it set the trees to dripping afresh, and muddied the trail anew. But Per Fendur led them keen as a scented hound toward their quarry.

Until . . .

He reined in his horse, glancing hither and yon.

"What's amiss?" Amadis asked.

"Confusion!" Per Fendur swung his horse around, swung from the saddle, threw the reins to Amadis and knelt to sniff the sodden soil. "Fends!"

"*Fends?*" Amadis stared at the priest, amazed to see the man sniffing the ground like a dog in heat.

Fendur rose, and wiped his nose. "Aye, fends. They've a sorcerer aiding them, and he's sent fends out to confuse us."

"So what do we do?"

Per Fendur snarled like a rabid dog. "We must follow

every trail. The gods damn whoever did this! But I'll find him and destroy him."

"And meanwhile?" Amadis asked, thinking of the keep and Vanysse. "What shall we do?"

"Hunt." Per Fendur indicated the tracks Eben's animals had taken. They spread in numerous directions.

Amadis sent men dashing to north and south, east and west, chasing trails that went off into the forest and disappeared into dens and burrows, setts and dreys, trees, so that all came back with no report. Per Fendur grew angry.

"We shall lose them soon."

Amadis glanced at the risen moon and wished he were back in the keep, in his mistress's bed. The gods knew, that was more comfortable than this cold ground.

"We go on. We must find them."

"Now?" Amadis stared at the priest and found the courage to dispute. "My men are weary; tired and cold and hungry."

"But nonetheless they'll go on. On *my* command."

Amadis shrugged and turned his eyes from Per Fendur's gaze, and called his reluctant men to their saddles.

❧☙❧

"WE NEED TO BUY TIME," Eben said. "The fends will have confused him for a while, but even so . . . ."

He picked animals from his stacked books, opening one and another, studying pages, sweeping more protesting beasts from shelves as he took down parchments and leather-bound tomes. Cullyn wondered that so many tracts existed even as Eben glanced at the pages and muttered to himself as he read.

"Not enough!" he told himself and looked to Cullyn.

"Not *enough*! We must do more. *I* must do more. You don't understand, do you?"

Cullyn shook his head.

Eben turned more pages; unscrolled aged parchments; shook out the droppings of animals. Paper crackled as he unrolled it, like old, dried flesh unwilling to give up its secrets. He studied each parchment and manuscript and book and threw them aside in a great confusion of movement and fluttering pages that set the animals still about the cottage to stirring nervously.

Then, "I have it," he declared. "At least, I hope I do. Come!"

Cullyn followed the man to the stable. Eben carried twigs and herbs, and Cullyn wondered what he did—what *they* did. But Eben urged him to mount Fey, so he did. They went out into the night.

Fey was eager to run, but Eben went afoot and so Cullyn must hold the stallion to a slow pace as Eben waved his branches and chanted, and they rode in what seemed to Cullyn circles until dawn. Then they returned to the cottage.

Cullyn could not understand how so old a man could run so long, but Eben seemed untired.

"I think," he said when they returned, "that I might have confused the priest long enough."

"So we're safe?"

"For a while. Hopefully long enough for Laurens to ride again."

"And then what?" Cullyn asked.

"If we remain here," Eben chuckled cynically, "then sooner or later he finds you and Laurens—and me. So we'd best hope Laurens recovers, and we see him safe."

"*We?*" Cullyn asked.

"It would seem that my lot is thrown with yours," Eben replied. "Not my choice, boy. But you brought this to me, so I've little other choice than to face the Church. And damn you for that!"

"I sought none of this," Cullyn protested. "I only did what Laurens asked, bringing him here."

"Even so," Eben said.

"So what do we do?" Cullyn asked again.

"Wait and hope that Laurens is well enough to ride before the priest finds us."

"And then?"

"We go where he can't—at least, not without difficulty."

"Where?"

Eben stared at him with a gaze that proclaimed him an idiot. "Why did you start all this? Was Abra somewhat to do with it?"

Cullyn nodded.

"And she's gone into Coim'na Drhu with Lofantyl?"

Cullyn nodded again.

"Then," Eben said, "I suppose we must go after her."

ELEVEN

❧❧❧

THEY HAD RIDDEN HARD, anxious of pursuit until they crossed the Alagordar, then eased the pace once the river was crossed. Even so Abra was wearied by the journey, and confused by the strange land they entered. It was simultaneously like and unlike Kandar: woodland and meadows, streams and rivers traversing the undulating landscape, save Kandar was winter-gripped and this place—this fey land—basked in lazy autumn, and more. There were trees she did not recognize, and weirdling beasts that roamed the forest. Birds far brighter than any she had seen before mingled with such ordinary avians as she did recognize.

She was both excited and afraid. Lofantyl assured her all was well and no harm should come to her, but Afranydyr frightened her. He seemed to her a dour man, who wished her no good, and since the rescue he had become even grimmer, hardly speaking to her at all—and then only in terms of hard courtesy. But Lofantyl joked with her and promised her ease and comfort once they reached his father's hall, and she could not help loving him.

"It shall be easier when we reach Kash'ma Hall," he said as they sat about a fire on which some animal she did not recognize roasted. "My father shall welcome you as my bride-to-be, and put Afranydyr in his place." He took her hands and bowed his head. "Please forgive my brother's intransigence, and trust my love."

Abra was not sure she could do either. She felt a great affection for Lofantyl—indeed such affection as might be love. But still he was a Durrym, and perhaps this was only seduction. Save when he held her hands and looked into her eyes, she felt her heart lurch and knew that she wanted only to be with him, man and wife.

But in Coim'na Drhu?

Could she live here? They certainly could not live in Kandar, for the Church would proscribe such union and execute them both as heretics. Her father might accept it, but never the Church.

She sighed and clutched Lofantyl's hands tighter. "What shall happen to us?"

"Why, we shall come to Kash'ma Hall and be wed. Do you not want that?"

"And Afranydyr?"

"Shall accept our father's decision."

"And if your father says you nay?"

"Then we'll go off and live like Cullyn. All alone in the forest between our lands."

"As outlaws?"

"If you like." He leaned toward her and they kissed. "I'd give up everything for you."

"Your hall? Your family?"

Lofantyl shrugged. "I don't much like Afranydyr, anyway. And my father has little time for me—he believes me too interested in you Garm."

"But still he'd see us wed?"

"He'd not deny my wishes. And my wish is to wed you." Lofantyl held her hands tighter. "Think on it! You and I married—Coim'na Drhu wedded with Kandar. Might that not bring us peace?"

"It might," she said as he kissed her again. And then, "Or deliver war."

They stared at one another as the fire spluttered and the night grew dark, sparks rising toward the many stars that speckled the fey lands night. Abra stared at Lofantyl and there came between them some understanding that they could not define, but only know. Lofantyl said, "I shall never betray you."

Then Afranydyr came to them, before Abra had chance to answer, all stern admonishment. "Best sleep—we ride out early."

"Sound advice, my brother." Lofantyl grinned. "And we shall take it in a while."

Afranydyr snorted and turned away.

Lofantyl said, "It *is* good advice," and took Abra's hand to escort her to her bed, where he left her with a courteous bow.

᭥᭥᭥

THEY WENT ON THROUGH impossible forests where impossible animals crossed their path, and came to Kash'ma Hall.

"My home," Lofantyl said.

Abra could scarcely believe it. How could such a place exist?

She was familiar with the confines of her father's keep—all stone, walled with granite, the village of Lyth below like some succored hybrid, the keep a defensive tower looming over the village.

This unbelievable place sat within a great swath of forest, isolated only by the meadow that spread around it like a great grass moat. The trees within which they stood halted on low, encircling ridgetops, and grew no farther, leaving the grass sway. It was a low bowl, encompassed by the forest, then the grass, which ran like some green sea to the walls of Kash'ma Hall, speckled with flowers, so that the emerald green of the grass was marked with blossoms of white and blue and yellow that filled the air with sweet scents that set Abra's head to spinning with their seductive perfumes.

"Is it not beautiful?" Lofantyl asked.

Abra could only nod her agreement.

She studied the keep—save was it truly a keep? It seemed more like some fairy castle, some fey fantasy. It seemed all wooden, as if trees were trained to ward the perimeters, and all the buildings inside those walls grown rather than built. All the buildings shone in the sun. It seemed as much forest as fortress. The grass sparkled, and the towers she saw carried the hues of wood, as if all were built of oak and ash and birch and beech, willow and aspen: every kind of timber imaginable, with great spills of flowers tumbling from the walls—as if it were all some great blossoming basket that shed happy colors into the latening day.

"My home," Lofantyl said.

"It's beautiful."

"Then let's go there and meet my father."

❧❧❧

THEY RODE IN THROUGH wooden gates all draped
with ivy and climbing plants that flourished blue and yellow flowers that filled the entrance with perfume. Men
and women and children watched them silently as they
followed an avenue that was lined as much with trees and
shrubs and flowers as with houses to—Abra was not sure
what it was: the central keep, or some unbelievably vast
tree? It seemed to have grown, rather than been built. It
boasted swirling branches so unlike the battlements of her
father's keep that she gasped in wonderment. It stood
taller than any tree could grow—in Kandar—and all its
boughs were cut with windows, its roots with doors, its
trunk with balconies. She felt awed, that the Durrym
magic could create so magnificent a hold.

She clutched Lofantyl as they approached a vast
doorway, where Durrym warriors stood.

"Don't be afraid," he urged her. "This is how we
live—with the land."

She nodded, unsure, and let him help her down from
the big bay horse, and took his hand as he led her into
the tree keep.

Afranydyr came after, and all their footsteps echoed
on wooden floors. Abra felt very afraid as they paced the
entry hall to a doorway guarded by two solemn-faced
Durrym.

"Now you'll meet my father," Lofantyl said, as the
guards swung the door open.

Abra swallowed hard and went with Lofantyl into
the central hall.

❧❧❧

ISYDRIAN WAS A TALL, hawk-faced Durrym, more akin to Afranydyr than Lofantyl in both appearance and manner. Abra felt quelled by his presence as he studied her, and Lofantyl ducked his head as he delivered their introductions.

"Father, this is Abra."

"Who is Garm'kes Lyn."

"And whom I'd wed."

The hall in which they stood was also timber, windows of some substance Abra could not define set in irregular places along the wide walls, like knots in the limb of some ancient tree. She was accustomed to the regularity of Lyth Keep, but this place was all curves and angles that tricked her eyes and set her head to spinning. Balconies ringed the room above, like intertwining branches within the central bole, smaller windows there, but all sunny, allowing in dancing shadows and shafts of brightness. It seemed to her that she stood within some massive tree, as might a squirrel. She caught the scent of wood, musky and heavy, and thought that she stood within a labyrinth.

Lofantyl's father sat at the center of the great, strange room, on a dais that supported a throne that seemed to be built of wood and bone. A shaft of light slanted downward to illuminate the planes of his stern face. She felt his cold gaze intimidating, and steeled herself to dignity.

"And how say you?" Isydrian asked.

Abra met his gaze. "I love your son."

"You are Garm. How can you love a Durrym?"

Lofantyl squeezed her hand and the answer came easy: "Because I do."

"And shall you stay here, in Coim'na Drhu, and forsake your own people?"

Abra hesitated a moment before she answered. "If I must."

She looked into Lofantyl's eyes and saw only love there.

"And you?" Isydrian studied his younger son. "How say you?"

"I'd wed her," Lofantyl said.

Afranydyr snorted.

"Then so be it," Isydrian agreed.

TWELVE

❧❧❧

Cullyn studied the trail, idly stroking the fox that sat beside him. The day was warm for spring, melting more snow and transforming the pathways to a mess of mud that must surely—or so he hoped—slow Per Fendur's pursuit. He listened to the birds: they'd bring him messages, Eben had said, but all he heard was their singing. He looked at the lures Eben had set and wondered if they'd work. He hoped so, for Laurens was not yet ready to move. And, indeed, he was not sure he was, himself, ready to go into Coim'na Drhu. It seemed a mighty venture that he'd sooner not attempt, save it seemed he had no choices left him.

Then a thrush settled on a branch close to his head and trilled a warning. The fox stirred, brush lifting as it moved from under his hand to stare into the woods. Cullyn crouched behind the cover of a bush and saw three horsemen coming slowly forward.

They were keep folk—he could tell from their

accoutrements—and they studied the ground. He thought one of them was the warrior called Drak, who appeared to lead the others. He remained in cover as they reached the division of paths and deer trails, and halted, staring around.

Eben had hung his talismans all around the wood, and Cullyn watched Drak stare at the feathers and dangling bones. He frowned and shook his head, and waved his men back as if confused. It seemed to Cullyn that he had not *seen* the magical workings, but was only turned away in confusion.

Even so . . . Cullyn waited until they had gone back down the trail and then ran to Eben's cottage, the fox at his side.

"They approach," he said.

"Then we'd best go." Eben set a fresh bandage around Laurens's ribs and motioned that the soldier rise. "I'd have given you more time, but the priest will find the way ere long."

"I'm well healed." Laurens struggled upright. "I've taken worse wounds and lived." Cullyn wondered at that, for Laurens's face was still pale and he moved unsteadily as he dressed. "Where do we go?"

"Into Coim'na Drhu, after this willful young woman." Eben gathered supplies as he spoke: potions and books that he stuffed into a satchel. "And you've a hard ride ahead."

"*Coim'na Drhu?*" Laurens paused in his dressing. "Are you mad?"

"Some say so," Eben returned cheerfully. "But what else?"

"Back to the keep and throw ourselves on Lord Bartram's mercy. He's a fair man."

"Who, from all this youngling has told me"—Eben

gestured at Cullyn—"listens to the priest and the adulterous captain."

"Even so," Laurens grunted as he struggled into his breeches. "Into the fey lands?"

"If we're to escape the priest's *questioning*, then yes," Eben said. "If we're to get this girl back—yes!"

"Have I any choice?" Laurens asked.

"You can stay here and die, when the priest finds you. Or—"

"Why are you doing this?"

Eben thrust a finger in Cullyn's direction. "He's syn'qui."

Laurens stared at Cullyn. "Him?"

"As best I can judge. Why else are you here?"

"I don't know." Laurens fastened his breeches. "But . . . if you believe that . . ."

"I do."

"Then we'd best be gone."

They gathered food and went to the stable. Cullyn saddled the mounts: Fey and Laurens's bay mare, Eben's mule. Animals darted about their feet—dogs and cats and badgers, and foxes. Eben spoke to them as he mounted the mule.

"All well, I'll be back. Until then . . ." He gusted a sigh. "Shall we depart before Per Fendur finds us?"

They rode north at first and then turned eastward, toward the Alagordar. They went slowly, for fear of opening Laurens's wound again. It was a full day before they reached the river. They forded at dusk.

"We're likely safe for a while," Eben said, "so let's make camp and rest."

Cullyn helped Laurens from his saddle.

"Shall I make a fire?"

"Why not?" Eben asked cheerfully.

"I wondered . . ." Cullyn gestured at the risen moon and the river. "Might the light not give us away?"

"I doubt it," Eben said. "I think that all Per Fendur would see would be mistlight. And the Durrym will find us, whether we hide our fires or not."

❧❀❧

"THIS MAN IS A HERETIC." Per Fendur tossed a parchment aside. "Burn it all."

Amadis stared at the shelves filled with books and scrolls and parchments, and gestured at Drak, who thrust a brand into the hearth and set the cottage alight.

"And kill all the animals you find," Per Fendur ordered. "They'll be familiars, and chained to fey magic."

So they set to slaughtering. Most of the wild ones escaped. The dogs and cats and badgers, the foxes and rats were too quick for the slashing swords. The bats exploded in fear too fast for the bladesmen to cut them. But the pigs and chickens were killed and cooked in the charnel house that had been Eben's home.

They ate well that night, leaving meat behind them to rot as Per Fendur took them onward across the Alagordar again.

❧❀❧

"WHAT'S THAT?" Cullyn asked as he looked westward. "Something's burning."

"Likely my home," Eben said. "I think your priest has found it." His voice was calm, his tone resigned, but Cullyn saw his eyes narrow and his lips draw tight. "It's not the first time; perhaps not the last. But something should be done about that priest."

Cullyn wondered if his own cottage still stood, or if

that were torched; and if he could ever return. He stared at Eben, wondering how the old man could accept such destruction so calmly.

"Shall we ever go back?" he wondered.

"If we can find the girl," Eben replied. "And if we can persuade her to return. It's our only chance—to bring her safely home and thereby gain Lord Bartram's patronage, his protection against the Per."

"And what chance have we?" Cullyn asked. "Three men against the Durrym?" He glanced at Laurens. "And one wounded?"

"I'll do my share," Laurens grunted. "I heal apace."

"It shall be diplomacy, not desperation," Eben said. "Subterfuge rather than sword work."

"I've never used a sword," Cullyn murmured.

"Then it's time you learned," said Laurens.

"Pah!" Eben shook his head irritably. "Do you never think, you soldiers? What shall we do? Go charging in with drawn blades to conquer a Durrym stronghold?"

"I'd hoped your magic might aid us." Laurens held out his cup that Cullyn might fill it with tea. "I'd thought you had some wizardly strategy designed."

Eben's laughter set roosting birds to fluttering in surprise. "Strategy? My only strategy was to escape the priest! Beyond that . . ." He shrugged. "It shall depend on Isydrian's humor. And that of the other families."

"Who is Isydrian?" Cullyn asked.

"Vashinu of Kash'ma Hall. Father of Lofantyl and Afranydyr. And . . ."—Eben's lips curled in a cynical smile as he stared into the fire—"myself."

"What?" Cullyn could not help gasping. He stared at Eben, whose silvery hair shone bright in the moonlight that etched his ancient face with lines and shadows. He looked, for all his vigor, an old man—so old as to be ageless, living on the edges of time, perhaps beyond chronology's constraints. Yet he named Isydrian his father, and Isydrian was Lofantyl's father. And Lofantyl had seemed not much older than Cullyn. Eben might have been his grandfather, even his great-grandfather.

Eben laughed at Cullyn's shocked expression, but softer. "I told you that I am a half-breed," he said. "And I suppose that now we embark on this great adventure I had better tell you the whole of it." He spat into the fire and turned his penetrating gaze on both Laurens and Cullyn. "Best you know what you face—at least, as much as I can tell you."

They waited as Eben fell silent, composing himself as if he gathered ancient memories.

"The Kandarians came to this land from across the western seas," he said. "The Durrym were already here, and lived in concert with nature—they used wood and bone, they did not hew stone or smelt metal. All they had came from the land. The newcome folk, however, owned only metal and determination to seize the land, and they came in their thousands. Why, I do not know, but they found a peaceful land, and for a long time lived beside the Durrym, who saw no reason to expel the incomers. But then—perhaps it's the nature of folk, I cannot be sure—they decided to expel the Durrym, and out of that the Church grew. A justification of territorial aggrandizement, perhaps? The desire to *own*? I don't know—only that Kandar moved against the Durrym and looked to drive them out. There were certain men— never women, which I have never understood—who rose in prominence and established the Church. And the Church decided that it should give the lordlings and petty kings what they wanted—which was to own all the land." He stared a while at the fire before continuing. "Perhaps it's Kandarian nature, but is it not true that the poor man wants to be rich, and the rich man wants to be king, and the king is unsatisfied until he owns everything?"

"I just want to be left alone," Cullyn said.

"You're odd," Eben returned. "That's all *I* wanted, but then you came along, and now . . ." He shrugged, continuing, "The Durrym objected to the Kandarian invasion and fought the newcomers, and were defeated. There were bloody battles fought, but in the end the Durrym were forced from their homeland into the east, across the Alagordar—the Mys'enh. But . . ." he chuckled, "they found the magic of the land there—of trees and rivers and rocks—and so were able to defend themselves with that confusion that denies men entry to the fey country."

He paused in his narrative and Cullyn asked, "Why could they not use that power before?"

"I think that the Mys'enh is a focal line," Eben said, "a division between worlds. There's no metal in Coim'na Drhu—only nature, and perhaps that divides the one land from the other. Perhaps the land welcomed the Durrym and gifted them with natural power." He shrugged. "I only know what happened after."

"Which was?"

"That the Durrym were safe across the river. Did Kandarians cross, they'd be turned back in confusion. None could find the Durrym."

"For that," Laurens said, "I'll vouch."

"So the Durrym felt safe," Eben went on, "but still resented the theft of their homeland. So they'd raid across the Mys'enh, and I was a product of such a raid: Isydrian crossed over and met my mother. And so, here I am." He raised his arms dramatically. "Born of a Durrym father and a Kandarian mother."

"Why did he not stay with her?" Cullyn asked. "Or take her back?"

"It was, shall we say," Eben suggested, "a *casual* acquaintance. But my mother was proscribed by the Church."

He fell silent then, and Cullyn saw pain in his eyes.

"What happened?"

"My mother was hung," Eben said flatly, as if he denied or blocked off hateful memories. "They built a gallows and dragged her off her feet. And made me watch as she choked. Then they burned her."

"And you? How did you survive?"

"I was a curiosity," the wizard said, "so the Church took me in. To study me. I was born of Kandar and Durrym, and I was therefore of interest—gifted with my father's Durrym magic and then taught the Church Kandarian magic, for which I had a talent. They thought I might find them a way across the river."

He paused again, staring at the fire. Cullyn waited no less eagerly than Laurens to hear the rest of the tale.

"I was held in a cell," Eben went on, "for eleven years. Priests would come to speak with me, to question me. I learned from them—and then I escaped. That's another story, for which we don't now have time—so suffice it to say that I escaped and fled into the Borderlands."

"And looked to find your father?" Cullyn asked.

"No." Eben shook his head. "Why? He'd deserted me and my mother. I despise Isydrian."

"But we go to him?" Laurens asked.

"What other choice?" Eben returned. "And he may feel guilt that we can use to get this Abra back."

"I do not understand," Cullyn said. "Isydrian is your father, Lofantyl and the other your brothers. But Lofantyl is young."

"Time takes different courses," Eben said. "Here, in Coim'na Drhu, it runs to a separate clock. It's a different world here, one set apart." He chuckled. "Have you never woken on some winter morning and thought it night because the sky is still dark and the birds not yet begun to sing? Or found yourself sleepy come the evening, because the light is gone? Yet time—do we judge it by clocks and candles—remains the same. It's like that: clocks run to men's accord, but the Durrym have no clocks, only the turning of the days. So perhaps they manage time better than Kandarians."

"How old *are* you?"

"The last time I thought about it," Eben answered, "I guessed at something like one hundred and seven, but I'm not sure. I lost count years ago."

Cullyn sat back, amazed. "And Lofantyl?"

"Younger," Eben said. "He can't be more than ninety."

"But Abra's younger than me," Cullyn gasped.

Eben chuckled. "I told you, no? Cross the river and time changes. Isydrian must be two hundred years old by now. The Durrym live long, eh?"

Cullyn fell silent, stunned by such concepts, wondering where he had come to, and what might happen to him in this unknown land. Then Laurens spoke, practical as ever.

"You talk of halls. What are they?"

"By all the gods, must I explain everything?" Eben sighed.

"Best you do," Laurens said, "so that we understand what we face here."

"You've a point," the wizard allowed. "So, the Durrym learned from you Kandarians. Or perhaps it's the way of the world. However, when they retreated into Coim'na Drhu they built fortresses, and divided into families. So the Dur'em Shahn guard the southern borders even as the Dur'em Zheit ward the north. The Dur'em

Jahnt own Dobre Henes, which is the greatest hall, and commanded by Santallya. But there are sundry others— the Dur'em Tys, the Dur'em Chan . . . Shall I go on?"

Laurens shook his head. "No, only tell me what it all means."

"That the Durrym fight amongst themselves," Eben said. "They vie for power. Isydrian would take Pyris's holdings and own all the Borderlands. That would make him strong—perhaps enough that he might overcome Santylla and take Dobre Henes, and become overlord."

"And we go into this?" Laurens stared at Ebens as if the wizard were mad. "Fugitives run from the frying pan into the fire?"

"What other choice do we have?" Eben asked. And gestured at Cullyn. "He's syn'qui, and we're sucked in, whether we like it or not. We are caught up in *his* destiny."

Laurens looked at Cullyn and said, "Damn you, boy. What have you delivered me to?"

Cullyn answered honestly: "I don't know. I don't understand much of this. I'm just an ordinary man."

Eben chuckled. "Far from it, youngling."

"Have I any choice in this?" Cullyn asked.

"None whatsoever," Eben said. "The gods picked you out and set you on your way; you've no choice save to go where they send you."

"And if I disagree?" Cullyn glanced at Fey, who cropped rich grass beside Laurens's bay and Eben's black mule, and thought of mounting the stallion and crossing back across the river.

"Then the priest would doubtless find you," Eben said. "Listen to me. You're now proscribed as I am, or Laurens. Your only hope is to bring Abra back, or stay in Coim'na Drhu. You have no others. Do you understand?"

"I could live elsewhere," Cullyn said. "I could build another cottage—if they burned mine down like yours."

"And then they'd find you," Eben replied.

"So I've no choice at all?" Cullyn asked.

"Save to accept your destiny," Eben answered. "And I pray that all the gods bless you."

It felt a heavy burden that he did not properly understand Syn'qui? Was that a blessing or a curse, or merely the ramblings of a mad old man? Save he did not think Eben mad. Indeed, in this unknown territory it seemed that Eben was his only hope of return to normality—if that still existed for him. For any of them. He stared across the river at the glow of the burning building and wondered where his life took him.

Eben interrupted his thoughts. "I doubt they'll cross by night, so let's rest. And be gone by dawn."

"Should we not set a watch?" Laurens asked.

"No need. Do they attempt a crossing, I shall likely know."

"Only *likely?*"

"Probably. And even if they do, all well the Durrym magic shall turn them around."

"Can you not set wards?" Lauren asked.

"Not save you want both Durrym and priest to find us," Eben returned. "For now, I'd prefer to stay anonymous. And if I set wards, then likely we'll be noticed. Best a plain watch, eh?"

Laurens grunted, stroking his wounded side. "Then I'll take the first watch." He looked to Cullyn. "You the second. Then . . ."

Eben was already settling to sleep.

"Wake him before first light, eh?"

Cullyn nodded.

He slept a while, albeit uneasily, and then relieved

Lauren. He stood guard until the moon was going down, and then, yawning, woke Eben.

"What?" the wizard demanded irritably.

"Your watch," Cullyn told him. "Until dawn."

Eben snorted and rose. "What have I got myself into?"

Cullyn found his bed and sank gratefully into sleep.

❧❧❧

Iᴛ ᴡᴀꜱ ᴀ ʜɪɢʜ, bright autumnal morning, the sun shining out of a clear blue sky across which birds darted. Squirrels watched them from the surrounding trees, and when Cullyn rose he saw sloe-eyed deer studying him from the margins of the woodland even as a big dog fox sniffed the air. He built the fire anew and set a kettle to boiling as he waited for Laurens to wake.

He went to find Eben—and found the ancient wizard slumped against a tree, his eyes closed and stentorian noises erupting from his mouth and nostrils.

Cullyn stared at him, anger stirring. Eben had refused to set wards about the camp and then fallen asleep on watch. He wondered just how much use magic really was as he nudged the snoring man. Eben stirred, muttering in his sleep. Cullyn shook him, and the old man woke.

"What is it?"

"You were supposed to be on watch."

"Are we attacked?" Eben rose stiffly, rubbing at his eyes.

"No," Cullyn said. "No thanks to you."

"Then all's well." Eben shook his dirty robe. "Is it time for breakfast?"

Cullyn sighed and went to prepare the food. Eben

stretched and rose. Cullyn could not help but think of a mummified corpse rising from its tomb.

"Excellent." Eben savored the odors of bacon and brewing tea. "Perhaps you're not so useless."

"I thought I was syn'qui." Cullyn resented the old man's sarcasm.

"That doesn't mean you're of any use," Eben declared. "Only that you're a focus of attention. I was syn'qui in my own way—which is why I chose to live alone . . . until you came along to deliver me all this aggravation."

Cullyn ducked his head. "Forgive me."

"Nothing to forgive," Eben returned cheerfully. "You've no more choice than I. But it does seem that you can make a decent breakfast. So shall we eat?"

Cullyn nodded and prepared the food as Eben woke Laurens, checking the wound and dressing it afresh as the morning air filled with the tantalising odor of bacon. The fox came closer and Eben absently took a slice from the pan and threw it to the animal. The fox snatched it up, swallowed, and sat watching them.

"This is a pleasant land," Eben remarked. "Where else might you sit down to breakfast with a fox?"

"Save you spoke of the fey houses fighting," Laurens said. "Is it so different?"

"Aye, there's that." Eben devoured bacon with gusto. "But perhaps the fey folk learned that from you Kandarians. They *do* live in concord with nature."

"And the lion shall lie down with the lamb," Laurens said. "And all shall be tranquility—so long as the Church approves."

"And its followers observe its rules, yes," Eben gave back. "The Church would rule, and set its own governance on kings and common folk."

"And there's no Church here?"

Eben shook his head. "The Durrym worship the old gods of tree and stone, of light and darkness."

"Which is much akin to us," Laurens said. "Bel, the light-bringer; Dasc, the moon goddess; Thyriam of the trees . . . Where's the difference?"

"In *thought*," Eben answered. "Kandarians think of their gods as allies, and the Church interprets the gods' thoughts and therefore determines what they say: so that all the gods' speaking comes from the Church."

"And here?"

"They look at the land, and consider that not all the gods are benign. And choose which to follow and which to ignore."

"Can we ignore the gods?"

"The Durrym do," Eben said. "When it suits them."

Cullyn swallowed his last mouthful of bacon, quickly, and said, "They're coming across the river!"

Eben's plate went scattering into the fire. The fox barked and darted away; the inquisitive deer fell back into the woodland.

Across the Alagordar, Per Fendur led his troop to the ford. He wore armor black under the flowing robe that covered the plates, a dark presence amongst the sparkling accoutrements of Lord Bartram's men.

"You were on watch," Laurens snarled. "What of your magic?"

"I fell asleep." Eben stretched his arms, rubbed his back. "I suppose we'd best leave now."

"So much for wizardry," Laurens grunted.

"I never thought . . ." Eben shook his head. "What power does he command, that he can find us?"

Cullyn said, "I don't know, but I think we'd best be on our way."

Fendur was into the river now, Amadis at his side;

the squadron behind, armed with lances and bows. They came splashing across, bright water rising from the pounding hooves, the early sun glinting on their armor.

Cullyn helped Laurens mount the bay, saw Eben clamber astride his mule, and swung onto Fey's saddle.

"Best we ride," Eben shouted. "And fast!"

"Where's your magic?" Cullyn asked. "Can you not halt them?"

"Lances and bows? No." Eben dug his heels into the mule's ribs and went off at a gallop.

THIRTEEN

THEY RODE HARD toward the rising sun, charging through woodland that disgorged startled animals at their coming. Most were ordinary—such creatures as Cullyn had seen daily across the mysterious river—but others were different. He saw birds decked in such plumage as he'd never seen before, and strange animals. There was a creature that seemed all fangs and claws, shaped like a ferret but several times a ferret's size, that stood ripping at the carcass of some kind of deer—save it wore more antlers than any deer he'd ever seen. And there were others. A creature that looked like a wolf, but sounded like a sheep; a vastly horned bull, or cow—they went by too quickly to tell—that watched them from the shadows and ducked its massive head and bellowed a mournful cry.

He paid them scant attention, intent only on following Eben and escaping Per Fendur.

Fey could easily have run ahead, but Eben's mule was not so fast and Laurens rode uncomfortably, clutching at his saddle and his wound as he followed the silver-haired man ever deeper into Coim'na Drhu. Cullyn rode after, wondering where they went, and into what?

When he looked back, he could not see the pursuers. Trees stood in the way, great willows and alders giving way to drier woodland, beeches and oaks, birches and hazel, spreading in impossible confusion. Coim'na Drhu was a conundrum that he could not understand.

Then they came to a glade where massive oaks gave way to tall beeches, and beyond that a steep-sided valley, its walls descending to a wide meadow through which ran a stream from which white horses drank, and cropped the grass. There were around twenty of them, a stallion and his herd. Save they were not like any horses Cullyn had seen, for they all bore a spiraled horn growing from between their ears. Which lifted as the refugees emerged from the treeline.

The stallion shrilled a warning and ducked his horned head in challenge.

Eben reined in, halting his mule at the rim of the slope. Cullyn heard Fey whinny an answering challenge and fought the stallion to a halt. Laurens stared at the spectacle, clutching his wounded side.

"Unicorns," Eben said. "Best be careful."

"Of horses?" Laurens asked.

"Not just horses," the old man returned. "Magical horses; fey animals. Are you virgin?"

Laurens laughed, shaking his head. "At my age? I'd hope not."

"Nor I," Eben replied, and looked to Cullyn. "And you?"

Cullyn thought of Elvira and shook his head.

"Then they'll kill us if we approach."

"Horses?" Laurens asked.

"Yes," Eben gave back. "Do you understand nothing? We've come into a *different* world. The rules are not the same."

"And Per Fendur is on our heels," Laurens said.

"If we ride down there the unicorns will kill us. They're savage beasts, the mares vicious as the stallions."

"So we're caught." Laurens rubbed at his side. "Fendur and Amadis behind us, unicorns to the fore. What do we do?"

Eben said, "Either wait for them to finish grazing, or go around."

Laurens grunted irritably. "We may not have time to wait."

Cullyn glanced back and wondered if he saw the glint of mail and lance heads amongst the trees. He studied the valley—it was long and broad, and if they were to continue on the way Eben chose, they'd need to ride for leagues to pick up their path again.

"How long might they graze?"

Eben shrugged. "All day; a few more minutes. Who knows with unicorns? They're unpredictable beasts."

As if in confirmation, the stallion shrilled another challenge and trotted a little way toward them. His ivory horn tossed a warning as he stamped the ground. The mares and foals looked up and moved to join him, presenting a threatening wall of horns that spread across their path. Eben motioned that they withdraw back into the treeline. Cullyn looked back again, and this time was sure that he saw sunlight shining on armor.

"I think," he said, "that we've not much time."

Eben and Laurens followed his gaze, and the wizard cursed as the jingle of saddle trappings tinkled through the woods.

"Damn the priest!" Eben's blue eyes narrowed irritably. "He's even more talent than I thought."

"Can you not use magic?" Laurens asked.

"Not here!" Eben glowered at the soldier as if Laurens were crazed. "We come clandestine, no? If I use magic, the Durrym will feel it, and come looking for us."

"But we're looking for them," Cullyn said.

"Do you understand nothing?" Eben favored him with a stare that reddened his cheeks. "We're looking for this damned girl, yes. But she's taken by Lofantyl, who's Dur'em Shahn. This"—he gestured at the landscape—"is the domain of the Dur'em Zheit. Who are in contest with Isydrian and his Shahn. Are we taken by the Zheit, Pyris could likely order us all slain for spite alone."

"Why did I ever look to you for help?" Laurens muttered. "Better to have thrown ourselves on Bartram's mercy."

Cullyn said, "We'd best decide what to do."

The jangle of armor drew closer. He could see shapes now, moving through the forest. His hunter's eyes began to pick out distinctions. Per Fendur and Amadis were in the lead, moving slowly but nonetheless inexorably toward him. And still the wall of unicorns stood before; and the valley's edge dropped steeply away, decked along all its flanks with trees and undergrowth that would inevitably slow their progress should they seek to skirt around. He believed that he could escape, mounted on Fey, but Laurens was wounded and Eben's mule could never match the pace of the Kandarian horses. It seemed they must be caught.

And then a pack of hounds exploded from the woodlands containing the farther edge of the valley. Cullyn had never seen such dogs. They were akin to wolfhounds, but heavier, more muscular, and taller. And they ran silently until they drew close to the herd of unicorns, and only then set to baying so that the horned horses turned to face them and drew their attention away from the three intruders.

Cullyn watched in fascination as the hounds raced toward the white equines. They did not attack, but rather set to herding the mythical beasts, baying and snapping, so that the unicorns were directed to the north. He watched the horns thrust and the dogs dart away, never drawing quite close enough that horn or hoof could inflict damage. He heard Eben mutter, not knowing whether the wizard gave thanks or curses. But the unicorns were driven away, so he said: "Do we cross the valley now?"

Eben looked back. "It's likely our only chance. So, yes."

They went down the steep flank and were onto the gentler slopes as Per Fendur led his troop out from the trees. The priest shouted and urged his mount to a gallop. Amadis couched his lance and beckoned the troop to follow.

They raced down the valley, and from out of the forest on the farther side there came a hunting party.

There was, as best Cullyn could estimate, ten of them, armed with lances and bows. Their leader was a slender boy, who carried only a bow and a long knife. They wore such dress as did Lofantyl—motley tunics and breeches, high boots of soft leather, some caps that hid their hair.

The boy-leader saw the three approaching riders and shouted something Cullyn could not hear. But he heard Eben's foul curse.

A rider raised a horn to his lips and blew a long call that brought the hounds back, off from the unicorns—which promptly swung around and set to chasing the dogs. And all became confusion.

Per Fendur halted his charge; the fey folk grouped together, staring at the newcomers; Cullyn, Laurens, and Eben galloped toward them. The boy shouted something and the fey riders spread out, nocking arrows and lowering lances. The unicorns, driven by the baying hounds, charged onward as if they'd run down the fey folk. Cullyn wondered whether the lances and the readied arrows were directed at the horned horses or at them.

Then Per Fendur raised his hands and mouthed a spell that sent a ball of bright fire hurtling after the escapees. Cullyn yelled a warning and Eben swung his mule aside and raised his own hands. The fireball swung away, exploding amongst the hunting party. There was a tremendous glow—as if the sun fell to earth—and a stench of burning that was accompanied by the screams of torched horses and men.

Eben mouthed a fouler curse. "He's even more power than I thought."

"I thought you knew Church magic," Laurens gasped as the air filled with the stench of burning flesh.

"As did I. But I underestimated him." Eben raised his hands and wove patterns in the air. "And this is no place for Kandarian magic."

He shouted, and it was as if a gust of tremendous wind erupted from his mouth, blowing back Per Fendur's firestorm as might a rain squall douse a blaze.

Per Fendur shouted and urged his followers on. The unicorns swung away from the explosion, and the hounds—those that did not halt, stunned—went after them. Cullyn saw the boy tumble from his mount, into the path of the panicked unicorns. There were men fallen around him, and the fey horses fretted—those still standing—unnerved by the smell of scorched flesh.

Cullyn did not think then, only reacted. He saw Eben mouthing words he could not hear and raising his hands again as Per Fendur sent a second fireball scorching through the air, and Amadis couched his lance and charged headlong down the slope with all the troops behind. And the unicorns thundered toward the dismounted boy with lowered horns, the stallion in the lead.

Cullyn heeled Fey to a charge, hoping to intercept the unicorns' attack. Fey was big enough he might deflect the white horse's attack—smash the stallion aside before the spiral horn pierced the fallen boy. Perhaps Cullyn might lift him up and carry him away from the hoofs and horns. Or not; but he felt no choice and drew his knife—his only weapon.

And then he saw the boy rise and snatch off his cap, and it was not a boy but a young woman, whose hair fell free as sunlight, flaxen and long. And she stood upright as the unicorn charged, and raised her arms and waited, as if welcoming her death. Cullyn urged Fey to an even faster pace.

But the unicorn slowed its gallop, reared up, then came to the woman at a walk. Cullyn reined Fey in, gaping in amazement as the white horned horse knelt before the girl, who stroked its horn and spoke to it, and then looked irritably at Cullyn.

"Who are you?"

He gave her his name as the unicorn rose and tossed its head, urging her to stroke its mane.

"And what do you here?"

"Escape," he said, still amazed. "My friends and I . . ."

"From them?" She jutted her chin in the direction of Per Fendur. "Those who spoiled my hunt?"

Cullyn nodded.

"Garm'kes Lyn," she said. "Like you."

Cullyn nodded again.

"Why do you not leave us alone?" She stroked the

unicorn as she spoke absently. "Why do you come across the Mys'enh?"

"We had little choice," he answered. "The priest would torture us, and slay us. So Eben brought us across the river."

"Eben?" He saw gray eyes set in a wide face above a large-lipped mouth open in surprise. He had thought Elvira pretty and Abra beautiful, but this fey woman was . . . He could not describe it. "You came here with *Eben?"*

"And Laurens, who's wounded." He looked to his companions. They were halted amongst the fey folk, Eben tending those hurt by Per Fendur's fireball.

"And chased by a Garm priest?"

Cullyn nodded, glancing back nervously to where Per Fendur and Amadis waited with their lance men. They had halted now and there seemed a kind of stalemate. Both parties stared at one another as the dogs sat panting and growling and the unicorns stood stamping warily.

Then: "I am Lyandra of the Dur'em Zheit."

"I am Cullyn of Kandar."

"And you came to my aid—even though I didn't need it."

"I didn't know that," he said. "Eben told me unicorns are vicious. Unless . . ." He broke off in embarrassment.

"I am," she said, staring at him defiantly. "I can command unicorns. The stallions, at least. They're fun to hunt—even if we don't kill them, they give us a good run. And the mares would horn me without a thought."

She turned to the stallion and whispered in its ear. It rose and trotted away, shrilling a call that gathered the herd. Lyandra shouted to her followers; she had a surprisingly loud voice, that saw all her surviving men mounted and readied for attack as the unicorn stallion gathered his herd and faced Per Fendur's men.

"I do not like you Garm," she said, "but even so, I think I like this priest less. So shall we drive him off?"

Her smile was like the sun rising. Cullyn offered her a hand and swung her behind him on the saddle. She shouted orders at her followers and a line of men and unicorns loped toward Per Fendur and Amadis.

It was pleasant to feel her hands about his waist. Better to see Per Fendur retreat as unicorns and armed folk charged toward them. Arrows flew over the cresting horns, and more than a few of the Kandarians were plucked by the shafts. He saw Per Fendur wave a hand, indicating retreat, as the wave of white horned horses charged toward him, followed by the Durrym, whose bows kept up a steady wave of arrows. He looked about and saw Laurens and Eben riding with them, albeit slower, as they drove Per Fendur and Amadis and all their troops back to the treeline, back over the ridge, and then toward the Alagordar.

More than one soldier was plucked from his horse by the unicorns, more still shafted by Durrym arrows as the great dogs snapped and bayed about the horses' heels. Then Lyandra raised a silver horn from her belt and blew a long, shrill call. The unicorns and the men ceased their pursuit and returned to the valley. The hounds went on baying as Cullyn halted Fey on the ridge.

"The dogs shall chase them off," Lyandra declared. "So you're safe for now—if you explain properly why you came here with Eben."

He looked down at her and said, "We came after Abra."

"The Garm who was taken by Lofantyl?"

Cullyn nodded and Lyandra threw back her head and laughed. Then called for a horse. "This," she said, grinning, "will fascinate my father." She swung astride the saddle. "I must take you to meet him. You and Eben, both."

Cullyn was not sure what to make of her glee until they rode down the slope to where Eben and Laurens waited, escorted by two of Lyandra's men.

Eben turned to Laurens and said, "As you told it— from frying pan to fire. And all because he's syn'qui."

"*Syn'qui?*" Lyandra's gray eyes darted from Eben to Cullyn.

The wizard shrugged and ducked his head. "Indeed— for my misfortune. Better I'd never met him, but—"

"Were he not, you'd likely be dead now."

Eben shrugged again. "Then perhaps he keeps me alive."

"Thus far," Lyandra answered. "But my father shall decide."

"Pyris still rules?"

"Pyris is Vashinu of Ky'atha Hall."

"And you still vie with the Shahn?"

Lyandra chuckled, staring at the wizard as if he were mad. "What else? It's the way of the world, no?"

"There's the notion of peace," Eben said. "Of concord and agreement."

Lyandra studied him with a scornful gaze. "Such as you Garm delivered us? Was that concord and agreement when you drove us from our homeland?"

"No," Eben allowed, "but not of our making." He gestured at Cullyn and Laurens. "We come only as fugitives, dependent on your mercy."

"That," Lyandra said, "shall be decided by my father."

"So be it," Eben returned. "Your father is, after all, a fair and just man."

"Who can also be cruel," she said ominously. "When it suits him."

Eben's ancient face creased into even deeper lines "I've no argument with the Dur'em Zheit. Indeed not with anyone—save that cursed priest who's disturbed my life, because . . ."—he glanced at Cullyn—"he' syn'qui."

She looked at him and said, "Are you sure?"

Eben nodded. "I'd not be here if I didn't believe it."

"Save he's told me his story, and it sounds like yo ran from the Garm lands as outlaws."

"Yes," Eben declared. "But how else did the pries find us here? Would he not have been turned back? Th lad's a compass; destiny's compass."

"There's that," Lyandra allowed. "It's surely strang that they could come so far into our country."

"As did we." Eben waved a hand at Cullyn and Laurens. "Is that not also strange?"

"You know the ways," she said.

"Yes, I do," Eben agreed. "But with two full-blooded Garm? Your magic should have turned us away, and Pe Fendur, also. But it didn't. What does that tell you?"

Lyandra shrugged. "I don't know." She studied Cullyn. "Best we speak with my father."

The dogs came back then, panting, and gathered about Cullyn as if he were an old friend. Lyandra stared at them, and at Cullyn, and sighed.

"I should slay you now," she said. "I wonder if tha were not the best way—the simplest."

"Then order it," Eben said. "You've enough mer left."

Lyandra shook her head again, setting long blond curls to tumbling, and said, "No. We shall go to my hal and talk with my father. *Then* your fate shall be decided."

Eben grinned.

Cullyn stared at him, wondering what deal had beer made that he did not properly understand.

But the surviving Durrym saw them mounted and led them off to Ky'atha Hall.

❧❀❧

IT WAS A LENGTHY TREK, across the valley and into the wooded ridges beyond, where they continued through dense, impossible forest. It seemed to Cullyn that the landscape was simultaneously natural and sculpted: one ridge might be clad with great oaks, the next with beeches, and in the bottoms between grew hazels and birches, with willows and alders along the streams, as if all the trees in the world had been set down in random profusion. There were looming pines and great maples, spruces and hickories. It was a fantastical landscape that was populated by no less fantastical beasts. Some few he'd seen before, but now he saw more watching from the treeline or rushing from their path. He saw creatures that aped the shape of man, but swung from tree to tree, and things that resembled squirrels, but large as the hounds that ran before the party. He saw wild pigs the size of cattle, and a massive snake that raised a head big as his own to hiss a warning before it slithered like a receding river into the undergrowth.

"It's a strange world, no?"

Eben interrupted his marveling and he nodded silent agreement.

"The Durrym own a different kind of magic to Kandar's," Eben advised him. "They created all this."

"Like a menagerie?" Cullyn had heard rumors of exotic gardens, populated with exotic creatures. But he could not imagine any like this.

"Yes, I suppose so," Eben replied. "It amuses them— to shape nature to their will."

"But surely no one can—"

"The Durrym can. Humans—the Church—canno Their magic is all belligerent." He chuckled, a sou sound. "Like the priest with his paltry fireball, eh?" H gestured at the landscape. "Two schools of thought—th one would live with the land and garner its magic; th other would seek only to control, and find ways to over come those who deny them that control. That's sad an paltry magic."

Cullyn thought of the dead and wounded. "Not s paltry."

"But still he was driven off by the unicorns."

"So why did he not send his fire against them?"

"I think it was because his magic works only agains his own kind," Eben replied. "I think that perhaps it doe not work so well here in Coim'na Drhu."

Cullyn pondered a while. "If the Durrym can do al this"—he gestured around—"why do they not exten their domain? Why do they not set their magic agains Kandar?"

"Excellent questions!" Eben chuckled. "I wonder i you don't begin to learn."

"Learn what?" Cullyn asked.

"That the way to knowledge is through observatior and asking," Eben replied. "So, listen: folk depend on dif ferent things for their survival. The Durrym own n steel, like Kandarians do. The Durrym live with the land Kandarians look to conquer it. Look about you—do yo see any metal here?"

Cullyn glanced around. It occurred to him that he' noticed the approach of Per Fendur's troop because sun light glinted off lance points and helmets and armor, an then he'd heard the tinkling of the metal through th trees. Yet none of the Durrym wore armor, neither di their lance heads shine in the sun, nor the trappings o their mounts rattle with any sound other than that o wood and leather. He realized that their lances were wooden-tipped, or bone, and that all their accoutrements—saddle gear and bridles, belts and quivers—were of the same natural materials. He turned, frowning, to Eben.

Who said, "Aye, no metal. But metal cuts wood—so Kandarian blades were stronger than what the Durrym had. And there were more Kandar folk than Durrym, so the fey ones withdrew—they had little other choice than to be slaughtered by steel. But . . ." He laughed. "When they were forced from their homeland, forced across the Alagordar, they crossed a kind of *line*. What do you call the river?"

"The Alagordar," Cullyn said. "Or the Barrier."

"Indeed: the Barrier. I think the world changes along that river. Do you know what *Mys'enh* means?"

Cullyn shook his head.

"The Place of Changing." Eben studied the trees a while and sighed. "As I've told you, time changes here. The seasons shift and strange beasts develop; trees grow together where they should not. I believe the Alagordar divides two worlds—that it's a line between the mundane and the fantastic. The fey country, if you like. And it made the Durrym fey."

"Which does not answer my question," Cullyn said. "About conquest."

"I'd thought you understood." Eben glanced at him. "The Durrym came to a new land, where Kandar could not find them. They settled here, and built their keeps and castles. They war amongst themselves, yes, but they've no great wish to invade: they'd sooner be left alone to pursue their own concerns."

"Then why did Lofantyl take Abra?"

"Perhaps," Eben said, "they simply fell in love. The gods know wars have started for lesser reasons. Or peace."

"What do you mean?"

"Think on it," Eben suggested. "Does this girl trul·
love Lofantyl, then perhaps a treaty might be forge·
through their marriage. Who knows, perhaps we migh
even unseat the priest?"

"But we only came to bring her back," Cullyn said.

"And met Lyandra, who's Dur'em Zheit—in contes·
with Lofantyl's Shahn. Why do you think that hap
pened?"

Cullyn shrugged.

"Because fate hinges on you, boy."

He pulled his mule away to fall alongside Laurens
who rode heavy in his saddle, a hand pressed to hi·
wounded side.

Cullyn rode a while confused, pondering Eben'·
words. Why, he thought, could his life not have re
mained simple? He had been happy in the forest with hi·
animals—happier to buy Fey—and content to remain
there. Yet now he chased Abra and was taken captive b·
Lyandra and the Dur'em Zheit, who were at war with
Lofantyl's Shahn.

His head slumped. He wished he had never me·
Lofantyl or Abra or Laurens or Eben. And then Lyandr·
slowed her horse to come up alongside.

"What ails you, my savior?"

"Savior?" he returned. "You had no need of saving."

"But you didn't know that, and still looked to rescu·
me. That counts, Cullyn of Kandar."

"Cullyn of Kandar?" He shook his head, embarrasse·
even as he felt flattered. "That makes me sound like som·
olden hero, which I'm not."

"Then what are you?" she asked.

"Confused. I'm a simple forester, taken from my lif·
by things I do not properly understand."

"But Eben says you're syn'qui."

Cullyn looked at her and laughed because she was so beautiful. "I'm some focus of destiny? Some hero? I think not!"

"We'll find out," she said. "My father will decide."

"Or decide to slay us."

"There's that, too," she answered cheerfully. "But you'll have at least one advocate."

Her smile told him who that would be. And Cullyn wondered at his fate as Lyandra urged her mount forward and he was left alone in a strange world.

᭸᭸᭸᭸

THEY CAMPED THAT NIGHT in a glade where great trees spread their branches over a smoothly grassed clearing, as if grown to accommodate the visitors. A little way off was a stream that gurgled over stones and filled up into such pools as were convenient for bathing, each one private for the willows and alders that spread out their overhanging branches. The fey folk set up fires and produced food from their saddlebags. Eben moved amongst the wounded, tending them, and Cullyn sat with Laurens.

"What have we come to?" he asked. "And what shall happen to us here?"

Laurens hesitated before answering, pressing a hand to his wounded side. "I don't know. They'll slay us or enslave us, or send us back."

"To face Per Fendur?"

"Perhaps." The soldier shrugged and winced at the movement. "But we've little other choice, eh?"

"You hurt," a voice interrupted.

Lyandra stood before them. Laurens nodded. "I do. I took one of your shafts."

"They can be painful," she said casually. "Usually they kill."

"I'm hard to slay," Laurens returned.

"I believe that." She smiled at him. "Has Eben no
tended you?"

"As best he could."

"But even so?"

"I've a hole through my gut, lady. Forgive me my cru
dity, but I piss blood, and I wonder if I shall reach you
hall."

"We've healers there," she said, "who can cure you
It's no more than another day's ride. Can you last tha
long?"

"Do you promise me healing," Laurens said, "ther
yes. I'd not leave this youngling alone. I doubt he car
fend for himself."

Lyandra chuckled. "I think he can," she said. "I thin
that Eben is right—he's syn'qui."

"Which is why we live?"

She smiled and ducked her blond head in agreement
then walked away.

Laurens stared at Cullyn. "Is this curse or blessing?
he asked.

And Cullyn answered honestly. "I don't know."

FOURTEEN

❧❧❧❧

THEY CANTERED through a thicket of oaks and ash and hazel and came to a ridge that was filled with long grass where deer grazed. The meadow was scattered with trees, spreading down the walls of the ridge to a small lake that was held like a blue jewel in the green cup of the encircling land. Lyandra paused there, staring down as if at some remembered treasure.

Cullyn could understand why.

He had traversed a wondrous land—such a place as defied imagination, all filled with impossibilities, as if every dreamed-of landscape or creature that might be encompassed by imagination existed. And now he looked upon a lake that was a perfect circle of pristine blue, reflecting back the late afternoon sun and the billows of white cloud that scudded overhead. It was an exact circle, and at its center, like a jewel in the blue ring, there

rose an islet as impossible as anything else in this strange
land.

Sheer cliffs of black granite rose from the lake's calm
waters, shining like jewels exposed to the sun. They
clambered from the mere to meet such walls as no natural force could have constructed. High they were, ringing
the islet, and beyond them lay a profusion of fantastical
towers, some squat and blunt, others like great needles
rising to meet the sky. Some rose up smooth and feature-
less, others were decked with balconies and walkways.
Some glittered as glassed windows shone back the sun's
rays; others were dull. But all were multicolored, so that
from the center of the lake the islet sparkled all blue and
green and white and crimson, purple and scarlet, silver
and yellow. Cullyn thought of a field of flowers, or a god's
handful of gems scattered over the rock to grow as they
would.

"It's beautiful, no?"

He turned to Lyandra and ducked his head in agreement.

"My home," she said, "Ky'atha Hall. Now let us meet
my parents."

She smiled and urged her mount down the slope.
Cullyn followed her, looking back to Eben and Laurens.
They rode together, seeming less eager than he to examine the wonders of this magical place. So he reined Fey
to their stride and glanced a question at Eben.

The wizard grinned sourly. "Pyris might not welcome
Isydrian's son. But"—he shrugged—"Laurens needs
better healing than I can give him. So we have no
choice, eh?"

"They've offered us no harm yet," Cullyn said. He
studied Laurens, thinking that the soldier *was* very pale.
He sagged in his saddle, a hand pressed constantly to his
side. "And Lyandra promised healing."

Eben chuckled. "There are *conditions* to Durrym promises."

"What do you mean?" Cullyn asked. "Surely a promise is a promise?"

Eben shook his head. "So young, so foolish."

Cullyn opened his mouth, but Lyandra went down the slope at a gallop before he could speak, and her followers gathered in the captives and herded them down to the lake's edge.

Two great trees whose nature Cullyn could not define grew on either side of a jetty that seemed a combination of woods. The platform extended a dozen feet into the water, set with lesser growths from which hung silvery chains. Lyandra reined in at the edge, took a horn from her saddle, and blew a shrill call.

From across the mere there came a response as wide gates swung ponderously open in the rock face of the islet. Cullyn could not understand; he could see no jointure—only the cavern between and the boats that came sailing out.

He gasped aloud, wondering if these things were natural or Durrym constructions. They were shaped like swans, with proudly vaunting heads and great spread tails. He saw no oarsmen, but only billowing wings and a disturbance in the water behind them, as if great webbed feet paddled across the mere.

"My father created them," Lyandra said. "Are they not splendid?"

All Cullyn could do was nod and gape.

Each one was large enough to carry five horses and their riders. Fey fretted as Cullyn led him onto the deck. Eben's mule bucked, protesting this unusual transportation. Laurens led his bay on board with a Durrym holding him upright.

They were all on board save Eben and his mule,

which snorted and continued to buck in protest at the prospective journey.

"Quiet, quiet." The wizard stroked the mule's head, and ducked an apology to those who waited. "He's not accustomed to boats. A moment, eh?"

He spoke in a soft whisper to the mule, dragging its ear close to his mouth, and the beast calmed, allowing Eben to lead it onto the swan-boat.

"He's a mind of his own," Eben said. "Best not stand behind him."

None did, for the mule argued the crossing with stamping hindfeet and other protests as they crossed the lake to Ky'atha Hall.

❧❦❧

GREAT BLOCKS OF GRANITE stood before them, the sheer rock faces opening on a tunnel that seemed to Cullyn as unnatural, and as acceptable, as any of Coim'na Drhu's wonders. The swan-boats floated on, propelled by powers he could not imagine, and came through the darkness into bright light.

They entered a harbor that had no right to be so large, where slopes decked with trees and squares and houses ran up to the keep that dominated the islet. The swan-boat docked, smooth as the bird it resembled, alongside the jetty. Lyandra took her horse off and motioned for Cullyn to follow.

Unsure of his footing, Fey stamped and fretted. Cullyn soothed the stallion and brought him off the curious boat.

Eben and Laurens came after, helped by Lyandra's escort.

"So now," she said, "we shall meet my parents, and your fates be decided."

She said it cheerfully enough, but Cullyn felt a chill run down his spine, aware that he was a stranger in a strange land. He looked to Eben for reassurance, but the wizard busied himself with the wounded, so all Cullyn could do was mount and ride Fey up the wide avenue that led directly to the citadel's central tower. Folk watched his passing, tall handsome folk who wore bright clothes that contrasted with the woodland colors of Lyandra's gear. He became aware of his own shabby clothing—much travel stained by now, and in dire need of washing. He heard the clatter of Fey's hooves and looked down at a roadway of such smooth stone as Kandar could never manufacture. It was all one surface that glinted green and black and blue, devoid of paving slabs—as if it were a carpet rolled out from the open gates of the tower toward which they rode. It was a marvel—as was all else about him. He saw plazas where fountains played, and shady gardens, houses and towers—surely far more than the islet could physically contain. It seemed as if space itself was rearranged by Durrym magic.

And then they entered the central keep.

It was encompassed with low walls, the entry beneath a vaulting arch that seemed fashioned from a single, massive piece of jade that filtered and shone back the sun's light. Beyond lay a courtyard filled with sweet-scented trees and pools of clear blue water. Birds sang amongst the trees and fat fishes swam lazily in the pools. The yard was paved with an intricate mosaic that he felt showed some picture, might he rise high enough above the place to observe it properly. But for now he only stared in wonder at the keep before him. It was larger than Lyth Keep, and infinitely more elegant. Lyth's hold was all gray stone and dull wood, built for defense rather than beauty. This place was a marvel. Sheer walls, unlined by mason's work, rose smooth as the avenue below to windows and balconies and terraced walkways. Plants hung from the outjutting terraces, trailing bright flowers down the smooth azure stone. Save Cullyn was not sure it *could* be stone, for it seemed like some vast candle, a thing melded and melted into place rather than built.

"It's pretty, no?" Lyandra swung from her saddle, smiling at his amazement. "I knew you'd like it."

He climbed down from Fey and handed the stallion's reins to a liveried man. "Be careful," he advised. "He doesn't much like people."

The man nodded, and was then hauled off his feet as Fey bucked, teeth snapping. Cullyn moved to calm the horse, but Lyandra grasped his arm and said, "No, wait."

The man spoke softly and Fey ceased his bucking, although his ears stayed back and his teeth remained bared. The man stroked the black muzzle, still speaking softly, and Fey calmed and allowed himself to be led away.

"Do you all have this power over animals?" Cullyn asked.

Lyandra chuckled—like clean water washing over stones, Cullyn thought—and said, "Yes. I think we understand them better than you Garm. Now come inside."

She waited until the wounded were taken off and Eben and Laurens stood beside them. Then she brought them into the keep.

There was a hall that seemed to Cullyn again for larger than the tower could hold, its floor a solid slab of pale green agate that shone bright in the sunlight coming through the wide windows, so that patterns of light glittered under his feet. Benches and tables stood around the walls, which were structured of impossibly smooth blue stone, decked with tapestries that depicted woodland scenes that seemed to move with the animation of the creatures sewn into them. Cullyn saw a unicorn kneeling before a woman, and would have sworn the horned horse moved as the woman raised her hand. He became aware that his jaw hung open, and closed it lest Lyandra think him some bumpkin.

"Come." She touched his arm and brought him across the hall to a door that appeared fashioned from pure silver. It was not guarded, and swung open as they approached. Lyandra hesitated, beckoning that Eben and Laurens follow.

She ducked her head and said, "My parents, I bring you visitors with a story to tell."

Instinctively, Cullyn bent his knee.

Facing him across a floor of black marble were a man and a woman of such regal demeanor that he could do naught else. They were tall and brown-haired as chestnuts in autumn. Gray streaked the man's temples, lending him a dignity that was supported by stance and visage. His hair was long, held off his aquiline features by a circle of silver. He wore a tunic strapped with gold and silver, and moleskin breeches that were set down the legs with fastenings of gold. The woman was an older version of Lyandra—still beautiful— her hair caught up in a net of silver filigree, her gown pale green and clinging. Cullyn thought that he had never seen such beautiful folk—save for their daughter.

"This is Cullyn." Lyandra touched his shoulder. "He looked to save me from a unicorn."

Her parents laughed, like tinkling water over stones.

"And this is Laurens—a companion of Cullyn's."

"Who's hurt," the woman said, and clapped her hands so that folk came hurrying to her side. "Tend him. Fetch the healers and see him healed."

"My thanks, lady," Laurens said.

She nodded graciously and watched as Laurens was led away.

"And this one you know." Lyandra gestured at Eben. Then laughed as she turned to Cullyn and said: "Forgive me, I forget my manners. These are my parents—Pyris and Mallandra—rulers of Ky'atha Hall."

"Who bid you welcome," Pyris said. "Even you, Eben."

Cullyn bowed. Eben stared at the fey lord. "Are you sure?"

"Why not? How often does Isydrian's son visit me?"

They stared at one another until Mallandra said, "Husband, they're weary and travel stained. Shall we not offer them baths, and clean clothes before we discuss what's brought them here?"

"Of course." Pyris acknowledged her suggestion with a lowering of his regal head.

"Let them bathe and find fresh clothes. Then dinner and conversation, eh, Eben?"

❧❧❧

CULLYN WAS ESCORTED to a chamber that seemed larger than his entire cottage, with high windows of clear glass that looked out over the keep and the lake beyond. A balcony stood outside, from which he could see the great spread of the forest. The floor was polished wood, scattered with magnificent carpets, and seats and armoires stood around the walls—which were hung with tapestries. Past this magnificence there was a sleeping chamber that contained a bed vast as some potentate's catafalque, and beyond that another room that Cullyn did not at first understand.

It was tiled in bright colors that depicted trees and

birds and hunting hounds, and at the center was a blue-tiled tub, with steps leading down and odd spigots set at one end. It smelled of soap and scent.

"Shall you bathe, then?"

He looked at the servant in surprise. The man wore livery he supposed belonged to Ky'atha Hall, but he seemed entirely human—Garm.

Cullyn asked him, and the man answered: "I am Fredryk. I was taken captive. Now I serve Lord Pyris."

"And would you not go back?"

"No." The servant shook his head. "Why should I? In Kandar I tended fields that grew good grain, but then the lord would come and take all I'd worked for. If I raised a cow that calfed, the keep lord would take the calf—and then demand the mother's milk. Here, I live well. Lord Pyris is benevolent."

Cullyn wondered, and let the man take him to the marvelous tub. He watched as handles were turned, spilling steaming water into the bowl. The servant set soaps and unguents beside the tub, and asked if Cullyn needed further help. Cullyn shook his head and dismissed the man.

"I'll see your clothes cleaned," the servant said, "and bring you fresh gear."

Cullyn waited until he was gone before he stripped off his clothing—which was, he must admit, filthy—and then descended into the tub.

The water was hot from one spigot, cold from the other: he lay there, playing with such wonders, scrubbing long days of travel dirt from his hair and body before—with some reluctance—he rose and toweled himself dry.

His familiar clothes were gone, but others were set on the bed: breeches and tunics, shirts and undergarments; such garb as only lords wore. He tugged on the latter and was making his choice of the former when he heard the knocking on his door.

Anticipating Eben or Laurens, he swung the door open, his chosen breeches in his hand and his torso bare.

And blushed as Lyandra laughed.

"Forgive me, I'd thought you might be ready by now."

He danced into his breeches, struggling at the same time to pull on his shirt. Lyandra pushed past him, setting him to dancing one-footed, as she strolled into the room, casual as if the sight of a half-dressed—or undressed?—man were entirely normal.

She wore a long green gown that flattered her body and made him wonder why he had thought her boyish. Her hair was caught up in a bun that exposed a slender neck decorated with a bejeweled silver necklace. Cullyn hurriedly buttoned his breeches and fastened his shirt, aware of the heat that possessed his cheeks.

Still smiling, Lyandra settled on the couch, carefully arranging her skirt.

"I should have sent word," she said. "You must forgive me."

"For what?" Cullyn stuttered. "I . . . I don't know . . . I'm pleased to see you . . . but . . ."

"Are all you Garm so shy?"

"I don't know." He fastened his shirt, pulled on a tunic and boots.

"My parents would see us at dinner," she said.

"Am I dressed right?" he asked, fastening a last button.

"You look splendid," she said. And rose from the bed to take his face in her hands and plant a kiss on his lips.

He felt his face grow hotter and wondered if he should put his hands on her. Hers, after all, rested on his

shoulders, and she smiled at him as if she both challenged and invited him. He caught wafts of perfume,
musky and sweet, like summer flowers and autumn's slow
decay. Her face was close enough he could smell her
breath: it was clean as fresh-cut mint. He hardly knew
what he did as he drew her closer and settled his lips on
hers.

She kissed him back, then pushed him away.

"They wait on us." She took his hand, leading him
toward the door. "And your future must be decided."

"Who shall decide it?"

"My parents, of course." She took him from the
chamber. "And I. After all, I found you."

"I don't understand."

She laughed, drawing him down the corridor to a
wide stairwell. "It's our way. The custom of Coim'na
Drhu. When you Garm cross the Mys'enh you are usually
turned back. Those who are not remain."

"As slaves and servants?"

She shook her head. "Not necessarily. Many hold
powerful stations amongst the families. Many choose
not to go back. And you"—she clutched his hand
tighter—"are syn'qui." She smiled again and led him
down the long stairs to a hall flanked with carvings of
Durrym and fantastical beasts. Cullyn followed, captured
by her hand and beauty, wondering into what strange
world he went.

They came to a door that seemed fashioned entirely
of melted gold. A liveried servant before it threw it open
to allow them access to the chamber beyond. It was inti-
mate. Small windows let in the sun's dying rays, candles
glowed in sconces along the walls—those carved with
friezes that depicted more woodland scenes: hunts and battles, strange beasts. The floor was covered with a single
massive carpet that reflected in its weaving the depictions

on the walls. Pyris and Mallandra sat at the ends of a table of carved oak, Eben and Laurens settled between them, servants—or guards, Cullyn wondered—standing behind.

He went to Laurens. "You're well?"

"Yes." The soldier ducked his craggy face. "These Durrym have fine healers. They've seen me well."

Cullyn looked to Eben, who smiled and winked.

Lyandra said, "Sit here, by me."

He took the chair and sat in nervous silence.

Pyris said, "Wine?" A servant filled all their goblets. Then, courteously: "Which first—talk or dinner?"

"Talk," Cullyn said bluntly. "I'd know my future."

"An honest Garm." Pyris chuckled. "So, then—talk."

"He's syn'qui," Lyandra said.

Pyris glanced at Eben, who nodded. "So we must take care of him, eh?"

"Best that you do," Eben said, wiping wine from his beard. "I believe the gods favor him—or curse him—but he's a pivot on which all our worlds turn."

"You're sure of this?" Pyris asked.

"I am," Eben replied. "How else could that priest have followed us so far into your kingdoms? Why else?"

"We need to talk," Pyris declared. "Privately."

He ordered their dinner brought in and dismissed the servants, so that the six of them could speak alone.

"The Kandarian Church finds new magic," Eben said. "Per Fendur was able to find us across the Mys'enh." He glanced at Laurens for confirmation, and Laurens said: "He boasts of new powers the Church has found, that shall allow them to cross the river. And he hates the Durrym."

"Why do they want to cross?" Pyris asked. "I'd thought we had some kind of truce."

"Kandar's grown too much," Laurens said. He smiled an apology. "Since we drove you out, all the land—save along the border—is given to farming, to vineyards, to mining and the like. Kandar prospers and the population grows. King Khoros would find more space, and the Church promises him that—it promises a way across the Alagordar, against a people we defeated before."

"And can it deliver its promises?"

"I fear so," Laurens said. "And surely the fact that Per Fendur came across proves it possible."

Pyris studied the soldier a while. "Why do you tell me this? Am I not your traditional enemy?"

"Perhaps once," Laurens returned, "but now?" He supped his wine and thought a moment. "I've met Cullyn and Eben, and my thinking has changed."

"And this one?" Pyris asked, glancing at Eben.

"I don't know, save he's a wizard and a friend."

"Who brought you here in search of this girl, Abra?"

"A damnably willful girl," Eben said grumpily. "And were Cullyn here not entranced, I'd be sitting at home in my cottage."

Lyandra kicked Cullyn, "Were you?"

"What?" he asked.

"Entranced."

He nodded, and felt her fingers close tight about the muscles above his knee. He winced—her grip was strong!—and said, "Until I met you."

And realized that it was true. He looked at her and she looked back at him, and there was something exchanged between them that he could not define, only *know*.

"However"—Pyris interrupted their exchange—"we face a dilemma. This Garm woman, Abra, is taken by Lofantyl to Kash'ma Hall. Willingly? Or kidnapped?" He looked to Eben and Laurens. "Is all you tell me true, then you Garm might come across the Mys'enh in search."

"I'd doubt," Laurens said, "that we could raise

sufficient men to threaten you. Khoros will hardly concern himself with the fate of a Border Lord's daughter."

"But this Church of yours?"

"Still develops its magic. I believe that Per Fendur is one of the few to own that ability." Laurens grew practical. "I think it must take years before there are sufficient priests to guide a real army. And then Khoros must levy his musters before he's sufficient men to threaten you."

"But the Church *has* found a way across," Eben said. "And perhaps Lord Bartram shall send all his men." He glanced at Cullyn and shrugged. "He's a beacon, after all."

Pyris laughed. "That would be no more than a raid; and easily defeated. I doubt this Lord Bartram has enough men to offer any real threat to Ky'atha Hall."

"Perhaps; perhaps not," Eben said. "But I'd not disregard the danger." He stared at Pyris. "My father is a cunning man, and by all accounts so is Per Fendur."

Laurens nodded agreement.

"There's that," Pyris allowed. "So what do you say?"

"That Isydrian might trade—ally with Fendur: Ky'atha Hall for his aid."

Mallandra gasped; Cullyn felt Lyandra's hand tighten.

"Think you so?" Pyris stared aghast at Eben.

Eben shrugged. "You know my father as well as I," he said bitterly. "Do you think him capable?"

Pyris lowered his head in agreement.

"And if Kash'ma Hall were to make an alliance with Lyth Keep," Eben said, "then you'd face a mighty foe."

There was a silence then. The room seemed to draw in, shadows lengthening. The candles flickered and the fire sparked as if in warning confirmation. Cullyn swallowed wine, feeling entirely out of his depth, but still compelled to speak.

"Why not act first?" he suggested.

"How?" Eben demanded.

Cullyn turned to Laurens. "Does Lord Bartram hate the Durrym?"

Laurens thought a moment and then shook his head. "Not hate them, but he's sworn to defend the border."

"And he's honorable?"

Laurens nodded. "A most honorable man."

"And his argument now is that—as best he knows— Abra was kidnapped by Lofantyl."

"That's why we're here," Laurens agreed. "To bring her back, and so escape the damned priest's attentions."

Cullyn felt his head swirl, a whirlwind of tumbling thoughts, Lyandra's hand warm on his thigh, her eyes fixed on him as were all the others. He was a simple man, only a forester, not used to such political games. He felt embarrassed as he studied their faces, all intent on his; but something he could not understand compelled him to speak.

"Suppose," he said, "that we offer both Abra and her father a choice. Let Abra decide whether or not she wishes to return to Kandar. Let Lord Bartram hear her decision, and make his choice. That might"—he eyed his audience, amazed at his boldness—"forge such a peace as could bring Kandar and Coim'na Drhu together."

"Out of the mouths of babes and sucklings," Eben muttered. Then louder, "Did I not tell you he's syn'qui?"

"But how," Pyris chuckled, "do you propose to do that?"

"There's a way," Eben said.

"Which is?" Pyris toyed with his goblet, studying Eben with a smile that looked for an answer he might not accept, save it serve him well.

"Do the old rules still apply?"

Pyris ducked his head in agreement.

"Then a challenge."

"A tourney?"

Eben nodded. "Why not? How else, save open warfare?"

"We might siege Kash'ma Hall," Pyris suggested. "That would be amusing."

"And useless," Eben said. "You'd waste men against Isydrian's walls, with no guarantee of getting Abra back. Do I know my father, he'd order her throat slit before he'd return her."

"That's true," Pyris allowed, "Isydrian's a mean temper on him."

"Unlike you."

Pyris laughed. "I am moderate."

"Of course," Eben said. "You are virtue personified."

"Which is why I listen to your ramblings."

"Save are they ramblings?" He stabbed a thumb in Cullyn's direction. "Or his?"

Pyris ducked his head in acknowledgment and studied Cullyn a while. "If I were to slay him, he'd not be such a signal to the Garm priest. Might that not be the wisest course? Let Lofantyl have his Garm woman, and we fight this Lord Bartram."

Eben said, "You'd slay a syn'qui?"

Laurens rose from his seat. "Do you threaten Cullyn, I challenge you."

Lyandra said, "Father!"

And Pyris chuckled. "So much talk of challenges." He stared at Laurens. "Do you think you could defeat me?"

Laurens shrugged. "I don't know, but I'd do my best were you to harm Cullyn."

"And you, daughter?"

Lyandra said, "Let him live. He speaks sense."

Cullyn felt insignificant. Even were he syn'qui he

heard his fate discussed as if he were not present. He said, defiantly, "I'll fight my own battles."

And Pyris roared laughter and said, "So be it! It shall be as Eben suggests—a challenge." He beamed at Mallandra. "Does a tourney excite you, my love?"

His wife studied Cullyn and her daughter. "Have you fought a tourney before?"

Cullyn shook his head. "What is a tourney?"

Pyris laughed again. Mallandra said, "Lance to lance; sword to sword."

"I've never fought with either a lance or a sword," Cullyn said as Lyandra's hand closed tighter on his thigh. "Indeed, I've never fought with anyone."

"But save you'd see the Dur'em Zheit besiege Kash'ma Hall," Pyris said, "that's what you must do—are you earnest in your desire to resolve this problem?"

Cullyn looked to Eben. "Is it the only way?"

"I believe so," the wizard answered.

Cullyn looked to Pyris, who chuckled as if relishing the prospect of combat. "We vie together," the Durrym explained cheerfully. "Isydrian would seize my hold, if he could. He'd defeat me and make Lofantyl master of Ky'atha Hall—and should he succeed in that ambition, then his clan would own such power as might challenge Santylla—he'd set himself or Afranydyr on the throne in Dobre Henes and rule all Coim'na Drhu."

"And this hinges on me?"

"Eben and my daughter say that you're syn'qui." Pyris sipped wine, staring at Cullyn across the ornate cup. "So, yes."

Cullyn met the Durrym's gaze. "I came after Abra, and then became a fugitive. Now I become your champion?"

"Perhaps." The smile faded a moment from Pyris's face. "But if you want—"

"To speak with Abra," Cullyn interrupted, wondering the while how he dared. "To find out what she wants; and Lofantyl. And perhaps . . ." He broke off, shrugging; uncertain of himself in such exalted company.

Eben murmured, "Speak on," and Laurens smiled encouragement.

"Perhaps," Cullyn continued, embarrassed, "that might broker peace between our lands. Were they wed . . . ?"

"What good to Ky'atha Hall?" Pyris demanded. "Some treaty between Lyth and Kash'ma serves me not at all."

"Save Lord Bartram swears peace with both." Cullyn supped wine, wondering what he said, amazed at his audacity. "That he accepts Abra's marriage to Lofantyl, and swears peace with both Kash'ma Hall and Ky'atha—which shall both agree to a treaty beforehand."

"Under whose aegis?" Pyris asked.

Cullyn swallowed deep, summoning up all his courage before he said, "Mine."

"To which end," Pyris replied, "you'll have to fight for Abra. Isydrian will agree to nothing else."

"Then I'll do it," Cullyn said.

"Excellent!" Pyris clapped his hands. "I shall send messengers out tomorrow."

FIFTEEN

❧❧❧

CULLYN STOOD WITH LYANDRA on the balcony outside his chambers. The night was warm, the lake glinting a silvery blue below, a soft breeze wafting forest scents from the woodlands. Overhead the sky hung star-pocked, glittering with the reflection of far-off worlds, the moon gone down to a slender crescent that tomorrow would fade to nothing—at least in Kandar. In Coim'na Drhu who knew what it might do. Perhaps the Durrym controlled even that.

"So I must challenge Lofantyl, who's my friend?" he muttered.

"If you wish to speak with Abra." Lyandra stared at him, almost coldly. "Are you in love with her?"

He looked into her eyes and shook his head. "Once I thought I was, but now . . ."

"Now?"

"She's too high above me. Like you."

Lyandra chuckled, a throaty sound, and her smile grew wide, like the sun emerging from behind storm clouds. Cullyn looked at her mouth and remembered that kiss she'd bestowed.

"You're syn'qui," she said. "I'm not above you."

"I came to escape Per Fendur's torture," he returned. "Had Laurens not broken us free—and found Eben to help us—we'd be dungeoned"—he shuddered at the thought—"and set on the rack."

"But you weren't," she said. "You escaped. Because you're syn'qui."

She leaned against him, and he felt the hard softness of her body through the thin gown. Her scent was enticing, her breath an invitation. He drew back.

"So everyone tells me." He set his elbows on the balcony's wall. "But no one tells me just what that means. That I'm marked by the gods? And therefore must fight a friend? Is that destiny? Have I no choice in it?"

"No," she said. "No more than I for . . ." She stilled her next words and took his hands and looked into his troubled eyes. "Abra is taken to Kash'ma Hall, where Isydrian will hold her like a trophy—a victory over the Garm. Lofantyl, it would seem, wants her, and Afranydyr will support his father. Are you to even discuss her fate with her father, then you must fight for her. That's the way of our world—and now you're caught up in it, like it or not."

"What if I went under a flag of truce?"

Lyandra chuckled. "Likely Isydrian would put an arrow in you himself."

Cullyn sighed, staring out at the pleasant landscape. It seemed, somehow, more benign than Kandar. Gentler, softer—yet just as bloody. "I'm caught up in events I do not understand," he murmured.

She touched his face, smiling at him. "You'll do what's right," she said. "Because worlds hinge on you, and I believe that you will make the right decision. If not . . ." She shrugged.

"I am a simple forester," he protested. "I know nothing of battle, of duels. I've fought no one—nor wanted to. I wanted only to be left alone."

Save as he looked at her he was no longer sure of that. Elvira faded away; Abra's beauty became a distant memory. He stared at this fey virgin and felt his heart swallowed up. He remembered her facing the unicorn, and before he knew it his arms were around her and their mouths together.

When they parted she whispered, "My champion."

He studied her face and wondered. She was beautiful and he desired her; but he had desired Elvira and Abra, and he was not sure what love meant. What it was. He felt a great confusion—and more than a little fear at the step he took. She was fey and he Garm'kes Lyn. He pushed her away.

"What's wrong?" she asked.

"You're . . ." He shook his head: he did not understand women. "The unicorn . . ."

"I've ensnared unicorns because I was virgin." She clutched his shoulders. "Now, however, I'd have you for my husband; my lover." She pulled him closer. "Likely I feel about you as does Lofantyl about Abra. I love you, Cullyn."

She closed her arms about him. She was strong, and he felt her body through the thin material of her dress, and responded helplessly.

Then pushed her away again, heat on his brow and heat in his loins. He did not understand why he said it, only that he must. "Before we . . ." He blushed; she laughed. "Before we . . . I must settle this business with

Abra and Lofantyl. And then ask your father's permission."

"He'll grant it," she said, "do I ask. And I shall."

He nodded. "Then after this thing is settled . . ."

She smiled and stroked his cheek. "I shall hold you to that."

❧☙

"IT'S TO BE LANCES," Laurens said. "Shields and lances. Are you dismounted, you'll have what hand weapons you prefer."

Cullyn stared at the old soldier. "I don't know how to use a lance," he said. "What of hand weapons?"

Laurens grinned. "You could use a sword."

"I don't know how to use a sword."

"A war axe?"

Cullyn shook his head.

"A hammer?"

"No."

"What *can* you use?"

"I'm handy with a bow . . ."

"We might," Laurens said, "suggest that. But I doubt your opponent would accept. And you are the one making the challenge—you have to accept his choice of weapons."

Cullyn swallowed, his throat dry.

"Then I must do what I must."

"He'll choose lances," Eben said. "They enjoy their tourneys, the Durrym. It'll be a formal affair—your opponent will be armored, and—"

"Armored?" Cullyn gaped at the wizard. "I've never worn armor in my life."

"What kind?" Laurens asked.

"Formal," Eben replied. "Full-bodied plate."

"That's heavy." Laurens studied Cullyn as if he were some specimen. "Still, he's big enough."

"Durrym armor's light," Eben said. "Remember, they don't use metal. The armor will be tended wood, leather—natural materials."

Laurens nodded thoughtfully. "How long do we have before this joust?"

"Who knows?" Eben shrugged. "Pyris must send a messenger to Kash'ma Hall, Isydrian must respond, the ground must be chosen. It could be weeks."

"That's in our favor. It'll give me time to train him somewhat." Laurens scratched his scarred cheek. "At least he has a fine, big mount. Was ever a horse built for battle, it's Fey."

Cullyn listened to them discussing his precarious future as if he were not there, and interrupted.

"I don't want to fight Lofantyl," he said. "I don't want to fight anyone. I just want to . . ." What he wanted to say was, "Go home," but instead he shrugged, thinking of Lyandra.

"Well, it's a fact of life that we don't always get what we want," Eben said.

"Why can't we just ask Abra?" Cullyn wondered. "Hear what she's got to say."

"Durrym rules," Eben replied. "One is that Lofantyl took her, and might not agree to returning her. Another is that *she* might not wish to return. Perhaps she's in love with him—who knows? And then there's my father to consider—Isydrian would do much to spite me, or Ky'atha Hall."

"Why?" Cullyn asked.

"Reasons," Eben said. "I'll tell you someday. But what I'll tell you now is that you have no choice—you're caught up in destiny's web, and can only dance on the puppet strings."

"No choice at all?" Cullyn stared at the wizard. "What if I refuse to fight?"

"It's gone too far for that." Eben fixed him with a bright blue gaze. "Pyris is committed—likely his messenger has already ridden off—and in a day or so we'll agree to the terms. Then you'll fight or become a prisoner here. To refuse a challenge is disgrace to the Durrym. It would leave you without honor, and you'd be outlawed—if not slain on the spot." He beamed wickedly at Cullyn and added, "As would we. So, you see? All our lives depend on you."

Cullyn frowned, and Eben's smile grew softer. "This is a different world, lad, with different rules. Pyris has set his heart on a tourney in hope of disgracing Isydrian—he knows that Isydrian cannot refuse the challenge. So you become Ky'atha Hall's champion—Pyris looks to you to upset his rival."

"And I've no say at all?"

"None," Eben replied cheerfully. "Save you'd risk Pyris's wrath. And lose Lyandra into the bargain."

Cullyn blushed.

"Win and you'll become a great man here," Eben said. "The clans will hail you, and you'll earn the right to wed Lyandra. Lose and . . ." He shrugged, his meaning clear.

Cullyn sighed. "Then let's do it."

❧☙❧☙

THE SUN STOOD HIGH and Cullyn found his armor uncomfortable. He wore a padded tunic that was over-layed with a breastplate of polished wood, pauldrons on his shoulders and vambraces on his arms. A tasset pro-tected his lower body, and cuisses and greaves his legs. The helmet sat hot on his head, and the visor obscured his vision so that he saw only a narrow slit of the world ahead. He carried a curved shield on his left arm and a heavy lance in his right hand.

Three times now Laurens had knocked him from Fey's saddle, leaving him sprawled on the grass. This time he rose angry, loosening the straps of his helm so that he might breathe clean air.

"I can't fight like this!"

"He'll be armored," Laurens said.

"And I'll be dead. I can't ride with this gear on me." He flung the helmet away and began to unbuckle straps. "If I must fight him at all, then I'll do it loose. As best I can."

"You'll still need shield and lance," Laurens said. "So get back up and we'll try it that way."

Cullyn stripped off his armor and mounted Fey again.

❀❧❀

"THE CHALLENGE IS ACCEPTED," Lyandra told him. "A week from now."

He sighed, stretching back on the wide bed as a Durrym healer rubbed unguents into his bruises. "Are you so eager for it?"

"To see you vanquish Kash'ma Hall? Yes."

"So you think I can?"

She stroked his hair. "You are my champion, and you are syn'qui. Of course you'll win."

Cullyn wondered. Lyandra, appeared to envisage him as some great knight—and the folk of Ky'atha Hall saw him as a champion, riding out for their honor. But he was not so sure. It was, in some ways, pleasurable. He was feted about the keep—admired and respected. The fey folk gifted him: he had a collection of swords that

Laurens examined daily, and his choice of armor. He had been offered horses, most of them decked in tourney armor. He dined with Pyris and Mallandra on such fine food as he'd never tasted, supping wine that set his taste buds to spinning, Lyandra close beside him. He wished he *were* a champion, and at the same time that he had never come to Coim'na Drhu. Save now he had no choice left and could only go where fate took him. He thought that to be syn'qui was a curse.

Then word came back, formally, that the challenge was accepted and the ground agreed. The tourney would take place midway between the two holds, where fine grass grew wide between a river and the forest. Both parties would arrive two days before the joust—time enough to set up their tents and feast in celebration of the combat. It would take them both two days to reach the ground.

❧❧☙☙

"YOU'RE LEARNING," Laurens said. "But when you swing the sword, use your wrists. Swing it, and then cut down."

Cullyn clambered to his feet. He ached horribly. He hated this training; he did not want to fight Lofantyl—or anyone. He wanted to go home—save that would take him away from Lyandra.

"And if he uses a war axe, or a hammer?"

"Then most likely you're dead."

"Cheerful news."

"I'll show you how to counter them."

"In a day?" Cullyn raised the unfamiliar sword.

"You learn fast," Laurens said. "The gods know, but you've learned to use a lance quick enough. How many times have you unseated me now?"

"Seven," Cullyn answered, not without pride.

From the edge of the practice ground Eben shouted, "You can achieve more than you believe yourself capable of." Lyandra applauded, and called for Cullyn to attack Laurens again. Cullyn looked at her and wondered at her appetite for bloodshed, but held up his shield and sword and went at Laurens again.

He battered the shield and forced Laurens back. Stroke followed stroke, some on shields, others on the deeply padded practice armor. Their blades were fashioned of soft wood, the shields real. Twice, Cullyn set his edge to Laurens's neck; thrice delivered cuts to the legs that would have brought a man down; once to the groin, where the armor divided.

"Enough!" Laurens stood laughing. "You've beaten me, eh? And you'll defeat your opponent. You're a natural fighter, lad. Only watch his lance, and if it comes . . ."

"You told me," Cullyn said.

"But if it's your friend Lofantyl on the other end?"

Cullyn shrugged.

Laurens said, "No matter what you feel, if he's on the other end of the lance, he's your enemy. You must unseat him—even kill him. Else he'll kill you."

"Defeat him, my champion," Lyandra called. "Slay him if you must, but defeat him. For Ky'atha Hall and my love."

Cullyn looked at Laurens and said, "I'd best win, eh?"

Laurens nodded: "For all our sakes, I think."

❦❧

ABRA LEANED AGAINST THE BALCONY of her chamber, watching Lofantyl and Afranydyr on the practice ground below. It was as if she stood on the bough of some immense tree, studying her fate being worked out for her. Isydrian and his court sat below, the lord of

Kash'ma Hall shouting advice and encouragement to both his sons. She could not, at such distance, see his face clearly, but she could imagine his expression. It would be bloodthirsty, eager for the coming tourney—and confident of victory.

She loved Lofantyl—of that she no longer had any doubt—but his family . . . Isydrian and Afranydyr seemed fish from a different sea. Where Lofantyl was gentle, they were hard. They extended her basic courtesy, but somehow made it clear she was prisoner, left alive only by Isydrian's whim. Had Afranydyr his way she had no doubt she'd by now have been made a slave, or a whore. She felt afraid in this strange, magnificent keep, where Lofantyl was her only friend. And he soon to fight Cullyn.

She returned inside her room as the practice ended, wondering what the outcome of the tourney should be.

❦❧❦

"I'VE NO LIKING FOR THIS," Lofantyl told Abra. "Cullyn is my friend, and I've no wish to fight him."

"Then don't," she said.

"I'm left no choice."

Her hand touched his mouth, closed it. "I'd stay here with you," she said. "I love you, so why must you fight Cullyn?"

"Honor demands it. Ky'atha has challenged Kash'ma, and we're caught up in the game."

❦❧❦

THE DAY CAME. It was a fine day, the sun riding a clear blue sky speckled with swifts and swallows and larks. To the left of the Dur'em Zheit pavilions, the river drifted wide and sparkling. Trout larger than any Cullyn had seen leapt from the water to snatch dancing insects from the air above. To the right, thick woodland grew, great oaks and solemn beeches, and between was a wide sward of grass, cropped down and greener than any in Kandar.

The pavilions were magnificent, multicolored and spacious, their interiors spread with silken carpets, each one fronted with the pennant of the occupying family. Cullyn shared with Eben and Laurens, theirs set beside that of Pyris and his wife—and Lyandra.

That night, at dusk, it had been agreed the formal confrontations would be made—challenger to challenged. The next day, at noon, the tourney would commence. Cullyn waited in uncomfortable anticipation as Durrym wandered about the encampment. Zheit and Shahn mingled as if it were a festival, placing wagers on the victor. Cullyn felt as if he were a horse on which they bet, and wondered at these strange folk who seemed capable of enmity and generosity, both.

He dreaded the combat.

❧§੭੩❧

"YOU'RE SURE YOU'LL NOT WEAR ARMOR?" Laurens asked him. "It'd be safer."

"It weighs me down, and I can't see out of that cursed helmet," he replied. "And if I really am syn'qui, I shouldn't need it."

"Being syn'qui," Ebens replied cheerfully, "doesn't guarantee your success."

"You're mightily encouraging."

The wizard shrugged. "I tell you only the truth. That's not always pleasant."

A trumpet sounded and Lyandra came. "It's time," she said, grinning at Cullyn.

He rose and went out of the tent to meet Lofantyl.

❧❧❧❧

THEY MET MIDWAY DOWN the jousting ground. Lofantyl wore a flowing robe, and Abra stood beside him in a gown of pale blue silk that flattered her red hair. Jewels decorated her coiffure, more ringing her fingers. She looked lovely—and concerned. Isydrian stood beside them, and by him a tall, hawk-faced man he introduced as Afranydyr, his elder son. Cullyn was accompanied by Eben and Laurens and Pyris, Lyandra standing to his left, her eyes measuring Abra.

The keep lords bowed formally and Pyris said: "We offer challenge."

"To what end?" Isydrian replied.

"That, do we vanquish, you shall allow Cullyn of Kandar to speak with the Garm woman, and heed their decision. Does she agree to return home, then you allow her to go."

Cullyn saw Abra clutch Lofantyl's arm and shake her head. But Pyris nodded: "It shall be so."

"Then on the morrow—" Pyris started. And was interrupted by Abra's cry.

"I don't want to go home! I love Lofantyl. I want to stay with him in Coim'na Drhu."

Isydrian ignored her outburst. "There are other settlements to be agreed."

"Which are?" Pyris asked.

"Does your man win," Isydrian said, "then the terms are yours to dictate. If not . . ." He eyed Eben with a cold stare. "My son and his companions are mine. To do with as I see fit."

"You were ever loathsome," Eben murmured.

Isydrian favored him with a contemptuous smile and looked to Pyris. "Agreed?"

Pyris nodded. "Agreed."

Cullyn felt the world spinning around him as his fate was decided. He stared at Abra and felt Lyandra's hand grasp his. He opened his mouth to say that he had no wish to fight Lofantyl, but his fey friend spoke first.

"I'll not fight him."

"What?" Isydrian stared aghast at his son. "Are you a coward? Has all that time you spent in the Garm lands changed you?"

"No." Lofantyl shook his head. "But I cannot fight him. It would be without honor."

"You're crazed," Isydrian said. "This Garm romance has destroyed your mind."

"I gave him the lyn'nha'thall." Lofantyl pointed at the knife on Cullyn's belt. "We swore friendship. I *cannot* fight him!"

He winked at Cullyn, who smiled back in relief.

"We must find some other way to settle this," he said.

And then his brother spoke. "With champions! Let me take Lofantyl's place."

Isydrian stared at his sons and shook his head, then turned to Pyris. "What Lofantyl says is right, do you not agree?"

Pyris nodded.

"Then Afranydyr shall be champion of the Shahn. Shall you accept that?"

Pyris nodded again.

"And yours?"

"Let me fight him," Laurens whispered. "I'd enjoy knocking that cockinjay off his horse."

"No." Cullyn shook his head. "I must do this myself."

Eben clapped his hands. "Well said, lad. Better to sort things out yourself."

Afranydyr stepped closer, an ugly smile twisting his lips, and said, "I take my brother's place. Do you agree?"

Cullyn nodded.

"Then at noon tomorrow we fight. Lance and shield, eh?" He grinned wickedly. "And I shall put my point through your chest and slay you. And the Garm woman shall be my brother's concubine, and your friends become my slaves."

"Perhaps," Cullyn answered. "Or perhaps not."

He felt anger grow inside him that he did not understand, save that he disliked Afranydyr for his arrogance and presumption. He had no wish to fight with Lofantyl: that Durrym was his friend, but Afranydyr . . . He felt a loathing for the man and even though he doubted he could win the combat, still he felt a sudden and great desire to defeat this arrogant fey.

"On the morrow," he said, "I shall bring you down."

Afranydyr laughed. "Dream on, Garm."

He sneered at Cullyn, utterly confident. Cullyn took a deep breath and turned toward the fey lords.

"I've terms of my own, do I defeat Afranydyr."

"And those are?" Isydrian asked.

"I'll state them after," Cullyn said. "Am I able."

Eben cried, "Well done, lad."

Afranydyr chuckled, confident.

SIXTEEN

IT WAS A FINE, BRIGHT DAY, as if the Durrym adjusted the seasons to their own purposes. Billows of white clouds sailed across a sky of pure blue, from which shone a sun that belonged to high summer. The grass between the pavilions shone emerald green and birds sang loud from the trees as Cullyn emerged from his tent. He wore a padded tunic, but was otherwise unarmored as he went to Fey and saddled the big black stallion. He had refused to accept horse armor in favor of speed and agility; he hoped he did the right thing.

Fey snorted and stamped as he set the saddle on, as if anticipating the combat, and Cullyn stroked the glossy neck.

"Remember," Laurens said, "you've two choices— aim at his shield and look to take him from his saddle. Or keep your lance low and your shield high, and aim for his groin. The armor's weakest there, and can you put your point in—"

"I thought this was a formal combat." Cullyn set the bit between Fey's champing teeth. "Shouldn't I aim for his shield? Aren't we meant to unhorse our opponent?"

"He looks to slay you," Laurens said, his smile cynical. "Didn't you hear him? Didn't you see his eyes?"

"He's right," Eben said. "Afranydyr's not like Lofantyl—he's no love for Garm. If you were facing Lofantyl it would be a true tourney. But this is a *fight*."

"But I don't want to slay him," Cullyn protested. "I thought that if I can unseat him—"

"He'll come at you again," Eben said. "He's cold as his father, and he'll not be satisfied until you're dead."

"Unseat him and ride him down," Laurens urged. "Use Fey. And if you must fight afoot, remember what I've taught you." He indicated the array of weapons set beside the lances. There was a wickedly spiked morning star, and a three-bladed mace, a massive broadsword, and the lighter sword Laurens had taught him—somewhat—to use. "Listen!" Laurens said. "If you can take him from his saddle, go over him. Then come back—I'll have the mace ready, and all you'll need do is smash his skull. He's better used to blade work than you, so try to avoid that. Just look to slay him, eh?"

Cullyn felt no wish to slay anyone, but it seemed he had no choice.

"The gods be with you," Eben said.

Laurens added, "Amen."

Then a trumpet sounded, shrilling into the morning, and Cullyn swung astride Fey. Eben and Laurens took the place of his squires, leading him to the tourney ground. He could see Lofantyl watching from the farther end, Abra at his side, clutching his arm. Both their faces were pale and intense, as if they'd no more taste for this combat than he. Isydrian, like Pyris, occupied a high seat midway along the path, which was warded by fences; a crowd of attendants lined the wicker walls. At each end of the ground there were six high lances set on frames, with shields beside, and all the other weapons that Cullyn thought looked too ponderous to wield. He found it hard to imagine swinging that dreadful mace against Afranydyr's skull. He wished he could avoid this combat.

Then Lyandra appeared, dressed in a gown of clinging white, took his hand, and handed him a scarf.

"Wear my favor, eh? For you are my champion, and after you've defeated that churl, we'll . . ." She smiled at him enticingly, and he felt his head swirl as he tucked her favor under his belt. He wondered again what he did—but then the trumpet sounded anew, and Lyandra set a foot to his stirrup and planted a kiss on his lips before she darted away. He was led reluctantly forward.

Eben handed him a shield that he fastened to his left arm. It was little more than a buckler, square-shaped and inwardly curved—intended to deflect a lance in formal joust. Eben whispered, "I've set what strength I can in this, but be careful."

Laurens passed him the lance, its tip pointed, the wood flaring out beyond the grip. He couched the farther end between ribs and elbow. And waited, his heart pounding as Fey stamped the grass, far more eager than Cullyn to attack.

Afranydyr appeared. He wore armor—a breastplate of polished black wood, pauldrons and greaves and vambraces, a helm fashioned like the face of the hawk he resembled, his eyes staring out above a hooked beak that was overhung with spread wings. The shape of a hawk was painted on his shield. He looked magnificent. And shouted a challenge as he took hold of his lance.

"No armor? Are you mad, Garm? I shall slay you—

save you surrender now. Surrender and I'll let you live. I'll take you for a servant—that's better than dying, no?"

Cullyn said, "No."

"He seeks to disconcert you," Laurens murmured.

"He's afraid of you," Eben whispered. "He knows you're syn'qui."

Afranydyr shouted: "Well? Shall you submit now, or must I slay you?"

"You're syn'qui," Eben said, "and you do what you must."

"Aim low," Laurens repeated. "Put your point in his gut, take the bastard off his saddle and kill him."

Cullyn said, "Shall we begin?"

❧❦❧

THEY DREW THEIR HORSES BACK and couched their lances. Pyris and Isydrian looked at one another and nodded. Each raised handkerchiefs; a trumpet sounded and the handkerchiefs dropped together. The combatants charged.

Cullyn drove his heels hard into Fey's ribs, for all the stallion needed no urging. He charged eagerly toward Afranydyr's mount, as if angered by this combat. Cullyn held his lance pointed as Laurens had taught him. Afranydyr crouched in his saddle, protected by shield and armor, his lance angled at Cullyn's shield.

Cullyn saw it coming and raised his own, so that both lances struck against the shields. He felt a tremendous shock run through his arm. It was far worse than the practice combats with Laurens. He felt his shield knocked aside and pain flash through his shoulder. He barely held on to his lance as he swerved Fey around before Afranydyr could recover, and found the farther end of the tourney ground and charged again.

Afranydyr had already brought his mount around, and had his shield up as Cullyn came toward him. They dashed at one another, Afranydyr crouched low in his saddle, protecting his body with the shield and his armor. Cullyn raised his own shield and wondered if he had done better to armor himself.

Then no time for thought: only the lance's point driving at him, and the impact of point on shield.

It was worse than before. Cullyn felt it through his entire body. He swayed backward in his saddle as splinters of broken wood flashed past his face and he felt his lance torn from his grip. Fey bucked under him and he barely held astride his saddle. He rode the stallion down the tourney ground with his opponent's laughter ringing dimly in his ears.

"Next turn I slay you, Garm!"

He reached the farther end and turned Fey to a prancing stop. Laurens threw him a fresh lance, that he caught from the air and couched, and charged again. It was only as he thundered toward Afranydyr that he realized his shield was broken, splintered by the Durrym's lance point. Briefly, he wondered if Eben was truly gifted. But . . .

Too late now to correct the mistake. He approached the Durrym and dropped his point as Laurens had advised. He wondered if it were honorable, and then Afranydyr's lance exploded through his shield and he saw splinters fly past his face as the world turned upside down and he realized in its spinning that he was pitched backward from his saddle.

He struck the ground and felt his breath smashed from his lungs. He tasted vomit in his mouth and smelled green grass and horse dung. He spat, which delivered him the taste of salty blood, and looked down at his torso. Afranydyr's point had gone in through his ribs, and when he took another gusty breath, he felt pain start through his side, and it seemed the world swung askew about him. He climbed panting to his feet. His side ached horribly, and his breath came thick past gobbets of dark and bloody phlegm. He saw his shirt colored and his shield was splintered, dangling uselessly from his arm: he tossed it aside. His ribs drove lances of pain into his side as he rose, and the tourney ground was misty and moving. The river and the trees and the pavilions swirled. And through the swirling, he dimly saw Afranydyr's armored bay charging toward him, his opponent couching his lance so that it drove into his unarmored, bleeding chest.

He staggered, weaving as the big horse came toward him, and he saw, in confused triple vision, the point of the lance that must surely pierce him, pick him up, pin him, and deliver him to death.

He had no defense, save the knife Lofantyl had gifted him. He drew it and prepared to meet his death.

Then Afranydyr's mount was smashed aside by Fey, turning Afranydyr's lance from Cullyn. The terrible impact flung the bay horse onto its side, pitching Afranydyr from the saddle. The Durrym fell trapped, the weight of his overturned horse pinning him to the ground. He bellowed curses as he raised his shield against Fey's stamping hoofs.

His head still spinning, Cullyn stumbled forward. His vision began to clear and he saw Fey rear up, screaming furiously, and smash his hooves down against the bay's ribs. The Durrym animal squealed as blood spurted from its nostrils and mouth. Its side was caved in. Fey bent and snapped teeth into the neck and shook the fallen horse as a terrier shakes a rat. Then reared again, preparing to strike Afranydyr.

The Durrym's shield was broken by the dreadful impact of the stallion's hoofs, bits and pieces of wood hanging from his upraised arm. He was still trapped by the body of his dead mount, and he could not draw his sword—for what good that might have done.

Cullyn forced himself to run, shouting at Fey.

"*No!* Leave him!"

The black stallion danced on his hind legs, the forelegs pawing air. Cullyn shouted again and Fey dropped, hooves crashing close to Afranydyr's face. He snapped his teeth a hand's span from Afranydyr's face and moved back, eyeing Cullyn as if disappointed.

Cullyn took his bridle and walked the stallion away. "Thank you." He stroked the velvet nose. "You saved my life. But now I must settle this."

Fey snorted and stared at him as if he were mad. His eyes and champing teeth said, Slay him and be done with it. Cullyn forced him back, stroking the neck now, smelling the exciting scent of horse sweat. He calmed the stallion and turned toward Afranydyr.

"Shall we leave this?" he asked. "I've no wish to slay you."

"No!" Afranydyr glowered at him, pride hot in his eyes. "Cede the combat to a Garm'kes Lyn? *Never!*"

"I only came here to bring Abra home," Cullyn said. "And now I'm not even sure of that."

"Cursed Garm," Afranydyr replied. "Do you think I want her? No, but my brother's stupid—in love with her."

"We can talk about that. We can talk about peace between Kash'ma and Ky'atha; between Kandar and Coim'na Drhu."

"*No!*"

Afranydyr heaved himself from under his dead mount and limped to where the weapons were racked. He picked up a broadsword. Cullyn said, "No!" even as the Durrym came toward him with the big sword circling above his head.

It whistled through the afternoon air, sunlight bright on the blade. Cullyn ducked under a decapitating swing and stepped away. His vision was returned now—no longer tripling—but his legs were unsteady, his stomach queasy. And he realized that his only weapon was the lyn'nha'thall Lofantyl had given him. He pressed a hand against his aching ribs and saw his fingers stained with blood. He saw Afranydyr bring the great blade back and danced away again as the blade cut air before his face, instinctively raising the lyn'nha'thall. It was smashed from his hand, the blade splintering as Afranydyr shouted from behind his hawk-featured helm, and raised the great sword again.

It seemed to Cullyn that the shattering of the friendship blade was a kind of symbol—as much as the giving. A gift from Lofantyl, it was earnest of *his* intent. That Afranydyr broke it so readily was indication of *his* intent. These brothers were very different: Cullyn might talk of peace with one, but with the other only of war. He fought Afranydyr only because the Durrym was blood-thirsty and proud, hating the Garm no less than so many Kandarians hated the Durrym—for no good reason that he could see. Yet here he was, locked in mortal combat simply to determine whether or not he be allowed to speak with Abra and find out if she wished to return home, or remain with Lofantyl. And perhaps from her decision broker some kind of peace.

He longed for peace even as he ducked under Afranydyr's great blade.

The sword whistled by his head. He felt hairs cut loose, raining on his face as he ran, as best he could, to the Zheit end of the tourney ground. It felt like swimming—his legs seemed to work only in slow motion as Afranydyr came after him, the broadsword raised to cut him down.

Laurens handed him a shield that he strapped to his

arm even as Afranydyr's blade came crashing down against the rack, hacking wood and sending weapons spilling in all directions. Cullyn grabbed the first he saw—a mace—and dropped and rolled as the broadsword came at him. It hacked into his shield, splinters falling loose as he fell down under the dreadful impact.

He tumbled over the grass as Afranydyr's blow landed on the sward. The force was such that the blade imbedded deep, and Cullyn had time to rise and swing the mace against the Durrym's helm.

A wing broke off and Afranydyr stumbled back. Cullyn raised his shield against Afranydyr's counter and swung again. His blow landed against the helmet and Afranydyr was knocked to his knees. Laurens shouted: "Slay him!"

Cullyn raised the mace in both hands, braced to bring the weight of it down against Afranydyr's damaged helmet. It would shatter the battered helm and the skull beneath and Afranydyr would lie dead and defeated before him. But it seemed without honor: he stepped back, lowering the heavy weapon as the Durrym rose. Dimly, he heard Laurens's snort of disgust, and Eben's weary sigh. From around the tourney ground there were shouts of approval and deprecation. He backed away as Afranydyr clambered to his feet and lofted the broadsword again.

Cullyn backed away from the swinging sword. "Can we not settle this?"

"With your death," Afranydyr snarled. And charged.

He was full-armored; Cullyn was not. The Durrym was protected, but Cullyn was more limber, even did his head still swim as if fishes danced inside his skull. It was a curious sensation, as if time slowed and he moved faster, indifferent to his fate as he watched the great sword cleave a path through the sunny air toward his head.

He ducked and swung the mace at Afranydyr's side as he raised his broken shield against the downswing of the broadsword.

He felt the wooden shield shatter, and a terrible pain lance his side. But Afranydyr was smashed away by his blow, stumbling back with the eyes Cullyn could see through the slits of the hawk's head helm opening wide in surprise and pain. Cullyn swung again, delivering a blow to the side of the helm that sent Afranydyr spinning away, his great blade waving wildly as he tottered back over the bloodied grass.

He shook his head and reached for the latchings of his dented helm. Tugged them loose and threw the thing aside, his visage furious as he stared at Cullyn.

"Now I shall slay you!"

He raised the broadsword.

Cullyn watched him, hefting the mace: no defense against so great a sword; and his opponent still armored, and he without a shield now. He was, he thought, about to die.

"Sword to sword!"

Laurens's shout broke his reverie. He flung the mace away and darted back to the weapons stand, where Laurens flung him a blade.

"Not the broadsword," the soldier said, "but faster. Duck his swings and cut him. Bring the bastard down with points and cuts—like I taught you."

Cullyn felt no wish to slay Afranydyr; not for all his temper with the recalcitrant Durrym. But Afranydyr was intent on killing him, so he took the sword and did as Laurens advised—and remembered his lessons.

Afranydyr swung his broadsword and Cullyn ducked, deflecting the blow, so that Afranydyr's cut passed over his head as he cut at the weakest points of the Durrym's armor.

He stuck his point between poleyn and greave, through the jointure of cuirass, and tasset, even as Afranydyr battered at him with his great sword. And all the time rolled and danced as the broadsword swung toward him and struck only empty earth.

The Durrym's armor became bloody. Cullyn's ribs hurt.

"Shall we not give this up?" he gasped.

Afranydyr snarled, "No!" And charged.

Cullyn ducked again under the broadsword's swing, and struck at his opponent's legs. Afranydyr toppled, falling onto his side. Cullyn set a boot on his great sword, pinning the blade to the ground, and set the point of his own blade against Afranydyr's throat.

"Shall you concede?"

Afranydyr cursed and shook his head. Cullyn looked up. He saw Eben and Lauren urging him to end the combat. Pyris and Mallandra stood with arms upraised, their thumbs pointed down. Lyandra clapped her hands.

"Do it," Afranydyr urged. "One blow, eh? I've been defeated by a Garm—to live on in disgrace? *No!*"

Cullyn said, "I can't."

"Then use that lyn'nha'thall my stupid brother gave you. Stick it between my ribs, Garm, and end my disgrace."

Cullyn said, "No, I cannot: you broke it."

"If you don't," Afranydyr returned viciously, "I shall dedicate my life to your destruction."

"Even so," Cullyn said, "I'll not slay you. So live."

"May all the gods damn you," Afranydyr spat.

Cullyn stared at the fallen Durrym, unsure of his next move. The easiest thing would be to simply lean on his sword and drive the blade through Afranydyr's neck. The easiest and the hardest, for he had no wish to take the warrior's life. But what else to do? Should he remove his point he'd no doubt at all that Afranydyr would rise and come at him again, and they fight to the death. And that, he thought, would surely confirm the enmity between Zheit and Shahn; between Kandar and Coim'na Drhu. He became aware of silence around him, as if all the world held its breath. It seemed that the birds had ceased their singing; even Fey stood silent. He looked to the pavilions and saw Pyris and Mallandra urging him to end the combat; Isydrian sat pale-faced, Lofantyl and Abra beside him, staring. Lyandra studied him with a quizzical expression, her lips pursed in a tight smile that he could not interpret.

He turned his gaze toward Eben and Laurens. The soldier clenched his fist, angling a thumb downward; the wizard shrugged and Cullyn saw his mouth shape words he could not hear, but guessed said, It's your choice.

Cullyn sighed, confused, then stepped back. "I'll not slay him," he cried, loud enough that all the company hear. "He fought honorably, and was honorably defeated. I grant him life."

Afranydyr mouthed curses; Isydrian shook his head, his face abruptly haggard, as if his son's survival were worse than his death. Lofantyl nodded, grinning in approval. Cullyn saw Lyandra's smile grow tighter.

Then Afranydyr clambered to his feet, clutching at the broadsword, hefting it in readiness to swing.

Isydrian bellowed, "No!" and the sword lowered, Afranydyr leaning on the hilt as if the blade were a crutch.

"Do you understand what you've done, Garm?"

Cullyn shook his head.

"You've taken my honor. I am your subject now."

"I'd not have subjects." Cullyn frowned, even more confused. "What do you say?"

"That I'm defeated in battle and you own my life, to command me as you will."

"Then I command you to live, and make peace with the Zheit. And that you have your wounds tended, and after we shall meet and speak of the future."

Afranydyr spat and nodded. "As you say." His voice was bitter.

They studied one another, still unsure. Then Eben shouted, "It's done!" and came to hold Cullyn up, with Laurens, even as Shahn came to escort Afranydyr to their pavilions.

Cullyn watched his opponent carried away, swaying on his feet. His side hurt suddenly in memory of his wounds. He took Lyandra's token from his belt and saw it all bloody. Then she came to him.

"Why did you not slay him? He'd have killed you."

He stared at this bloodthirsty virgin he loved and asked her, wearily, "Why should I? Better to make peace, no?"

"Better, indeed," Eben said, fixing Lyandra with his blue-eyed gaze, "that all be peace."

"Zheit and Shahn?" she returned. "Durrym and Kandar? You voice impossibilities, old man."

"Listen to the syn'qui, eh?" Eben smiled at Cullyn. "Listen to him, and follow his advice."

Cullyn coughed then, and blood came out of his mouth. Lyandra gasped and tenderly wiped his chin. He clutched his side, which hurt horribly, and the worse for Lyandra's arms about him.

"He needs healing," Eben declared.

"I need to speak with Lofantyl and Abra," Cullyn muttered through the heaviness that filled his mouth and throat. "We must . . ."

Then he could speak no more, because the world spun away and he felt terribly weary. He fell against Lyandra and saw her gown all stained with blood, which he supposed was his own. He was faintly aware of her voice calling out in alarm and of hands grasping him, but then it all went away into darkness.

SEVENTEEN

HE WOKE TO THE GLOW of candles, burning, the tent misty before his eyes, so that it took him a while to discern the shapes before him, even to feel the moistened cloth Lyandra pressed to his fevered brow. He forced his eyes to focus on her face and tried to smile, but his mouth seemed incapable of movement, and all that escaped his lips was a groan that he heard like some far-off echo uttered by another. He thought that Eben knelt beside her, and Laurens, and another figure he did not recognize. Then he slipped away again, into the darkness and the swirling dreams.

He fought Afranydyr again, save sometimes his opponent wore Lofantyl's face, or was Per Fendur. Sometimes he died; sometimes he was victorious. He saw Kandar and Coim'na Drhu join in battle, both lands wasted by the strife. He saw weeping women, Durrym and Kandarian both, and keeps and castles burning, wood reduced to ashes, stone to rubble. He wondered, in his fevered dreaming, if he wept.

Then light came and he opened his eyes again and raised his head.

"At last." The smile on Eben's mouth betrayed the wizard's stern tone. "We had wondered, you know."

"About what?" Cullyn saw Laurens, the soldier's arms easing him up against soft pillows, smiling fondly. Then Lyandra, clutching his hand, touching his face, tears on her cheeks.

"Whether you'd live."

"Why not?"

Eben chuckled. "You took some sore wounds—things broken, torn up, pierced. But Durrym healers are most efficient."

"Afranydyr?" Cullyn asked.

"Also lives, thanks to you. You had the right to slay him."

"I'd not slay anyone," Cullyn murmured as Lyandra brought a cup to his lips and urged him to drink the potion. It warmed and strengthened him, so he eased farther up against the pillows, for all it took both Lyandra and Laurens to aid him. "Not save I'm forced to it."

Eben nodded approvingly. "He's in little better condition: pricked and bled, and sorely wounded. Laurens taught you well."

Cullyn turned his face toward the soldier, which took an effort, for his head felt weighted and all his muscles weak. "Thank you."

"It was you, not me," Laurens said. "You fought a brave battle."

"And now?"

"You have the choice," Lyandra said, smiling as she

wiped his brow. "You own Afranydyr's life. You won a great victory. Do you not understand?"

He shook his head and wished he'd not, for the movement sent the faces spinning.

"You can dictate your own terms," he heard her say, echoed by Eben.

"You *own* Afranydyr's life. He must obey you, and through him, Isydrian. You can dictate a peace between the Zheit and the Shahn."

"And between Kandar and Coim'na Drhu?"

"Perhaps that, too. Isydrian is bound by honor to hear you out."

Cullyn was not sure who spoke. A mist closed over his mind and he felt weary. He watched the faces of the people he realized he loved grow dim. He felt a kiss— Lyandra's?—against his cheek, and went back into the darkness.

❧☙

CULLYN LED A SQUADRON into battle then, Durrym riding against Kandarians, and he unsure which side he supported. Per Fendur rode at the head, and was opposed by Lyandra, who rode a shining white unicorn that halted as the Kandarian arrows flew and was plucked from her mount. Lofantyl was there, and Abra, reaching down to lift him up and hand him to Eben and Laurens, even as he felt the same shafts as pierced Lyandra pierce him. They said together, Do what you must, and were echoed by Eben.

He woke sweaty and fevered, troubled by the strange dream. Was this what Eben meant, when the old man spoke of him being syn'qui?

He sat up and saw that Lyandra slept in a chair beside his bed, and Eben and Laurens snored loudly on the other couches. He saw a cup on a table beside him and found it contained water that he drank in copious drafts, gulping it down so that Lyandra woke and smiled at him, bright as the sun that rose beyond the confines of the pavilion.

"I need a bath," he said. "I feel dirty."

She put her arms around him, carefully, and said, "I'll bathe you, my love."

And eased him to his feet and ordered a tub be drawn, and washed him as might a servant, laughing at his blushes, and then helped him dress as Eben and Laurens woke. Then, laughing anew at his recovery, she brought the news to her parents.

❧❧

THE DUR'EM ZHEIT HAILED HIM as he entered the pavilion. They rose to their feet behind the long tables set down the length of the tent and shouted his name, clattering knives against goblets as he halted in confusion, staring nervously around. It was full night by now, but the pavilion shone bright from the silica globes that Cullyn now understood held glowworms. In his cottage it would have been firelight and tallow candles. In Lyth Keep it would have been smoky lanterns and blazing sconces. This was a brighter, more mellow light that matched the magnificence of the pavilion, as if the Durrym simultaneously lived in concord with nature and exploited it.

The floor was grass, but cropped short as any carpet and greener than any grass he'd seen, softer underfoot than rich wool. The tent was all silk and linen, its roof and walls fluttering softly in the gentle night breeze, panels of blue and gold and white. Down both sides ran tables of carved—or was it *taught*—wood, with high-

backed chairs behind, decorated with ornate inlays of
shells and stones and gems. And all the folk there on
their feet and hailing him.

At the farther end was a dais, a raised platform on
which was set a solitary table large enough to accommodate all who sat there. Pyris and Mallandra held the center, Lyandra on her father's left, Eben and Laurens
beyond her. Then Isydrian, with his sons beside, and
Abra, who sat with nervous visage as Lofantyl grinned
and Afranydyr scowled. The pavilion smelled of roasting
meat and rich wine, and Cullyn felt his head spin.

Then Pyris rose and came down the aisle between
the tables, bringing Lyandra with him, and Mallandra,
one to either side in formal procession. He held their
hands and halted before Cullyn. The pavilion fell silent,
anticipatory.

Cullyn waited, wondering what transpired, and
nervous.

Then Lyandra's father said formally, "I am Pyris of
Ky'atha Hall, Vashinu of the Dur'em Zheit. You delivered us a great victory, for which I thank you. You defeated Afrandyr of Kash'ma Hall, champion of the
Dur'em Shahn, and won us much respect. I am obliged
to you."

He bowed; Cullyn gaped. Then he saw Eben motion-
ing to him that he return the gesture of respect, and
ducked his head.

Pyris beamed and said, "You have set a mighty geas
on the Shahn. You now own Afranydyr's life, so they
cannot attack us again so long as you are with us."

Cullyn wondered what such a geas might be, but—
perhaps learning diplomacy—he said only, "I am happy
to have pleased you."

"More than me," Pyris returned. "You've pleased my
daughter, and she'd wed you—even though you be

Garm'kes Lyn." There was a measure of doubt in his voice, but even so he swung Lyandra forward toward Cullyn, who instinctively took her hand. She smiled at him, and he knew he loved her.

But still wondered what future they might have together.

"And I approve," Pyris said. At his side, Mallandra said, "And I." Then Pyris asked, "How say you, Cullyn of Kandar?"

Cullyn hesitated a moment as he wondered where this might lead him. Then he looked into Lyandra's eyes and felt all his doubts dissolve, and said, "Yes."

The hall erupted once more as the Zheit lifted goblets and shouted his name and Lyandra's. She pressed against him and kissed him and whispered, "The unicorns shall be dangerous after we're wed."

He blushed and took her hand as her parents escorted them formally toward the high table. He saw Laurens there, smiling his approval, and Eben with an expression of satisfaction on his aged face. Lofantyl smiled his approval, as did Abra. Isydrian sat stark-featured, and Afranydyr, beside his father, glowered.

Cullyn was abruptly aware that the shouts of approval and the raising of cups had come from the Zheit, not the Shahn, who sat sullen and defeated at the feast.

He stepped to the dais, pausing a moment behind Afranydyr to touch the Durrym's shoulder and ask, "Are you healed?"

Afranydyr scowled through a proud smile. "Well enough."

"I'd make peace," Cullyn said. "I'd not have you for an enemy."

"You shall not," Isydrian interjected. "You defeated my son—the champion of the Shahn—and now you may dictate your own terms."

When first Cullyn had seen the Durrym lord he had looked young—even were he Eben's father—but now he appeared aged, his eyes avoiding Cullyn's as he studied his older son.

He glanced at Pyris and sighed. "We must discuss this. Does the Garm understand?"

Cullyn took his seat, not properly understanding.

Lyandra whispered, "Dictate your terms."

Pyris said, "The Garm? Does he not own a name—especially now?"

"Cullyn of Kandar." Isydrian's voice rang hollow. "Or is it now Cullyn of Ky'atha Hall?"

The Zheit voiced approval of that latter title, and Cullyn felt Lyandra's hand squeeze his. He stared out at the tented hall and saw the Shahn imitating smiles that offered neither approval nor humor.

"What's expected of me?" he asked Lyandra.

Lyandra answered, "A decision."

He turned to Eben for answers, and the wizard quit his own chair to kneel by Cullyn's and whisper in his ear, "You defeated Afranydyr in honest battle—now you own his life and can dictate your own terms. You can take him for a slave—"

"No."

"Or bind him to peace; him and Isydrian, both."

"That should be better." Cullyn felt decision fill him. It was as if he were a flask that until now had not been properly topped. Now he *knew* what he must say, albeit he did not yet understand where the words came from. Only that they burst from him. He rose to his feet and stared at the gathering. "I defeated Afranydyr, who is a great warrior."

There was a shout of acclamation from the Zheit, a reluctant nodding of agreement from the Shahn.

"And I'd wed Lyandra of Ky'atha Hall, just as Lofantyl of Kash'ma would wed Abra of Lyth Keep."

The pavilion fell silent then, murmurs running like waves down the tables, like the sea rushing over pebbles that clashed together under the impact. Cullyn looked to Pyris and Mallandra and said, "I am honored that your daughter would consider me for a husband. I am honored that *you* consider me suitable." He looked to Lofantyl. "How say you?"

"That we are friends." Lofantyl rose, still holding Abra's hand. "That when I went into your Kandarian lands I found a true friend, and a true love."

Afranydyr scowled, and his father sat blank-faced.

"So let us wed," Cullyn declared, wondering at his presumption. Was this what it meant to be syn'qui? "I shall marry Lyandra, and Lofantyl shall marry Abra." He paused. "And Zheit and Shahn shall make peace." He stared, surprised by his confidence, at Pyris and Isydrian. "How say you?"

Pyris nodded. "I'd not see us go to war. I agree."

Isydrian scowled and shook his head.

"There are further terms," Cullyn announced. "You are Eben's father, and I'd see you make peace with him."

"No!" Isydrian muttered.

"Then I claim Afranydyr's life."

"You cannot!"

"By right of combat, I can."

Isydrian gusted a windy sigh. "As you say." His face collapsed into deeper wrinkles. "Name your terms."

"Acknowledge Eben as your son, and make peace with the Zheit."

Isydrian nodded reluctant agreement. "What else?"

"That we all speak with Lord Bartram, and forge some kind of peace with Kandar."

Both hall lords stared at him then, as if he were mad. "It can be done," he said, wondering where his confidence came from, aware that Laurens wore the same expression as the Durrym.

And Eben smiled as if all his dreams had come true.

"Now swear the peace," Cullyn said. "You two embrace and declare it—that Zheit and Shahn no longer fight, but live together."

He went to where Afranydyr sat scowling and set his hands on the Durrym's shoulders. "I name this man my brother, as Lofantyl is. Do you accept?"

Afranydyr sat a while, uncomfortable beneath Cullyn's grip. Then ducked his head in reluctant agreement.

Lofantyl clapped his hands in accord. "Well done, my Garm brother!"

Abra kissed his hand. "Thank you."

Lyandra took it and kissed his lips. "You are truly syn'qui."

Eben murmured, "It's not done yet. There's still Per Fendur to think of."

"And," Lyandra added, "our wedding."

EIGHTEEN

TIME MOVES LIKE A RIVER. Sometimes it rushes forward, as if in spate; at others there are eddies, swirling sideways to slow and revolve in backwaters. Time was different in Coim'na Drhu and Kandar: men and Durrym danced to different rhythms. So it was that Cullyn and his companions might live for weeks in the fey lands even as Per Fendur and his defeated company made their way back across the Alagordar to deliver their news to Lord Bartram.

The priest was not pleased with defeat.

"Your daughter is kidnapped by the filthy Durrym. Taken captive into the fey lands! Can you allow that?"

Per Fendur's voice rang harsh and the feasting hall, already glum, fell silent. Lord Bartram stroked his gray beard and thought a while. Vanysse stared at her husband even as she found Amadis's hand and clutched it tight.

"It's sacrilege," Fendur continued angrily. "And not only your daughter, but also the heretics—Laurens, the forester called Cullyn, and Eben the wizard. We must hunt them down!"

"To what end?" Bartram asked.

"That they be put to the questioning."

"Torture, you mean."

"If necessary."

Bartram sighed and turned his eyes from the priest's cold black glare to study his wife. She smiled agreement, and beside her he saw Amadis grin. He wondered, suddenly, what fate they had planned for him, these three conspirators. Fendur and Amadis he thought he understood: they desired power. But Vanysse? The gods knew that Khoros had sent her to him as a bride to bind the south and the Border together, but he'd loved her—and even thought that she loved him, despite the difference in their ages. He'd not argued her affair with Amadis. He acknowledged that he was too old to satisfy so young and lusty a woman, and had turned a blind eye, content to have her with him. But now it seemed she turned against him.

He asked her, "What do you think I should do, wife?"

"Follow Per Fendur's advice," she said. "Would you not have your daughter back?"

He suddenly wondered where her true allegiance lay, and if some deep plan rested behind her words.

"We must go across the Barrier." It was Fendur who spoke now, Vanysse and Amadis nodding their agreement. "We must go in force and bring Abra back. Her and the others."

"And you believe such an expedition is possible?"

"You know," the priest said, "that I can find a way. I did before."

"And were sent running."

Fendur's sallow face darkened. "I had only a squadron of horsemen then. And even so it was a narrow fight." He looked to Amadis for confirmation and got back a nod of deceitful agreement. He did not hear Drak, seated amongst the soldiery, snort laughter. "Give me enough men and I'll bring your daughter back."

"To the Church's questioning?"

"Perhaps not her," Fendur replied. "But the others . . ."

"And you believe this possible? That we might bring Abra home?"

"Do you cede me enough men."

"I'll cede you all of them," Lord Bartram returned, "if I can speak with Abra again and know what *she* desires."

In his lust for conquest Fendur missed the inflection. "Then we go," he said. "When?"

"Two days to organize," Bartram answered. "That many to provision."

"And you'll ride with us?" Fendur glanced at Amadis.

"Of course," Lord Bartram said. And to himself: to discover *her* wish.

❧❦❧

"I NEVER THOUGHT I'd want to live here," Abra told Lofantyl. "I was taught that you fey folk were strange— our enemies."

"And now?" He took her hand, hopeful of her reply.

"I think not. I think that we Kandarians are *your* enemies." She frowned. "This lust for conquest troubles me. You'd not overcome Kandar, eh?"

He shook his head. "We're happy here. The land favors us, and gifts us with ever stronger magic, so why should we want to go back? Besides, we are far fewer in numbers than you Garm; should it come to war, you'd outnumber us."

They strolled beside the river, where the water babbled merrily and fat trout jumped at dancing, unwary flies. Abra looked about her and saw what he meant: this was a green and pleasant land, where folk lived in accord with the terrain. Save for the halls' rivalries.

"Shall your father and brother accept Cullyn's ruling?"

Lofantyl nodded. "All well."

"You sound doubtful, my love."

Lofantyl brought her to a place where willows draped massive limbs over the benches of the river. They were so large their central trunks had split to drape the great branches to the ground, providing comfortable seating. They took places on a down-swinging limb and watched the water go by. A blur of bright color that was a kingfisher flashed by, chased by another as if the birds gamed, or flew some avian ballet.

Then Lofantyl chuckled, shrugging, and added: "I do not much trust my father or my brother." He laughed. "I never got on with either of them, much."

"But Cullyn's sworn them to peace, no?"

"Perhaps . . ." He turned his eyes toward the river. "I hope it be so, but is it not . . ." He looked at her, fear and honesty in his gaze. "If it is not, what shall you choose?"

"To stay with you."

"Even does it come to war with your father?"

Abra swung toward him, cradled by the willow's branch and his knees, his hands on her shoulders, and said, "Yes. I pray it does not come to that, but if I must make a choice, then it shall be to stay with you. I love you."

Lofantyl said, fervently, "Thank you."

❦❦❦

"SHALL IT WORK? Can it work?"

Cullyn held Lyandra close as they stared out over the river, unaware that Lofantyl and Abra did the same. The sun was setting now, fading like some vast smiling face toward the horizon, the sky painted all red where the smile decorated the clouds and the blue that announced the rising of the moon. To the east, past the forest beyond which lay Kandar, it was a velvet blue, a sickle moon lofting, accompanied by courtier stars. A breeze blew fresh, but warm, and he felt Lyandra's body heated against his. A squadron of geese beat westward toward the setting sun, its honking musical as the instruments that played in the Durrym encampment. He watched as the V-shaped flight westered, and in a way wished he might join them—to fly away careless. But Lyandra's hand was warm in his, and her body soft as his grew hard, so he watched the geese fly away and kissed her cheek.

"You're syn'qui," she said, "so I suppose it shall."

"Peace between Ky'atha and Kash'ma; between Kandar and Coim'na Dhru?"

"Perhaps, if you govern it."

"*Govern* it?" he stuttered. "What can I govern?"

"The world's fate," she answered. "Now kiss me, eh?"

There were times, he thought, that it was best to obey.

❦❦❦

"WHAT IN THE GODS' NAMES is going on?" Laurens asked Eben. "We came here to fetch Abra back. I understood that, but now . . . ? What are we—emissaries or prisoners?"

Eben grinned at the soldier, settling himself more comfortably on the couch. "Do you really want to go back?"

Laurens frowned.

"Back to your barracks in Lyth? Is the food better there, the wine? Is that cold keep warmer than this tent?" Eben gestured at their confines. "Is your bed softer? Is the company so fine?"

Laurens shook his head, grunting as he filled a glass. "I'm sworn to Lord Bartram's service. What's comfort to do with it?"

"Much, I think." Eben stretched his legs down the length of his own couch and fell back against the pillows. "In Kandar I lived as an outcast. You know what happened to my cottage, and likely Cullyn's, too."

"Even so," Laurens grumbled.

"Even so," Eben answered, "consider the advantages. Cullyn is to wed Lyandra, and we are, in a way, his liege men. Lofantyl shall wed Abra, and Kash'ma and Ky'atha Halls swear peace. Perhaps even Kandar and Coim'na Drhu, does the syn'qui succeed."

"He's but a lad," Laurens returned, "and I'm a soldier."

"Would you see peace forged?"

Laurens nodded.

"Then trust me," Eben said. "And him. He knows not what he does, but the power's in him, and I place *my* trust in that."

"And Per Fendur?"

"Shall be defeated."

"And even if he is, then shall the Church not send another?"

"Perhaps, but if the Zheit and the Shahn can be brought to peace, then perhaps so can Kandar and Coim'na Drhu. It's at least a start."

"Perhaps." Laurens sighed and poured himself more wine. "I leave these ponderings to such as you. I'm only a simple soldier."

Eben chuckled. "You're hardly simple, my friend."

"Where is he, anyway?" Laurens wondered.

"Walking with his love," Eben replied. "What else would a young man do on his wedding eve?"

Laurens laughed obscenely.

❧❀❧

IT WAS A CURIOUSLY SIMPLE ceremony for a folk so given to display.

Pyris himself came to Cullyn's tent and asked, formally, for permission to enter. That granted, he asked if Cullyn was ready—would he attend in a hour? The suitor was—for the last few hours, nervously. He was dressed in the outfit Pyris had gifted him: a shirt of soft white linen with golden embroidery about the collar and cuffs, surmounted with a tunic of green dark as oak leaves in high summer, and all stitched with silver thread around the edgings. Breeches of dark blue fit almost embarrassingly snug, and slid into knee-high boots of white deerskin. A leather belt was chased with gold and silver, and equipped with an ornate sheath for his shattered lyn'-nha'thall. Servants had come to shave him and dress his hair, and he had never felt so much the popinjay.

Or been so much laughed at, for Eben and Laurens had taken much pleasure in commenting on his outfit, albeit they were little less splendid. Eben's ancient robe had been washed and mended, restitched where cabalistic symbols had disappeared under the weight of time. He had even allowed his beard to be trimmed and his own hair washed, so that now he looked like a true wizard. Almost, Cullyn thought, regal.

And Laurens had shaved himself and let a servant crop his hair even shorter. He had accepted a white linen shirt and a blue tunic, breeches of matching blue, and boots like Cullyn's. He wore a weaponless belt, and seemed uncomfortable for the absence.

"In the names of all the gods," he grunted when the barbers were done, "I smell like a whore."

It was true that perfumes had been washed into their hair and unguents applied to their skin, but Cullyn wondered if they did not smell better than any time since leaving Ky'atha Hall. Nonetheless, he paced the confines of the tent plucking at his finery, aware that in his wake he left a trail of scent unlike his usual smell of must and leaf mold.

Eben said, "It shan't last long. Before the day's out you'll stink of wine. And then"—with a sidelong glance at Laurens—"we'll be on the road again and you'll smell as usual."

"Do I smell?" Laurens filled a goblet with the rich Durrym wine.

"Do horses drop road apples?" Eben extended a goblet that Laurens filled.

"When shall we leave?" Cullyn asked.

"In due course." Eben stroked his fresh-washed beard as if he could not quite believe it so clean. "The Durrym have less sense of time than you—they'll likely celebrate for a week or more. This is a momentous event."

"It's my wedding," Cullyn muttered, wondering if his breeches were indecently tight.

"It's the marriage of Garm to Durrym." Eben drank more wine, carefully, a hand covering his beard that he not spill on its pungent silkiness. Cullyn could not help smiling, for all his nervousness. "You to Lyandra, Lofantyl to Abra. This is such an event as has never before happened. This is a turning point for the world."

Cullyn groaned. More ominous talk of fate and destiny. "Where shall we live?" he asked.

"Abra with Lofantyl, in Kash'ma Hall," Eben replied. "You and Lyandra, where you choose."

"I can't take her back to the cottage—even if it still stands. She's accustomed to better accommodation. And . . ." He frowned. "There's still Per Fendur."

"Who shall be dealt with," Eben said calmly. "One way or the other."

"And those ways are?"

"Worry about that later." He drank more wine. "You're syn'qui: you shape destiny."

Cullyn shook his head and took up a goblet, drained it in one long gulp, and looked to Laurens.

"How say you? You came into all this in my defense, would you go back?"

Laurens paused before answering, downed a goblet of the rich red wine, and then shook his head.

"Save Lord Bartram demands it, no. I've thought this over and decided I've no love of that priest or Amadis. I'd as soon stay here—Coim'na Drhu seems a most pleasant country, so why go back?"

Eben chuckled.

Laurens ignored him, continuing: "I threw in my lot with you, and I believe this old man"—he shaped an obscene gesture in Eben's direction—"is wise. So I'll stay here so long as you remain."

"And if I don't?"

"Then I'll follow after. You need someone to watch your back."

"Well said!" Eben clapped his hands. "Even syn'qui need bodyguards."

Cullyn ceased his nervous pacing, staring at them, knowing he had true friends with him. He took their hands. "Thank you."

❧❧❧❧

PYRIS CAME AGAIN.

He wore a black shirt topped with a long tunic of white trimmed with silver embroidery and pale fox fur. His breeches were white and his boots black as deepest midnight. His long hair was gathered in a tail by a knot of oak leaves, and Cullyn thought he had not seen so splendid a figure as Pyris bowed formally and asked, "Are you ready?"

Cullyn gulped down the last of his wine and nodded.

Pyris smiled and reached beneath his shirt to extract a package that he extended to Cullyn. "I'd give you this."

Cullyn unwrapped the parcel and found himself holding a magnificent knife, sheathed in a no-less splendid scabbard. The hilt was ivory—a unicorn's horn, he suspected—the quillons fashioned from some golden wood he did not recognize that matched the inlay of the butt. The blade was long and wickedly pointed, fashioned from stone or wood—he could not tell—but sharp on both edges, with a fuller running from tip to choils. It was the finest knife he had ever seen, far better than the one Lofantyl had gifted him. He stared at it, turning it in the light.

"It's superb."

He stared at Pyris, who said, "No more than you deserve. That lyn'nha'thall Lofantyl gave you broke in defense of Zheit honor. This will not. I fashioned it myself, and it marks our bond."

Cullyn heard Eben gasp, and from the corner of his eye saw the ancient wizard's smile grow wider. He sensed a tremendous honor was done him and ducked his head and sheathed the wonderful blade. "You do me too much honor, Lord Pyris."

"No more than you deserve." The Durrym smiled. "Now, shall you and your spokesmen follow me?"

Cullyn wondered why his mouth was so dry and his knees so weak as he went after Pyris. Eben and Laurens came after, their faces grave, as befit the ceremony.

Outside stood an escort of Zheit warriors, and beyond them, waiting, a similar squadron of Shahn, surrounding Lofantyl, who grinned and waved at Cullyn. He seemed far less nervous, and far more splendidly dressed in a tunic of oaken color above a shirt that seemed sewn from gold, so that it shimmered as he moved, belted over breeches of dawn's dark blue, and boots of pale hide that were akin to the sun's rising.

"Do we not both look splendid?" he called. "Who could not love us?"

Then stilled his smile as his father glowered.

Afranydyr stood beside Isydrian, and both their faces were blank, devoid of any expression save, perhaps, doubt or disapproval. Or resignation.

"Shall we go on?" Pyris asked Isydrian.

"We go on," Isydrian said. "Honor binds us. You dictate the terms."

Pyris ducked his head. Afranydyr scowled at Cullyn.

"Beware that one," Laurens whispered, "for he'll put a blade between your shoulders does he find the chance."

"He'd be slain for that," Eben murmured, "for Durrym honor."

"Even so." Laurens glowered at Afranydyr. "I'd not trust him."

"Do you trust anyone?"

"You," Laurens answered, "and Cullyn. Lord Bartram. Otherwise, no."

Cullyn ignored their bickering as he strode with his escort amongst the colorful pavilions. Folk came out to cheer him on his way, and also Lofantyl. They sang, and plucked on stringed instruments, or banged gongs, or shook rattling drums, so that all the morning was filled up with sound, and birds took shrilling flight from the trees and the gurgling of the river was overcome by the sounds of celebration.

❧❦❧

THEY CAME TO THE GREATEST PAVILION. It was tented in pale blue, like dawn's rising or the sun's setting. Men of the Zheit and the Shahn stood about the entrance, bearing spears and shields in honor, and behind them it seemed that all the Durrym women and their children were gathered, singing their approval of this odd double marriage.

Pyris led Cullyn into the tent, Isydrian bringing Lofantyl.

Lyandra and Abra waited for them, at the high table set at the end of the pavilion.

Cullyn gasped as he saw Lyandra. Her hair was taken up in a pile decorated with pearls and silvery filigree, a silver chain around her slender neck, from which was suspended a green gem that matched the color of her clinging gown. She was smiling demurely, and Cullyn felt his heart lurch.

Beside him, he heard Lofantyl gasp, and saw that Abra looked no less lovely. Save his eyes were fixed entirely on Lyandra, who was, he decided in that moment and all the others he'd seen her, the most desirable woman in the world. His or hers: Kandar or Coim'na Drhu, it made no difference. He loved her.

He bent his knee, unbidden, not knowing what ceremony was demanded, but only asking: "Shall you wed me?"

Her answer was firm: "Yes."

The crowd gasped as Durrym tradition was over-turned. Then gasped again as Lofantyl followed Cullyn's example and knelt before Abra, and asked, "And shall you wed me?"

Abra lowered her head and said, softer than Lyandra, but no less surely, "Yes."

"This is not how it's done," Isydrian muttered. "This is not the proper way."

"Times change," Pyris murmured. "Shall you argue it now?"

Isydrian sighed and shook his head. Both bride-grooms rose, grinning at one another, and were escorted onward.

They halted before the high table from which Lyandra and Abra stepped down to face their suitors. Pyris took a blue cloth woven with gold thread from his tunic; Isydrian did the same. Pyris took Lyandra's right hand in his and held it out. Unthinking, Cullyn took her hand, and Pyris wound the ribbon about their wrists.

"Do you wed?" he asked. "Do you take you each to be one, in bed and life, forever?"

Before Cullyn could speak, Lyandra said, "I do."

Cullyn was aware of Pyris's bright blue eyes on him and nodded. "I do."

He was faintly aware of Abra and Lofantyl exchang-ing the same simple vows. But mostly he was aware of Lyandra's smile and the promise that rested in her eyes.

And then of the shouting that filled the pavilion, a great explosion of acclaim that seemed to come from all of them, Zheit and Shahn together, as cups were banged on the long tables and all stood in toast and approval. It was as if a war had ended and the combatants celebrated.

He wondered what he should do next, and was grate-ful for Lyandra's hand in his, and Pyris's on his shoulder as they guided him to the high table.

Mallandra sat there, beaming, her chair to Pyris's left. Cullyn was seated beside her, Lyandra to his left, Eben and Laurens beyond her. Isydrian sat to Pyris's right, with Lofantyl and Abra at his side, and then Afranydyr, still sullen-faced.

Pyris rose, holding a cup of blue glass set round with ivory tracework, and gestured that Isydrian join him. The Shahn lord rose slower, still reluctant. Pyris set a hand on Isydrian's shoulder and raised his cup, smiling.

"We celebrate a great occasion. Such a thing as has never been seen before. Peace is made between Zheit and Shahn. Durrym weds Garm'kes Lyn. Perhaps even peace with Kandar. Is that not worth a feast?"

He embraced Isydrian as the pavilion exploded in approval.

Cullyn laughed and turned to Lyandra. She kissed him, but when he opened his eyes he saw Afranydyr staring at him, past Lofantyl and Abra embracing, and felt a chill.

Then the feasting began, Pyris and Isydrian urging their people to the tables, and the food was such as Cullyn had never tasted before, not even in Ky'atha Hall. There were rich soups composed of fish or meat or vegetables; hot bread basted in honey or garlic; fried fish golden in their coating of crumbs and herbs; succulent steaks and roasted fowls; whole hares, spit-roasted; venison burned over fires or served in sauces that plucked at his tongue.

It was a magnificent banquet, accompanied by far more wine than he was used to. He felt his head swim and clutched at Lyandra.

"Shall we find our bed, wife?"

She smiled and asked, "Are you ready?"

"I might disappoint you. I think I've drunk too much, but even so . . ."

"Let's find out, eh?"

They rose and all the folk in the pavilion rose with them, and Cullyn was vaguely aware that Lofantyl and Abra also rose and quit the tent, with smiles and laughter and shouts of approval.

Laurens clapped him on the back and said, "Well done, and do it better now," and settled back laughing.

"I wish you well," was all Eben said.

"You'll not come back to the tent tonight?" Cullyn asked.

And Lyandra clutched his hand tighter and said, "We've our own pavilion now we're wed. Come see it, eh?"

Drunkenly, Cullyn took her hand and followed her into the night.

It was alive with song and laughter, drums and guitars and zithers, playing approving hymns to their jointure.

Lyandra brought him to a tent that was stained blue on all its edges save the canopy, which was purest white.

"The wedding tent," she said, and brought him inside.

It was a simple canopy, but spread with luxuriant rugs across the floor, a wide bed at the center, covered with linen sheets and exotic furs. There was a brazier on which was set a kettle of mulled wine.

Cullyn gaped, and Lyandra said, "Come to bed, my husband."

He obeyed.

NINETEEN

❧❧❧

L ORD BARTRAM SIGHED as his armor was buckled on. It had been a long time since he was engaged in battle, and the armor fit tighter now, crushing the bulges of his body so that he must suck in his belly and feel his face grow red, and wish it had not come to this. It was both an irritation and an embarrassment that his daughter had fled the keep with Lofantyl, as well as concern for her well-being. He cared for Abra. She was his only child, daughter of his long-dead wife, and he wondered how she fared. But he felt that if she had chosen to go with the Durrym, then she knew her own mind—and it should be no bad thing to see Lyth Keep allied by marriage (if that was what Lofantyl planned) to the Durrym hold. If it were other than that— he gasped as the bucklings of his armor were drawn tighter—then he'd deliver such vengeance on the seducer as would leave him unmanned and dead.

But still, he wished none of it had happened.

He sheathed his great sword and decided that he would ask Abra what she wanted—and did she choose to remain with the Durrym, then so be it. But meanwhile he was committed to this expedition; he had no other choice. He had sooner sent emissaries, but Per Fendur denied him that right, and he began to wonder who ruled in Lyth Keep now.

So he went out into the yard where his charger waited, trying not to pant as the armor pressed against him, his wife seemingly dutiful at his side. Vanysse brushed his cheek with her lips. "Farewell, husband. Bring our daughter back, eh?"

And then she was gone, smiling at Amadis. And Bartram thought, Our daughter? Surely only mine, for you've no great love for her.

Then he set foot to stirrup and two servants came to help him mount, and he swung astride his charger, which snapped and bucked somewhat because they'd not ridden out in too long, and Bartram suddenly felt a wild excitement that he'd not known in too many years of ease and prosperity. He was unsure what faced him, but he felt alive, younger—and that some great decision was soon to be made. So he took the reins and eased his prancing mount to the head of the column.

Amadis and Per Fendur sat there, the one in splendid, golden armor, the other in black, surmounted by a flowing cloak. Amadis carried a lance, Fendur a broadbladed knife and no other weapons save his magic. Bartram swung his horse before them.

"I command this sortie, and you shall obey me, eh?" They ducked their heads, but their eyes gave back other answers. "So let us go find Abra, but heed me—we parley first. I'll not foment a war if it can be avoided."

He gestured that the gates be opened and they thun-

dered down the road to Lyth and beyond, through the
village and across the fields toward the forest that, across
the Alagordar, hid Coim'na Drhu.

❧❧❧

"THE GODS KNOW but these Durrym hold fine
feasts." Laurens lay back, rubbing at his belly and belch-
ing as he stared at the sky. "Where's Cullyn?"

"Where do you think?" Eben rested against a down-
hung willow branch. "Where do you think Abra and
Lofantyl are?"

Laurens chuckled and poured himself more wine.
"Oh, old man, to be young again, eh?"

"With all youth's problems?" Eben shook his head.
"It's hard enough to grow old and find there are still problems."

"But we're surely settled, no?" Laurens rose on an elbow, that he might see Eben's eyes. "We remain with
Cullyn in this handsome land, liege men to the syn'qui."

"Save for the priest," Eben replied. "I doubt he'll give
up his pursuit."

"Across the Barrier? He'll surely be confused."

"He came across before."

"And was driven back. I doubt he'll attempt it
again."

"Perhaps, but keep your sword sharp."

❧❧❧

"HERE; WE CAN CROSS HERE."

Per Fendur indicated the ford and heeled his mount
into the river.

The water was shallow, spraying up light sparkling
waves beneath his mount's hooves. Amadis followed

him, and then Lord Bartram, and the warriors of Lyth
lancers and swordsmen and archers, as great a force as
had crossed the Barrier since the wars.

The priest halted on the farther bank and looked
around, sniffing the air, then pointed and said, "This
way," and they rode into Coim'na Drhu. Across the
Alagordar—the Barrier that was no longer a barrier to
the priest's magic.

Lord Bartram felt his skin prickle as Fendur brought
the war band on into the deceiving woodlands across the
river, into the forest beyond the banks, and then deeper
to where new and ancient trees grew together, willows
and oaks and birches and hazels all combined in impossible gatherings, with meadows filled with grass between
and strange creatures watching them from the edge of
the woods. But the priest rode on confidently, aware of
the power rested in him. He could *see* the way. He knew
as does a scented hound, where the prey had gone. And
he would track it down.

But that was for another day.

This night a thin moon hung over Coim'na Drhu, a
judging sickle, and the air grew chill as a wind blew up
from off the river, so they made camp, hacking down
trees to make their fires, setting up their tents and settling for the night. They built their fires high, ignoring
fear of Durrym magic to find protection against the creatures that surrounded them, which were unfamiliar and
strange.

Lord Bartram sat before a blazing fire, listening to the
rustle of odd wings that flapped across the starlit sky. He
wondered if the shape he saw flitting past the sickle
moon was a dragon, or some gigantic bat. Sometimes
they hovered above the Kandarians' fire, and he wondered if they carried messages back to the Durrym. Crows
cawed from the trees, and faces showed from the under-

growth and brushwood, horned and fanged, sometimes like vast bears, at others like enormous serpents that hissed a warning.

Go back!

Per Fendur stalked the perimeter of the camp, voicing incantations about each watchfire, assuring the guards that all was well, that they were engaged in holy quest—to bring back Abra and defeat the Durrym.

"What do you think?" Bartram asked Amadis. Less from interest than want of conversation to fill the frightening darkness. "Shall we succeed?"

"I place my faith in the Church," Amadis replied. But his eyes were fixed on the rustling night. "Per Fendur guides us."

"To what?"

"To bringing your daughter back."

"And should she not wish to come back?"

"What choice has she?"

"We all have choices." Bartram faced his wife's lover. "Abra, hers; you, yours; me, mine."

"What do you say, my lord?"

"That there must be a deciding," Bartram answered. "And soon. I cannot let this go on."

"I do not understand," Amadis said, protesting innocence.

Bartram returned, "You shall, soon enough."

And then great wings flapped above them and great dark shapes filled the sky, so low that their passage gusted the fires into spiraling sparks that rose up and were then driven down by the slapping of the leathery wings.

Amadis crouched, brushing embers from his tunic. Bartram laughed and said, "I think they know we're coming."

And Per Fendur returned from his inspection and said, "Tomorrow, eh? They know we're here, but do we

travel by night, below the trees where these beasts cannot find us, we shall find them and deliver them the
Church's justice."

✤❧❦✤

CULLYN WOKE from contented sleep to the pounding
of Lyandra's fists. "What is it?" He rubbed lazily at his eyes

"An alarm!" She shook his head. "Wake up!"

"What?"

"Can you not hear?"

He raised himself, preferring to put his arms around
her again and go back to sleep.

"Get dressed! And quickly."

He sat up and heard the muffled beating of great
wings, a squealing in the sky. Lyandra was already tugging
on her clothes. She flung him his.

"And wear that knife my father gave you, and a
sword."

"I don't understand," he muttered, even as he tugged
on his breeches and buckled up his belt. The urgency of
her tone disturbed him. "What is this?"

"A warning!" She was already dressed in the motley
leathers he'd first seen her in, a blade at her side, her hair
put up beneath that boyish cap. "Come, hurry."

✤❧❦✤

"I MUST GO." Lofantyl kissed Abra and rose from
their bed. "There's peril coming for both of us."

No less aware than Cullyn, she asked, "What peril?"

"I've not the time to explain," he said. "Trust me, eh
And stay safe. Go across the river if you must, and I'l
find you later."

And then, fastening his shirt, his sword belt flapping about his knees, he was gone.

❧❧❧

OVER THE RIVER VALLEY where the water ran in satisfied confusion vast bats and winged serpents beat heavily against the moonlit sky. The trout ducked down, seeking refuge. The bats and dragons howled their warnings and winged away, their task done.

Cullyn came stumbling from his pavilion, still fixing his clothing, Lyandra at his side, and saw Pyris, armored, staring at the western ridge.

Isydrian came to them, and Afranydyr, both armored, and all their men with them in various states of disarray, some barely dressed, others in half their armor, some in full battle kit, others naked save for shields and swords, or lances or bows.

"What is it?" Isydrian asked.

"An attack," Pyris answered.

"It's the priest—Per Fendur." Eben joined them, Laurens standing red-eyed with wine at his side, but still kitted with a blade in his right hand, and a Durrym shield in his left. "I told you he'd found a way past the Barrier, no?"

"I should have believed you," Isydrian allowed.

"Matters past," Pyris said. "We face a common enemy now. Do we stand together?"

Isydrian nodded. "Shahn and Zheit? There's a first, eh?"

"A start," Pyris said, smiling.

"So let's order this rabble into battle lines."

Isydrian set to yelling orders and Pyris joined him, their men shaping a defensive wall between the wood-topped ridge and the encampment where the women—those not holding weapons and standing with their men—gathered in children and old folk.

It was close on dawn, the sky a pearly gray not yet decided between light and darkness. A good time to attack, when people slept, or woke lazy from the feasting. Birds sang now that the bats and dragons had gone, and to the east the sun began to stain the horizon a bloody red.

❧❧❧

A LINE OF HORSEMEN came out from the trees, halting on Per Fendur's command. The priest rode a little way forward and raised his hands. Lord Bartram shouted, "No! We'll parley first," but Fendur ignored him, pointing at the Durrym clustered below.

Bartram turned his horse toward the priest, but Amadis moved to block him, dancing his charger before Bartram's so that his lord was held away from Fendur.

"You defy me?" Lord Bartram shouted, outraged.

"I obey the Church, my lord."

"Damn you," Bartram growled. "I'll have an accounting for this betrayal." He drew his sword.

Which Amadis knocked from his hand, settling his lance point against Bartram's chest to topple the older man from his horse.

"Your day is done, old man. I follow Per Fendur now."

Bartram landed on his back, winded. He struggled to rise, but his armor was too heavy and all he could do was shout for help as his men stared in confusion and looked about to see who commanded them. Drak began to dismount, but Amadis shouted that the soldier ignore his fallen lord, and smiled from under his golden helmet as Per Fendur commenced the fashioning of his magic.

Lord Bartram lay like an overturned turtle, helpless and furious as the battle began.

❦❧

"BEWARE!" EBEN YELLED, his bellow near deafening Cullyn. He raised his own hands, muttering furiously as light seemed to gather about the priest so that Fendur's black-clad form grew indistinct, like a shimmering mirage. Power gathered, palpable, about him, and then he was hidden altogether as the light became incandescent and erupted.

It was akin to that other attack, when Cullyn had first encountered Lyandra, but far more powerful. Myriad fires shot from where the priest stood his horse, great licking tongues of flame that seared the morning and struck like lightning at the Durrym ranks. Cullyn kicked Lyandra's feet from under her and flung himself on her even as she protested, cursing volubly. Laurens dropped to the ground beside them as the morning was filled with a sulphurous stench, as if some great furnace gate had been opened. Durrym died without a sound, torched by that dreadful fire too swiftly to cry out. Rather, they were reduced to crisped corpses that collapsed into drifting ashes. Tents took fire, the grand pavilions burning so that for a while flame held the Durrym trapped. Some sought refuge in the river, more followed Cullyn's example and fell to the ground. Cullyn looked up, wondering if his hair burned, and saw Eben standing like some ancient monument, his hands thrust out even as little flames danced over his robe and across his hair. And then it was as if a great wind blew, conjured from his hands to gust against Per Fendur's magic and drive the flames back

toward the priest. Cullyn gasped as the light died to re-
veal Fendur again, seated angry on his black horse. He ignored the fallen men, gazing furiously down the slope.

Eben slapped at the embers scorching his robe and
shook his head, sending ashes and hanks of burning hair
to fall in a cloud around him. "The priest is strong," he
muttered, "but it shall take him a while to recover."

"And you?" Cullyn rose warily. It seemed to him that
Eben was suddenly aged, his already ancient face now
haggard.

"I'll survive. I've lived too long to die now. But until
that bastard gathers his strength again, it'll be sword
work."

As if to confirm his words, Per Fendur shouted a
command, and from over the ridge came the might of
Lyth Keep, a flood of horsemen that thundered down toward the Durrym pavilions, armored and bearing lances,
waving swords as the bowmen shafted arrows that
pricked men and tents in equal measure.

Cullyn saw a Shahn taken through the throat by a
shaft, and ran forward, toward the charge.

"No! This is madness!"

He ducked as arrows flew past his head, and turned
to Lyandra.

She crouched beside him, holding a shield and her
long knife. Three shafts stood upright on her shield; a
fourth plucked at her cap, and Cullyn felt madness en-
compass him. He saw a golden-armored horseman thun-
dering toward them, riders on his flanks, and all charging
with couched lances that seemed angled entirely at
Lyandra. He sprang to face the assault.

The leading rider held a lance and a shield, all armored in gold, and his horse was kitted with gilded mail.
Cullyn saw the lance angled at Lyandra. He chopped it
aside, and saw her toppled by the charger's path even as

he was flung away and the rest of the charge went past in a confusion of hoofs and sound and trampled sod. He tumbled, dizzied by the impact, his head spinning as the lancer brought his horse around in a tightly dancing circle and charged again.

Cullyn glanced to where Lyandra still lay and saw the lance's point aimed at his chest. He raised his sword, thinking that he was about to die.

Then Laurens was there, swinging a Durrym blade against the horse's muzzle, against the armor, so that the animal swerved away from Lyandra and Cullyn and came crashing down, screaming in pain.

The rider staggered to his feet, his armor dented and bloodied. He lofted a sword that Laurens smashed aside, then delivered a cut that sent sparkling pieces of golden armor lofting like jewels into the rising sunlight.

He chopped again, a butcher's game, down into the helmet, and through, and Amadis died.

"Thank you. You saved my life," Cullyn gasped

"I enjoyed it," Laurens answered. "I never liked him."

Then the battle raged about them and it was all survival, parry and cut, hack one man down and avoid the next blow. Cullyn lost sight of Lyandra, who darted limber amongst the Kandarians, her long knife flashing until it was all bloody.

❦❦❦

LORD BARTRAM FOUND HIS FEET with difficulty. Shame filled him as he located his sword and sheathed the blade. He caught his nervous horse and, with an effort that seemed to take what little breath was left him, mounted. He turned to Fendur. "I gave no order to attack. We might have spoken with them!"

"With Durrym?" The priest's face was sallow, his eyes hollow and reddened. "Durrym are only good for slaughtering."

"And Abra?"

"What of her? Her only importance is that she brought us here."

"My daughter is no pawn." Bartram's sword was suddenly in his hand, as if he were young again. He saw the battle before him, his men and Durrym dying needlessly. He wondered how his daughter fared amongst such carnage, and what betrayal was planned by Amadis and the priest.

"Of course she is," Fendur sneered, "as are you. Only pawns."

"I command here," Bartram growled, and reached for the horn that would call his men back.

"Think you so, old man?" Fendur laughed wickedly. "Your wife sleeps with your captain, and your daughter takes a filthy Durrym for her lover. What command does that leave you? No, *I* command here. In the name of the Church."

Lord Bartram raised the horn.

Per Fendur said, "You'll not call them back," and stuck his blade into Bartram's side, between the joining of the pauldron and the breastplate. The horn fell from fingers that were abruptly numbed by the terrible pain that filled the old man's body. It was as if the horn became filled with cold and heat simultaneously, running down his arm into his throat, his chest, his ribs.

He was dimly aware of his charger prancing beneath him, bucking and shaking its head. The terrain swirled before him and then he was staring at the freshly blued sky, all the breath smashed from his body. He realized that he was dismounted, stretched on the trampled grass, his sword gone. Fendur danced his black horse around the fallen lord, laughing.

"Your time is past, old man. You grew too soft, eh? To contemplate alliance with the Durrym? *No!*"

He left Bartram and set his horse to moving down the slope, already fashioning a further spell.

❧❦❧

"THE WOMEN AND CHILDREN?" Isydrian parried a Kandarian blade and smashed his own against the soldier's ribs.

"Tended." Pyris drove his sword's point into his attacker's throat and spun to stab into the back of the man assaulting Isydrian. "Mallandra takes them to safety." He chanced a glance at the burning pavilions. "And Abra, too, I think."

Isydrian looked toward the river. A pall of smoke hung above the tents, swirling where it met the breeze coming off the water. Folk splashed through the shallows, ushered on by the two women, gathering on the farther bank, where nervous animals watched from the trees.

It was one of those curious lulls that occur in the midst of battle, so that for a moment the two Durrym lords stood alone, the fighting raging bloody around them but they cupped in a moment of solitude.

"You fight well," Isydrian said.

"As do you."

"We might be friends."

"Are we not, now?"

Isydrian nodded, then raised his sword and returned to the combat.

❧❦❧

CULLYN STOOD back-to-back with Laurens. Both their blades were sheathed in blood and Cullyn feared he might vomit. How many Kandarians had he slain, men he might have known in other circumstances?

"This is madness."

"This is war."

"Then war is madness."

"Likely, but . . ." Laurens brought up his shield as a javelin arced at Cullyn. He caught the missile and hacked off the shaft. "What choice have we?"

"If I could talk with Lord Bartram . . ."

"I doubt he's in the mood for talking." Laurens took a sword blow on his shield, parrying the counter to drive his point hard through chain mail, into the man's belly. Then gasped as the dying man fell back. "Drak? Is that you?"

Drak tottered, sword forgotten, his shield too weighty now to hold up. For a moment they stood facing one another. Then Drak said hoarsely, "You've killed me. Damn that foul priest."

"Yes, forgive me," Laurens answered, and stabbed Drak's throat that he die swiftly. He turned to Cullyn: "I've no more liking for this than you. I'm killing men I knew—drank with; men I'd name as friends—but destiny names our paths, and mine runs alongside yours. So . . ."

He ducked, raising his shield as arrows flew, and then they were again encompassed by the battle and there was no time for further debate: only the business of bloody survival.

❧❦❧

LOFANTYL SAW ABRA and Mallandra take the defenseless ones across the river, saw them gather on the far bank and prayed they be safe.

Afranydyr said, "You fight well, brother. Better than I thought you capable of."

"I don't enjoy it," Lofantyl replied. "This is stupid."

"The Garm delivered it." Afranydyr swung his sword as one of the few still-mounted Kandarians thrust a lance at his chest. He knocked the lance away with his shield and ducked to deliver a blow that broke the horse's knees. The beast screamed and fell, pitching its rider from the saddle. The man landed on his face in the bloodied grass, and Afranydyr hacked at his neck, breaking it, then plunged his blade into the wounded horse that it suffer no longer. "We have no other choice," he said.

"We might have talked with them. I think they came to find Abra."

"Or conquer Coim'na Drhu."

"Even so, we might have spoken."

"With Garm'kes—"

Afranydyr was unable to finish the sentence because an arrow drove into his throat and his mouth filled up with blood. It spurted from his gaping mouth as his eyes opened wide in disbelief. He coughed gobbets of crimson and dropped his blade as he reached for the projectile that pierced his windpipe.

Lofantyl gaped, for a moment stunned. The shaft protruded from under the cheekpieces of his brother's helmet, the fletchings set firm against the neck, the bloody tip jutting from the jointure of Afranydyr's spine and skull. Streamers of blood flooded from his nostrils as he fell to his knees. He clutched the arrow and snapped the shaft, then tugged it clear.

"I'm slain," he mumbled through the flooding of his mouth. And then fell down on his face and lay still.

Lofantyl turned. The archer was dismounted, nock-

ing a fresh shaft. Lofantyl raised his shield and charged.
An arrow hit the shield, driving through hide and wood,
the tip protruding through the inner side. He ignored it,
slamming the shield into the bowman's face as the archer
snatched at his narrow sword.

He had no time to draw the blade, for Lofantyl was
caught up in the battle madness. He smashed the archer
down and plunged his blade into the man's chest, twisting it as his victim screamed, then hacking at the
writhing body. "For Afranydyr!"

❧❧❧

"THIS IS MADNESS." Eben watched Per Fendur
bring his black horse down the slope. "Why do you do
this?"

He knew the answer: power; dominion; conquest.
All the stupid, pointless ambitions of petty men. And all
of them delivering other men to death.

Am I any better? he wondered, and then dismissed
the question: I *know* that I must oppose him, because I
believe he is evil, and it becomes his belief against mine.
So I have no choice save to hold my own beliefs and oppose what I *believe* is wrong.

So he faced the priest.

Behind them the fighting slowed—too many dead,
sword arms weary, archers' fingers sore from the plucking
of the bows, arrows used up; men on tired horses that
panted for want of water finding their lances heavy. The
morning stank of blood and burning. Armored men—
Durrym and Kandarian—rested on their swords as a great
stillness filled the valley.

And Per Fendur rode toward Eben.

TWENTY

❧❦❧

CULLYN WATCHED afraid as Per Fendur brought his black horse down the bloodied slope to where Eben stood. Bodies lay about him and the air stank of blood and dying, and the foul aftermath of Fendur's magic. He squinted as he saw a brightness shimmer about the priest—as if the man were girded in mirage-light. He was suddenly aware of Lyandra at his side, and the tremendous relief he felt that she was alive; nor less when Laurens joined them.

"What now?" he asked. "Is there not an archer can put a shaft into that black crow?"

"It's between Eben and him," Laurens said. "I think it's what Eben wants."

"And if Eben is slain?"

"Then I'll face the priest." There was honest loathing in Laurens's answer.

"Or I, were that possible. Save it's not."

Cullyn realized that Pyris had joined them, and Isydrian, who said: "And if not you, then me. I believe that man deserves to die. But it's as Pyris says."

"Surely he cannot face us all?" Cullyn asked. "What of your magic?"

"Useless against this priest." Pyris shook his head.

Cullyn frowned, frustrated and afraid for Eben. "What do you say?"

"His magic is of a different kind," Isydrian explained. "Ours is of wood and stone, the animals." He grimaced. "Could I aid my son, I would. But . . ." He shook his head helplessly.

"Give me a bow," Laurens suggested, "and I'll put a shaft into the bastard."

"He protects himself too well," Isydrian returned. "He's shielded against harm. Do you not see?"

Laurens cursed and Cullyn narrowed his eyes again, and saw the shimmering brightness that enveloped Per Fendur extend farther as he approached Eben. The priest dismounted and waved his black horse away as he faced the older man. It seemed that they stood contained within a faint, flickering globe that simultaneously absorbed and reflected the bright morning sunlight. It was as if silvered gnats darted about them, holding them within a dancing sphere that somehow defied entry.

"Is there nothing we can do?" Cullyn gripped the hilt of his bloodied sword, urgent to fight, to aid his friend. Then felt Lyandra's hand gripped hard on his arm, urging him to remain still.

"I sense it now." Isydrian looked to Pyris. "You?"

Pyris nodded. "He owns even more power than I'd thought." He turned to Cullyn. "Only one blood-bonded with the priest can approach him now. A blood relative, or one whose blood he's shared or shed."

"He tortured me," Lofantyl said, sword ready in his hand.

"But did he cut you?" asked his father.

"No. Only stretched me."

"Then you'd die," Isydrian said. "It must be blood. Only blood can break that protection."

They watched helplessly as the two men faced one another, priest and wizard, one in the prime of his power, the other old. Drawn to different callings, youth and rampant ambition confronting age and wisdom.

"I'd not thought my son so brave," Isydrian said thoughtfully. "Afranydyr, yes." For a moment his eyes misted. "Lofantyl, perhaps. But Eben?"

"He has no less courage." Pyris clutched his sword's hilt as if he'd draw and charge.

Indeed, the blade came partway from the scabbard. Then he sighed as Isydrian touched his arm and said, "It's between them, my friend."

"And all our fates dependent on it." Pyris let the long sword slip back into the scabbard.

"Pray that my son wins. The gods know, but I've lost enough already."

"And found new friends."

"Yes," Isydrian said.

"Then let us pray together for Eben's success."

᥍᥏᥍

"SO WE COME TOGETHER." Per Fendur swept his cloak back, exposing his black armor. "A final settlement, eh?"

Eben stood before him, his hair scorched so that strands of discolored silver flared about his aged head. He looked a tattered figure, his robe all burned by Fendur's magic, his beard ragged from the burning. "You can go back," he said. "Take your folk back to Kandar. We want no war here."

"No."

"Then what?"

"You and I, old man. And after, all of Coim'na Drhu."

"I cannot agree to that."

"So die!"

Per Fendur raised his hands, his strength returned, summoning magic again.

Eben smiled sadly and brought up his own hands as they mouthed incantations, calling on what powers they had.

Those watching could not tell what forces they summoned, only watch, for there were no gusts of flame and fire, no great demonstrations of magic; only two men facing one another, their hands outthrust, their eyes bulging, their lips drawn back from clenched teeth, spittle falling from their lips. They were like two bulls, or large-horned stags contesting mastery.

A stillness filled the valley. Across the river the women watched, warded by Mallandra and Abra. Wounded men sat up, ignoring the ashes that filled the air from the smoldering pavilions. Kandarians and Durrym, who not long before had fought one another, watched.

It was as if a great decision filled up all the world, and that the world awaited its fate.

"YOU ARE OLD," Fendur grunted. "Too old to defeat me."

"And you are too young to know wisdom," Eben answered.

"I am stronger than you!"

Eben staggered back.

Fendur laughed, and then was halted as Eben sent another spell against him.

"Not so much stronger, boy. Age brings wisdom, and you've none of that. Only foolish ambition."

❧❧❧

CULLYN WATCHED a man rise from the slope above the battleground. He had no idea who it might be, only that the armored figure rose up and came tottering down the ridge with a drawn sword that he used as much for a crutch as a weapon. Whoever it was staggered as if sorely hurt. He supposed it was some early-wounded Kandarian come to join, too late, the battle.

❧❧❧

LORD BARTRAM SAW the black-clad figure of Per Fendur before him, facing an old, silver-haired man in tattered robes, and a group below, watching. He wondered what transpired here—beyond the thoughtless slaughter of his men—and wove his way down the slope.

❧❧❧

"I'M STRONGER THAN YOU, old man." Fendur flung such magic against Eben as sent his opponent staggering back. "I shall defeat you and destroy you, and you shall be nothing. Only dust."

Eben countered the spell. "Not yet; not ever. Not while I live."

Fendur laughed as he, in turn, countered Eben's spell. "Old fool, who shall not be for long."

He flung fresh magic against Eben's, watching and

laughing as the older man was battered by the invisible storm. Eben tottered, his hands trembling as he angled gnarled fingers at Fendur. He braced his shoulders as if he stood against a terrible wind. His lips stretched back from gritted teeth and his breath came in short, panting gasps as his eyes narrowed with the effort of his casting.

"Can we not help him at all?" Cullyn turned to Pyris and Isydrian.

Pyris shook his head, his face a mask of frustration.

"This is between them alone," Isydrian said, "and likely our fates decided by the outcome."

Cullyn felt himself close to ignoring the Durrym lords' advice. He could see Eben wavering inside the strange globe, and it pained him to stand helpless as his friend fought alone. He felt Lyandra's hand, firm against his sword arm; Pyris clutched his shoulder.

Then suddenly Laurens gasped, "That's Lord Bartram!" and Cullyn recognized the armored figure moving ponderously toward the combatants.

❧❦❧

LORD BARTRAM FOUND IT HARD to get his breath. He could feel blood washing down his side and his left arm was numb, unlike his ribs—which hurt abominably. Anger motivated him as he stalked toward the two men facing one another with the Durrym looking on. He wondered why none moved to end the sorcerous combat. The sun was up now and heating the river valley that was, he noticed absently, a most pleasant place. It beat against his helm and set sweat to trickling down his face, so he unlatched his cheek straps and flung the helmet away. He wished he might do the same with his armor, which now felt dreadfully heavy. But no time for that: he was not sure how much longer he could stay on his feet, and there was a thing he'd do before he fell down.

He wondered where Abra was as he drew closer. Safe, he hoped, and were it with her Durrym lover, then good luck to them. He recognized Fendur's black armor, and saw it glinting behind some curious shield that seemed like a balloon of light that encompassed both men. He wondered who the other was. The renegade wizard Fendur had mentioned? What was his name . . . Effen, Evin, Elric, something like that. It didn't matter: Bartram could feel the blood flowing from his wound and doubted he had much longer to live. But before he died, he was determined to make one last stroke.

No one should endanger Abra.

None moved to halt him as he staggered to where the sorcerors faced one another. Fendur stood triumphant, chuckling as he flung his invisible magic against his opponent. The old man was haggard, his face contorted with pain. Bartram thought the old man likely looked as sore hurt as he. Then he took a deep breath, knowing that this must cost him much effort, and forced his numbed arm to grip the sword's hilt. He almost toppled then, but pride and outrage kept him on his feet as he raised the blade double-handed.

And brought it down through the oddly shimmering light against Per Fendur's back. It was not, perhaps, an honorable stroke, but all Lord Bartram wanted to do was slay the priest and end his power.

The globe of light parted as easily as cut cloth. Fendur gasped, turning in time to see the sword descending and Bartram's face behind the blade. He opened his mouth, but before any words could escape his lips the blade was buried in the jointure of neck and shoulder, cleaving bone and carving deep into organs, so that only a gargling scream escaped. Bartram twisted the blade and stabbed at

Fendur's ribs, driving the point in between the breastplate and the tasset, and turning it again that the wound be open and bloody. Then he fell down, exhausted.

❦⟳❦

FENDUR'S MAGIC CEASED as his life bled out. He endeavored to fashion a final spell, but only blood came out of his mouth and he could not lift his right arm. Dimly, he saw Eben smiling grimly, and then the supine figure of Lord Bartram. And realized who had slain him.

"You?"

He struggled to lift up his left hand, struggled to fashion a destroying spell, hatred lending him unnatural strength. He rose awkwardly on his sundered arm, fashioning an incantation through blood-flecked lips.

❦⟳❦

EBEN FELL TO HIS KNEES, then put his hands on the ground else he taste earth. He panted, sweating, not yet confident he lived. He felt horribly weakened and knew that his power was terribly depleted. Save for one last casting: that he'd make even if it killed him. He saw Per Fendur stretched bloody on the ground before him, and sensed the power the priest summoned. He mouthed his spell and white fire blazed from his fingertips.

Per Fendur opened his mouth to scream, but the fire struck too fast. It consumed him—and in the blink of an eye he was gone. Only ashes drifted in the sunlit air, dispersing as the breeze blew them away.

Eben gasped and stretched full length on the charred earth. Then folk were running toward him, lifting him up, and carrying him and his savior both back to what scorched remnants of the pavilions still existed.

"Who was that?" he managed to ask. "Who put the sword into the priest?"

"Lord Bartram," Laurens answered. "A fine man."

"Indeed," Eben grunted, "for he saved my life."

"I think perhaps," Cullyn said, "that he saved us all."

"I'd have beaten him," Eben declared obstinately. "Sooner or later."

"Better sooner," Laurens said, "with Lord Bartram's help. Eh, old man?"

"Perhaps. He lives?"

"As yet." There was doubt in Laurens's voice, and his eyes hovered anxiously on both men.

❧❦❧

THEY WERE LAID ON THE GROUND, settled on what bedding could be found from amidst the wreckage of the encampment. Pyris and Isydrian both called for healers as a crowd gathered, Durrym and Kandarian mingling in uneasy truce. Laurens knelt beside Lord Bartram, loosening his bloody armor.

"The bastard priest defied my command," Bartram grunted irritably, "then stuck a blade into me."

"As well he did," Pyris said, "else you'd not have been able to touch him."

"What fey talk is that?" Bartram asked.

"It was a bonding," said Isydrian. "He shed your blood, and that—because you were not slain—bound him to you."

"So you could penetrate his defenses," Pyris continued, "which we could not."

"I wondered why you stood watching when honest blades might have ended it." Bartram sighed. "Still, no matter, eh?" Then he frowned. "He is dead?"

The Durrym lords nodded. Laurens said, "Near clove

in two. I've seldom seen such a blow. Then Eben sent him up in smoke."

"That's fitting." Bartram winced. As the healers came, examining his wound. "Abra's safe?"

"She comes to you now." Laurens pointed across the river, which the women and old folk and children forded again. "Unharmed."

"Good." Bartram smiled. "I only came to bring her back or see her happy. I'd no great wish for war."

"That was the priest's idea?" Eben asked.

"Indeed, he had a lust for it," Bartram confirmed. He looked to Laurens. "Help me up, eh? I must speak with my folk."

"Wait," Laurens urged. "Wait until the healers come."

"No time," Bartram returned. "I'd not see battle break out again."

Cullyn followed the direction of his gaze and saw the truce uneasy. Durrym and Kandarians stood together, but all held weapons, hands firm on sword hilts and spears. It seemed to him that a fire had blazed and then faded, but still smoldered, threatening fresh flames. He quit Eben's side and joined Laurens.

"It shall be for the best."

"He's right," Eben declared. "They're both right."

"It could kill him," Laurens argued.

"We all must die." Bartram sat up, groaning as fresh spillings flooded over his side. "And I'd see my mistakes rectified before I go." He tried to rise to his feet, but was too weak. He looked to Cullyn. "You, boy, help me, eh?"

Cullyn set an arm around Lord Bartram's back, feeling the blood settle sticky on his hand. Pyris and Isydrian joined him, then Laurens, so that Bartram was lifted to his feet. Then he shook them off.

"I'll stand alone."

They let go of him, but huddled close for fear he'd collapse as he faced the mingled crowd.

"Hear me," he shouted, "you soldiers of Lyth Keep, and you Durrym, also. There is no more war between us. We Kandarians came here falsely, deceived by the priest, Per Fendur, who is now slain. We are now at peace. I, Lord Bartram of Lyth Keep, declare that there shall be no more enmity." He paused to wipe blood from his beard. "Do any of you disagree, go home. I believe our conquerors will allow that."

He swung his head to Pyris and Isydrian in turn, and they both nodded.

"Those who'd remain, lay down your arms."

None left, even did they look askance at their new-found allies. They sheathed their blades and grounded their spears, unstrung their bows and looked to Bartram.

Who said, "Good," and then: "I feel somewhat weak," and collapsed.

Laurens caught him before he fell, and Pyris and Isydrian helped ease the wounded man to the ground.

The healers applied their skills as Laurens fretted. "Hold on, my lord."

"I thought," Bartram said slowly, through the bloody spittle that frothed from his mouth, "that you found other allegiances, now."

"Not against you," Laurens declared. "Only against Amadis and the priest."

"And against Kandar?"

"No." Cullyn knelt beside them. "Now that Fendur's slain, perhaps there can be peace."

"And who are you?"

"He's Cullyn," Laurens said, "he's syn'qui."

"A *focal*." Eben rose onto his elbows. "A cursed or gifted man, but one who shapes worlds whether he likes it or not. A simple man, in many ways—"

"Only a forester," Cullyn interrupted.

"Who brought about this battle," Eben said. "Without which—"

"I wish I'd not," Cullyn announced.

"Save had you not, there'd not be peace now."

"Is there?" Cullyn looked to Lord Bartram.

"So far as I am concerned—though I cannot speak for King Khoros. This venture was all Per Fendur's doing, and him aided by Amadis. I'd only see my daughter safe and happy."

"Which I promise," Lofantyl said.

"And you are?"

"Lofantyl of Kash'ma Hall, son of Isydrian." He paused, kneeling to touch Bartram's hand. "By our laws and your daughter's wish, I am Abra's husband. I love her, and she loves me."

"The Durrym prisoner." Bartram chuckled. "Forgive me, but my eyes grow dim. Abra chose this?"

"She did."

Bartram glanced at Laurens, who nodded his confirmation. "Then I wish you happiness. But remember—do you fail her, you shall answer to me."

"I'll not fail her," Lofantyl declared. "Ever."

"Then we're in accord." Bartram looked to where Pyris and Isydrian waited. "And we, I think. I cannot speak for all Kandar, but this promise I make you—there shall be no more war between Lyth Keep and your halls. And do I live, I shall endeavor to broker peace between our lands."

The Durrym lords nodded solemnly, and took the hand of the wounded man in token of agreement.

"Enough!" The healer spoke with authority. "No more talk—only leave us to tend these hurt friends."

"Indeed," the second added no less sternly. "Have we not enough wounded to aid? Leave us."

They walked away—Cullyn and Lyandra, Laurens,

Pyris and Isydrian, Lofantyl—all grave and fearing neither Bartram or Eben would survive. Then Abra came, all wet from the fording of the river; all fearful for her father. Lofantyl caught her in his arms and swung her round before she could run to Bartram.

"Slowly, slowly. He's sore hurt."

She struggled against his grip. "He dies?"

"Healers tend him. And he gave us his blessing."

"I must go to him."

"There's nothing you can do."

"Save see his face! Allow me that."

Isydrian said, "Let her," and Lofantyl released her.

"Is it not strange?" Isydrian turned a face on which Cullyn saw tears shining toward the ravaged encampment. "I've lost a son this day, but found another—and a daughter."

"And new friendships," Pyris said.

"That, too." Isydrian stared at Cullyn. "What have you brought me, syn'qui?"

"Peace between Shahn and Zheit," Pyris said. "Perhaps even between we Durrym and the Garm'kes Lyn. Perhaps hope for a brighter future."

Isydrian began to reply, but then Abra came racing toward them, her face lit by hope, announcing that the healers believed her father would live, and Eben. So Isydrian only said, "Which first? Afranydyr's funeral or a celebratory feast?"

"Can it not be both?" Cullyn asked, wondering at his audacity. "Perhaps Afranydyr was a sacrifice to a better future. Can we not mourn him and celebrate at the same time?"

Isydrian thought a moment, then nodded. "Yes, you speak wisely."

"He's syn'qui," Lyandra said, holding tight on Cullyn's arm. "Of course he does."

EPILOGUE

❧❧❧

T IME HEALS: scars form on wounds, broken bones mend, aches ease. Old hurts are forgotten, ancient enmities are appeased.

Lord Bartram learned this as he lay in Kash'ma Hall, tended by Isydrian's healers—more like an honored guest than any kind of captive. It was a wondrous place of wood that seemed to grow in accord with the Durrym's wishes, as if the timber spun itself eagerly about the keep, entwining halls and chambers and corridors to shape walkways and windows, balconies and gardens where flowers grew and fountains played. Birds sang from amongst the bushes and the trees, and the sun shone from a cloud-scudded blue sky that was speckled with the darting shapes of swifts and swallows, and such other creatures as he'd not seen before entering Coim'na Drhu.

He rested, and mended, and thought of Lyth Keep.

There, he thought, the gray stone would still be cold, those chimneys he'd joked about with Abra all bundled up with blazing firewood. He wondered how his wife fared, and decided he did not miss her so much. He wondered what Ky'atha Hall was like, and looked forward to visiting there. Pyris had invited him, and he had taken the Durrym's hand in friendship—no sense of deceit or entrapment, only honesty.

The god—or gods—knew the Durrym had tended him well. He was no longer sure which gods existed, only that he found his ancient enemies now his best friends, kindly and caring. The healers had tended him daily, healing the wounds Fendur had delivered; and Abra was clearly in love with Lofantyl.

Nor were Isydrian and Pyris and Mallandra poor companions. They were Durrym, but they visited daily, several times, and brought him such wine and sweet-meats as he'd never eaten, and gamed with him when he could once again—the gods be blessed for Durrym heal-ers—raise his left arm. A thing they called the Game of Stones was subtle and intrigued him. It was a thing of shifting tablets of wood over a board, all black and white, and jumping to gambits. Abra was adept, and Eben—whom Bartram came to like quite apart from the old wiz-ard's habit of boasting his own prowess and teasing Bartram about the duel with Per Fendur.

Laurens tended him no less than the healers. The master-at-arms delivered his food more often than the servants, sitting with him and—until Bartram was able again to use his left arm—feeding him. It embarrassed Bartram that he was so weak, but also he felt flattered by such loyalty, and they spoke of many things.

"This Cullyn," Bartram asked one day as Laurens cut his food, "who is he?"

"He was a forester," Laurens answered, "an orphan,

making himself a living in the woods. But he's also syn'qui—that's why all this has happened."

"The Durrym," Bartram returned, "speak of this. What does it mean, what is a syn'qui?"

Laurens shrugged and said, "Eben can explain it better than I."

"But you liege with him. You followed him here."

"Didn't you?"

"I came with Fendur; I came after Abra."

"And saw the truth, no?" Laurens set the plate down, looking toward the window. The sun shone in through whatever material the Durrym used to cover their embrasures—surely sturdier than the flimsy glass of Lyth Keep, surely cleaner; it lit the chamber with dancing light that set the rugs decorating the wooden floor to colorful patterns. "I think he brought us all together, that we make peace."

"I believe you're right," Bartram said. "But peace shall not be easy."

"When ever was it?" Laurens asked. "War is always the easier option."

"You become a philospher in your age."

"Perhaps I do," Laurens chuckled. "Perhaps I learn from Cullyn and Eben."

"As, I think, do I."

❧❧❧

EBEN EXPLAINED IT scarcely better: "The boy hardly knows what he does. He only acts, or reacts, but he's chosen to make decisions that influence us all. Think on it— why did Lofantyl befriend him? Why did Abra fall in love with Lofantyl? Why did Cullyn aid them, or Laurens? It's fate, my friend, and he pulls fate into patterns that he does not understand, only shapes. That's what a syn'qui is: a *shaper*. I've the power of magic, I can advise, but I cannot *shape* the future. He can, even if he doesn't understand how or why. Perhaps it's his innocence that grants him that gift—or curse—but that's why he's syn'qui."

They had become friends, these two old men, and Bartram enjoyed Eben's company no less than that of Laurens or his Durrym hosts, or Cullyn himself. He found the young man a most pleasant companion, and Lyandra delightful. But his greatest pleasure was to see Abra, who came with Lofantyl—whom Bartram now accepted as his son.

"I wonder what shall happen when I go back," he said one day as they walked away from Afranydyr's funeral.

Isydrian's elder son had been consigned to the ground. A pit had been dug and his body, dressed in the armor he had worn when he died, set inside. Then the earth had been piled over him and a sapling oak planted. Bartram had gasped as he watched the young tree grow, sprouting leaves, its roots spreading visibly, to take hold of the corpse and the earth before his eyes.

"Shall you go back?" Abra asked. "Why not stay here?"

"There's Vanysse," he said.

"Mourning Amadis?"

"You knew of that?"

"Everyone knew."

Bartram sighed. "I was a fool."

"No." She took his hand. "You were always an honest husband, and a good father."

"But my wife?" He shook his head. "Besides, I'm sworn to guard the Borderlands."

"Against what enemies?" She gestured at the solemn group that stood around the sprouting oak. "These? Have you not already sworn friendship?"

"Yes, but . . ." Bartram hesitated. "I cannot speak for Khoros or the Church. Likely the Church shall send another priest to Lyth Keep."

"Who might be kinder than Per Fendur."

"Or not."

"Aye, there's that."

"And you'll remain here?"

Abra nodded, squeezing her father's hand. "I'm wed to Lofantyl, and I love him."

"And with my blessing—he's a fine fellow. But I've still a wife in Lyth and a sworn duty to Khoros."

"Why do you not speak with Cullyn and Eben?" she asked. "Between them, they seem to speak much sense."

❧☙

THE CHAMBER WAS LIT with late afternoon sunlight that painted the floorboards and the walls with dancing patterns of light and shadow. Tapestries and rugs shimmered, the scenes depicted there coming alive. They sat around a circular table more akin to a mushroom than anything carved by human hands. Lord Bartram occupied one chair, Abra and Lofantyl beside him; Pyris and Isydrian sat beyond, then Cullyn and Eben and Laurens, facing him.

Lord Bartram's hands were clutched about his head as he agonized over his decision.

"This is not easy," he said. "I am sworn to guard the Border against—"

"Sworn friends," Isydrian interrupted.

"Who shall no longer look to invade you," Pyris added.

"That, I believe." Bartram shook his head in anguish. "But even as I swear that Lyth shall never come against you again, I cannot guarantee my king's word. And I've a wife there."

"As best I understand it," Eben said, "your wife—forgive me if I speak bluntly—will not mourn you."

"That's likely true," Bartram allowed, and sighed, "I think her heart was ever with Amadis."

"Who's now dead." Eben was ever blunt: Bartram liked that in him. "So what reason to go back?"

"I'm liege lord of Lyth Keep. I'm sworn to guard the Borderlands."

"Against . . . ?"

Bartram started to say, "The Durrym," then broke off as Eben laughed long and loud and gave him back, "Those who've healed you and tended you and made you welcome? Do you truly believe them enemies of Kandar?"

Bartram shook his head. Concepts spun there, inside his mind, that he'd never before properly considered. He said, "No, they seem good friends."

"They are. They've no wish to invade Kandar. Perhaps once, when Afranydyr dreamed, but now . . ." The ancient wizard shrugged, leaving Bartram to make his own decision.

"Stay here," Pyris suggested, echoed by Isydrian. "You should live well here—honored as the man who slew the invading priest."

"And Vanysse?"

"Slept with Amadis," Abra said, blunt as Eben. "Do you go back, then name her adulteress and give her to the Church's arms."

"I'd not do that," Bartram said. "She was, I know, but even so . . ."

"Then stay here," Pyris suggested again. "Be welcomed and honored."

"I'd name you a commander," Isydrian said, "and make you greater than ever you were in Kandar."

"Save I took vows," Bartram returned. "I thank you both for the honors you offer me, but I must go back."

"Why?" Abra gasped.

"Because I must confront my traitorous wife," her father replied, "and tell her that her lover is dead, and the priest who supported him. And then I must let King Khoros know that there shall be no more war between Lyth Keep and Coim'na Drhu. And perhaps that shall end this warfare."

He looked at Cullyn. "How say you?"

Cullyn swallowed hard, embarrassed. "Why do you ask me, my lord?"

"Because you're syn'qui."

"Only a forester."

"Syn'qui! Now answer."

All the eyes around the table fixed on him. He wanted to look away, to go away, but he met their gazes and fastened his own on Bartram.

"Must I," he said, "then I'd say go back and deal with your wife as you see fit. And then look to broker a peace between Kandar and Coim'na Drhu. And does the king not listen, then either rise against him or come back here—to friends."

"Young and foolish, but wise in his simplicity." Eben nodded his silvered head. "He sees the way to the future, even if he doesn't recognize it. He's like a blind man who can take you safely through the darkest night. He might not see it, but he *hears* and *knows*, in his blood and bones, and can therefore lead you to safety."

"I hope so," Lord Bartram said. "And I shall do my best."

"And we shall all see where that leads us," Eben returned.

About the Author

ANGUS WELLS was born in a small village in Kent, England. He has worked as a publicist and as a science fiction and fantasy editor. He now writes full time, and is the author of The Books of the Kingdoms (*Wrath of Ashar, The Usurper, The Way Beneath*) and The Godwars (*Forbidden Magic, Dark Magic, Wild Magic*). *Lords of the Sky*, his first stand-alone novel, debuted in trade paperback in October of 1994, and was followed by the two-book Exiles Saga: *Exile's Children* and *Exile's Challenge*. He lives in Nottingham with his dog, Elmore.